Hard to Get

Cynthia Dane & Hildred Billings

BARACHOU PRESS

Hard to Get

Published: 29h September 2016
Publisher: Barachou Press

Part 1

HARD TO GET

Chapter 1

"Mr. Ethan Cole's office, please hold."

The phone slipped through Nadia's sweaty hand as she attempted to transfer yet another caller to the hold music. More lights flashed on the machine. Already there were five people trying to get through to Ethan Cole, who was currently in a hush-hush meeting with one of his business's key investors. "*Absolutely no calls,*" he had said. "*Should only be an hour.*" Two and a half hours later, Nadia was still fielding men and women who grew increasingly irate.

Good money came with being the receptionist at the most prestigious office in the city. Ethan Cole was the CEO of the biggest business around, and Nadia's job was to do nothing but handle appointments, phone calls, and smile at every person coming through the doors. From nine until five she sat at that desk greeting Saudi princes and Japanese bankers. Sometimes the occasional Brazilian billionaire or European son of aristocracy made their way in there too, but those were a dime a dozen. Nadia was a lot more likely to remember men in robes and men who bowed before her, mistaking her for Mrs. Cole.

Usually this time of day was slower, allowing Nadia to catch up on work abandoned in the middle of the morning or even – gasp – take a break. Nobody in that office was getting a break that afternoon, though, labor laws be damned. From the moment they walked in from lunch, everyone in the executive office was smacked with an avalanche of people and documents in need of a CEO's body part.

Hope he's enjoying his stupid meeting. Nadia knew how important these business deals were behind the closed doors of Ethan's office, but the man often lost track of time, especially since he lost his last assistant months ago. Sometimes Nadia filled in when pertinent. Most of the time, however, Mr. Cole took more time in his meetings, recording conversations and asking someone in the office to transcribe for him.

Nadia stared at such an audio file on her computer. Thirty-five minutes of Mr. Cole discussing stock prices with an investor. She couldn't *wait* to transcribe that bullshit, what with her chunks of time open to such things!

Another call came in. "Mr. Cole's office, please hold."

Two of the hold lights switched off. *Good. Everyone hang up and leave me alone.* Nadia was about to break. She didn't care how good the money was. There were days where she seriously thought about marching into Mr. Cole's office and slapping down her two-week's notice. She'd been in that office going on two years… surely that would look good enough on her résumé.

And do what? Go to work for some other asshole who will probably hit on me? One thing about Mr. Cole was that he was never anything other than professional with Nadia. A miracle, considering how young and rich the man was. Now, as for the men who walked through the office doors and immediately started charming the lovely young receptionist? They were another story. A really annoying, skeezy story.

What Nadia would give for a hard drink and a harder woman to soothe the stress of this shit day!

Then again, her mother always told her to be careful what she wished for. Because a pretty hard woman was walking through the door now, her millions of dollars oozing from every strand of frosted hair and diamonds gleaming from her ears and hands. And sunglasses. Those were some seriously blinged-out sunglasses.

Oh. No.

Nadia pulled the day's schedule toward her, panic striking her heart. *Fuck, fuck, fuck!* When she went over the schedule first thing in the morning, she hadn't thought much of the initials E.W. penciled in at 3:30 in the afternoon. That could've been at least a dozen people in the office address book. The name "Eva Warren" never registered in Nadia's addled mind.

Don't acknowledge her. Don't! Nadia kept her head down and pretended to write something on the giant calendar to the left of her desk. Maybe Eva would simply have a seat in the reception area while she waited for her appointment with Mr. Cole. Someone would be by to offer her cucumber water or champagne. Someone who was not Nadia, because *hell no.*

"Good afternoon," came a chipper voice right in front of Nadia's desk. "For the both of us, to be sure."

Nadia had no choice. She looked up, briefly making eye contact with Eva Warren, a young heiress who was business as usual for the city's super-rich world… except for the part where she was a butch lesbian who enjoyed leaving scandalized hearts and eyes in her wake.

A *high-fashion* butch lesbian, that was. Eva wasn't like the blue collar women who hung out at the city's only lesbian bar on the far side of town. She would never be caught dead in a band T-shirt or jeans a size too big. Her hair was short and bright blond, a trademark of her family but the style pure *I will fuck you up.* Her clothes were Dior, Givenchy, Valentino, Armani… all tailor-made pantsuits to give her a masculine edge while still showing off her feminine form. Like hips. And breasts.

And a tight ass Nadia would kill to have – and maybe touch. A little.

"I said…" Eva removed her Chanel sunglasses and leaned in toward Nadia. Oh. Frosty blue eyes to match the frost in her hair. What was with

Scandinavian beauties, anyway? Never content with blue eyes or light blond hair. Had to have both, didn't they? *Calm down, you thirsty asshole.* Nadia had no idea if she was talking to herself or broadcasting to Eva. "Good afternoon."

Nadia was used to dealing with women of extreme means. They came in all the time, usually with husbands, but sometimes on their own too. Such women were reluctant to pass up any form of validation, especially from a woman like Nadia. How many times had some woman reeking of French perfume reached across the desk and gotten in Nadia's face about saying *hello?* If she ever received complaints that Mr. Cole felt compelled to address, they almost always came from rich women. "*She is so rude! Why didn't she say hello to me in the way* I *wanted?" "Does she have a brain in there, or do you hire beautiful women for your collection of supermodels, Ethan?" "My husband was leering at her when he thought I wasn't looking. You should replace her with a homelier woman."*

Eva, however, was on a different level. She was used to getting validation and being fawned over like any other heiress, but her greetings to Nadia were always – *always* – laced in flirtations. From the first time they met over a year ago, Eva had made it her personal mission to outrageously flirt with Nadia every time she came into Ethan Cole's office.

Men flirted with her all the time too. They were easy to politely ignore or shoot down when necessary. What did a gay girl do when one of the hottest and most eligible bachelorettes came waltzing up implying romantic walks on the beach and screaming in the middle of pound town in city high-rises?

She reverted to what she learned in the School of Passive-Aggression, of course.

"Good afternoon, Ms. Warren." Nadia's voice was more reserved than usual. Was she constructing a high enough wall between them? God only knew. "Here for you three-thirty appointment? I will be more than happy to check you in, but I'm afraid that Mr. Cole is still tied up with his previous appointment and it may be a while still."

"No kidding. His meetings always run over like an abandoned bathtub." Sighing, Eva took the tablet Nadia handed her and signed her name. "You think I didn't count on that? I came early so I could see your gorgeous face."

The tablet clattered to Nadia's desk. "I… thanks." Was she blushing? She was totally blushing. *Fuck!*

Eva wasn't walking away. Why wasn't she walking away? Nadia braced herself for the come-on about to smack her in the face – and in the loins.

"What are you doing this Friday? I know the holidays are about to start and everyone is *so* busy this Christmas, but a girl is always looking for ways to pass the time before playing mind games with family. So what do you say? You, me, a bottle of red wine at *Le Ciel…*"

"I have other obligations this weekend, unfortunately." Boom. Shot down again. Nadia was becoming a pro at being one of the only lesbians in town who could shoot Eva Warren down right out of her higher-than-life skies. "Sounds lovely, though."

"Hm." Eva stood up straight, French-tipped nails tugging on the hem of her navy blue jacket. Yup. Those were breasts outlined in her jacket and beneath her skinny black necktie. Yup. Breasts. She had them. *You fucking pervert.* Again, Nadia had no idea who that was addressed to anymore. "You're such a busy woman. Every time I ask you out, you happen to be doing something else."

Nadia forced the fakest smile she could muster. "It's almost like my time is precious."

A male coworker hustled up to the receptionist's desk with papers in hand – and then promptly turned and scuttled off the moment he saw the scene unfolding. *This woman and I are legendary around here.*

"I admire precious things. Perhaps someday I will introduce you to my collection of precious gemstones from all over the world. Handed down through my mother's family. Jewels unlike you have ever seen. Some used to belong to queens, empresses, duchesses…" Eva slapped both hands against the top of the desk. "You would look even more gorgeous with them bedecking that soft skin of yours."

That smirk on her face didn't merely imply letting Nadia try on necklaces and earrings. It meant stripping her naked and pouring rubies and emeralds on her until people were blinded by her sparkling nudity.

"You're such a generous woman, Ms. Warren."

Finally, Eva stepped back, turning as if to sit in the reception area. Her phone popped out of her jacket pocket and flashed a bright pink screen in Nadia's direction. "Perhaps you could learn something from me? About being generous, that is."

"I'll let you know when Mr. Cole can see you, Ms. Warren."

Eva graciously accepted defeat for, what, the tenth time in a row? Even now, as she sat in a leather chair and swung one long, lean leg over the other, she gazed at Nadia from the corner of her eye. *Why does she have to be so hot?* It made turning down her advances even harder to do.

Nadia didn't *dislike* Eva. Sure, she was heavy-handed with the flirting, but she always knew when to stop and get on with her life. Some days Nadia was really not in the mood and felt the burning urge to smack the smirk off that heart-shaped face. Most days, however, she found it increasingly more difficult to not melt like she was being flirted with by the hottest girl in school. *I'm sure I would've thought that about her too.* Not that Nadia went to a hoighty-toighty private school like Eva did, though.

She had her reasons for always turning her down. *I can remember the first time she came in here.* Nadia's second month on the job. She was still getting the hang of the office's phone system when an Amazonian queen sauntered through the doors and sent Nadia into a state of shock. *I didn't realize she was my type until I first saw her.* Usually Nadia went for the lipstick femme types like herself. Then she saw what a "diamond dyke" was and disappeared into the hazy fog of lust.

Yet it was the principle of the thing. Years working in offices around the city had taught Nadia something: people wanted to take advantage of her. She wasn't humble enough to think she wasn't as beautiful as people said she was. From the time she was an adolescent her peers always fawned over her wavy red hair and pale complexion – the freckles went away with puberty, though. Thanks to her job, Nadia was also no stranger to designer clothes that accentuated her figure and made her look way more expensive than she actually was.

This created a perfect storm of perverted men always trying to get in her pants. Men with wives, no less. Pride made men of all ages go after the pretty receptionist. Shit, even Mr. Cole asked her out shortly after she started working there. Since he hired her, Nadia was under no delusions that she was hired merely for her work merits. Sure, she had a résumé that landed her an interview… but there were dozens of more qualified women. Something about Nadia pinged Mr. Cole's fondness for beautiful women.

He backed off the moment she made it clear she was not interested in him. Or any man, for that matter. Now he had some other young girlfriend to pass the time away with, leaving Nadia with a parade of multimillionaires to endlessly flirt with her. Some were grosser than others. None of them actually got through to her like Eva Warren did.

Being jaded prevented Nadia from making a huge mistake, though. She knew that she would be nothing more than a conquest to a rich person like Eva. The tabloids were always going on about Ms. Warren's sordid love life with young women all over the world. Half the time they were huge scandals because nobody ever guessed the woman she was with swung that way. They were also stunning beauties who made regular modeling and acting appearances – in Hollywood, no less.

Yet another woman she can claim to have fucked. That's all Nadia would be, and she would not allow it… no matter how appealing a night with Eva Warren sounded.

Nadia glanced at her as she flipped an appointment book over and penciled something in. Eva texted on her phone, her slender body relaxed in that chair in the only way her height would allow. Limbs for miles… everywhere. Nadia wasn't too short, but she was definitely shorter than Eva. What would it be like to be trapped beneath her body and feel nothing but her carnal power?

She needed a cigarette thinking about it.

The door to Mr. Cole's office opened. Out came an older gentlemen shaking hands with the younger Ethan Cole and promising to call him back later that week. The man stopped by the front desk to schedule an appointment while Mr. Cole turned to the reception area.

"Ah, Ms. Warren, sorry to keep you waiting…"

He and Eva disappeared into his office without either one saying a thing to Nadia. Suited her fine. Until Eva returned half an hour later, lingering by the desk under the guise of making another appointment. Hold lights disappeared from the phone directory.

"Can I schedule you a month from now, Ms. Warren?" She made a habit of coming in once a month to check how her family's investments were doing with the company. "Or did you have another date in mind?"

She didn't realize what she hadsaid until the word "date" fell from her lips.

"I've got a million dates in my mind. All of them include you."

Nadia received a confident wink before Ms. Warren excused herself from the office, taking her perfect ass and gait with her. *I'm going to crack sooner rather than later.* She needed a girlfriend. A really hot one, so Eva would never, *ever* tempt her to make a huge mistake.

***

"A moment, Nadia?"

The receptionist finished putting on her coat before grabbing her purse and leaving for the night. Mr. Cole was likewise dressed in his travel wear, except he got to hop into his limo instead of the bus. "Yes, sir?"

Thankfully, it was work talk instead of personal business. Mr. Cole wanted her to join him and girlfriend Jasmine on a weekend to the mountains. Not for anything *like that,* but to act as his personal assistant while he tackled his backlog of work.

"Sounds like it's supposed to be a romantic getaway, sir." Nadia cleared her throat. "I mean… not with *me*…" She couldn't stop the blushing today.

Ethan waved that away. "It is. I've been promising Jasmine that I would spend more time with her, but you know how the workload is right now."

"Of course." Not only was it the end of the year and people wanted to get business out of the way, but Ethan had the double problem of losing his assistant *and* his business partner earlier that year. Neither had been replaced, meaning a plateful of work for Mr. Cole to handle by himself.

"I'll pay you the usual overtime rate for the whole weekend. You won't have to work the whole time, of course. You can rest assured that your bonus this year will be quite… hefty as well. For your efforts."

Nadia nodded. "Say no more, Mr. Cole. I had no plans anyway." Regardless of what she told Eva to turn her down, Nadia's life was hardly exciting. *I Netflix and chill with myself. Yay.* "Tell me when and where you're picking me up."

After they went over the details, Nadia was finally released to go home for the night. Apparently, someone else had taken that elevator earlier too.

Paper fell at Nadia's feet the moment the elevator began its descent. She picked it up, unfolding it to reveal a note written in sophisticated, clean cursive.

"You have witched my wishes… dressed up in your pretty clothes."

Nadia crumpled up the paper and took a deep breath. Most people wouldn't think anything of that. But as someone who had gone through the same "*I must read every lesbian artist's work ever*" phase as every other gay girl before her, Nadia recognized a spin on the legendary Sappho's work. The pristine handwriting was another giveaway.

"She's going to kill me," Nadia muttered. At least she knew what she would be fantasizing about while watching Netflix later.

Chapter 2

"No," Eva sighed, changing the channel yet again, "no, no, *no.*"

Eventually she shut off the 72-inch flatscreen in her living room. Even at that size the poor, piddling monitor looked positively tiny in her cave of a room. No matter how many sofas and coffee tables she shoved into it, however, it still looked ridiculous. She was about to start investing in huge art pieces to hang on the walls at this rate.

"Why can't a girl watch a trashy reality show anymore?" She downed the last of her evening wine before tossing her glass onto the other end of her couch. "What else do I reward myself with?"

Stacks of papers and books cluttered the table. Finals were coming up sooner than she would like to admit. *I'm going to pass them all with flying colors. Watch me, world.* Eva considered it bad enough that she was taking three years instead of two to finish her business degree. Her brother and professors told her to take a full four if necessary – so she could help with the family business, of course – but Eva was tired of wasting time. If she was going to be formally employed by her own family by the time she was twenty-seven, she *better* finish her graduate degree. Tomorrow, preferably.

It's all Henry's stupid stipulations. Her dearest older brother and the heir presumptive of the family fortunes. He was in charge of everything after their father retired to some dirty ranch in Montana. Eva had every intention of cutting herself a piece of that pie as well, but her brother insisted she get her degrees in line first. While Eva didn't disagree with Henry's logic, she always lived on the precipice of suspicion. Was he stalling? Was their family too traditional to employ a woman, let alone a woman like *her?* Did everyone still think she was some flippant playgirl who couldn't be trusted with the keys to the kingdom?

Shit, she needed another drink.

And a woman, but that was a constant in her life. Eva whipped out her phone and stared at her contact's list called *Ladies.* Women she had either already slept with or promised to sleep with sometime very soon. Most of the names she didn't recognize any longer. Others needed to be deleted for one reason or another. *This one's dating some European athlete. The male kind.* A few were possible contenders for a getaway that weekend, perhaps to the family island in the Caribbean, but Eva quickly lost interest.

There was only one woman on her mind. There was *always* one woman on her mind whenever she went to bother Ethan Cole for an afternoon.

Nadia was one of those rare beauties. Not rare in that she was beautiful, but rare in that she had *something* sparkling about her. Eva had met countless supermodels and other pinnacles of femininity since she was a little girl. Boring. If Nadia's gorgeous red hair wasn't eye-catching enough, there were those pretty hazel eyes that always gave Eva a testing look. Or how about her impeccable sense of style? Those dresses and blouses were criminal. The only thing missing was one of Eva's choice pieces of jewelry resting on top of those exquisite breasts.

Ten times Eva had asked her out. Ten times she had been rejected as if she were some college girl begging for attention.

Eva was no stranger to rejection. She had to be used to it. Just because she sweated money didn't mean any woman she fancied would be willing to sleep with her. Men? Yeah, they could do that. Even the staunchest "open-minded" woman suddenly played for no one but the opposing team when it came to all that money other millionaires had. Sure, the occasional girl decided to give the ol' clit rub a try when Eva slathered the flirtations on hard enough, but for the most part, she had a limited dating pool no matter where she fucked off to in the world.

Now, other out lesbians turning her down? That was rare. If Eva didn't know better, she would think Nadia had someone else she was devoted to. Everyone she asked, however, couldn't think of anyone.

So why did they always banter until Nadia found a way to shut the mating dance down?

Women. Eva was one and couldn't figure them out.

"Do you need anything else, Ms. Warren?" One of the maids – was it Claudette? Florette? What the fuck was this one's name? – bended over Eva's couch and picked up the abandoned wineglass. "Or would you like to be left alone for the evening?"

Eva was frustrated – yes, that way – enough to quip that ClauFlorette should do anything but leave her alone for the evening. She was a pretty young woman, but Eva had a staunch rule about not schtooping the family help. *At least I can't knock them up.* She fondly remembered that episode four years ago when a maid claimed to be pregnant with Henry's child. Her brother copped to sleeping with her, but DNA tests were… not in the woman's favor.

"I think I'll be turning in for the night soon." Eva bit one of her nails. "Thanks."

"Yes, ma'am." The maid stepped back. "By the way, Mr. Warren is on his way here. Thought you might like to know."

Eva said nothing. *Great.* The maid departed, taking the wineglass with her. *Wonder what he wants this time.*

Henry arrived two minutes later. He took one look at his sister's academic mess and said, "I thought you were done with this term already."

"Next week." Eva motioned to the other end of her couch. Henry sat, trousers still crisp against his legs even though he had been wearing them all day. "To what do I owe this pleasure, brother?" She made it sound like she never saw him. Which was hilarious even to her, considering they technically lived in the same house. Henry lived over in the East Wing, however. Eva took her residence in the West Wing ever since she reached the age of majority and her mother gave up trying to remodel the place. Now Mommy Dearest was in Montana, and Eva could do whatever she wanted to *her* space. Even so, she usually only saw her brother at dinner, assuming they were both there. That only happened twice or thrice a week. They both had busy lives that made his appearance in her wing a rare occurrence.

"I wanted to check-in with how your meeting went. I didn't get a phone call."

Shit. Eva had been so distracted by pussy that she forgot to send her brother the update. "Everything's fine. We're five million dollars richer thanks to Cole. Well, you and Daddy are."

Surely Henry caught that edge in her voice. "Only five million?"

"Things slow down this time of year." She didn't have to tell him that. Come on.

"Nevertheless, I appreciate you taking the time out of your schedule to speak with him."

"Spit it out, Henry."

His posture relaxed. Always the rigid man, even though Eva wouldn't give a fuck if her brother farted in her presence. *Has that ever happened? If a Warren farts and no one is there to experience it, did it truly happen? Are we that special?*

"Starting next month I will be taking over the task of checking in with Mr. Cole. I'm sure you understand."

Eva snorted. "What is there to struggle to understand? You and he are best pals now. You're marrying his ex-girlfriend." With Mr. Cole's blessing, no less. "He went to your collaring ceremony. We're all family now."

Neither Henry nor his sister were secretive about their personal lives, although they certainly didn't announce perversions either through conversation or through registered mail. So what if Henry was a lifestyle

Dom with a fiancée who was more submissive than a single maid in that mansion? Eva didn't see anything weird about it. She dabbled in the BDSM world too, and her brother knew it. They were both members of the club downtown, although they used coded words to announce they were going so the other wouldn't show up the same night. Some things had to remain sacred.

And, to be fair, Eva had gone to her brother's collaring ceremony to represent her brother's best interests. If their parents ever found out? That was one more stroke for their dear mother. She wouldn't be able to make her boring jewelry any longer with such shaky hands.

"That may play a part in it." Henry brushed something off his sister's couch. Probably the oodles of lead Eva's nerves were always ejecting from her mechanical pencils. "Anyway, didn't want you to take it personally. I'll find something else for you do on the family's behalf soon enough."

Thank you, oh gracious brother. Eva tried to not roll her eyes. "You better find loads for me to do soon. I'm graduating in a year."

Henry didn't respond to that. *He never does. Fucker.* "What are you doing this weekend? Any exciting plans?"

"What? No. Finishing up my final papers." Eva was mostly done with them, but she was the type to get her homework out of the way early and spend her time all the way up until the deadline perfecting it. "Although I thought about doing that down on the island before you spend all of New Year's down there with your fiancée."

"That could be nice. I hear the weather is beautiful right now."

"But?"

"But I was going to ask if you wanted to go to the mountains with Monica and me this weekend. A friend is lending us his vacation home. It's a big house, so you don't have to deal with us if you don't want to. Would get you out of the house for a while."

"I get out of the house all the time." Eva laughed. "Sometimes I go to my apartment in the city." It was a quaint studio downtown. Perfect place to take overnight lovers without family or house staff getting in the way.

"That doesn't count.

"Shopping like crazy when I'm stressed out doesn't count? I hate to break it to you, Henry, but you're about to get really acquainted with that once you're married. Good thing your little woman makes a lot of her own money so she's not spending all of yours."

"*You're* jealous because you don't have anyone to spoil. Our nature to want to spoil someone with our money. What else is it good for?"

Trick question. Eva wasn't falling for it. "Fine. I'll go with you, but only because sitting in front of a mountain fireplace editing my papers sounds cozy."

Henry smiled for the first time since coming into her residence. "Great." He stood, slapping his hands against his thighs. "See you at breakfast?"

Eva shrugged. "I suppose." She didn't have any out-of-house plans for the next day. Sheesh. Henry had really picked up on her being quite boring, now hadn't he? A girl couldn't help it if she was focused on her academic pursuits, though. "Good night, Henry."

"Good night, Eva." He made it halfway to the living room entryway before turning around again. "Going with us will be good for you, I promise. Who knows? Maybe there's a nice lady for you to meet there."

Eva rolled her eyes. "Don't tell me you're playing matchmaker again, Henry." Last time her brother meddled in her love life, Eva ended up having dinner with a widow twice her age and twice as confused about her sexuality. *Henry swore she was DTF. I don't think so.*

"I would never. I have no idea who else may be there." He left.

Eva threw herself across the couch, hands cupping beneath her chin and feet kicking out behind her. Her phone rested on a pillow beneath her face. "Siri," she said, waiting for the chime to pop up on her phone, "any messages?"

"No, Ms. Warren," came the robotic voice. "You're all alone tonight."

"So are you, asshole."

"I concede to your logic, Ms. Warren."

Eva closed out some background programs on her phone. This included her browser opened to a list of translated poems by her favorite classic lyrist, Sappho. *I'm so pathetic.* And clichéd. Of course, Eva had felt pretty suave leaving that note for Nadia to find later. *Did she even find it? Probably not.* It wasn't fair. Was she so hung up on the redhead because she always rejected her? Or because she really did fancy her?

Probably both. Eva was the first to admit that she liked a good challenge – as long as her challenger was up for the game as well.

Chapter 3

Only Ethan Cole would have a super powered cell phone that could get reception anywhere in the world. *Anywhere.* Nadia figured they could be on a ship in Antarctica and this call from Hong Kong would still get through, let alone at the top of a wintery mountain.

Nadia passed the work phone across the limousine, her boss snatching it from her hand and attempting Cantonese. Beside him, girlfriend Jasmine gave Nadia a look that suggested she was a traitor. Fair enough. Ethan and Jasmine were supposed to be on some holiday getaway before the holidays actually started. But after Nadia was invited to tag along and get paid some hefty overtime, well…

Mr. Cole swore she would get her fair amount of rest this weekend, but after seeing the amount of notes and other files she was asked to parse through in two days, Nadia wasn't sure about that. *The view will be nice. It's also quiet up here.* She crossed her fingers that she wouldn't have to hear her good friend and boss have sex. From the way Jasmine talked, that was her and Mr. Cole's *favorite* past time. The more crops and ball gags, the better!

Think I'd rather die.

Aside from work materials, Nadia had packed a book and her personal laptop. Who knew? Maybe there would be time to wrap up in a blanket and take a few minutes for herself. Or maybe she would spend the weekend trapped in the mountains with two randy billionaires and a stack of monotonous work that no amount of overtime could ever pay for.

At least she didn't have some kind of life to miss out on. *If I stayed home, I would read this book and… finish it.* It was too cold to go out. Dark too early to have a life in the city. Nadia briefly missed having a boyfriend. The only thing she could say about those days was that she and a guy could go anywhere without worrying about much. By herself? Sigh.

They pulled up to their destination shortly after Ethan got off the phone. *What a lovely manor.* To billionaires, this was probably a cottage, not a simple vacation home. Nadia had seen her fair share of mansions and the like by now – she had certainly seen the various places Ethan Cole called home in the city – but it always galled her to hear rich men and women go on about hiring enough staff to maintain these otherwise empty properties that were visited maybe once or twice a year. *Sounds like the kind of place Eva Warren would have.* Nadia had never been to the expansive Warren Estate outside of town, but she had certainly heard of it. Those old money families always had the most traditional mansions filled with European-trained staff. Last Nadia heard it wasn't uncommon to hire one maid per bedroom. And those were live-in maids!

Yup. There are people here. Nadia didn't think for two minutes that her boss would bring them to an isolated place in the mountains that didn't have the appropriate amount of staff. Maids spilled from the front doors, hustling to Mr. Cole's limo and unloading the suitcases and other bags brought along. Nadia's suitcase was the smallest. A carry-on bag, really. When she was only staying two nights, what the hell else did she need?

"We're going on ahead," Mr. Cole said as soon as the three of them stood in the frosty mountain air. While crisp, it made Nadia's nose turn blue in about three seconds. "Could you stay out here and test the cell phone reception? I've been assured that there is Wi-Fi inside, but I need to know if I'll be able to make more private calls out here. Thanks."

He and Jasmine went ahead into the house. Nadia stood by the limo, the driver popping out for a cigarette break before heading back into the city and the maids quibbling over who had to carry Jasmine's thirty-pound monster of a suitcase. Nadia pulled out the work cell phone and walked around the front driveway, searching for a signal. She didn't find much of one.

Shit. He won't be happy about that. Mr. Cole wouldn't get angry at her, but his displeasure would be palpable. It would probably trickle down to his girlfriend, who would later whine about it to Nadia. So the cycle continued.

"That's mine." Nadia insisted on helping the maids by taking her own suitcase. She walked along a snaking path between another limo and a Ferrari. *Did the owners of this place leave their cars here?* Nadia heard it was a vacation home. Why would the owners leave such nice cars here? Especially all the way up in frost country? Seemed like a great way to fuck up such priceless automobiles.

Nadia pushed open the front door and stepped into a well-heated foyer. Right away, her boss handed her his briefcase to "put somewhere." *How about up your ass?* She turned and passed it on to another maid before proceeding farther into the room. There she met five other guests – all a surprise, of course.

"Oh my," came a voice that struck Nadia's heart. "Look who else showed up."

She glanced to her left and made eye contact with Eva Warren, sipping on a drink and looking as if it was her birthday.

***

Henry was right. I sure met a girl here.

Eva had been ready to write off the whole shitfest of a weekend. Her and the rest of her immediate family were the first to arrive at the winter villa, mistakenly believing that that they would have the place to themselves. Then Eva was pleasantly surprised to find Kathryn Alison, her best friend in the *whole* world, and boyfriend Ian stumbling in with confusion on their lovesick faces. "*What? We were told that we would be alone! What the fuck are you doing here?*" Ten minutes later? Here came the Coles in their fancy suits and day dresses – and that pretty redhead Nadia.

James Merange, the owner of the villa, was an infamous prankster. It didn't take long to figure out that something was amiss here, and it was probably done on purpose. *He is the type to loan his villa to a bunch of alpha personality billionaires and make them think they would be alone.* With their women, no less. Eva was perhaps the least surprised by these turn of events. Until Nadia sauntered into the foyer, anyway.

Even touched by the cold, she's beyond pretty. Nadia's pale cheeks now turned beet red. Was that from the sudden heat punching her? Or from bumping into dear old Eva? *Dare I be self-centered enough to think it's about me?* Why not? Seemed like the natural thing to do.

The consensus was that this was a huge mistake. Why, everyone had been told that they would be the only guests there that weekend! The butler and the maids wouldn't commit to any comments, but it was quite suspicious that eight place settings were set for dinner. Eva finished her drink and turned to her friend, the coldest blond beauty she ever had the chance of knowing. "This could be my lucky weekend."

Kathryn glanced over Eva's shoulder and rolled her eyes. "You're going to get yourself thrown out of here if you try something with her. It's in the 20s out there. Do you really want to do that to yourself?"

"I knew I had to refrost my tips."

"Oh, shut up." Irritable Kathryn was adorable when she looked so fed up with the unjust world. *Came here for some weekend mountain nookie with your boyfriend, hm?* Eva had endless fun giving Kathryn shit for her relationship with Ian. The two were about as compatible as night and day. Apparently, that made them super compatible. Complements, opposites… something. The two of them hadn't seen each other in what, a month? Eva only knew because Kathryn called her every other day to whine about how sexually frustrated she was. Poor dear was in a serious relationship and couldn't simply go to the sex club and find her a stud to take the edge off. *Good. See how it feels.* Eva knew all about prolonged frustration between rolls in the hay. Contrary to popular belief, she did *not* get laid every weekend.

She was really feeling that frustration now as she looked at Nadia, who hid behind the rest of the Cole party.

The resigned guests moved into a lounge where more alcohol was handed out like water on a hot day. Eva accepted a glass of brandy and sat on the nearest loveseat. She quickly noticed that her brother and his fiancée had disappeared from the bunch.

I'm gonna need another drink. Looking around the room showed two – would be three if Henry hadn't absconded with his fiancée somewhere – couples who looked ready to pounce their lovers if there weren't so many witnesses. Apparently the theme of this weekend was choking on heterosexuality, because Eva was already drowning under that pressure.

Nadia came into the room last and sat on the opposite side of the room. What was she even doing here? Not that Eva was complaining. She could use some eye candy in this room full of heterosexual femmes. Nadia was the prettiest one, of course. Something about a girl being gay made her hotter than the straight ones. *Wonder what it is?*

Eva quickly gathered that Ethan Cole was behind and making his receptionist play catchup on boring admin work. *Poor dear.* Eva would have paid her plenty of overtime.

Too bad Nadia didn't see things that way. Oh well. Sometimes it was good for Eva to not get what she wanted. Kept things in perspective.

She spent the next ten to fifteen minutes talking to Kathryn about Christmas plans. Mommy and Daddy dearest had called the night before to suggest the Warren clan rendezvous in New York City for the holidays. Like Eva felt like doing that! Going to Montana to see her folks would have been bad enough. Dragged to New York, of all places? During the coldest, most crowded times of the year? New Year's alone would kill Eva's patience. *I've done the whole watch the ball drop from my hotel room thing.* Not like she got along with her parents, anyway.

Henry and his fiancée Monica reappeared with the most languid faces Eva had ever seen. *Oh, gross.* She turned back to Kathryn. "They totally did it. The perverts."

"How can you tell?"

Oh, to count the ways she knew! When Henry was in love, he did everything possible to keep sex an open possibility 24/7. Not that Eva wanted to think about her big brother's love life, but when the man was ten years older than her, a girl was going to hear about his affairs from the time she was five. *I remember him bringing some country club girl home for my seventh birthday party.* Their mother squawked to find Henry and his girlfriend making fools of themselves in an empty room. "*Stop fornicating this instant! There are children present!*" That was Eva's first time hearing about sex. Freud would probably have something to say about that.

Ever since Henry started dating Monica several months ago, their life had followed a similar pattern. The two were one of the staunchest BDSM couples around, taking the lifestyle to new heights whether someone was watching or not. Eva didn't care about that. What she cared about was watching those two sneak off wherever the family went so they could get in trouble with management. "*Stop fucking this instant! We're in public!*" Eva had that on standby for the next time she caught them where they shouldn't be.

"I can tell. I unfortunately know all about it by now."

"At least some people around here are getting laid."

"Tough luck about your romantic weekend."

"Yeah, yeah…" Kathryn looked wistfully at her boyfriend, currently playing chess with Ethan Cole. *She could do so much better.* Eva didn't hate Ian, but Kathryn had made a lot of concessions to be with him. Like giving up most of her Domme lifestyle so she could start submitting to that fuckboy. *Okay, he's not that bad, but what good is a guy you can't boss around?* One reason out of many Eva could never be straight.

Her eyes went back to Nadia, already at work. "Hey, speaking of getting laid."

Kathryn sighed. "No, I don't know how you can bag that hot chick over there." Her tone implied that Eva needed to give it up. As the only person in the world Eva openly talked about her crush on Nadia with, Kathryn had heard it all. Every attempt at getting at least a date was ran by Eva's poor best friend, who could only shake her head and suggest that hey, maybe Eva wasn't the girl's type. "*You're rather intimidating. You verbally castrate Ian every time you two are in the same room. I have to sew his dick back on for him.*" Yeah, but that was some piss-ass guy! Women were different. Totally.

"Ladies and gentlemen, dinner is served."

Finally. The crowd got up to follow the butler into the dining room across the hall. The savory scent of roast alerted Eva that she was hungrier than she thought. Three glasses of brandy wasn't enough to fill her stomach.

At least dinner distracted her from the mess that this weekend already was. On one hand, her best friend was there, but on the other, she was being tempted by a redheaded goddess and teased by the stench of heteronormativity. She especially was not impressed when, halfway through the meal, she glanced over and saw Ian and Kathryn playing a sly game of "grab the thigh!" beneath the dining table. Eva couldn't roll her eyes hard enough – it helped that they landed on Nadia, who pretended to not notice a single person in the room as she ate her supper.

It's a crazy sex party weekend, and we're the odd ones out. How about that?

"Excuse me," Kathryn said, getting up and dropping her napkin onto her plate. She left without a look to anyone else.

It took about two minutes for Ian to get up and head out the same exit.

"Oh, for fuck's sake," Eva mumbled. Her brother gazed at her from the other end of the table. She had half a mind to call him a hypocrite. *Everyone's running around getting laid but me.* She looked at Nadia again. At least someone was none the wiser around there.

Testosterone ruled this winter villa. Eva eyed every man in that room suspiciously – yes, even the butler on standby. Asshole probably had a sidepiece waiting for him as soon as his shift was over. What maid was it? A cook? A gardener? Eva was going to be good this weekend. She was going to follow Henry's advice and avoid flirting and the pursuit of carnal pleasure in favor of editing her papers and appreciating the mountain views. Then two other couples showed up, full of more sexual desire for one another than Eva could tolerate. One thing if it was her brother and his fiancée. She was *used* to that polluting her environment. Dealing with her best friend and her boyfriend? And the Coles on top of that? Ludicrous!

To add insult to injury, Nadia was there. Beautiful, *frigid* Nadia. Eva had better luck going after one of the maids flitting about the place.

I was going to be good. I was going to be good…

Nadia happened to glance up. They made eye contact, shivers visibly taking the other woman over. Eva smirked. It was the only thing she knew to do.

Chapter 4

Nadia had worked in worse environments. Really, being cooped up in a cozy study with a fireplace on a December evening was *far* from the worst environment. The only things making it awkward were the vacuum of testosterone and the six and a half feet of estrogen manning the bar.

She's so tall! Nadia knew that Eva was one of the tallest women around, like her brother was one of the tallest men in the region, but she never paid attention to how commanding a woman with the last name of Warren could be. *It's because she's not wearing three layers of clothing.* As the fire continued to roar through the evening, more of Eva's clothing fell off her body. First her black jacket, now draped across the back of the nearest loveseat. Then her royal purple vest, wherever it went. Now she stood with only a white blouse to grace her lean torso. Black slacks ran down the length of her supermodel legs.

Not that Nadia was staring. Nadia never stared. Especially not at Eva when she wasn't looking back.

Charts, dumbass. Nadia turned back to the work spread out before her. She had commandeered a small table in the corner of the study and made good use of the high-speed Wi-Fi on Mr. Cole's work tablet. The man was currently engaged in a game of charades. And by "engaged," Nadia meant he looked drolly on while the rest of the guests tried to be good sports.

Nadia liked charades. That didn't mean she was in a hurry to join in. Not only did she have a ton of work to make a dent in, but the types of things these rich people wanted to act out required a graduate degree to understand. Nadia may have been in the top five percentile of her university class, but it was *just* a Bachelor's. *Was good enough to get me this job.* That's what she told herself when she didn't want to admit how much her looks played a part in getting hired.

There were charts to analyze, quantify, and put together in small reports that Mr. Cole could hand out at his next board meeting. Nadia had a background in graphic design that allowed her to do this task with little effort. However, even a little bit of effort was almost too much right now.

The only way she would be able to concentrate on her work was if she stopped being in the same room as Eva Warren.

Nadia rose from her seat and went to her boss. "What should I do about the charts due on Monday?" she asked, kneeling beside his seat so she could lower her voice. "Do you want them tonight or tomorrow?"

"Tonight would be best," he was quick to respond in his usual gruff manner. "Don't tax yourself."

Nadia nodded. "I think I'll go up to my room and work on them." It was probably colder up there, but at least she could put on her pajamas and curl up beneath the covers of her guest bed. Maybe play some music too. *I'll need the music to drown out all the lovebirds in this nest.* Nadia went back to her table and cleaned up her materials. *And my own thoughts.*

Halfway out the room Eva approached her with a glass of cognac. The wordless invitation was there. Not the first time Eva offered her a drink that night. She was offering everyone an endless supply of drinks.

"No thanks," she mumbled, forcing a small smile of appreciation on her way out.

Sure enough, it was cold in her room. An unlit fireplace offered promises of warmth, but Nadia played with the heater instead. Something softly clanked to life as she grabbed a quilt off an armchair and wrapped it around her at a desk.

Charts. Charts were easier to comprehend now that she had some privacy. No distractions. Just her, a thousand dollar tablet, a binder full of printouts…

And a head full of naughty, naughty things.

Nadia had no idea where those images came from. Certainly not from her subconscious! Just because a girl suddenly had sex on the brain did not mean she was a nympho.

Even if that sex included the only other available woman in that house. Who was most definitely a lesbian.

Why am I thinking about her? Nadia tried to concentrate on a graph showing the steady increase of profits with some investor. *Get yourself together, Nadia.* True, she had never been in Eva's vicinity for this long of time before. Usually they only saw each other at the office, and that was for ten minute intervals. Intervals full of flirting, but manageable intervals nonetheless.

The longer Nadia stayed around someone like Eva, the more she realized *she had a type.*

Until now, Nadia had only dated one type of woman. This "type" consisted solely of women like her: femmes. While Nadia didn't openly identify with her label, she did take it to heart. Frilly things. Feminine things. *Pretty things.* That was her. When she wasn't threading her fingers through her long, red locks, she was shopping for big purses, high heels, makeup, and the cutest designer dresses her budget allowed. Basically, Nadia was a glutton for all things feminine. While she didn't find masculine women *un*attractive, they rarely did anything for her.

She liked soft curves. Giggles. Hair that went on for miles right along with a strong pair of lean legs. Her last serious fling was a Midwestern gal with auburn hair down to the small of her back. She always wore it up in a loose, flirty bun. *Our favorite kind of date was going to the spa and spoiling ourselves silly with pedicures and facials.*

Eva was a different woman. At the same time? Not different at all.

There was a dark femininity about her. No, not sinister. *Lovely* dark. Mysterious? Perhaps. Eva Warren wasn't a woman most would call mysterious, though. More like brash and brazen. Beautiful. Bold. *Beyond compare.* When you were one of the richest butch lesbians in the country, you truly were a legendary Diamond Dyke. Eva wore a lot of diamonds. Diamond rings. Diamond earrings. Diamond-studded watches. Her clothes were the same designers as her more feminine, heterosexual friends, but they were cut drastically different and accentuated various parts of her body. Those collars were meant to show off the length of her neck and the crop of her hair. Those pants gave her the illusion of more hips and the promise of the longest legs. Her heels gave her a gait that was rivaled only by master seductresses. Jasmine often talked about meeting women like Eva at the local sports club and seeing them train, both in cardio athletics and strength. Eva worked as hard on her appearance as Nadia did on hers. The outcome? Too radically different to comprehend.

"Okay!" Nadia leaned back in her chair, hands on top of her head. The quilt fell to the floor. "She's hot!"

Not exactly a new revelation, but admitting it out loud like that helped Nadia put the whole thing aside and get back to work.

She took a bathroom break an hour later. Unfortunately, she was in one of few rooms that didn't have its own guest bath. Price one had to pay when she was the hired help. Nadia recalled the bathroom across the hall and chose the ten o' clock hour to pay it a visit.

Five minutes later, she emerged to find a *scene.*

A maid giggled at the other end of the hall. She was young, perhaps twenty-two, and had a healthy tan that glowed beneath her simple black uniform. The woman was also ridiculously short compared to the giant looming over her and making her laugh.

"You get used to it," Eva said, after the maid touched something on the taller woman's hip. "At first it hurts a lot because of where it is.

Anywhere that has a good chunk of bone is going to hurt like the devil. Totally worth it. You want to see more? It goes on a good ways."

More giggles. That maid was going to send herself into a fit at this rate.

Nadia, meanwhile, couldn't figure out why her cheeks were on fire.

Blushing? *Probably*. Didn't take much to make her blush these days. Definitely wasn't jealousy. Nope.

Because why would Nadia be jealous that the hot woman who always flirted with her would be flirting with someone else? Someone *younger?*

"See?" Eva pulled her pants out farther from her hip. "Wraps all the way down my thigh. I'll have to be careful for the rest of my life that I don't stretch it out too much. Good thing I like to work out."

The maid stifled a squeal. *Hussy!* What was Eva showing her? A tattoo? She had a tattoo on her hip? Her thigh? Why hadn't she ever told Nadia that? Why hadn't she ever offered to show *her* a hot tattoo?

Eva glanced up and caught Nadia looking in their direction. "Garnet Rose Studio is who did it. Hardest place to get an appointment. Of course I got one the day after I requested a consultation."

Were women any different from men in this regard? Always flaunting their power and wealth…

"Excuse me," Eva put her hand on the maid's shoulder. "I'm keeping you from work."

The maid was not happy to shuffle away and get back to her duties. It may have been night at a winter villa, but there were seven important guests who demanded careful attention. Doubtlessly the maid would be needed downstairs to make sure the wet bar stayed stocked and all messes cleaned up in a timely manner. How kind and thoughtful for Eva to consider this on the maid's behalf.

Even more thoughtful of her to bridge the gap between her and Nadia with a few lazy strides. With legs that long? Accomplished in as little as seven steps.

"Fancy running into you here." Eva leaned against the wall, body acting as a barricade – not that Nadia had to move more than a few feet to walk around her. "Roam the halls much?"

Nadia had two options. She could continue to be her standoffish self around Eva… or she could let her guard down a teensy bit. Wouldn't want to give her the wrong idea. "Sometimes. You flirt with every woman you come across, or just the cute ones?"

"Close." Eva didn't flinch. "I flirt with every woman who looks open to being flirted with." Her eyes narrowed at Nadia.

Don't take the bait. Don't take the bait! "So you think I'm open to being flirted with all the time, huh?"

"That would be the interpretation, yes."

Nadia shifted from one foot to the other. Eyes averted. The only thing she managed to *not* do was bite her lip. That was a habit she punted to the sun when she was in college and determined to have the hardest face in her sociology class.

"But…" Eva did a half turn. "If you don't want me to flirt with you, I won't. If that's the case, you will also be happy to know that I won't be coming by your office anymore. Henry decided he should take that chore over from now on. I'm sure you understand."

Vaguely. All Nadia knew was that Eva's brother was the fiancé of Mr. Cole's ex-girlfriend. In some circles that would make them enemies.

Nadia wasn't paid to know that kind of information. She was paid to know who was coming by the office that day and field any calls coming in. Anything more than that and she risked getting called nosy and having her Christmas bonus lowered. As it was, she was looking forward to sending her parents on a nice trip for their upcoming thirtieth anniversary.

Now Nadia was presented with two possibilities. She could let things go, and Eva would probably disappear from her life. The flip side to that was… Eva would disappear from her life, rarely to flirt with her again.

They weren't even at work right now!

When she first started working for Mr. Cole, Nadia had to sit through half an afternoon's worth of HR drivel. Most of it was about how bad it was to fraternize with coworkers – especially Mr. Cole, ahem, not that it stopped him from opening a flirtation with her shortly after she started working – and clients. However, as Mr. Cole had told her in their one-on-

one at the end of the day, Nadia would soon find herself in a unique situation. "*Forgive me, Ms. Gaines, but you are a conventionally beautiful woman, and you are young. There will be many unscrupulous people who come through that door with the intention of making you uncomfortable with their advancements. Please know that you are under no obligation to return such flirtations. If you are made to feel uncomfortable, let me know, and I will deal with it. Your comfort and ability to work in peace are a priority.*"

Nadia was able to handle the rich old men – and some of the young ones – without much issue. It was the *women* her little gay heart was never prepared for.

"You won't be coming by anymore?"

Eva shrugged. "Family business, dear. Don't have much control over it. I'm but a pawn in my family's games. It's amazing I have as much freedom as I do."

"I suppose." Nadia could shrug too. "Too bad. I was starting to look forward to you coming in and making me feel special."

Was that spit choking Eva's throat? Ha!

"Special, huh?"

"What, you think it's easy being a pretty girl like me?" Nadia tossed her bushy red locks over her shoulder. "Every day all these rich men come in and act like they are the best thing to ever happen to me. Do you know how many flirt with me? I could have my pick of billionaire dick. Even when I was dating men," she didn't mention that was as little as a year ago, "I turned them all down. You know why? I was waiting for a woman instead. A woman who could compete with those small-dicked fuckers and show me what it's like to *really* be flirted with."

She knew she had pushed some powerful buttons. What Nadia didn't expect, however, was that she would soon find herself against the wall, staring up into Eva's bright blue eyes.

Eva and her brother were giants of genetics in any world, let alone the one Nadia had started working in two years ago. Not only height, either – anyone could say that the Warrens were infamous for being over six feet tall. Monica was the first addition to the family who didn't come anywhere near that height at a petite five feet. No, what shocked whole rooms into silence was the ridiculous Scandinavian genes that would make the ignorant think that blond hair and blue eyes were dominant. Like the pair of eyes Nadia stared into now. Big. Bright. *Icy* blue. Nadia knew lots of women who would pay big money to have contacts that made their eyes that color. To actually see real ones? Glowing? *Gazing?* It was enough to make a lesbian's knees buckle beneath the erotic pressure.

Cheekbones that could slice the air she breathed. Ears as long as they were dainty. Perfectly groomed hair that looked so effortless Nadia almost bought that Eva didn't spend an hour a day on it. And that was from the neck up.

Anyone who told Nadia that she was an "exotic" looking beauty (because strong Irish genes were exotic now?) had never met a Warren.

"You still don't know what it's like. If I think I have a real chance, I won't back down. You'd have to slap me."

An excuse to touch those smooth cheeks? Dare Nadia be tempted?

"Men, women… we're not too different in the end," Eva continued. "When we want a woman, it's with the same amount of fervor. We women are merely conditioned to hold our passion back. You think my mother didn't try to smack the flirtatious nature out of me? You should've seen me in high school."

I should have, yeah. Nadia had accepted her desire for girls when she was a mere sixteen. There was no way she would have been able to turn Eva down back then like she was accustomed to now.

"I bet you got all the girls." Was she trembling? Nadia better not be trembling.

"Sometimes. There certainly are a lot of pretty heiresses out there right now who will never admit to having slept with another girl, let alone this one. I've forgotten them, though. Women who won't own up to who they are don't interest me. Unlike you. Everyone knows you're gay too, and you've never denied it."

"Why would I deny it?" Truth be told, Nadia *never* openly told anyone but Mr. Cole and later his assistant Jasmine (now girlfriend, and HR could suck it) that she was gay. She didn't believe Mr. Cole was the kind of man to spread that information around. *It was probably one of the other men in the office who overheard me.* Nadia had to shoot the boss down in the executive office break room as some guy waltzed in.

"Maybe it's because of my world of privilege," Eva began, "but it takes balls we weren't born with to be open about that sort of thing. So I admire a woman of any appearance who completely owns who she is."

Any appearance?

Eva leaned against the wall. No wonder. Not only was another maid approaching, but Eva's friend Kathryn was rushing by with her boyfriend, en route to their room. Good thing the rooms were padded enough that Nadia didn't have to listen to it. *I'd die.* And blush. Like now. Fuck.

"Straight people. Hmph."

Okay, that made Nadia chuckle.

"Don't you get sick of it?" Eva's arms were crossed. "Everyone is pairing up in the straight world. I'm telling you, my brother and Monica are only the tip of the iceberg. After their wedding in February, there are going to be a lot more coming up."

"You know something about those two that I don't?"

"Huh? Oh my God, *them?"* Eva laughed. Nay, *guffawed.* "The day Kathryn marries any guy will be a cold one in hell. She'll marry me first. In fact, she's more than once drunkenly implied we should get hitched now that it's legal."

"Is she…?"

"No. Trust me, I've tried. Many drunken times."

Yeah, that was too good to be true. Nadia always wanted to hear about more heiresses coming out, but it rarely happened. Eva was the most high profile one. Also one of the most reviled, based on the gossip Nadia unfortunately heard here and there.

Once the coast was clear, Eva said, "So, anyway, what I meant by appearances is that women like me," she gestured to her hair and clothes, "don't have much choice about coming out if we really want to express ourselves. I admire you more feminine types for owning it."

"Of course I do. Don't you think there should be more femme lesbian representation?"

Eva gave her a cursory glance. *Hot damn those lashes.* Eva sure knew how to use makeup to her advantage. Nadia felt like a bumbling mess in comparison. "I think we should have *all* the representation. Every kind of lesbian and bisexual girl. Let's take over the media. You, me, everyone." Her hand grazed Nadia's. "Wouldn't mind getting papped with you in Miami."

Nadia played with a chunk of her hair. "I've never been to Miami."

"Hm? That so? It's a fun place. Going there in February for the bachelorette party."

Nadia glanced at her. "Do you actually like me? Or do you flirt with me because you flirt with everyone who pings your radar?"

Maybe it was the words. Maybe it was the tone. Either way, Eva snorted incredulously. "I would never flirt with a woman I wouldn't want to take things to the next level with."

The words were out of Nadia's mouth before she could check them. "I was hoping you would say that."

"Uh huh. So she *does* like me." Eva may be crossing every limb she had, but her casual posture was more than inviting. "Why are you always playing hard to get, then?"

"What can I say? I'm a romantic at heart. I want a woman to work to have a piece of this."

Eva's eyes went up, then down. Up. Down. *Up.* Down. Face. Tits. Hips. Ass. What piece was she thinking of taking? Even Nadia was impressed that she had said something like that. *It's like admitting I want her too.* Her lips twitched. Suddenly, poor Nadia was hyper aware of her body and what it looked like. Oh, God, Eva couldn't see the cellulite, could she? That didn't show up through a dress, right? Or the fact her breasts weren't as perky without a bra as they used to be? Would someone like Eva care about that? In Nadia's experience, hungry women like Eva fell into two categories: those who loved every part of every woman's body, and those who could make a girl cry with one mean comment.

"Time to cut the crap." Whoa. Where did that growl come from? And how could Nadia hear more of it? It went straight to her stomach and lit a fire in her thighs! "Do you want to do it or not?"

It certainly wasn't romantic, but for a woman who declared herself a romantic, Nadia sure didn't care about such things now. Sometimes blunt and direct dirty talk was more arousing than the flowers and bullshit.

Chapter 5

Where the fuck was the light switch? Did they need a light switch? *Yes. God, fuck me, where's the light switch!* Eva wasn't going to do it with a babe like Nadia and *not* see her naked. Where was the light switch!

Fuck it. There were lips to kiss and clothes to rip off.

"Ah!" Nadia found her back against the wall and a ravenous woman pushed up against her. Not that she ever said anything other than, "*Do it. I dare you. Take what you want and then take everything else too.*" Was that a challenge? That was a challenge. The best kind of challenge!

Eva was going to take all of it. Now.

"Should I get a stepstool?" the cheeky woman said as Eva bent down lower to kiss her lover's throat. More like maim it, but whatever. "Or should I stand on my tip-toes for you, Ms. Warren?"

Fuck, that's hot! Not enough women called her Ms. Warren like that. *That's right. Know who I am.* There was a reason her family was one of the most powerful in the area. She may be the redheaded stepchild nobody liked to talk about and begrudgingly left alone, but that didn't stop her from having a birthright. The Warren birthright wasn't just money and property, either. It was commanded respect. A regal aura that transcended the masses and made Eva carefully cultivate her image every time she left her residence.

Good to know Nadia recognized that. In turn, Eva would recognize the perfectly crafted body, the heavenly voice, and silky hair before her.

But not before kicking off her heels so she was finally short enough to kiss Nadia's lips without breaking someone's spine.

There was nothing shy about the way Nadia kissed. This wasn't her first round with another woman. Nor did she harbor inhibitions that were unique to their kind of relationship. Sometimes that happened. Sometimes Eva came upon a woman who wanted to have sex but spent the whole time comparing the experience to men. Eva didn't care what women did after they parted ways. What they did *before* they met. But like hell her pride allowed a woman to think about men when there was a perfectly good woman in the room!

"Why are you wearing clothes?" Eva's hands were determined to find a zipper, buttons, anything that would give her access to Nadia's hidden torso. "You should be naked right now."

Nadia grabbed Eva by the blouse and pulled it far from her trousers. "Could say the same thing to you. I've been staring at your ass for months. Let me see it."

Her ass, huh? Eva knew she had a decent derriere. To have it be the first thing a woman talked about? That was new.

"No, no, you first." Eva pulled her mouth off Nadia's soft skin long enough to tug on her bodice. "You show me yours, I'll show you mine. We get wound up and do it in fewer than ten minutes."

"Is that supposed to sound appealing? I know you can go longer than that."

"Oh, I can. It's going to be many ten minutes tonight."

Nadia reached behind her back and tugged on the buttons Eva couldn't find. The light switch remained elusive, but Eva's eyes adjusted to the newfound darkness of the bedroom and appreciated the shadowy skin appearing before her.

The bust of the dress fell to Nadia's waist. *Holy. Shit.* Those were some breasts, all right. That sure was a black pushup bra, all right. Man, wasn't it great that someone invented the pushup bra? Eva wanted to spend the rest of her life undressing women like Nadia and seeing their breasts spill from their bras. It was one of the simplest pleasures in life.

Nadia's tongue clicked when Eva went to rip down that bra. "Nuh uh. Your turn. Show me what kind of panties you wear."

"Panties?" Eva's hand was already on her waistband. "*Panties?* Those are fighting words in some lesbian bars."

"So, you wear panties?"

"Honey," the falling zipper was louder than the thumping of Eva's excited heart, "I get them tailor made to fit my hot ass."

That… was not a lie. All of Eva's everyday underwear were handmade by a seamstress in New York. The same one her mother took her to when she began developing breasts at ten. Since that day, some old yet stylish New Yorker was tasked to create simple – yet *so* comfortable – undergarments for a woman who wouldn't be caught dead buying packs of cotton underwear from the market.

Good thing, too. That meant her hips and thighs looked extra good in her cotton black pair she wore today. Nadia wanted to see her ass? She would see Eva's glorious ass the moment it popped out of her trousers.

"Behold. My ass." She turned her hips for extra effect. "Now do I get to suck on your tits or what?"

"Why are you in such a hurry? We've got *all* night."

Yes, and Eva was going to do things to her, so help her Sappho, patron saint of all things… Sapphic. "I'm not in a hurry." She surrounded and splayed her hands above her lover's head. "I'm starving to devour you. You want to go nice and slow? I'm the wrong girl tonight. All I've been thinking about is throwing you on that bed and tasting every inch of your body. I'm going to make you feel the kind of orgasms that will make you addicted to me. There is no hurry versus taking one's time. There's only doing what feels right, and let me tell you, ripping all the clothes from your body and making you see stars is the only thing that feels right."

She tipped Nadia's chin up to see her reaction. Excellent. Those eyes were clouding over in fantasy. Hopefully, they were fantasies that included Eva doing what she was born to do with gorgeous women like Nadia.

"So what are you waiting for?" Her fingers sauntered up Eva's blouse, teasing her buttons and the hard nipples beneath. "The more you talk, the more I think you're all bluster."

All bluster?

All bluster?

Enough bantering. Time to take Nadia away from this reality and into the one where Eva was the only one who existed. Because Eva sure as hell was convinced that Nadia was the only one who existed now.

***

Nadia had never landed on a bed so damn hard before. Her whole body jerked from the impact, but instead of fear, she felt *alive.* The dress choking her waist disappeared. Down her legs. Over her bare toes. Onto the floor where it would shortly be forgotten.

She may still be wearing her underwear, but Nadia felt most definitely exposed – in the best ways, of course. Ways that brought her the undivided attention of a woman who swore to devour her, bit by bit. Or more like gulp by gulp, gauging how quickly shit was going now.

"Do you know how fucking hot you are?" Eva abandoned her lover long enough to turn on a lamp by the bed. *Wow. Those legs.* Nadia's first time seeing Eva's bare legs did not disappoint. What her trousers always hid was the amount of hard muscle lining the otherwise lean limbs. *And a nice tattoo.* Nadia was gazing at a runner. Hopefully she'd put those legs to better use soon. "Because you've been killing me for months."

Nadia hid her shy grin behind her hand. Eva climbed onto the bed and went straight for ear nibbling. Oh, hi, tingles! "You're just saying that," Nadia murmured. "You forget about me the moment you leave the office."

"Wrong. I never stop thinking about a woman as stunning as you." Those words rolled right into Nadia's ear. How could breath be so hot?

"So there are other women?"

Eva drew her nose across Nadia's cheek. "Do you see any other women here?"

"Mm-hmm."

"That so? I'd love to know where. If I have to put on a show, I get advance warning."

"I'm talking about you."

"Oh, of *course* you were." Eva pushed Nadia down and grabbed the front clasps of her bra. "How could I forget how gay this is?"

"Indeed. How dare you?" Nadia wrapped her hand around Eva's wrist. "Do you need an invitation? You were going to devour me, Ms. Warren."

She had said the magic words. No sooner were they past her lips did Eva throw herself on top of Nadia and make good on every promise she had dropped over the past year.

She also wasn't kidding when she said she was going to devour poor Nadia. That was "poor" only in the sense that Nadia was but a mere mortal who didn't have the physical or mental capacity necessary to do everything she wanted in bed. One second she wanted to rut like a crazed animal in heat. The next? Give Eva a taste of her own medicine by climbing on top of her and making *her* the bottom. There were a million positions to try and words to say. Why did she have to do one at a time? Plus, her body was going to give out at some point! What took priority, anyway?

Oh. Eva ripping apart the front of Nadia's bra took priority.

The sound echoing in the room was involuntary. A million nerves fired up in Nadia's breasts. How was she supposed to process a ravenous mouth right on her nipple? And how was she supposed to process the damn woman *smacking* the side of her breast and giving her a delectable taste of mild pain? It was impossible!

"Tell me you want it," Eva growled, pinching the nipple her mouth abandoned. "Don't hold back on me. You're exactly the type of girl I want screaming and writhing."

"I want it." Fuck, did she! Any apprehension she felt before was long gone. Even if a light clicked on in her head and told her that this was a terrible idea, she would never listen to it. Not when the sexual experience of the year was right here in front of her. *Maybe of my 20s. Maybe of my life!* She didn't think Eva was all bluster. She did, however, want a thorough demonstration of her prowess. Now. "Fuck me."

"Fuck me, what?"

The game began. Nadia had inadvertently walked into a situation she had never witnessed before, let alone participated in. Didn't she know what kind of woman Eva was? She had certainly heard plenty of rumors over the years. *Everyone* knew what her brother and his fiancée got up to, let alone in public. Apples didn't fall far from trees. The whole Warren tree was probably nothing but kinksters.

"Ms. Warren."

A moment passed between them, heavy with mutual desire and the establishment of their roles tonight. Even if Nadia suddenly had the gumption to give Eva what she gave in turn, it wouldn't suit the mood. Not tonight. Maybe not any night.

Eva thirsted for more than a pretty woman that struck her fancy. She craved a woman who would offer her some level of submission.

They weren't in the office. They weren't at a party covered in tabloid photographers. They were in the bedroom… and Nadia still called her Ms. Warren.

"Say it." Every time Eva spoke like that, Nadia quivered. "Say the whole thing."

She swallowed. What, she had no idea, because both her throat and her mouth were dry. "Fuck me, Ms. Warren." When did her voice get so meek? "I deserve it."

Eva's stoic face cracked into a wide smile. "I bet you do." Both of her hands wrapped around Nadia's breasts – and squeezed. "You know exactly what I want to hear."

Nadia didn't know whether to smile or keep a straight face. "Helps to have someone who knows what she's doing in the lead."

"Oh, don't worry." Eva squeezed. Harder. Nadia shut her eyes and concentrated on the sweet feelings swelling inside of her. "I know what I'm doing." Long, naked legs brushed against Nadia's. *Oh my God. She's so soft.* "I trust that you do too. If not? You will soon enough."

Nadia couldn't speak. Not because she was speechless, but because someone kissed her so hard the words were knocked right out of her.

Chapter 6

Once Nadia completely let go, everything turned to instinct. That primal bullshit that made people lose their minds and do things they otherwise wouldn't. Or at least would never admit to doing. She wouldn't be able to lie later. What Eva did to her? What she did to *Eva?* It was the only way things could have happened.

There wasn't much talking. Either Nadia's lips were covered with another woman's, or she was so far gone from the world that the thought of saying anything other than empty words was impossible. She knew she was gone when Eva slipped between her legs and unleashed all the energy culminating between them.

They may not have removed all of their clothing, but that only made it hotter. Eva wanted her so badly that she couldn't wait to take off the last of her clothes before thrusting between Nadia's opened legs. *Shit!* Nadia had been on the receiving end of her fair share of encounters. None of those men or women compared to the way Eva's body lingered on hers, pulling, pushing, taunting, *teasing.* Her breaths became hotter. Her grunts were louder. One moment Nadia was telling her to put up or shut up, and the next… this was as close to tribbing as Nadia ever got in her life, and she was pretty sure it was the only way to have sex from now on!

When they *did* take off their clothes… yeah, that couldn't be an average affair either. Eva yanked off the black bra still clinging to Nadia's shoulders. It joined the other clothing over the edge of the bed, shortly followed by Eva's white blouse. *Oh my God. Congratulations on the physique.* Eva's ivory white bra didn't leave much to the imagination. Already her nipples were piercing through while the whole of her cleavage begged Nadia's tongue to explore its depths. *Okay.* She launched herself up and went for it before Eva could say "Down, girl."

All Nadia wanted was to feel that wonderful mixture of physical pleasure and the emotional elation she received for having so much attention focused on her. It wasn't just about who Eva was or how she could have had anyone she put her mind to. It wasn't only about the way she kissed, blew, or snaked her fingers past Nadia's lingerie and slammed right into her, eliciting the loudest cry Nadia ever emitted. *She's got me now. Boom. Having sex with this woman.* No, what it was really about was feeling like the only woman in the world, let alone the only one who mattered. Didn't matter if Eva made love like this to every other woman she was ever with. Nadia didn't know, and she didn't care. Because Eva was like this *right now,* and Nadia was luckier than she had any right to be. No matter how much she asserted that she deserved it.

Eva didn't comment on how Nadia felt inside. She didn't have to say a damn thing. Her look of elated determination and the brace of her hand beside Nadia's head did all the talking. Their eyes locked in the docile light of the room. Nadia didn't know what else to do with her hands, so she grabbed the bedding around her, arching her back and feeling everything inside come undone. There was no mercy. From the moment she called her lover Ms. Warren, mercy left the bedroom.

"You gonna come?" Eva was either amused or aroused, but not both. "I want to see what you look like when you come from only my fingers."

Nadia found the breath for one short phrase. "Then fuck me harder."

Her request was honored. Within five seconds Nadia was officially on the way to sharing her most intimate moment with a woman named Eva Warren.

It shocked her how quickly she came. This woman, who knew nothing about her body other than what general female anatomy tended to dictate, had managed to fire her up in fewer than what… ten minutes? Five minutes? No, there was no way it was *just* finesse on Eva's part. Not even the greatest sex goddess on Earth could do that on her own. It was a team effort. Nadia had to be so in the moment that she couldn't help but look for excuses to come. She had already been on the verge when Eva was biting her nipple and dry-humping her. To have her actually inside? Nadia never stood a chance. Between one woman's skill and the other's willingness to experience this kind of unique pleasure, a quick orgasm was only inevitable.

She simply didn't anticipate how *crazy* it would feel.

Eva wasn't the only one unleashing energy. Nadia did her part too, and it wasn't the mere energy of a woman in desperate need of a good lay. Or how hot Eva was. It was more. It was the heat of the moment. The sweet addiction of feeling so close to another human being. No longer was Nadia merely having sex with someone. She was *with* her. Nadia could have gotten off on her own just fine. Yet only another woman – let alone one like Eva – could bring this level of intimacy and emotional satisfaction.

"Holy shit!" That cry came from both the pleasure overtaking her and from her subconscious blooming with a greater need.

Nadia was not satisfied. If anything, she came down from her brief euphoria needier than ever. The walls had been torn down. Eva had seen her at her most intimate, her most vulnerable. There was nothing Nadia could do or say to turn this woman off now. Not to mention what endorphins did to a woman's brain.

"Come here and use me. Now."

Perhaps it was her cloudy head that made time go by so quickly. A blur. A whirlwind of feelings, both internal and external. She swore that one moment Eva still had her underwear on and the next she was completely naked, a glint of pale white skin in the dark room. Nadia also swore that they were softly kissing one moment and then going at it like rabbits the next.

This was the real moment she had been waiting for. Their bodies entwined, strength and need crashing against the bed as legs wrapped around legs and the familiar feeling of a woman's heat hit Nadia near hers. She had no idea what Eva would do to her after being given so much liberty to do what she wanted. To have her slide on top of her and do what two women had done since the dawn of time, whether people wanted to admit it or not? It was unreal.

Their kisses, their movements, and the way Eva wrapped her arms around Nadia as they undulated together was what she had always wanted without having ever admitted it. *I can't believe she feels like this!* Nadia was drowning beneath Eva's body. And when she wasn't drowning, she was inhaled, clawed, and *owned.* There was no escape, not that she wanted to escape. No world outside of the one they created, not that she wanted to go to any other place. Nadia was perfectly content to have this woman deliver what was promised not too long ago.

Too overwhelming. Nadia rode a high from the moment Eva slipped between her legs, and now she cried out, nails digging into strong shoulder blades and thighs shaking around a relentless leg. Every time Nadia got the smallest breather, Eva came back, rubbing her slit until poor Nadia's clit tore her apart.

While Nadia lost her mind again, Eva thrust as hard as she dared against her lover's thigh. Nadia had barely regained sense of the world outside of them when the woman on top of her emitted a sound that shook them both in their cores.

Wow. That's all she could think as her fingers threaded through Eva's short hair and caressed the top of her ear. The feminine cry of orgasm bursting against Nadia wasn't what she was expecting. Everything about Eva was so craftily put together to create an image of dominance and no bullshit that sometimes Nadia forgot she was with a *girl.* A woman, sure.

But like Nadia's experiences made her the person she was, Eva too had experiences that went as far back as a girl trying to make sense of the world. Who cared if she cried out in a way that made Nadia think of her more "feminine" partners. Wasn't it more endearing than anything else? What better time to show a trace of shared humanity than when in a situation like this?

Nadia caught her partner's fall the moment Eva lost her strength and collapsed on her. "You okay?" she whispered, fingers still entwined with Eva's hair.

"Fuck yeah I'm okay," came an exasperated breath. "Shit. After that? You think I'm not okay?" She rolled off, their legs still coiled together at the ankles. *Geez, she's gorgeous.* Naked Eva was as alluring as fully clothed in designer suits Eva. "I'm so okay it should be illegal."

Nadia folded her hands on her stomach. Felt weird to not have someone on top of her. *Are we taking a breather or is that it?* Eva had made some other promises. She better deliver.

"Should be asking you if *you're* okay," Eva continued. "I smothered you half to death. Guessing you liked it, though."

"Liked it? You should do it again." Here came the tingles again. *I should do something for her. I wonder what she tastes like...* "Although."

"Although what?"

Nadia sat up, pulling the covers back from the bed. "I like being under the covers."

Eva grinned. "And cover up that gorgeous body of yours?"

"I like the feel of the sheets when I do it. I bet this bed has really nice sheets."

"Hmm." Eva felt them with her fingertips. "All right, I guess. *My* sheets are much nicer."

Nadia's grin disappeared. She had forgotten what a privileged nugget Eva was. *Of course she has nice sheets. She probably has no idea what I'm talking about.*

Eva was the first to get under the covers. "Get in here. I haven't tasted your pussy yet."

Nadia couldn't get under the covers fast enough. *This is what I want.* There really wasn't anything cozier than enjoying some comfy sheets with a beautiful naked woman. Especially when that beautiful naked woman was wrapping around her and gently sucking on her throat whilst rubbing her mound with nimble fingers.

"Ho God!"

That was not Eva's voice. It definitely was not Nadia's.

The covers flung back so Nadia could have the fright of her life. There was Jasmine, standing in the bedroom's unlocked doorway and staring at the spectacle before her.

Oh my God.

Oh my God!

Time was not Nadia's friend. The bastard had completely stopped. Neither Eva nor Jasmine moved – not until Eva leaned back and wrapped her hands behind her head. "Caught," she muttered. "By your boss's girlfriend, no less."

"Get outta here!" Nadia shouted, panic, anger, and a healthy dose of fear hitting her right in the chest. *Oh my G o d!* Mortified, she grabbed one of her books off the nightstand and flung it at Jasmine. The door quickly closed.

Eva lowered her hands, a wicked smile emblazoned on her face. "What a turn of events. I haven't been walked in on like that in a while. Think she saw my good side?" She gestured to her ass hanging halfway out of the bed.

Nadia couldn't look at her. *Jasmine saw me with Eva. One of my best friends saw me in bed with Eva Warren.* Hard to say if she was more than embarrassed. Nadia was far from an exhibitionist, that was for sure. She could trade sex stories with friends, but actually being caught in an intimate moment like that? Horrifying! *How can I look at her again? How can I…* She turned to Eva, still grinning as if she had her trophy validated.

"What are you smiling about?" Where had the fun gone? Never mind. Nadia didn't want to know. She crawled out of bed and began searching for her clothes. When she realized this was *her* room, she froze.

"You okay?" it was Eva's turn to ask.

Nadia narrowed her eyes. "I'm embarrassed."

"Yeah, that is kind of embarrassing. Come back, though." She patted the empty space next to her. "It's not a big deal. She knows we're both gay. So what? Could've been worse. Could've walked in on *her*."

Don't put that in my head. Jasmine talked enough about her and Mr. Cole's sex life to stun Nadia forever. "Do you have to be so laissez-faire about this?"

"Hon…" Eva shrugged. "It's sex. Millions of people are having it right now."

Nadia flung open her suitcase and pulled out her silk robe. She couldn't get it on fast enough. "I think you should leave."

Eva sat up with a start. "Huh?"

"Come on. You got what you wanted." Nadia stood next to the bed but didn't dare get too close to the woman she had sex with. "You can leave me alone now."

"Excuse me?"

A thousand thoughts swarmed Nadia's head. No denying that Eva's pursuit of her was purely about bedposts and notches. She was what? The hundredth girl? The tenth redhead? Probably. Sounded like good figures to go by. "I'm not dumb. This was a quick bang. So, you got your bang. You can leave now."

"Whoa, whoa." Eva stood up, although she was in no hurry to grab her clothes. "Did I do something wrong? Did I offend you? Please tell me if I did. I didn't mean to."

Nadia looked away from that naked body. "Leave, please." Her voice softened. "You didn't do anything wrong. I can't do this right now."

Eva lingered, perhaps waiting for Nadia to retract what she said. "I see." She walked over to her clothes and picked them up, one by one, putting her bra on first. So much for admiring the way her breasts moved when she walked. "Guess I misinterpreted. Wouldn't be the first time."

Her terse voice didn't suit her. *Stick to your guns, girl.* Nadia sat on the edge of the bed and waited for Eva to finish dressing. *I've never kicked a woman out of my room before.* Ever since Jasmine walked in on them, though? Something sour simmered in Nadia's throat. She wasn't sure what it was yet.

"Enjoy your night." Eva showed herself out. "You might want to lock this door." It shut.

Alone, Nadia flopped onto the bed. Sad thing? She recognized Eva's perfume and was sad when it began to disappear.

***

What a farce of a weekend.

After being booted from Nadia's room – whatever *that* was about – Eva drowned herself in more cognac from the study and the papers she brought with her. They were crap, of course. It would be a miracle if her professors passed her at this point.

She didn't see Nadia all day Saturday. That almost pissed Eva off more. It certainly drove her to her guest room and ensured that she wouldn't emerge except to have a five-minute chat with Kathryn about *boys* and bullshit. Eva muttered about her poisoned good fortune, but her best friend barely responded. She had half a mind to go up to Jasmine Bliss and tell her to mind her own damn business for the rest of her life, but every time they crossed paths, Jasmine hurried, as red as Nadia's hair.

Shit, she was so gorgeous. Eva had seen her fair share of beautiful women in bed, but Nadia was something else. Almost otherworldly. Angelic. That was it! Wow. How sappy.

You're only hung up on her because she rejected you in the end. Eva refused to get out of bed in a timely manner Sunday morning, even though Henry had knocked on her door more than once to tell her to get her ass moving so they could go home.

She saw Nadia in the foyer as everyone got ready to leave. Nadia fluffed her hair in the hallway mirror and caught Eva's reflection. Squeaking in surprise, she rushed to Jasmine's side. Apparently things had been forgiven between the two of them.

Like that would stop Eva from giving it one last try.

"You should give me your number," she said as she walked past Nadia. "I'll take you on a real date." When that didn't get a response, she tried, "I can't get how you felt beneath me out of my head."

Nadia was the only one who heard her, yet she looked as if everyone chatting in the foyer had eavesdropped right then.

"Fine." Eva wandered off, bumping into Kathryn – alone, for once.

"I haven't been able to walk since Friday night," she said with a sniff. "I even stayed in bed all day yesterday and my everything is *still* sore." Good to know someone got laid all weekend. Gag.

"I don't wanna hear about your fucked pussy." Eva couldn't look at her. There were times it was not fun being best friends with a straight woman, and this was one of them. "Think about me. I finally got that hottie in bed, and now she won't talk to me. Says we had some fun but now she's going home. Fuck my life. Thought I could at least take her on a proper date…"

"Oh, excuse me regarding your Sapphic plight, but you're not God's gift to *every* woman." Kathryn winced as she turned and shuffled toward the coat rack, grabbing a scarf she almost forgot. "And here I thought I had missed my boyfriend that much."

"You can fuck your dumbass anytime you want." Eva lowered her voice. "Do you know how long it's been since I had sex before Friday night? Two. Months." Fuck grad school.

Kathryn rolled her eyes. "Sorry it didn't work out. Think I'm gonna leave now. See you at lunch on Tuesday?"

Eva snorted. "Sure. Lunch on Tuesday. If you can walk by then."

"At any rate…" Kathryn continued. "You have good taste, as usual. She's the prettiest one in here. Aside from us, of course."

"Regardless of what I've told you before, honey, I'm not into other blondes."

Kathryn rendezvoused with her boyfriend before getting the hell out.

Eva couldn't wait to leave either. If Nadia wanted nothing to do with her? Fine. She didn't want anything to do with Nadia either. As soon as

Henry and Monica had their shit together, they were out of there. Eva didn't even look over her shoulder as they left. Okay. Maybe she did. Once. Just because she appreciated the way Nadia's coat fell on her body.

"What's your problem?" Henry asked her in the limo. "Didn't get what you wanted again?"

Something about the way he said that implied he knew what happened. *That's absurd.* "Oh, I got what I wanted." Eva didn't take her eyes off the window.

"Good." Henry turned to his fiancée and said something that Eva couldn't hear. It probably wasn't for her, anyway.

Still, it was merely another day of her watching everyone else in her life have what she so desperately wanted deep inside: someone to share the morning with. *I would've shared it with her.* Whatever Nadia's problem was… well, it wasn't any of Eva's concern.

Nope.

Not at all.

Not even a little bit.

Shit. She needed one of her mother's happy pills.

Chapter 7

Nadia spent an early Saturday morning enjoying the first real break of sunshine that year. Since Christmas, the city had been a dark and dreary place, with rainstorms thrashing the evergreen trees and threats of snow always on the horizon. One potentially nasty freeze covered the landscape in ice. Nadia wasn't falling for it. Not too many winters ago she had slipped and sprained her ankle. Now she knew where to look for dark patches of otherwise invisible ice on the sidewalks.

Today, however, was a clear and serene day. Not the warmest, by far, but nice enough to sit on the porch swing and enjoy the morning with hot tea and a thick coat.

Hopefully it stays sunny all day. Nadia had a wedding shower to go to out of town as soon as she was finished with her tea. No, not her own… unfortunately. Worse. She was going to Monica Graham's wedding shower, hosted by mutual friend Jasmine, who had asked Nadia to attend for the moral support. *She's in way over her head.* Jasmine spent more time trying to figure out how rich people lived instead of living her own life. *Sounds like a rabbit hole I never want to fall in.*

A crisp breeze blew by. Chills rattled down her body. For the briefest moment, it gave Nadia memories of that cold night in the mountains when she was seduced in her own guest bed.

There had been no word, no sign of Eva since that weekend. Felt strange to be at work and never anticipate her walking through the door. Instead, Henry Warren was the familiar face coming in and out of Mr. Cole's office. Nadia had spent more than a few hours at her desk wondering if Mr. Warren would give her a message from his sister. Such a thing never came.

She was of two minds about that. At first she was relieved. The last thing she wanted was to be harassed after she told Eva a final no. On the other hand… would it have killed her to put in a little more effort?

Stop it. Stop it right now. Nadia got up and went back into her rental house. For years she lived in a crappy studio apartment downtown. A few months ago, however, an old friend of the family retired to the countryside and asked Nadia to rent this nice house in the suburbs for cheap. At the time, she had jumped on the opportunity. Two stories with three bedrooms? A full kitchen? A bathtub? Sweet. The old town neighborhood was also a fun, bustling community for art types and those who liked to pretend to be living in the '60s. What Nadia hadn't anticipated, however, was the longer commute in and out of downtown, as well as the incredible emptiness she felt late at night.

It was even worse when she had to go up to the Hills, where Mr. Cole and Jasmine lived. Although the Hills weren't too far out of town, they were exclusive – and buses only ran so far up into them. Usually Jasmine would pick her up if they were going to hang out. Jasmine was way too busy to do that today, though. Nadia dithered between a convenient Uber or a less expensive taxi. She ended up taking the taxi since that was less suspicious in the Hills.

The taxi idled at a notoriously long red light in the middle of downtown. Nadia glanced out the window and saw a trendy street bistro stuffed with brunchers. *Rather be doing that today.* The wedding shower was sure to be a total snore, complete with cucumber sandwiches and old biddies who had spent most of their lives balancing million-dollar checkbooks. Probably some of the same cranky women who came into the office. They weren't ever nice to Nadia then. Why would they be now? They'd probably treat her like the help anyway.

Something caught Nadia's eye. A sleek, black Jaguar with the top down. Two beautiful blondes, complete with designer sweaters, trousers, and handbags, sat in the front seat, one twirling curls around her finger and the other staring through the windshield, wearing a pair of Prada sunglasses. Nadia would always recognize Prada. It was one of her favorites.

The woman wearing the Prada sunglasses? Neither her favorite nor her most despised.

Nadia was relieved when the taxi pulled far away from the parallel parking nightmare. She was pretty sure she had seen Eva, and was not in the mood… until they were far enough away to not be bothered by her, of course. Nadia was easiest to get when she was farthest away.

***

"There better be booze," Kathryn said, taking off her sunglasses now that the hood of the car was back up. It looked too much like rain on the horizon for Eva to risk her precious leather interior. "If you're dragging me to this, then there better be booze."

"Didn't know you were such a lush for wedding showers." Eva slowed the Jaguar down as they went around the widest bend up in the Hills. Her GPS's robotic voice announced that she would be at her destination soon. "I'll keep that in mind for when I throw yours one day."

"If I ever get married, you can be sure that you will not be throwing the wedding shower. You'll be throwing the best bachelorette party ever, as God intended."

"Duly noted." Eva bit her lip to keep from thanking Kathryn for coming. Eva was the one with the obligation to attend, since the bride was her future sister-in-law. Yet she wasn't about to spend half her afternoon sipping tea and listening to old women tell the future Lady Warren what she should do with her married life. As fun as that would be, since Monica had no intention of selling her business of debauchery. Even so, Eva would soon lose interest. And patience. And when she lost interest and patience? She was liable to make the biggest ass out of herself. Kathryn helped offset that.

They arrived at Ethan and Jasmine's mansion shortly thereafter. "Shit," Eva muttered, noticing the amount of cars already parked in the front. "We're late."

"Could've told you that."

An attendant appeared to show Eva where to park. As soon as they were out of the car, she said, "Let's go find you some booze."

The cider and champagne served at her future sister-in-law's shower was not strong enough to deal with what she did that day.

Sure enough, the usual suspects in Ethan Cole's salon emerged. Middle-aged women of Eva's mother's generation who were convinced that their shit didn't stink and that they controlled the very social sphere everyone found themselves in. Jasmine certainly was not friends with these people. In fact, she looked relieved to greet Eva and Kathryn, even though they did not know each other well either. *We're not total assholes to her, though.* Eva had heard it all ever since Ethan Cole went public with his low-class girlfriend Jasmine. Oh, the woman *tried* to fit in. She wore the right designers, went to the right hair salons, was driven by the right drivers, and visited the right venues, but fact of the matter was… she was poor, with parents no one had ever heard of, and manners that would fly in the blue collar world but not this one. She was pretty and sweet, and that was enough to endear her to some of high society. But not enough. Just because she was a tabloid photographer's darling didn't mean she was getting invitations to the Women's Society and bridge club.

Eva saw these women first. Primarily, she saw Francesca Blake, the Queen Bee of the room and an old, dear friend of Eva's mother. Those two women conspired to get Eva dating Benny Blake, Francesca's son.

Did not work. In the slightest.

However, Eva knew how to handle these women. So did Kathryn, who was a pro at bullshit and fitting in wherever she went. Everyone knew she was the aloof ice queen who could silence even one of these assholes with one, cold glance. They deferred to her, too, even if they didn't like it. Kathryn was richer than any of them. She was also the only heiress of their children's generation who had made her own name for herself, so she commanded respect from a business front. *I'll be like that one day.* Kathryn was two years older than Eva and had already put in her time at grad school. *I'm going to be like that one day!* To say she was sometimes jealous of her best friend was an understatement.

Then Eva turned and saw the other side of the room.

Jasmine and Monica had set up shop over there. So had Nadia. A most surprising addition to this otherwise drab party.

Eva reacted the only way she knew how: with a dazzling smile that would strike *something* into that pretty redhead's heart. Inside, however, Eva's own heart beat fast enough to jumpstart her Jaguar. *Hi. Remember me? I'm the woman you had that awesome sex with two months ago. What? Have you already forgotten me? No way. I can't believe it. You've thought of me every night before you go to sleep. Maybe you don't want to think about me that often, but you have.* For as dumbstruck as she was in the moment, Eva still managed to convey that with one smile toward Nadia.

The other woman squeaked and turned away with wide eyes blazing. Whatever she said to Jasmine was lost to Eva's ears. Yet she had noticed her, and that was all that mattered.

Suddenly it was a *very* interesting party.

Oh, the mechanics of it were still as dull as math class, but at least Eva had something that struck her fancy. While Kathryn self-medicated with champagne, Eva ignored the ramblings of old, wealthy women and instead stole glances of Nadia, dressed in a simple yet gorgeous lavender dress that bore all the markings of an exclusive design of The Crimson Dove, one of the city's most celebrated boutiques. *Bet Cole bought that for her.* The man was notorious for buying all the pretty women in his life dress after dress. Eva wouldn't be surprised to find out that Ethan Cole was one of the manliest boys to play dress-up with Barbie dolls as a child. *Perv then, perv now.* At least they had something in common.

I wonder if she's slept with him.

Pangs of jealousy exploded in Eva's gut, and she was forced to look away. *So what if she has? All those women in that office have slept with him.* Another thing the randy billionaire was notorious for. He staffed the prettiest women around to fuel his own male ego. His personal harem, if one willed. Eva had seen the rotating door of "personal assistants" who lasted a few months before running off with millions of dollars and a new hole blown between their legs. Nadia said she was gay, but Eva had seen it before: a powerful man and his money could change almost any woman with neither. It was survival of the peasantry. Or something.

"And how about you, Ms. Warren?" Francesca Blake asked at the end of the social hour. She looked at Eva through the usual critical eyes. "What are you up to recently? Your mother told me that you're still in school."

"Indeed. Hope to graduate at the end of the year." Eva sipped her second glass of champagne. "After that, I'll be joining the family business." *I better be, Henry.*

"Really? How nice."

Francesca turned her attention to Monica on the other side of the room.

"You better put in a good word with your future husband, Monica. Don't let him work this one too hard. It would break her mother's heart."

Eva exchanged a bitter glance with Monica. The petite woman who looked more old Hollywood than any other Warren tugged on her coiled locks and imparted a serene smile upon Francesca. "I dare not get in their way. As an only child myself, I think it best to stay out of the affairs of siblings."

Always with her diplomatic answers. Not that it was *her* Eva ever held any ire for. Nope. That would be Francesca in this case. Dragging up Eva's mother Isabella was a great way to try and put the Warren heiress in her place. *Mother hates what I'm trying to do.* Eva never had an ounce of pressure to go into the family business placed upon her shoulders. That was Henry's job, because he was the oldest, and male. Eva only existed because Henry grew sick in elementary school and scared their parents into having a spare heir. When he fully recovered and Eva turned out to be female anyway, everything changed. Before she was even born.

I was no longer needed to be a spare. My parents had no use for me. She was mostly left alone growing up. At most, Gerald and Isabella Warren saw her as a potential bartering chip for wealthy marriages. Unfortunately, she was not interested in any of the rich heirs she went to school with, nor did she take a liking to any of the young men – like Benny Blake – who came to have dinner here and there. Turned out she was too gay for that shit, much to her parents' chagrin.

Perhaps Francesca still harbored dreams of her only and still single son marrying into the Warren family. *We certainly have more money than the Blakes.* Yet if Eva were to marry anyone, it would be a woman. She decided that the day gay marriage was declared legal in their state, let alone the whole country.

She caught Nadia's gaze. The woman quickly looked down at her notepad and pretended to not have been staring at Eva.

I knew it. Flames licked at Eva's maddening heart. *She wants me.*

With this knowledge, Eva's mind began turning and turning and *turning.* How to get her attention in a positive way? Better yet, how to score a real date with her? Was she open to that? She had refused to give Eva a number. Then again, that was two months ago. Maybe she had cooled down by now. She didn't have a girlfriend, did she? That would be shitty. Eva didn't want to have to woo pretty Nadia away from some hussy. She was too busy for that bullshit.

Why do I even care this much? I slept with her, didn't I? Usually that was enough to make Eva stop obsessing over a girl. Sure, the sex had been great. What they had of it, anyway. *There's still so much I could do with her.* No. Better not have those kinds of thoughts in present company.

Alas, Eva had next to no chance to flirt with Nadia. Not even when the party ended two hours later. Nadia chose that exact moment to get up and leave the room, sparing no glance for Eva. At least it gave her a chance to stare at Nadia's ass on its way by. It was torture now. Eva knew what that ass felt like in her hands.

She knew what Nadia looked like when she came.

Knew what she *sounded* like.

Felt like.

Tasted like.

"Helloooo," Kathryn snapped her fingers in front of Eva's face. "You getting me out of here or not? I'm too tipsy to drive your car. Drank waaaay too much champagne. Holy fuck, I hate these things." Anything related to marriage and weddings gave Kathryn hives. "Never mind. You've got those big butchy eyes going full speed."

Eva clutched her friend's arm. "Why won't she talk to me?"

Kathryn looked way too confused for this question. "Because you're an intimidating bitch. Stop leering and start chatting." Kathryn was so antsy to leave that Eva had no choice but to follow her lead outside. "You're no stranger to seducing women like her into your bed. I'm sure you'll figure it out. You know every trick in the book."

Eva stopped at the top of the front steps, drinking in the mid-winter sunlight. "I do, don't I?" She batted her lashes behind her Prada sunglasses. "Guess it's time for me to put everything I know to work." Plans were already formulating. Nadia had her taste of Eva Warren. Soon she wouldn't be able to say no to a full, satisfying course.

Chapter 8

"Starting today," Mr. Cole said at the Monday morning staff meeting, "Miss Amber Mayview will be working as my personal assistant. Please make her feel welcomed, and help her in any way she needs."

A courtesy clap went around the desk. More than one person leaned in toward another to whisper something. Probably about how hot this Miss Amber Mayview was. While Nadia had no issue with a hot coworker, she *did* take issue with her best friend's boyfriend hiring yet another modelesque hottie as his new personal assistant. *He's living with the last one. What's going on here?* Nadia furrowed her brows when Mr. Cole made eye contact with her. He cleared his throat and looked away.

"Looking forward to working with all of you." Amber was already tall *without* the six-inch stilettos. Nadia would dare say the new blond bombshell of the office was taller than Mr. Cole if he slouched too much.

"And on that note, I have something else serious to mention." Amber sat back down in her chair and continued taking notes of the staff meeting, her first task on the job. "What I am about to say is highly confidential. I don't have to remind you all of your NDAs."

Some shoulders bristled. Everyone at the conference table shut up.

"It is highly possible that I will be taking on a new business partner soon." Everyone remained *shut up,* because everyone – except Amber – remembered the last piece of shit business partner Mr. Cole eventually booted out of his life last year. "You will be seeing *many* prestigious and brilliant people coming in and out of this office. It's possible one of them may be a new boss in the near future. I would appreciate the best professionalism possible."

Nods and murmurs of agreement went around the room. Nadia barely registered this information. Of course Mr. Cole would take on a new business partner, like he took on a new personal assistant once he had time to go through the interviews to hire one. Nadia was more interested in *who* he chose. Amber briefly looked at Nadia before going back to her notes. At least she had brown eyes and wasn't another hot example of Scandinavian bullshit.

The meeting adjourned shortly thereafter. Since Mr. Cole was a busy man who had phone calls to return, Nadia was tasked with showing Amber around the office and getting her acquainted with how things work. Amber would be using the empty desk in the far corner of the room, and the only one within Nadia's range of sight from the receptionist's perch. *Jasmine used to work there.* Nadia acclimated to an empty desk. Seeing a Victoria's Secret model plant her perky breasts behind a desk and fling her long, stringy blond hair behind her shoulders? Ridiculous. And distracting.

"This is the break room." Nadia gestured to the machines on the counter and the two large refrigerators along the far side of the wall. "Please put your name on all items and make sure nothing stays in there for more than a week. This is your cabinet. Please feel free to store any kitchen items you think you will need in here. Fred keeps a hand mixer in his, so you know… it's pretty much a free-for-all."

"Hand mixer. What, is he baking cakes in here? And who's Fred?"

The bastard who outed me. "Someone who shouldn't know your secrets."

Amber snorted and rolled her eyes. "Pretty sure that's everyone, yeah?"

I sure don't want to know your secrets. Perhaps it was petty of Nadia to already hold a grudge against Amber. Sheesh. The only one to ever work in that office with a bigger stripper name was Jasmine. *That's who I'm looking out for.* Nadia didn't want to believe that a man who claimed to be so in love would cheat, but men were men, and Nadia was on the front lines of seeing the latest pussy Ethan Cole was fucking. *Does Jasmine know about this woman?* Perhaps a lunch break phone call was in order.

Nadia showed her the restroom and supply closet, complete with copy machine. Nadia had insisted on having it replaced shortly after Jasmine told a drunken tale of being fucked against it. *Gross. Gross!* Straight people. Seriously.

"Sooo… pretty sure I should finish up my desk stuff." Amber returned to said desk without a thanks or goodbye. Suited Nadia fine. She plopped herself at the receptionist's desk and began the Monday morning toil of clearing weekend messages and confirming that week's appointments. So happened that "H. Warren" was scheduled to come in shortly after lunch.

Unfortunately, lunch consisted of taking Amber down to the building cafeteria and eating with her. Nadia made sure to mention Jasmine no fewer than ten times. Amber, in turn, talked about her sorority and her last job being the personal assistant to Loretta Clyde, the vice president of a large shipping company there at the waterfront. In fact, Amber was quite meticulous going over her credentials. Did Nadia know that she was the vice editor for her large high school newspaper? Oh, by the way, she graduated from Columbia. Had administrative internships out her ass. Loretta Clyde? Pfft. Mr. Cole may have been the biggest name yet, but Loretta was small stuff. How about Christopher Samson? Yeah. That one. Amber had been *his* personal assistant before he retired. Did Nadia know that Amber could type 150wpm and developed her own much more efficient form of shorthand? Because she had.

Once she finished running her mouth, Amber took a sip of iced tea, those whirling brown eyes never once leaving Nadia's.

"That's… impressive." Nadia cleared her throat.

"I got this job on my merits alone."

Oh, here they went. Nadia sweetly smiled. "I like to think that about myself as well."

"Really? Being a receptionist is tough."

"It is. I am good at it, but there were people better than me applying for the position. Don't kid yourself, Amber. You weren't the only qualified person to be Mr. Cole's assistant."

Their silent impasse was deafening.

"I'm not sleeping with him."

"Didn't say you were."

"I'm not. I have a boyfriend."

"You don't have to convince me."

"Hm."

They went to their separate stations after lunch: Nadia to her usual work, and Amber to typing up reports for Mr. Cole. Indeed, she was a fast typist. Her slender fingers flew over the laptop keyboard. *I know a few jokes about fast typists.* Nadia sighed. She better find a way to get laid soon before she started dreaming about a woman's typing skills.

The H. Warren appointment showed up twenty minutes early.

It was not Henry.

What it *was* could only be described as "utterly ridiculous."

Nadia was the only one in the executive office who seemed to notice Ms. Eva Warren leaning in the open doorway with her golden sunglasses still perched on the bridge of her nose. What in the world was she doing? No one came to Mr. Cole's office to display herself in this fashion! Speaking of fashion, what in the world was she wearing? Gone were the pantsuits. What Nadia gazed upon was Eva Warren at her most casual – in public, anyway. Dark wash designer jeans hugged her hips and disappeared into her huge leather boots covered in golden zippers and buckles. A baggy silk white blouse hung from her torso. Was that a *sweater?* Nadia dropped her pen. Eva wore an open black cardigan, the sleeves smartly rolled up to her elbows and her breasts poking through both silk and cashmere. *Oh. My. God.* Had Nadia stepped onto some European runway? Nordic hair and skin clashed with Eastern European no-nonsense over there. Eva could've either passed for a Norwegian supermodel or a Ukrainian she-devil. Until that moment, Nadia hadn't realized she was so stricken by such images.

Eva stepped away from the entrance with a slight roll of her hips. *You know, those hips weren't so bad when they were crashing against my pussy.* Nadia picked up her forgotten pen. She needed to check herself before the woman on a mission reached the desk.

"Ms. Warren," she said. "I was not expecting you. Here in place of your brother, Mr. Warren?"

Eva curled her hands around the edge of Nadia's desk and leaned down, sunglasses falling down her face. Those striking blue eyes made Nadia's cheek pale, as if frozen over in an unforgiving tundra. *Am I turning purple? I'm turning purple.* Choking on that rose and… was that sandalwood?... perfume.

"Henry's indisposed today." Eva pushed her chest up. Nadia stared at that cleavage much longer than was kosher. *Right. She has breasts. Remember breasts? They were in your mouth at one point. Fuuuck!* "Still recovering from the honeymoon."

"Right. The honeymoon." Nadia had attended the Warren wedding two weeks ago. *I saw this woman in a dress.* Somehow, Monica had convinced her sister-in-law to wear a dress for the bridal party. *She was gorgeous.* That deep, lusty red was a color Eva should sport more often. Not that Nadia was complaining about this current ensemble. *I could go on a date with her dressed like this. A real people date.* Dinner and movie was real, wasn't it? Nadia imagined them at an intimate restaurant overlooking the river. Candlelight. That delicate yet curdling laugh ringing in her ears every time Eva thought she said something funny.

Snap out of it!

"Congratulations on the announcement, by the way. I'm sure your family is very happy."

That flirty look faltered for the briefest instance. "Oh, you mean the baby thing?" The big event at the Warren wedding was the revelation that it was a shotgun marriage. Not that the groom had any idea until the bride revealed that they had a gestating heir attending the wedding. "It's fantastic. No pressure on me to ever have babies." Eva stood up straight. "Not that Mommy and Daddy were hounding *me* to do that."

Nadia didn't respond.

"Anyway, I know I'm early and that Ethan can't be bothered with me right now. So how about I stay out here, hm?" She crossed her arms beneath her breasts. *Mine are bigger, but hers fit her frame better than mine do.* Would she stop thinking about boobs already?

Nadia gestured to the sitting area. "You're welcomed to stay, Ms. Warren."

Eva glanced at the couches and then back at Nadia. "But you're not over there, are you?"

"Do you mean to imply something, Ms. Warren?"

Down Eva went, crossed arms leaning on top of the desk so her crisp bangs were inches away from Nadia's forehead. She could smell her minty breath. *Feel* her minty breath right against warming skin. Nadia inched back and refused to look Eva in the eye. That perfume was stronger now. Definitely roses. And sandalwood. Hints of spices. What was that other scent? Nadia didn't dare think about it.

The scent was so maddeningly feminine that Nadia spent the next few seconds thinking about what *else* was so feminine about Ms. Eva Warren. Not merely her womanly physique, either. Or the light tone of her voice. The way she walked, hips swaying in tune to heels. Searing looks boiling in owned womanhood. *Her name is really feminine too.* Everyone, including Nadia, knew that Eva's full name was Evangeline. Somehow it fit her.

"I imply whatever you want to infer, my dear," Eva said with a heavy whisper that only Nadia could hear. "But if you prefer me to be more blunt, I was going to ask if you get to go on break soon. There's a parlor in the women's restroom with our names on the door."

Nadia should have guessed. If Eva was going to waltz in here and try to seduce poor her for ten minutes, then the only place for them to go was the small parlor adjacent to the restroom. It wouldn't be Nadia's first time making out in a bathroom. Probably not Eva's either.

"I'm not that kind of girl, sorry." Nadia crossed the Warren name off her calendar. "Now, if you'll excuse me, Ms. Warren, I need to get back to work. I just got off lunch, so no breaks for me anytime soon."

Eva didn't budge. "Give me your number and I'll be out of your hair."

Not this again. Eva had been after Nadia's number for ages. After their first night together, Nadia had been inclined to give it… and then thought better about it.

"No? That's all right." Eva pulled out one of her calling cards and slid it across Nadia's desk. "Keep it. Call me sometime. I'll always keep my schedule open for you."

Nadia glanced at the card but paid it no mind as she turned to her computer.

"Do you like French food? Hm? Me neither. How about authentic Chinese? Thai? I bet you're a Peruvian kind of girl. How about we go sometime?"

Nadia opened a spreadsheet and began running formulas, adding up numbers she barely knew the sources of. Mr. Cole would want them by the end of the day.

"My family has a yacht on standby down at the marina. Weather's supposed to be clear this weekend. How about we take it out for the evening and watch the stars?

What! How dare the program give her these glaring red errors! Who fucked up the formulas while she was out at lunch? Damnit. Nadia's fingers hovered over the keyboard as she tried to think of how to fix this bullshit.

"Haven't I seen you in this dress before? Of course it looks gorgeous on you, but wouldn't you like to go on a little shopping spree? I don't mean here. Milan. Dubai. Beverly Hills. Hong Kong. You tell me where, and we'll go there. Tonight."

"Ms. Warren, I'm afraid that I will have to ask you to please step back. This is sensitive information on this computer."

That pretty smile disappeared on Eva's heart-shaped face. She slowly pulled back from the desk, frown growing.

"All right," she finally sighed. "I see that you're busy. Still, give me a call if your schedule opens up." Eva looked as if she were going to the sitting area, but at the last moment she bent back down and whispered in Nadia's direction. "You think I'm the kind who seduces and runs? You are *sorely* mistaken, Nadia. If anything, I want you more now. What we had was only the tip of the iceberg."

Nadia stared at her computer monitor. "I'll keep that in mind, Ms. Warren."

"Hmph." Eva left the desk… and veered right instead of left toward the waiting area. "And who might you be? New to the office? I've never seen you around before."

Nadia glanced up from her computer and saw something that made her brain melt: Eva, sitting on the edge of Amber's desk, giving the new assistant a generous view of some heiress's cleavage. Amber? She was *looking.*

A lump went down Nadia's throat as Amber giggled. *You told me you had a boyfriend!* Instead of thinking it was a cover for banging the boss, however, Nadia should have thought of it as a cover for something else…

After all, hadn't she used a boyfriend as a cover? Her boyfriend in Canada, as it were?

Nadia needed to get a grip. Of course Eva was going to wander off and flirt with the first hottie she came across. She probably would have done it even if Nadia gave her a number and a promise for a date. Pshaw. That's how these playgirls and boys worked. Especially the ridiculously rich ones.

Eva could have anyone she wanted. Just because she wanted Nadia one moment didn't mean she didn't want someone else *more* the next. Nadia went back to work, completely rest assured that she made the right choice in not pursuing anything more than a hot one night stand with the eligible bachelorette.

That didn't stop her from being temptingly hot, though. Nadia caught herself looking up more times than she could count until Eva finally left

Amber alone and entered Mr. Cole's office. When she disappeared behind the doors, Amber looked most pleased with her first day at work.

Jerk. Nadia furrowed her brows. Score another one for Mr. Cole and his amazing ability to staff hot queer women left and right. All the beautiful women without the real temptation. Clearly, Jasmine had nothing to worry about. Nadia, on the other hand? This was going to try her poor, already stressed out heart.

***

"You keep striking out like this, we won't be able to be friends anymore." Kathryn was halfway to claiming the whole basket of French fries to herself. Someone was on her period. "I can't be friends with someone who doesn't have the suave skills of Dona Juana herself."

"First of all, that's not a real person. Second of all," Eva snatched the basket and grabbed the longest fry she could find. Where was the consommé flakes? Ever since Eva's last trip to Japan, she was obsessed with consommé spiced potato chips and fries. Mayonnaise? She could do without that on her fries. "I can't help it that I'm crushing on the most unavailable lesbian in the city. Seriously. What gives?"

Kathryn watched in dismay as Eva poured half a small bottle of consommé on the fries. Out of all the spices and sauces available on the table, that was her least favorite, and here Eva guaranteed that her best friend would not be hogging all the fries to herself. *What? I left her half the basket!* They ordered the biggest one to share. Kathryn could get her own if she was that upset about it.

"Maybe it's because your breath smells like ass."

"Excuse you." Eva stuffed her mouth with fries. Whoops. Got one on her cashmere sweater. Whatever. Wasn't good enough to seduce Nadia, so into the trash it would go. "I had a mint before I went in there."

Kathryn slipped a fry out of the basket. "Maybe she's not into you."

"Oh, honey, she's *into* me." Eva would quip that it was quite literal, but Nadia did not have the wonderful chance to finger her one night stand. *I did. That's all that mattered.* Eva looked wistfully into the basket of fries as she remembered the way Nadia's whole body shuddered around two fingers. *These ones right here.* Pop went another French fry into her mouth. At least her fingers were versatile.

"Be that as it may, you're creeping her out, I guarantee it. Stop showing up at the office so you can spread your ovaries all over the place and leave her alone. If she wants to go out with you, she'll let you know."

"Spread my *what?*"

"Sorry. Got ovaries on the brain."

"Let me guess. Aunt Flow and Animal Planet?"

"I spent all day yesterday on the couch crying over baby animals with a pint of ice cream as my only friend."

"Don't you have a boyfriend?"

"He's in Holland."

"And I should be in the Caribbean with the most beautiful redhead on this planet."

"The Caribbean? Wouldn't she burn there?"

"She's not *that* kind of redhead."

"Oh."

Eva sighed. "You're probably right. I've gotta let her go. At least I got to fuck her."

"That's the spirit." Kathryn found a whole section of clean fries and pulled them onto a napkin. "Time to move on."

"Maybe I'll move on to Cole's new assistant."

"Oh? He's already replaced Jasmine Bliss?"

"Oh, he's replaced her. Job wise, that is. Some beautiful blonde with legs that go on for miles. She was very receptive to my flirting, too."

"Which means…"

"She's either got the gay gene too or she's an indiscriminate gold digger." Eva kinda hated those types. It was fun to date a gay-for-pay for a few weeks when she was hot and the sex was more than okay. Eventually, though, the woman either wanted a big payoff or the guarantee that there would be dick on the side… because it was never about *Eva* to begin with.

Finding women she fancied who were also genuinely into the idea of her was harder than a multimillionaire had the right to experience. Even ugly men didn't have this much of a problem at her income level. "I might take the latter though, if it means a palate cleanser."

"Just make sure you know that Cole isn't responsible for curating a dating pool for you."

Eva stuck out her tongue. How else was she supposed to respond to that?

She needed to go home after this late afternoon snack with her friend. Schoolwork called, as much as Eva dreaded it at the moment. One of her professors up and disappeared to Germany for reasons unknown. That fucker was good at that. Now Eva was in limbo for many of her assignments and projects. That didn't mean she wasn't still working on them, though.

Eva always parked her Jaguar near the West Wing entrance of the Warren Estate, as opposed to in front of the main entrance like her brother did. Now was an especially poor time for parking anywhere else. A vintage 1965 Ford Mustang took up two spots by itself, a reminder that at least one of the elder Warrens was in residence.

Sure enough, a maid approached Eva the moment she entered.

"Lady Warren is waiting for you in the den," the middle-aged matron said in her gruff voice. *This woman practically raised me from four to six.* A dark time for nannies around the Estate. "She's asked to see you as soon as you've returned, Miss."

"Thank you." Eva didn't have to ask which Lady Warren the maid meant. There may be two with that title now, but with that Mustang out front, only *one* commanded the primary title. "See to it that we're not disturbed. I'm sure she wants to wring my neck over something."

The maid didn't smile. Nor did she frown as she wandered off to return to her duties.

Eva removed her sunglasses before stepping into her den. *Hello, Mother.* Isabella Warren sat on the far end of the longest couch in the house, long legs crossed with one stiletto heel digging into the Persian rug beneath it. Scary long nails flipped through one of Eva's fashion magazines while Isabella's other hand held an electronic cigarette that already made the room smell like cloves. For a "lady," Isabella wore a skintight gold dress, her stringy brown hair fried from years of bleaching abuse. Not even her tits were natural anymore.

"Mother," Eva greeted, placing her wallet on the coffee table. "I hear you wanted me?" What a loaded question. Were they talking about now or when Eva was in utero?

Isabella looked up with the plainest expression. Was she even capable of expression now? Or was the Botox too fresh? "Have a seat, Bee."

Eva's heart stilled. Color washed from her face. Bee, huh? That's what Isabella called her daughter before elementary school. Back before she became a "problem" child. *I used to think she was a good mother.* What little kid didn't want to believe that about her mother? Fathers came in different varieties, but mothers were supposed to be kind and nurturing. Failing that, they could at least be supportive in other ways. Poor baby Eva had assumed that her mother's attentions had everything to do with maternal love and little to do with her potential.

"*There's my little Buzzy Bee! Did you work hard at ballet? Come, we must go to French class! If you do well, we'll get you ice cream at Petrulio's.*"

All baby Eva had heard was ice cream. What Isabella meant was "and see if you can't get along with the Tanaka fortune heir who gets ice cream there at this time of day." Turned out they didn't get along, and it had nothing to do with a Japanese language barrier.

Eva sat a few feet away from her mother on the couch. "This must not be a pleasure call."

At least Isabella was good at cutting to the chase. "Why haven't you responded to Rossi's invitation? I spoke to Sofia yesterday, and she says that you haven't called to schedule a lunch at all. It's been four months, Eva! You're getting too old to ignore these opportunities."

Eva's hands curled into fists in her lap. No sense losing it, though. Her mother did not respond to "theatrics," as she called them. "I have no interest in the Rossis. Especially not what you're talking about."

"Why not! They are a very respectable family. True, a bit green in American ways, but there's a lot to be said about having an old European family in your personal tree. Your father's been pursuing an alliance with them since…"

"Father, huh? I didn't realize he made business decisions around here anymore. Thought that had fallen on Henry ever since Father botched his investments." Something the Warrens didn't like to talk about. The public story was that Gerald retired from the public eye "for his health," when in truth he had ran away from debts and left Henry and Eva to clean them up. Even then, Gerald was always calling his son to suggest some crazy scheme that would certainly lose the family millions of dollars. *My future niece or nephew better not be an idiot.* More reasons for Eva to start making most of her own money.

"Your father has a sense for people. The Rossis are one of the most powerful families in northern Italy. Humor us and at least meet their son?"

As much as she didn't want to admit it, Eva took after her mother in many ways. Her inability to beat around the bush was one of them. "No."

"Eva!" Isabella tossed the fashion magazine onto the coffee table. "I've had enough of this. Stop being a selfish brat and think of this family before your own… proclivities." Is that what they were calling the lesbianism now? One day Isabella would figure out that Eva popped out of the womb this way. Then again, that would mean having to blame herself. "I just sat through your brother's embarrassing wedding. Don't make me sit through your even *more* embarrassing wedding."

There were a lot of things to latch onto there. *You would come to my gay wedding?* To keep appearances, for sure. Eva didn't mention that. Instead, she said, "Henry is happy with whom he has chosen to marry. Monica is a shrewd businesswoman who makes her own money and has endless connections. Isn't that the kind of woman you wanted your son to marry?"

Yup. Botox was too fresh. Otherwise, Isabella would be frowning like a cat trapped in the rain. "That woman is a whore."

"Tell me how you really feel about the mother of your grandchildren." It was a public secret that Mr. and Mrs. Warren did not care for the new

Mrs. Warren. First of all, she was the ex-girlfriend of the family's biggest debtor. Second, she was a self-made woman, meaning she had no family money or prestige to bring to the Warren fold. Thirdly? Her very successful business was a pleasure house for the elite of the world. That was how she and Henry met! *Still, don't think they would like her being called a whore.* Eva may or may not have to let that slip to her brother later. Isabella's biggest problem, however, was that she had been trying to play matchmaker for her children since they were too young to tie their own shoes. Unfortunately, she had terrible taste in potential suitors. Even if Eva were straight – or bisexual – she would be greatly disappointed with the men her mother suggested.

"When are you going to get over this fear of boys?" That's what it was, huh? "I was married by your age. Men may not be pleasant, Eva, but they're necessary for a balanced life."

"I've been trying to get as many men out of my life as possible. I like life *unbalanced.*"

"Yes, you've made it clear that you insist on this lifestyle."

Eva stood up. *I've had enough of this for today.*

"How is a woman going to provide for you?" Isabella made to get up as well, but her heel wobbled. "Who will protect you when you become old and frail?"

Don't pretend you give a shit about my protection. This was about marriage alliances. It always had been. "I'm going to make my own money in the family business," Eva announced for the fifth time that year already. "Henry's promised that…"

"Henry! Your brother is stringing you along like that dumb girl you are. Do you really think he's going to let you play businessman in this family?"

Eva faced her mother, lips turned down. "No. I think he's going to let me be a business*woman.* You're getting crazier every time you inject that shit into your face."

"I take it all back." Isabella had *that* tone in her voice. The one she unleashed when her intent was to kill her daughter's spirit. "Your brother's wife isn't the whore in this family."

Eva turned again, warnings shooting from her eyes. "You're right, Mother." Her lips curled into a devilish smile. "*I'm* the whore, aren't I? Oh, it would burn you to know how many pussies I've buried my fingers in."

"Eva!" At least the woman could flush in horror.

"Don't worry about having to attend my embarrassing wedding one day, Mother." Eva escaped into the hallway, hellbent on hiding in her chambers. "You won't be invited."

Eva managed to not cry until she reached her private chambers, blessedly devoid of life. Even so, only a few tears fell, which she wiped away before starting her homework.

Chapter 9

Because one extra woman in the office wasn't enough, Ethan Cole soon announced that his new business partner was Adrienne Thomas, one of the biggest female names in the game – and his ex-girlfriend. *I don't get rich people.* No room for love loss in business, Nadia presumed.

Adrienne made herself a little too much at home. The first day on the job she waltzed into the office and tossed her coat on Nadia's desk. "Take care of that, would you?" Before Nadia could come to instantly resent the new partner at Cole Enterprises (soon to be Thomas-Cole, because Nadia needed to learn how to answer the phone and type letterheads all over again like she needed five million bee stings) yet *another* new face showed up. Todd Payne, Adrienne's personal assistant.

Nadia foolishly assumed that a male assistant wouldn't bring too much drama to the office. It soon became apparent, however, that the man was in a relationship with Ms. Thomas. A submissive one, because Nadia had never met a man so up the ass of a woman like Todd was.

At least it proved a bonding experience for her and Amber.

"The bastard is *so* insufferable in meetings," Amber lamented over lunch one late March afternoon. "The way he licks Ms. Thomas's ass is like a dog licking its own butthole. I'm pretty sure he would do that if she asked him to."

Nadia sipped her tea and watched the rain fall outside. "The other day he told me that my shoes were last season." She rolled her eyes. "Of course they're last season. Duh. I *bought* them last season. What, does he think I get paid enough to go shopping at The Crimson Dove every month? Fuck him." Nadia loved those red pumps. They cost a grand, but she bought them the last time Mr. Cole treated her.

"Right? I can't keep up with how many outfits Ms. Thomas wears. I thought I had a big closet. Even Miss Bliss rewears some of the same clothes in front of me. At least there's that. Thought I might have to step up my wardrobe game, not that I can afford it! Not at this level!"

Nadia thought of something. "Hasn't Mr. Cole offered to buy you some work clothes yet? He did that for all his other assistants…" Nadia stopped. She wouldn't tell Amber this, but Mr. Cole had been *sleeping* with those other assistants. Probably why he really spoiled them.

"He has… but… don't you think that's weird? I would feel so uncomfortable letting him pay for my clothes."

Nadia shrugged. "He bought me that green dress you liked so much the other day."

"Really?"

"Yeah. Whenever an assistant goes shopping, *I* get to go with her. And get a few things of my own 'for my trouble.'"

"Pfft! Trouble!" Amber made scare quotes with her fingers.

"Don't worry about him buying you clothes if that's what he wants. The money is nothing to him. You can't spend enough at The Crimson Dove to piss him off." Surely, Amber had seen some of his financial information by now? The man was so loaded he couldn't even give enough away to charity every year. Not even with Jasmine now finding more and more charities to dump money into. What was it this month, again?

Probably something to do with cats. Jasmine *loved* cats… and now Mr. Cole did too, if he knew what was good for him.

"Then what the fuck are we waiting for?"

"I don't know. What are we?"

They hurried to finish lunch and get back upstairs. Mr. Cole was already in his office. When Amber emerged five minutes later carrying a black AmEx and sporting a "IT'S FUCKING CHRISTMAS" face, Nadia knew to grab her coat and hit the pavement.

"*Your boyfriend is paying for Amber and my clothes at TCD. Where you at?*" Nadia texted Jasmine on their way down in the elevator. Amber could take or leave the boss's girlfriend in tow, but Jasmine was one of Nadia's favorite people to shop with. *One of the few newly minted rich women who don't mind shopping in the slums with little ol' me.* Jasmine was a pro at finding ridiculous deals in department stores. Not that she needed to anymore… but it was fun to do for her friend.

She received a reply once they stepped onto the cold avenue and waved goodbye to the doorman. "*Sorry! L I'm not feeling well and staying home. You have fun spending his money. Think of me!*"

Jasmine hadn't been feeling well a lot lately. Mr. Cole had a nasty flu earlier that month, and Jasmine never seemed to shake it off. Nadia was glad she got through the winter with only a couple sniffles. Better than last year's ankle mishap.

Amber nearly fainted when they walked into The Crimson Dove down the street. The place was the nicest, most exclusive boutique in the area, and Nadia never got over how ridiculous the experience was every time. Champagne! Attendants out their asses! The most luxurious one-of-a-kind looks that a personal seamstress could tailor to almost any body. Which was good for Nadia, whose curves had a tendency to bust out of dresses that should've otherwise been her size. Lean Amber did not have this issue. She could grab a look off the mannequin and be dressed flawlessly within five minutes.

"What do you think?" she asked, admiring herself in a mirror as she twirled on a dais. "Is this too slutty to wear at work?"

Nadia wanted to snort into her champagne flute. "Slutty" was in the mind of the beholder, and the beholder around the office was Ethan Cole. He would definitely not mind Amber strutting around in a tight dress that showed off her cleavage. Neither would most of his associates. Still, better to err on the side of professionalism. After all, she wasn't sleeping with him, right? "Probably. But you should get it anyway. For those hot dates."

Amber smiled at herself in the mirror. "I would go clubbing in this, but I can't think of any nightclub where this isn't *too* much."

"How about for your boyfriend?"

Amber flinched. Nadia didn't press it.

"Actually…" Hm, were they officially friends now? "I don't have a boyfriend. Not anymore. He dumped me after I started this job."

"That sucks."

"Yeah. We weren't that serious, but it didn't feel good. Not like this dress does!"

"Why would he dump you because of this job?"

Amber shrugged. "He thinks I'm sleeping with the boss. I'm getting used to that assumption." She caught Nadia's look in the mirror. "Truth be told, he's not my type. Plus he has a girlfriend, and I'm not that gross."

Now *that* piqued Nadia's interest. "What's your type?"

"I dunno, Nadia, what's *your* type?"

They came to an impasse in the middle of the boutique, in time for the attendant to return with more suggestions for Amber's wardrobe.

She had a different style from Nadia, for sure. Whereas Nadia was a fan of the Queen Anne and peplum styles, Amber was all about sheath, spaghetti straps, and skirts as short as anyone would dare in an executive office. The more fringe, the better. To be fair, she could pull it off. If Nadia tried wearing any of these clothes? Everyone would laugh at her.

Everyone.

Even Eva.

Nadia turned into a statue in the middle of the boutique. She must have been paler than the moon, for Amber asked, "What's wrong? You sick?"

Nope. Unless love sick for a woman who wouldn't be compatible with Nadia in the long run counted.

Love sick? What am I going on about? Nadia wasn't love sick. Especially not for *Eva.* Just because she was really hot… and good in bed… and knew how to flirt… and was rich…

The faraway door to the boutique opened, admitting a small group of women talking about classes and how they were ready to blow off steam with some shopping. Nadia didn't pay them any mind since some other attendant would take care of them.

"Oh," Amber muttered. She had been dithering between the black or the blue version of a dress when the new party caught her eye.

"Oh, what?" Nadia turned. She happened to catch Eva's gaze from across the room.

Really, now.

"Friend of yours?" Amber stepped off the dais and helped herself to some champagne from the tray. "I ask because she was *really* friendly with you the last time she was by the office."

"And with you. She's friendly with anything that has tits and a skirt."

"So I've noticed." Amber finished off a glass. "She almost asked me out. Almost."

Nadia couldn't bring herself to look at the front of the room. "Would you have said yes?"

"No. Why would I? She was using me to make you jealous."

Amber walked into the changing area, although she was still within Nadia's earshot. "It didn't work."

"You don't need a player like that anyway. Don't care how rich these bastards are." Amber laughed. "Okay, maybe it depends on the bastard. A girl is gonna get tempted *once* in a while, you know.'

"Oh, I know…"

Amber poked her head out of the room. "So you and her?"

Nadia couldn't look her in the eye. "Once."

"Ooooh. Sexy." Amber disappeared again. "But not as sexy as my ass in this dress!"

Nadia had already chosen what she wanted to buy. A black dress… but not *any* black dress. Flecks of diamonds covered fabric and came with a solid gold belt that would drape heavenly on Nadia's hips. *I could never wear this on the bus.* She sighed, fingering the soft fabric that easily contoured her body. *If only I had a car. And a dowdy trench coat to cover this dress.* Rich women could get away with it because they lived on tightly secure properties and had drivers who took them in and out of town for shopping trips. They didn't even have to deal with the TSA at the airport. The few times Nadia was treated to private flying made her even more bitter about her pauper lifestyle.

She stole a look at the group of heiresses fawning over the latest hot designer. Eva had disappeared. Maybe she went home. Was she the type to get excited about shopping at The Crimson Dove? Probably not. The only time Nadia ever saw her in a dress was at last month's wedding. *She should at least wear shorts in the summer… her legs are to die for.* If only Nadia had more time to explore them with her tongue before her senses came back to her.

Those women explaining their fashion plights to the attendants never had to worry about people groping them or trying to steal their shit on the bus. They never had to think about the safest routes they would take between work and home. Most of them didn't even have to work! They were heiresses for a reason.

Before disgust could ruin her afternoon, Nadia went to the restroom. This was too much bullshit for her to handle.

"Hello."

Nadia had barely shut the door behind her when she heard that familiar voice in the powder area. The woman standing in front of the gilded mirror was not, however, powdering her nose in any sense of the phrase. Instead, Eva was in the midst of applying some blood red lipstick, mouth pursed toward her dazzling reflection.

Nadia released the door handle behind her. "When you said we should rendezvous in the bathroom, this wasn't what I had in mind."

Eva lowered the tube and gazed at Nadia over her shoulder. The tall woman had to bend over the sink in order to see her full reflection in the mirror. This meant her ass pushed out far enough for Nadia to slap on her way by – if she dared.

"That was a while ago. You've been thinking about me, huh?"

Nadia approached the sink next to Eva's. Warm water poured from a golden spout. Nadia removed her rings before rinsing off her hands. "You're a hard woman to forget."

Makeup disappeared into a small black handbag. Eva spun around and hopped onto the counter, legs dangling and fingers drumming on the black marble. "All the more reason to give me your number."

Nadia shut off the faucet and patted her hands dry with a complimentary white handkerchief she soon deposited into a discreet hamper. "You're still on about that?"

"Do I have a reason not to be?" Eva held her hand out, waiting. When Nadia didn't tell her to back the fuck off, the Amazonian heiress curled some red locks around her finger. "I think it's fate we've met here. You shopping with Cole's new mistress…"

"It's not like that." Nadia didn't mind some banter, but she was not letting Eva start rumors that would eventually get back to an already insecure Jasmine. "And this may surprise you, but I've experienced a few things in your world before. I have quite a few pieces from this shop by now." All bought by either Mr. Cole or Jasmine. Who was counting, though?

"My world, huh?"

"Don't know if you've ever noticed, but you're in the 1%. I'm in the bottom 99%."

"I've noticed." Eva leaned over, elbow scraping the counter. "But you're not in the bottom 99% of everything. You're definitely in the 1% of beautiful women on this planet."

"Still going on about that?"

"Why wouldn't I be?" Eva sat back up, taking her rosy perfume with her. "What's your deal, anyway? You have someone else? Was I that bad in bed?"

Nadia snorted. "No." She averted her eyes. "And… no."

"Ah. Then I'm even more flummoxed why you won't date me."

"I think I have more claim to that sentence than you do."

To her credit, Eva didn't follow that up with something so profoundly stupid that Nadia would have to run to save face. *She's something else, all right.* Didn't help she was wearing those designer jeans again. No cardigan, this time, but her pale green blouse had long enough sleeves to keep her warm in heated cars and rooms. Nadia turned her head slightly enough to catch another whiff of that perfume. The scent of sandalwood was more prevalent than ever.

"You like it?" Eva grinned through her ruby red lips. *I like kissing waxy lipstick…* Not something she thought she could say about a woman like Eva. But that red… yowza. "It's Dolce & Gabbana. There's this perfume shop in New York I always go to, and they insisted I try this last time I was there. Maybe I'll take you sometime. I bet you go well with a more rustic scent."

Nadia bumped her hip against the counter as she attempted to turn around too quickly. She was going to ask "*Why do you keep thinking you're taking me places?*" when she caught the silliest smile on that face. Sheesh. Eva looked like a kid being told she was about to meet her idol. All that over the thought of taking Nadia to New York? Impossible. *She'll take me to New York, wine and dine me, lick my pussy until I can't scream anymore… and then be over me. Why would I want that drama in my life?* Even if all that other stuff sounded awesome.

"Hey," Nadia began, refusing eye contact once again. "Why do you always flirt with me like this? Even in a freakin' bathroom. You got no shame?" Nadia sure didn't have any shame.

Eva bit that bottom lip as if her teeth could scrape off that lipstick. *As if.* Eva was definitely paying for no-smear lipstick. Top of the line, probably. "Why wouldn't I flirt with you? Like I'm going to let a gorgeous gay girl get away from me that easily. You want me to stop flirting with you forever? Say the word."

Nadia considered that idea for one hot second. "Would you be sad if I told you to leave me alone?"

"Heartbroken. Crushed."

She couldn't tell if that was sarcasm or not.

"Look." Eva turned toward her, elbow resting against the counter. "I ain't the one with a problem here." So she spoke low-class scoundrel too? "In fact, you seemed pretty happy that night we were together. I seem to recall a certain redhead game for round two… until her hot friend entered the room. So what gives? You threw me out after Jasmine Bliss caught us in bed together. As much as I think Cole gets his jollies from women boning one another, I somehow doubt he's condoning a Sapphic affair between you two."

"I… what the fuck?" Nadia didn't even want to consider that. Where did Eva get these ridiculous, perverted ideas? "Absolutely not."

"Relax. Just joking." Eva slipped off the counter. "All I want is one reason you won't go out with me. Otherwise, I'm going to assume you're playing a friendly game of hard to get. One you will lose, by the way."

Nadia stared at her through incredulous eyes. "Will I?"

There she was. Eva Warren, pressing Nadia against the black marble counter of a women's restroom in the fanciest boutique in the city. Nadia braced herself against Eva's chest, both thrilled and mortified to be touching those breasts again. *Fuck. That's not a padded bra she's wearing.* Nadia's mouth parted at the thought of kissing those oncoming lips of deliciously red poison.

Then she *was* kissing those poisoned lips, and everything disappeared around her.

Only Eva existed. Only the counter pressing against her ass existed. Only this kiss and this perfume swarming her senses existed. A lot of things may have been the only ones existing, but they came one at a time. Sometimes she only felt the pressure of the counter's edge. Other times she only smelled roses and sandalwood. Most of the time, though? She tasted those sweet lips and felt the erotic dance begin in her mouth.

When Eva kissed her harder, Nadia whimpered. Too much? Too fast? This wasn't a romantic mountain getaway. This was a bathroom in the middle of the city.

Shit! Those girls – *Amber* – could come in at any moment! Sure, everyone and their dog knew that Nadia and Eva had an agonizingly long mating dance going on behind the scenes, but nobody wanted to actually walk in on them copulating like common animals!

She was left in a daze when Eva backed away. "Oh, yeah. You're gonna lose." Eva nipped Nadia's ear. "Hard."

Eva moved. What was it? Some will of the universe? Or was Nadia truly in control of her actions? Because she found it hard to believe that she was snatching Eva's wrist and imploring her to stay instead of going back out to talk fashion designers and flirt with the attendants.

"Hm?" Eva chuckled, gazing at Nadia's small, pale hand. "Don't go?"

Nadia shook her head.

Eva reclosed the gap between them, although those lips remained an agonizing distance away. "See? Look who's losing already."

"Shut up and kiss me."

Nadia missed those blasted lips by three inches – Eva was already turning around and pulling Nadia away from the sinks. "Fuck me beneath the bleachers," she muttered, heading straight for the handicap stall. "Because that's what this feels like."

I can relate. Nadia may be no stranger to risky public sex, but this seemed… dirtier? No, not the bathroom, which was probably cleaner than Nadia's back home. All Eva had to do was stick Nadia in the far corner away from the toilet to make her forget they were in a bathroom. No, what felt dirty – okay, maybe more scandalous than dirty – was the fact some rich bitch could walk through the bathroom door at any moment. The stall door was floor to ceiling. Nobody could see them.

But could they be heard?

"Relax," Eva whispered in Nadia's ear. Now she was shuddering. So much for relaxing! "Nobody will know we're in here." She snorted hot, intoxicating breath against Nadia's skin. "I'd offer to take you back to my apartment and make love to you for the rest of the day there, but you're technically on the clock, aren't you?"

Oh my God, she's right!

"Wouldn't want you to get in trouble with your standup boss." Eva licked the nape of Nadia's outstretched neck. "Besides, you've got his card to pay for his assistant's clothes with, right? Oh, right." She lifted the hem of Nadia's skirt and kissed the tops of her breasts. "I'll make sure you get back to business as usual in a timely manner. More so than you are right now."

"Shut up," Nadia whispered again. "You should be doing something else with that mouth of yours."

"You mean this?" Nadia didn't have a chance to respond. Nadia was on her, kissing her lips and the whole of her mouth as if there was nothing else in the world for a girl to do. Right now? Nope. There sure wasn't. Nadia was convinced that Eva was put on that planet to kiss girls.

And she didn't just kiss her lips. Why would Eva do that, when Nadia had perfectly soft cheeks and a throat to cover in attention? This woman had the softest lips in the universe. Or maybe that was her top of the line lipstick making them feel so soft. *Where can I get some?* It was definitely no smear. Otherwise Nadia would be covered in it right now.

Like she was covered in kisses. And hands, coming at her from every direction.

One would have thought that Eva had never touched Nadia before. She grabbed her ass, her hips, curled around her shoulders, and – yes – ripped at her bodice so she could admire those breasts once more. Not that Eva was getting to breasts trapped in such a tight pushup bra. But, hey, it was a pushup bra! Quite the view!

"You are *so* fucking hot." The desperation in Eva's voice was almost enough to lull Nadia down to her knees. "Do you realize that? Do you realize what you do to me?"

"I…" Nadia could barely form words. Why wasn't her tongue doing other things? Like exploring the far corners of Eva's? "I don't know…"

Eva opened her mouth to retort. Someone opened the main door leading into the bathroom.

Heels clacked on the floor. Purses hit the counter. Nadia froze in fright. Eva? She kept going, of course!

"Does she really think she looks good in a dress like that?" One feminine voice asked the void. Water rushed from one of the sinks. "I mean, when you have tits like that, you have to keep in mind what you're doing with them. Who does she think she is, letting them flop around for every bus boy to see?"

A giggle floated on the air. Kisses floated on Nadia's skin. "You're jealous you're not a DD… and didn't have to pay for them."

"I don't care if Carrie grew them herself or got Dr. Garrison to do them for her. You've gotta contain those things!"

It was one of the most inane conversations a pair of young women could have in a bathroom in a high-end boutique. After that, Nadia couldn't be bothered to listen to what they said. It was none of her concern. Nothing to do with her. The only thing she had to think about was Eva's fingers dipping between opening thighs and rubbing against the breadth of a pair of cotton underwear.

"Fuck," Nadia whispered. No, no, don't make any noises! Don't alert the girls out there that someone was getting fingered in the handicap stall!

"You've got it," Eva whispered back, fingertips pushing aside the fabric and parting Nadia's nether lips. "I'll make it quick. For you."

Nadia gasped as two fingers slipped right into her. *How is she this good?* If Nadia tried to finger Eva, it would take a good two minutes to find the right angle for *one* finger. Two right off the bat? In the corner of a bathroom stall? Shit! Someone had plenty of practice at this. *I wonder how many women she's done this to… let alone in a bathroom…*

"And in the end, Carrie's gonna look better than all of us at that gala."

"Truth."

Someone swung open one of the adjacent stall doors, heels pounding like the drums of war. That same someone blew her nose and turned on a noise machine to drown out her other sounds. Meanwhile, Nadia was halfway to an orgasm just from the thrill this gave her.

"If you come before those girls leave," Eva murmured, "you *have* to give me your number. Deal?"

Nadia would agree to anything right now if it meant getting her ultimate way. Which was, namely, an orgasm.

She didn't know if it was a good or a bad thing that she started to come as the girl flushed the toilet and slammed the stall door behind her on the way out. It was enough commotion to drown out the whimpers coming from Nadia's throat. She wrapped her arms around Eva's shoulders and hid a silent scream in her shoulder. Fingers pounded into her below, making her legs shake and her heart rush in crazy palpitations.

"Get tighter, I dare you."

Nadia's eyes rolled back in her head as she rode out the height of her climax. Words? Sounds? People? What were those?

The girls disappeared, closing the bathroom door behind them. Eva chose that exact moment to back away, two wet fingers touching her lusciously red lips. "Give me your number," she said, before pushing one finger between her biting, porcelain white teeth. "I've earned it."

Nadia slipped down the wall and landed with an unceremonious *thwump* on her ass. She was so warm and calm that an earthquake could open the ground beneath her and she would remain as still as a tree on a quiet summer day. *Fuck me.* So much for playing hard to get.

Chapter 10

If April showers brought May flowers, then Eva hoped a whole rose garden bloomed as soon as April 30th came and went.

Not that she had anywhere to go. Midterm papers were due and she had to pull her part on a group project by the end of the week. Watching the dreary, cold rain fall outside her apartment window was a good incentive to sit her ass down, blast some Finnish folk music, and get work done before the cleaning lady showed up.

Unfortunately, the weather also made her extremely lethargic. What else made her lethargic? Memories of Nadia and the way she kissed.

Eva held up her phone against the dripping window in her reading nook, sighing. Nadia's phone number had no fewer than five fours in it. Bit ridiculous, really… but made it easy to remember. *Should I call her now?* It was mid-afternoon on a sleepy Sunday. Surely, she wouldn't be that busy. Had Eva waited a few days for nothing? She looked at the number again.

Fuck! What would she say? "*Hey, gorgeous, how about you come over to my swank apartment and let me fuck you in my king-sized bed?* Eva may have called a studio apartment her second home, but it was still a respectable size. Big enough to hold a king-sized bed, a walk-in closet the size of the bathroom, and a full, stainless steel kitchen she rarely touched. It was a good love shack when she needed somewhere to go late at night with a date… or if the girl was from a humble enough background to still be impressed by a bachelorette pad. Lots of those girls were intimidated by the Warren Estate.

Eva wasn't going to call about a date until she had the perfect one lined up. Something that Nadia would enjoy and didn't *have* to revolve around sex. So that left the sex club, The Dark Hour, out. That also left out the erotic film house. What about the planetarium? That place was all the rage lately because that's where Ethan Cole finally proposed to his little love muffin. No doubt Nadia would be one of the bridesmaids at the biggest wedding of the summer. The Coles were not wasting time getting hitched. Eva had already received her invitation in the mail.

If the weather were better, Eva would suggest a trip to the beach or a romp at the docks. Henry never used the family yacht, and their parents sure as hell were never bothered… living out in Montana these days and all. Eva tapped a pencil against her cheek until she realized it hurt. How many times had she offered to take Nadia shopping? On a weekend trip anywhere in the world? Maybe she should keep things simple. Suggest a nice dinner and a trip to the opera. Or a movie here at the apartment? Surely, that would pass Nadia's muster?

Ask her what she wants to do, dumbass. Seriously! Eva never had this much trouble calling a girl before. Back in high school, she called them left and right, flirting with anyone who was silly enough to give her a number back in 2007. Undergrad? Pfft! Eva had a whole directory in her pocket… including women from around the world. Most never lasted more than a night here and there. Back then? It was enough.

Eva gazed at Nadia's number again. This one would be different. It had to be…

Because?

Just… because!

Eva cleaned her coursework from her nook and finally worked up the nerve to call a woman she had already been two knuckles deep in – twice. The quickie in the bathroom was good fun, but it didn't go farther than the heavy kissing and the one-sided fingering. Eva would make sure that changed next time.

She hit the green button patching her through to Nadia's phone. And waited.

Silence.

Eerie, gut-wrenching silence.

"*Hey, Nadia… how about we go out this next week? I've got a paper due Wednesday, but after that it's smooth sailing through the weekend. Speaking of sailing, do you like the water?*"

The phone started to ring. Abruptly, it cut off.

"Fucking rain." Eva tried calling again. The same thing happened. One ring and *click*. She didn't have time for this. A text message would have to suffice.

Except the message she sent failed to deliver.

Eva stared at her phone, acknowledging its ability to betray her. Or was it Nadia's phone betraying her? Evangeline Warren didn't get into her prestigious colleges on name alone. She was pretty damn smart too.

Smart enough to infer that her number had been blocked.

Chapter 11

Having lunch with friends was supposed to be fun. Yet Nadia found herself in a constantly precarious position. On one side she had her blue collar friends who could barely afford to have lunch at fast food chains once a week. On the other, she had friends like Jasmine, engaged to a billionaire.

Strange to think of those two engaged now. Nadia was one of the first to hear. Then the whole world found out when the news was leaked to the press. Not only was the wedding heralded to be that June – which Jasmine informed her friend was *not* the original plan – but the papers dared to misprint that Adrienne Thomas was the bride, not Jasmine.

Poor Jasmine was planning a wedding in less than three months. The first thing she asked was for Nadia to be one of her bridesmaids. The second? "What do you think of my ring?"

Nadia stared at it now. It twinkled every time Jasmine lifted her fork. Diamonds and rubies… how like Jasmine. The way she told it, Mr. Cole had presented her with a selection of rings that he vetted first. Naturally, Jasmine had chosen her signature color of bright red.

The rubies made Jasmine think of Eva's lips the last time they met. *I can't believe I let her do that.* How low was Nadia, anyway? Fingering in a bathroom stall! Sure, it was the cleanest, nicest bathroom stall in the city, but it was the principle of the thing. *I can't believe I gave her my number.* Blocked Eva's right away. For the best.

Nadia cut her Swiss cheese and mushroom panini into fourths before eating. The sourdough bread crunched between her teeth before she tasted a hint of seasoned turkey. This was her favorite sandwich and salad shop in the city, but she never bothered coming unless she had someone like Jasmine in tow. When she asked to get lunch on a Friday afternoon, Nadia couldn't say no… as long as they were coming here. For a $15 sandwich? Worth it.

"We've got a date with a wedding planner coming up," Jasmine reminded her friend. "I want you and my other friend Selena to be there. You gonna come?"

"I'll try." Nadia was still trying to wrap her head around it. Jasmine, a woman who had only worked for Mr. Cole for six months before moving in with him. Nadia didn't even know they were sleeping together until a few months in. *I try not to think about it.* How many of his assistants had Mr. Cole slept with before settling on Jasmine? Nope. Not thinking about it.

Jasmine talked about the trials and tribulations of planning the wedding of the year, as it was already being heralded. Guest lists. Menus. *Dresses.* No expense would be spared when the guest list included heads of states and the occasional royal family member. Jasmine was in way over her head, but that's what the best wedding planner in the region was for.

Jasmine ran out of breath and asked for a refill of water. While the server disappeared to get a pitcher of ice water, Nadia stared at her half-eaten sandwich and asked, "What's it like dating a billionaire?"

She became aware of their sunshiny environment. Light poured through floor-to-ceiling windows, bathing the well-dressed diners in vitamin D. Cream leather chairs and ivory tablecloths dotted the dining landscape. The sweet sounds of recorded piano music filled the aural air. It was the kind of place friends came to have lunch, all right. But only if they realized how much it cost to be serviced by women in black tie.

If I wanted to come here every day, I would have to date a billionaire, for sure.

Jasmine stared at her soup and salad with foggy eyes. "It's quite something, that's for sure."

Nadia sighed.

"For one, you don't have to worry about money. Ever. That's the craziest thing to get used to. Need to go to the hospital? No worries. Even if you don't have insurance – and you get the best insurance in the world, duh – you can still afford to be told it's a cold and that you should get some rest and drink water. All my loans were paid off in a few days." Jasmine tilted her head, lost in thought. "Obviously, there's the shopping. Flying on private jets. Going anywhere in the world because you feel like it and staying in the nicest hotel. Honestly, the scariest thing is realizing that you're used to it. Although it feels weird to spend your boyfriend's money willy-nilly. I still worry that he's going to get mad at me for putting food on his tab. He doesn't even look at it, though. His accountant takes care of it and sends him a monthly report on what he paid."

"That's nuts." Nadia imagined Eva having no idea how much she spent when she went out to eat. Hand over a credit card and let someone else transfer the funds. No worries about overcharging. No worries about interest. No worries about being able to pay it off! Nadia had so many things she wanted to drop thousands of dollars on. Not just her student loans, which she paid the minimum amount on every month. She wanted a car. A new bed. A week in the Caribbean. *I always wanted to go there…*

Jasmine added more salt to her soup. "Why do you ask? Doesn't have to do with a certain someone, does it?"

"Hm?" Nadia looked up with a start. "Don't know what you're talking about."

"Please."

Nadia was going to let the conversation end. None of Jasmine's business. What did she understand? Sure, she liked to talk about that one time she fooled around with a co-ed in college, but Jasmine had never *dated* another woman before. There were politics involved. Nadia wasn't sure what politics in this case, but there never *was a* case of lesbian dating without politics!

"She ask you out again?"

Water gargled in Nadia's throat. *Fuck!* She grabbed a napkin to stop the spew of liquid flying from her mouth.

"I'll take that as a yes." Jasmine refilled Nadia's water glass for her. Poisoned stuff!

Once Nadia had her bearings – and a sore throat – again, she said, "When is she not asking me out?"

"Dunno. You tell me."

Nadia swallowed her water more slowly this time. Too bad it wiped out the delicious taste of cheese and mushrooms. "I may or may not have given her my number recently. But then I blocked it before she ever contacted me."

"What? Why?"

"Why did I block her?"

"Or give her your number in the first place. Unless…" Jasmine waggled her freshly plucked eyebrows. "You like her."

Groaning, Nadia forgot her sandwich and instead paid attention to the people one table over. A mother and her teenaged daughter. The daughter was enamored with her phone while the mother flipped through a copy of *The Daily Social.* The front page promised that the paper contained the whole scoop on today's Monegasque billionaires. Sun! French! Yachts! Casinos! Yay! *Does Eva speak French? I don't remember.* She only remembered Mandarin and German. Shit. Why did she even know that much?

"It's complicated," was all Nadia would say.

"Hmmm. She likes you. You like her. You two spent a night together I'm sure wasn't *that* bad… so what gives? Why keep turning her down?"

Nadia shrugged. "She's not really my type."

"Really?" Jasmine back her next slew of words and stabbed some of her salad instead. "I mean, if I were gay enough… I'd date her. She's hot!"

"You think so?"

"Everyone thinks she's hot."

"That's not true." Right?

Jasmine leveled a heavy gaze at her. "Give it to me straight, girl. Or gay. Which is it?"

"Er…" Nadia had no idea how to respond to that. "I guess my main thing is that she's not serious about me. I don't mind casually dating someone, but on her level? Sounds like a mess."

"I suppose. What makes you think she's not serious, though?"

"For one, she dates lots of girls. Why would I be any different? She thinks I'm pretty and that I'm playing hard to get. It's probably a game for her. You know those types." Surely, Jasmine knew by now! "They're used to getting their way and whatever they want. You see it all the time in the office. I don't know how many men have flirted with me and then upped their game when I told them no."

"Unfortunately, I do know about that."

"So you get where I'm coming from. She's not actually interested in *me.* She's interested in getting her way. If I had said yes from the very beginning, I'd probably be dumped already. Then there's that other thing."

Jasmine pushed her empty soup bowl aside. "What other thing?"

"You know…" Nadia lowered her voice. "The *other* thing."

It took Jasmine a while to figure it out, but when she did, she jerked back, eyes searching for anyone who might overhear their conversation. "Not into BDSM, huh?"

"No thanks." Nadia paused. "Hm… it might be fun to dabble a little bit. But she's not like that, right? She wants it all the time. Everyone knows that." There were three things one quickly found out about Eva Warren. 1) She was rich as flying fuck. 2) Gay. Really gay. So gay she and her friends had coined the phrase Diamond Dyke to describe how rich and gay they were. 3) She was a self-professed Domme in the BDSM scene. Nadia had ran into a couple of women at the local gay bar who had "played" with Eva. Some of them had nothing but nice things to say. The others had ran far, far away because it turned out it was *not* for them. With Eva's personality type? No kidding. "What do you call those types again? Lifestylers?"

"Yeah. Ethan's not like that," Jasmine was quick to say. Great. More details Nadia didn't need. Not knowing about her boss's sex life included not giving a shit that he liked BDSM too. What rich fuck didn't these days? Talk about power tripping. Blech. "There are some people like that though. Like Monica and…"

She stopped. *Like Monica and Eva's brother?* "Apple doesn't fall far from the tree."

"I guess not."

"So, yeah, I like a woman who takes charge, but not like *that.* I know that Monica is lovely, but I don't want to be related to…" She stopped. Holy shit. If, by some crazy chance of the universe she married Eva… she would be related to Monica! Her boss's ex-girlfriend!

This rich people's world was *way* too small and insular!

"So she's too domineering and rich for you. Got it." Jasmine giggled. "I'll keep my eye out for middle-class sweethearts for you."

"You do that." Another sigh. Nadia couldn't even bring herself to talk about her last encounter with Eva. The encounter she could never stop thinking about.

Those lips.

Those eyes.

Those *fingers.*

That intoxicating voice whispering in her ear, telling her when to come.

"Yo, Earth to Nadia." Jasmine waved her hand in front of her friend's face. "What kind of dress do you wanna wear for the wedding?"

The kind Eva wore. Nadia shook out her head and made a noncommittal remark. What it was? She never remembered. She was still fighting away images of that jaw-dropping Domme.

***

"Gwen wants to know if we'll play badminton with her tomorrow."

Eva looked up from the table. Kathryn sat down across from her, eyes glued to her phone. French-tipped nails tapped a response in the body of text messages. "Badminton? Tomorrow? I guess." Eva pulled her planner over to make sure she had nothing going on at that time. She had classes in the morning and a family dinner in the evening. These days, the Warrens had to *plan* their family dinners in advance. "I should be free. Can we play badminton with three people?"

"It's at the sports club, so I'm sure we could find a fourth." Kathryn continued to text with clacking fingers. "You're my partner, though."

"Aw, I've been waiting *years* to hear you say that."

"Uh huh. Oh! She says she's invited Jasmine too. So there we go. Four people for doubles."

"Jasmine? Jasmine Bliss?"

"Is there some other Jasmine I don't know about?"

"No, just…" This could work. Eva got up from the table and went to her desk. Where was her stationary? Fuck. She only had the plain kind here. Oh well. It would have to do. "Never mind."

"What are you up to?" Kathryn called from the table.

"Nothing!" Nothing? *Nothing?* Yeah, right. For days Eva had been plotting how she was going to throw a Hail Mary pass in Nadia's direction. She had given up on going to Cole's office. That would only piss her off more. Instead, she would have to find an indirect way of speaking to Nadia. The final attempt, as it were. *If she gives me a real rejection, I'll walk away. For good.* There were tons of fish in the sea, or something like that.

Eva put aside her stationary. She'd write a letter after Kathryn left. No need to have her best friend look over her shoulder and critique a *love* letter. If that's what it even was.

One of the only ways Eva would get to Nadia was through Jasmine. Contrary to what many may think, their paths did not often cross. It seemed like a fortuitous sign to rendezvous with her tomorrow.

As soon as Kathryn was gone, Eva pushed aside her reading homework and attempted to write the first love letter of her life. *That's not what it is.* Or so she told herself as her pen slowly moved across the paper.

Chapter 12

Eva had to admit, there was almost no better way to release the stress than to hit the badminton courts. The ones in the sports club downtown were particularly nice. Always clean, always springy, and *always* teeming with beautiful, sporty women who liked to sweat.

She was a bit preoccupied at the moment, however. Namely, she was in the middle of a serious volley between herself and Gwen on the other side of the net.

This was supposed to be doubles, but the two other women struggled to pull their own weight. Kathryn was seriously distracted by things going on in her own life. As for Jasmine? The poor dear tried to exert some decent athleticism, but it was truly not her strong suit. Not like Eva, who was once a formidable force on the soccer field. Or Gwen, for that matter. That girl definitely played her fair share of high school sports as well.

The birdie tossed from one side to the other, Gwen dive-bombing with grunts and screams of triumph. Likewise, Eva had no problems shoving

Kathryn aside and smacking the birdie back. The best part? Eva usually won the volleys, giving them a sizable lead halfway through their match.

"Fuck!" Kathryn had launched during a volley and let the birdie hit the ground, giving the other team a point. "What is wrong with me today?"

While the other women stood expectantly on the other side of the net, Eva looped her arm around her friend's shoulders and took her to their corner of the court. "You okay?" she asked, glancing at Jasmine, currently twirling her racquet in her hand. "Or do you need a time out?"

"I'm fine," Kathryn mumbled. "Freaking out, that's all."

"I'll say. Boyfriend need his ass kicked?" Eva always volunteered for ass-kicking duty.

"He's the least of my problems. Work."

"Ah." Kathryn loved to run herself ragged with the charity projects. In another life, she was a social worker who spent half her days tearing out her hair and crying in the bathroom from all the stress. "Sounds like a great opportunity to hit the shit out of some birdies. You gonna get your head in the game or what?"

"I've got my head in the game."

"All right. Let's go."

They went back to their spots, Jasmine's serve.

Another long volley ensued. Kathryn started to pull her own, racing back and forth on the court with her eye always on the birdie. She hit a few good swings that *almost* scored them a point. Almost. Gwen was too fast and too strong.

The birdie flew over Eva's head. "Get it!" she shouted.

"Mine!"

Kathryn smacked the shit out of the birdie, sending it soaring over the net… and right into Jasmine's waiting face.

"Ow!"

The birdie hit the floor. Jasmine Bliss went down, hand covering her face. "Shit," Eva mumbled, ducking beneath the net. *There goes my chance. Thanks, Kathryn!* "Look what you did!" she said to her friend. "Felled the one brunette in the bunch. Isn't that discrimination?"

"Sorry," Kathryn muttered.

"It ain't broken, is it?" Eva knelt in front of Jasmine and pried her hand away. Gushes of blood fell down the other woman's face. "Ew! I don't think it's broken. Just a bit busted."

"Thanks," Jasmine muttered.

Hm. This might be my chance. Never let it be said that Eva didn't have her share of that classic Warren opportunism. "Come on. Let's get you cleaned up." She helped Jasmine to stand, brushing off some dirt from her sports top and leading her to the ladies' locker rooms. Gwen wandered in their direction. "No, no, I got this. Besides, Miss Jasmine and I need to have a chat anyway." Oh, yes, a sweet chat about *love.* And blood. Because there was a lot of it coming out of that little nose.

As soon as Jasmine sat down on an empty bench, Eva raided a first aid bin. She returned to Jasmine to find her worrying over her nose.

"Nasty, but don't worry. It looks messy. Painful. Don't think it's broken, though. Yikes."

"Don't say that," Jasmine whined, refusing to remove her hand. When Eva finally pried it away, she saw a giant, bloody mess. The nose was not misshapen, however. That was a good sign. Even so, Jasmine wiggled every time Eva tried to clean up the blood. It got everywhere. Mostly on her hands. *Lovely.*

"Hold still. Let me get this cleaned up and see what we're dealing with." Blood was better than a truly busted nose. Blood eventually stopped flowing. A busted nose? Good thing Jasmine had that good Cole insurance now. "*Tch.* I played soccer in high school. You think I don't know broken noses? Or how to take care of them?"

"I didn't say anything…"

"Blood everywhere in soccer," Eva continued to mutter as she dabbed Jasmine's face. "Skinned knees… bruised tail bones. Nobody gets out of it without a scar or two. See?" She pulled her leg up and pointed to a white line on one of her long limbs. "Sophomore year of high school. Some bitch shoved me so hard my father nearly sued the pants off her father." That was a slight understatement. Gerald Warren only took an interest in his daughter's high school athleticism when she came home with a gash in her leg. *Made me even more ugly to the men they were trying to set me up with.* Grown men, too! Her parents truly had no shame. "*A few decades ago it wasn't unusual for girls your age to marry men in their thirties. They need time to make their fortunes, and you need time to make their children. See?*" Such a sweetheart, her father was.

Jasmine didn't speak. She was probably in shock.

Eva sat back and admired her handiwork as soon as she was satisfied with how well she cleaned Jasmine's face up. *Nice blood splats.* "Your nose isn't broken. It might bleed a little, but it's not broken. Gonna hurt like fuck for a few days, though. Oh well, if anyone asks, tell them I smacked you. People expect me to be too gruff for my own good."

"Thanks." Jasmine pulled out a compact. She sighed in resignation.

My chance. Eva looked around the locker room before pulling her folded up letter from her pockets and putting it in Jasmine's hand. "You've got to give this to Nadia. I'll owe you."

Jasmine's eyes widened. "What?"

"Shh!" Eva closed Jasmine's hand over the note. "Come on. Spot me this favor. Like I said, I'll owe you one. *Come on.* I'm going crazy! She won't talk to me!"

Jasmine stared at the now crumpled note in her palm. "Dare I ask what this is?"

"What the fuck do you think it is? Pages from the Marquis de Sade's diary? Pfft. Hey, though, don't read it. Seriously." That would be more embarrassing than having her seventh grade diary read out loud to her current grad school class. Ew.

"All right." At least Jasmine put the note in her pocket. "I don't make any promises about her. She's made it pretty clear she doesn't want to date you."

Ouch. "I know. That's why I'm going through you, her friend, and her boss's fiancée. She's gotta at least take the note from you, because she sure as hell won't take it from me." Eva grunted in frustration. "You know, she didn't have anything bad to say about that night you caught us stealing the sheets. She even gave me her number, although she ended up blocking mine. What the fuck gives? I never got an explanation." Blah. She probably revealed too much.

Jasmine snorted – or at least tried to. "You got it bad for her, huh?"

"Have you seen her?"

"A few times, yeah." Jasmine smiled. "If you want to know what she's told me…"

"Duh?" Holy shit, what had Nadia been gabbing about? Eva needed deets. Now.

"She's said that you're too domineering for her." *Excuse me?* "You intimidate her, and she thinks you're into lifestyle stuff like your brother. She's not."

"Shit." Eva sat back, crossing her arms. "I'm not either! That stuff's fun for the bedroom, but I'm not into stuff outside of it like my stupid brother. Give me that note back. I'll make an addendum." She reached for the note in Jasmine's hand.

"Oh, no." Jasmine scooted off the bench. "I'll take it from here, thanks. Like I said, though, I make no promises. If she keeps telling you no, you need to let her go."

Thanks for that, Dr. Phil. Eva didn't need to be told to back off – unless it was a final ultimatum. She wasn't exactly into upholding the predatory lesbian stereotype, no matter what people liked to say. *Nadia doesn't think that about me, does she?* Eva watched Jasmine finish cleaning up and head out. Eva stayed behind, wondering if she had made a mistake.

A lot of mistakes. From the beginning.

Nadia's problem had nothing to do with Eva, after all. Only her preconceived notions of Eva. *My reputation continues to precede me.* Sometimes it was hard having such an outgoing personality. People were quick to judge. Especially the women one wanted to impress the most.

***

Work was chaos, as usual. Although the office should've been through transitioning from a single enterprise to a partnership between Ethan Cole and Adrienne Thomas, such a thing had yet to transpire. For one, Nadia could still not answer the phones correctly, no matter how many times she reminded herself to say "Thomas-Cole" instead of "Cole." It didn't help that personal assistant Todd kept flouncing about the office as a stark reminder of the change. Sure, Nadia could remember that things *had* changed… but what those changes were escaped her as she answered her ninth phone call in twenty minutes. Everyone wanted a piece of the Thomas-Cole pie, and they were going to take the receptionist down with them.

She had hung up when Jasmine entered the office. Her eyes went straight to Amber's desk. The boss's assistant sat tall and straight in her chair, fingers clicking and tapping on a keyboard as she checked Mr. Cole's Wikipedia page for the second time that day. *I remember when that was Jasmine's job.*

"Hey," Nadia said, slamming a pencil upside down on her desk. "He doesn't have anyone in there." She referred to Mr. Cole's office, of course. Why else would Jasmine come in unannounced? "You can probably go in. If not, tell him you barged in without my say so I don't get in trouble."

Jasmine perched on the edge of Nadia's desk. She pulled something from her pocket and jammed it into Nadia's hand.

"What's this?" Wrinkled paper filled Nadia's fist. Okay, then.

"Don't shoot the messenger. I owed someone."

Nadia unfolded the note and perused the first few words written in Eva's flamboyant handwriting. "*It's been nearly four months since we…*" The note immediately folded again, Nadia's face turning as red as her hair.

"Remember what I said! Don't shoot the messenger." Jasmine hopped off the receptionist's desk. "By the way," she hissed in Nadia's direction, "you should really go on another date with her. She's got it *baaaaddd* for the lipstick style."

"What are you trying to say?" Nadia hissed back.

Jasmine put her hand on the door handle behind her. "That she's still clit-drunk on you. Or whatever the phrase is for you all." The door gave way, and she disappeared into Mr. Cole's office like a shadow in the dark.

Nadia remained dumbstruck. The phone rang. She ignored it.

She caught a look from Amber over at her desk. "What's that?" she mouthed.

Nadia opened the note in her lap, also ignoring Amber. It was none of her business. What *was* Nadia's business, however, was knowing how Jasmine got a hold of a note like this. From Eva. For Nadia.

There were strange forces afoot. Those forces should've been enough to keep Nadia from reading the letter. Nothing good could be in it…

"*It's been four months since we first made love,*" the letter began. *Wow, her handwriting is gorgeous.* Rarely did Nadia come across such beautifully legible cursive handwriting. Seemed almost a shame that the whole paper had been wrinkled. "*Do you remember? It feels like a dream now. I know that I dream about it a lot. There are few women who linger in my head as much as you do, Nadia. I'm not merely talking about your lovely hair or the softness of your skin. Nor do I speak of your wonderful breasts and…*"

Nadia lifted her head, making sure no one read over her shoulder before continuing.

"*I hope you think of that night as fondly as I do. The dance we've engaged in since then has me both energized and perplexed. Do you not want me? I keep thinking you don't, that I have no chance, and then you come to me with your kisses and unforgettable seduction. Perhaps what happened at The Crimson Dove wasn't romantic, but it was real. I thought that it was a sign you wanted me. Not as a one-night stand. Something more.*

"*I'm not asking you to marry me. I'm not even asking you to go steady with me. I want to take things slowly with you, yes… but this molasses-paced game we're playing has me losing my mind. I suppose what I'm really asking is for you to make a decision. If you don't want to be with me at all, simply say so. I'll be sorely disappointed, but I will respect your decision. But, if you do decide you would like to try dating me, I humbly ask that you tell me what you want. I want to get to know you. I want to know what you like, what makes you tick. What are your dreams, Nadia? I'll happily tell you mine, whether it's in my home or on a rooftop in Paris. I have so many things that I can give you. Perhaps you do not believe it, but there are many things you can give me as well.*"

Nadia stopped reading there. Not because she didn't want to continue, but because a shadow loomed over her desk.

"Are you on break?" Adrienne Thomas asked with her semi-shrill voice. "If you are, you should probably do it *away* from your desk. If not, then you need to be paying attention."

Nadia jammed the letter into her desk and hoped her cheeks weren't exploding in shame. "Yes, ma'am. What is it that you need?"

"I…"

Amber appeared, sneakily wedging herself between the receptionist's desk and the feminine half of Thomas-Cole, Enterprises. "Yes, ma'am, what is it that you need? Nadia is very busy today. Me? Not so much. Perhaps there's something I can help you with?"

Silence befell the front of the office. Adrienne glanced between the receptionist and her partner's personal assistant. *What a trio we make.* The curvy redhead, the supermodel blonde, and the brunette royalty. Any man – or lesbian, Nadia presumed – walking into the executive offices would think he had died and gone to sexual heaven. *Gag me.*

"Why, yes. Thank you, Amber." Unlike Mr. Cole, Ms. Thomas was allergic to people's last names. Probably thought it made her more approachable. "Let's discuss it in my office."

Once they disappeared, Nadia pulled the letter back out and finished reading it.

"I look forward to hearing from you. XOXO, Evangeline Warren."

Evangeline was a ridiculously pretty name.

Nadia spent the rest of her day trying to think of anything but Eva. Every time she did? She giggled and thought of the letter. How delightfully sweet! No one had ever written Nadia a letter like that before.

Then the doubts settled in.

Eva only wrote that because she wanted Nadia badly enough to say she once had her. That's what women like her did. That's what the men would do. There reached a point in fame and fortune where women weren't so different from men. *She wants me, but only because she thinks she can't have me.* Nadia was so lost in thought that she almost over poured her coffee. It was only because of Amber's sudden appearance that a giant mishap was avoided.

"Earth to Nadia," Amber said with a goofy grin. "What's up with you today?"

Nadia slightly turned her head, ignoring her coffee. She also ignored the other employees entering the break room only to depart again, traveling coats wrapped around their frames. Was it five already? *I should be catching my bus…* "You ever been in love?"

Amber took a step back, face pale. "What?"

"Oh, sorry…"

"Is it a girl?"

"Yeah."

Amber grinned again. "Is it that hot Warren woman?"

Nadia couldn't look her in the eye. "Maybe…"

"Ha! You've got the hots for her! Hasn't it been months since you two hooked up?"

"Kinda." Nadia never told Amber what happened at The Crimson Dove. She never told *anyone.* At first she thought it was out of shame. Now she considered that… perhaps it was something she merely wanted to keep to herself? "She keeps asking me out. What do you think?"

Amber laughed. "What do *I* think? I think you should ride that pony until it collapses."

"What does that mean?"

"It means…" Amber leaned in, her flowery perfume much more insufferable than Eva's ever could be. "You have your fun and milk her dry."

"I don't want to do that!"

"*Or* you fall in love along the way, I dunno." Amber grabbed her coffee cup. "All I know is that if a hot rich bitch like her was hitting on me? I wouldn't think twice about it."

Nadia stared at the roaring coffee pot. "You gay?"

"Oh, honey." Amber stepped back as her cup filled with the bitter elixir of life. "I play for whatever team benefits me the most."

That didn't quite answer Nadia's question.

***

She had many more questions as she went home and sat on her porch swing, watching the sun set over the horizon of evergreens.

Eva's letter lay in her lap, still crinkled, still filled with unbelievable handwriting. Every word was carefully crafted, the ink even, the curls and lines exquisite. It told of a well-bred woman who took pride in her work. Sometimes it was easy to forget that a brusque woman like Eva was one of the wealthiest heiresses around. Beneath the designer threads and expensive perfume, Nadia only saw and heard someone who was personality first, background second.

What was the worst that could happen? A whirlwind romance filled with sex and spoiling? Ha! Sounded like the kind of life Nadia needed. But was it what she wanted? Sometimes the two conflated.

Her hand hovered over her phone. A chilly breeze started up, almost driving her back inside. However, the sun was too alluring. It reminded Nadia of the crazy hue that was Eva's hair.

She picked up her phone and dialed one of its forbidden numbers.

It rang once.

Twice.

By the third ring, Nadia had almost lost her nerve. As she was about to hang up, however, the other end clicked.

"Hello?" Eva's voice was as clear as it was deep. Nadia froze on the porch swing, throat suddenly dry. "To whom do I owe this extreme pleasure?"

Nadia snapped back to reality. "Like you don't have the best caller ID a person can get."

So started a new chapter in their ridiculously unconventional relationship.

Chapter 13

"What are you doing standing there?". Eva gestured to the woman loitering in her kitchen. "You gonna help me wipe down these counters?"

Kathryn, with a teacup in hand, looked as if Eva had asked her to whip out the vacuum and get to work picking up lint with chopsticks. "Pardon?"

Grunting, Eva pushed her friend out of the way and grabbed a paper towel. What next? Did she put that Clorox stuff on the paper towel? Or was she supposed to use the powdery stuff? Fuck! There were a million cleaning supplies beneath her sink, but Eva never had anything to do with them. She paid for the cleaning lady to bring them over and store them there. *Then* the cleaning lady used said supplies to wipe down Eva's kitchen once, sometimes twice a week. *Oh my God. The bathroom.* Eva dropped the paper towel. When was the last time the bathroom was cleaned? How many times could a toilet be flushed before it was imperative it be cleaned again? *I don't notice if other people have dirty toilets…* Because the other toilets she sometimes used, belonged to people who had regular cleaning ladies too.

"I can't get over this. You. Cleaning." Kathryn sipped her tea with a chuckle. "You have it that bad for this girl."

Eva looked between cleaning spray and powder. "Which one do I use again?"

"Oh my God." When Eva gave her one last exasperated look, Kathryn finally pointed to the powder. "That one. I think. Maybe."

While Eva made a valiant attempt to clean her own studio apartment, Kathryn pointed out that it probably wasn't necessary. Wasn't this place professionally cleaned on more than one occasion? Nadia wasn't going to notice if Eva had a smudge on her counter. Nadia's kitchen was probably dirtier than this, and that wasn't a bad thing. She just didn't have, you know, *a cleaning lady.* Or had Eva forgotten how privileged the lot of them were again?

Don't start on the privilege thing again. Kathryn's perpetual self-guilt over being one of the richest women in the city knew no bounds. This was the woman who, when she wasn't freelancing for her boyfriend's real estate legacy, spent most of her time either remodeling charities or starting up new ones. It was admirable, but Eva was not in the mood to have her fellow heiress lord over her because she knew the difference between eating on a thousand dollar budget for one and a one hundred dollar budget for four.

"Don't you have somewhere you have to be?" Eva tossed out the paper towel and washed her hands in the kitchen sink. *Do I have to wash this again now?* "Cutting the ribbon on a soup kitchen? Crushing someone in a board room? Sucking your boyfriend's dick?"

"I've got all three scheduled for this evening," Kathryn said dryly. *Sad thing it's probably true for at least two of them.* The charity and the dick, definitely. "Plenty of time to stand here and make you nervous."

"I'm not nervous!"

Kathryn clicked her tongue. "You haven't even changed. You're still wearing your PJs."

Eva looked down at her T-shirt and sleep shorts. "Fuck."

"Uh huh. Fuck."

What commenced, with a whole hour until Nadia was supposed to arrive, was Eva turning her closet and dresser drawers into complete disarray. *I could've sworn I had an outfit picked out last night!* Where was it now? Oh. Blue jeans and a black blouse. Was that cute? Would Nadia think she was hot in that? Or would she be expecting Diamond Dyke Eva 24/7? *So much pressure!* Eva mussed up her hair overthinking her sparse closet. Sparse compared to her closet back at the family house, anyway. That closet was almost the size of her living space here.

"What do you think?" She held up a jacket and a designer cotton T-shirt. "Sexy enough?"

"Sexy? You think you gotta be sexy?"

"Not all of us are effortlessly smokin' hot in jeans and a T-shirt, Kat."

"Nope. We sure aren't. You've got the market cornered on that."

Eva blushed. Sometimes her friend's compliments went straight to her heart. Oh, she wasn't crushing on Kathryn these days. That was a long time ago. *High school's dumb.* Kathryn was two years older, which meant she was Queen of Winchester Academy when Eva was first trying out for the girls' soccer team. *The only things her boyfriend and I have in common is that we both love her and soccer.* Unlike Kathryn's boyfriend, however, Eva never made captain.

"Dress like yourself."

"'Myself' takes forty-five minutes to do her hair and makeup. I ain't got time for that."

Kathryn rolled her eyes. "Put on some cute casual clothes and comb your hair. Seriously. Comb your hair. You look mad."

Eva stopped in front of a mirror. In her frenzy, she had managed to go straight for the Dr. Frankenstein look.

"Here." Kathryn unhooked a pair of jeans from a hanger and pulled the first T-shirt she encountered in the top dresser drawer. "Perfect. Chic but not overdone. You'll have her up your shirt in fewer than five minutes, guaranteed."

Eva grinned. "Then what's the point of even getting dressed?" To reiterate her point, she pulled her current T-shirt over her head and pranced around in a sports bra. It was better than fretting over her date.

Her. Date.

Not only had she been shocked to eventually get a call from Nadia, but she was even more shocked that Nadia agreed to meet her Saturday afternoon. Normally Eva went home on the weekends. For Nadia? She would permanently move to her studio apartment if it meant getting to see her every weekend.

When Eva asked her what she wanted to do, she was not expecting, "I'd like to see where you live."

Kathryn had agreed with Eva that dragging poor Nadia all the way out to Warren Estate was not the way to go. Nadia would feel much more comfortable in a cozy studio apartment in a neighborhood she at least passed through on her commute. Eva informed her brother that she would be downtown all weekend and to, for the love of God, *not bother her* unless Dad was dead or Monica had gone into super premature labor. Even then, it could wait until Sunday night. Maybe. Better make it Monday to be sure. *I will steal her time all weekend if I can.*

"So what do you have planned with your destined mate?" Kathryn pulled her jacket on after depositing the empty teacup in the dishwasher. "Movie? Reading her your high school poetry?" She shrugged with puffy cheeks jutting out of her collar. "Sucking her clit?"

"I've got all three scheduled, thanks!"

Kathryn laughed. Eva didn't realize why she was laughing until she actually thought about what her friend said.

"I'm not reading her my poetry!" There was a reason Eva had not pursued a passion for creative writing. Her poetry was like dragging one's nails across vinyl.

"Kisses." Kathryn waved before heading toward the door. "Have fun with your lady. I'm sure you'll tell me all about it either way."

"If you don't hear from me all weekend, it's great news."

"Or you're dead. Whichever."

"Dead from happiness!"

The door opened. "See ya."

Eva was left in her empty, quiet apartment. Not that her head wasn't full of extraneous noise. She had jeans on, but she dithered between changing her bra or putting something frillier on. *I almost never get this worked up over a date.* She also didn't usually worry about impressing the women she dated. They either thought she was cool and sexy or not. No skin off her back if a fling decided Eva wasn't what she was looking for.

Nadia, though? She was different. Even if she liked Eva, superficially, she wasn't totally on board with dating her. Not seriously, anyway. *Fuck.* Eva hadn't been this nervous about a date since she first had her gay awakening in high…

The receptionist downstairs buzzed her.

"Ms. Warren?" came a masculine voice. "There's a young lady here who says she's expected. Ms. Gaines."

"Oh my God," Eva muttered. She *actually* came. "Send her up!"

Eva had about five minutes to get the last of her shit together. Forget a frilly bra. She pulled the dark gray college T-shirt over her sports bra and called it good. Eva grabbed a comb and attacked her hair. Wetting it, covering it in one of her tamer products… should she totally comb it flat? Or should she let it fray a bit? What was hotter?

Did anyone clean the bathroom?

Her door buzzed.

"Fuuuuck." Eva gave herself one last look over in her vanity mirror before launching toward the door. "Coming!"

She peered through the peephole. Parted red hair looked back at her.

Deep breath. This is only the first girl in years to make you lose your mind. Whatevs, right? Eva opened the door.

"Ah… hi." Nadia, dressed in a pretty navy blue peplum dress, stared at Eva's more casual wear. "I hope I'm not too early. The buses were running late and I left early…"

Eva leaned against her doorway, trying to play cool. "No troubles. I like your dress."

"Oh!" Nadia looked down. "I wasn't sure what to wear. Didn't know what we're doing."

Neither am I. Eva was good at playing by ear, but that only worked when she wasn't a nervous wreck. "You look great. Come on in."

Eva moved out of the way. Nadia slowly entered, taking in the size of the apartment and emitting a tiny "Wow," from her lips. "This place is huge!"

"Is it?" That was not a word Eva would have ever used to describe her apartment. In fact, weren't studio apartments supposed to be smaller? Like, wasn't that the point? "I never noticed."

"It's bigger than the first floor of the house I live in."

I wanna see your house. Eva cleared her throat. "I got it a few years ago when I started going to college. It's… kind of a mess. Sorry."

Nadia gave her a look that insinuated that in no world was this a *mess!*

"Would you like something to drink? Tea? Water?"

The most pregnant of pauses ensued. "How about some coffee? I need caffeine."

"I could make coffee." Eva was already heading into her kitchen. "Do you like lattes?"

Nadia helped herself onto one of the stools at the counter. "You have a latte machine?"

"Hell yeah I do." What else was a girl going to do when she wanted a latte at midnight? Go down to the nearest 24-hour café? Yeah, right. Not when she was in the midst of studying. Making her own lattes was a great way to take a break while getting her buzz on. "Gimme a few."

Nadia spent most of her waiting time fixing her dress and hair, as if either weren't perfect already. Eva was trapped between wanting to rip off the other woman's clothes and preserving her in this moment forever. Who knew how this date would go? Maybe this was her only chance to see Nadia like this. Was she even really in Eva's apartment? *I'm losing it. Certifiably losing it.* Sighing, Eva hurried to make a latte. On top of that, she wanted to make it cute. *I'm not great at latte art…* Aha! A heart. Or at least it was a recognizable heart. Okay, one side was bigger than the other. Okay, it was starting to melt into the rest of the latte. Um…

"Here." Eva pushed the cup across the counter. "It's nothing special. Sorry. Eh…"

Nadia stared into the cup as the heart drifted apart in two. "Aw. You broke my heart."

Eva would never be able to swallow again.

Nadia blew on the drink, her lips creating the perfect round O to entice Eva with. She looked away. Might as well make her own coffee. Because what she needed was more jitters.

"So… come to this neighborhood often?

Eva regretted that right away. Nadia's incredulous face was the epitome of "*Why the hell would I come around here?*" Eva's apartment was near her campus, yes, but it also happened to be in one of the most expensive neighborhoods in town. It hadn't even been gentrified – that's how far back money and power went in that area since the city's founding in the 1700s. Eva kept forgetting that because Nadia worked directly beneath one of the richest fuckers in America didn't mean she was one of them herself.

"I pass through on the bus to work."

"You don't have a car?" Eva's Jaguar was parked in the garage down below. Guarded by 24-hour security. She needed a damn keycard to even access that part of the garage.

"No." Nadia shrugged. "Too expensive."

"Oh." Eva didn't understand *too expensive.* This apartment alone cost as much as some big houses farther out in the country. Eva knew. She had looked.

"That's all right. I bet you have lots of cars."

Nadia gazed at her over the rim of her latte cup. *Is this some sort of accusation?* "I have two." The Jaguar and her lesser-used Lambo that spent most of its time up at the house. Sometimes she lent it to her brother when he said it fit "the aesthetic of his day" and the Rolls-Royce wouldn't do. *He can keep that fuddy thing.* Eva would never be caught dead in that old-man car. "I don't really collect them like some people do." She knew for a fact that Nadia's boss collected Italian sports cars as if it were his life's mission. *That and fucking every assistant to come into his employ.* Maybe that was another reason Eva never used her Lambo and sometimes thought about selling it.

"Oh." Nadia was still smirking into her cup. Her eyes? Absolutely merciless.

"Anyway." Eva put her cup of coffee on the counter and leaned in front of Nadia. Time to crank up the flirting. This was a date, wasn't it? "Nice of you to come by. You picked a great time, too. Right before end-of-semester hell."

"You're graduating, right?"

"Not until the end of the year. I took a semester off a while back." Eva burnt herself out after her first semester of grad school. Took things a little *too* seriously.

"What are you doing afterward?"

This was not Eva's idea of date talk. *Can't we talk about how beautiful she is? How much fun we've had before?* Eva's fingers itched to touch those intimate places again. That night up in the mountains wasn't enough. That bathroom at The Crimson Dove was *definitely* not enough. She had a perfectly good bed over there. Why wasn't Nadia already writhing all over it? *Dumbass. This is a date, not a booty call. Plenty of time for that.*

Right. Nadia was making small talk. "I'm going to work for my family's business."

"Doing what?"

Eva bristled. "That's a good question. I haven't received a solid answer about that yet."

"Oh."

A hand waved between them. "I'm sure he'll put me wherever I'm needed most. I'm specializing in both sales and corporate investments. There's talk about us going into the jewelry business. What better way to start my career than buying up jewels and gold around the world?" Sounded pretty sweet, honestly. Eva was already planning the trips to Cambodia. A hop, skip, and a jump away from the family vacation home in Thailand.

"He?"

"My brother. Henry." Surely, she knew Henry? Everyone knew Henry… er, right?

"I've met him a few times. Seems nice?" Nadia fished for the right tone. "Not that I know him well at all."

"He is nice. Passive-aggressive, but nice." When Nadia cocked her head – red curls spilling everywhere, of course – Eva explained, "He has to be passive-aggressive. It's part of the family image. He tries to check it with people he actually likes." Contrary to popular belief, that was *not* a lot of people, and most of them were women.

"I don't think you're passive-aggressive."

"I'm too aggressive. Yup." Eva stood up. "I get away with it, though. I'm a girl, and the baby of the family. And, um…"

Nadia leaned against her hand. "Gay?"

"Hella gay. They already have super low expectations for me."

"That's sad."

Eva had said it as matter-of-factly as she always did when explaining her situation and family life, but the way Nadia sighed was so… pitiful. *Nobody pities me.* That was both an assertive thought and a realization. Nobody found anything pitiful about Eva – well, unless they were bigots. In the real world, though? They were more likely to be a Kathryn and say, "At least she's got all that money and assets. Can't take too much pity on her." Not that Eva wanted anybody's pity. Empathy was nice, though.

"So you don't *have* to go into the family business, huh?"

"It was never expected of me, no." That's all Eva wanted to say.

"So why bother? Sounds like you could do anything you want."

Eva knew what she meant by that. "*You could be an artist! Make a life traveling the world or having fun! Why aren't you like other heiresses? I saw that Paris Hilton TV show. That's the life! You're even blond!*"

"Because it's all I've ever wanted to do." That and play soccer, but those athletic dreams went by the wayside after that one thing that happened junior year. "When your whole family makes their living a certain way, you either embrace or reject it, right? I guess I don't know what's good for me. I want to be a businesswoman, and my family is the perfect way to get my foot through the door." She shrugged. "One of the few times nepotism is great."

"I see." Nadia set her cup to the side. "Admirable. I like hard workers."

Was Eva blushing? She totally wasn't blushing. "So!" she exclaimed, slapping a hand on the counter. "What should we do? I've got the whole day off. You too, yeah?"

Nadia nodded. Noncommittal, but open to some ideas. Eva did not lack for ideas.

"I don't know. What's good around here?"

"If you weren't wearing that dress, I'd suggest heading to the park down the block and kicking a ball around." She once had a girlfriend into that. One of the grandest flirting sessions ever was teaching a petite brunette how to play soccer.

"Except I'm wearing this dress." Nadia flashed a grin and then quickly hid it again. "For now, anyway."

That was a good sign, wasn't it? Sheesh. Eva was not supposed to be this far off her game. She must have looked so foolish in front of Nadia.

"I've never really been around this neighborhood before," Nadia supplemented a few seconds later. "I'm guessing you know it pretty well?"

"Sure." She knew the best cafés, the best markets, where to catch a movie… there was a pharmacy and her dermatologist was in this area too. Hm. Not exactly date stuff. "What did you have in mind?"

"How about we go for a walk?"

Eva peered around the counter, checking out Nadia's footwear. "A walk and then dinner?"

That got her a bigger smile. *Damn, she's gorgeous when she smiles like that.* Not the fake smile either, or at least that practiced, plastic smile flashed at Eva every time she went into Cole's office. "Sounds nice."

"Hope you like Greek food. My favorite restaurant around here is heavy on the Mediterranean."

"The more olives, the better."

Eva couldn't help but grin back at her.

Chapter 14

The air may have been cool and breezy, but the sun itself was out and hotter than the fire burning in Nadia's chest. She dithered between sweating to death every time they rounded a concrete corner or shivering and asking to borrow the black blazer Eva wore over her cotton T-shirt. Because of *course* she was going to be that ridiculously hot. She even had Dior sunglasses that sparkled in the light!

Nadia felt like the Queen of the Frumps next to the cool and stylish heiress. Every time they passed a panel of store windows, Nadia caught their reflection. Eva was tall, lean, and wearing clothes – yes, even those damn denim jeans – that were tailored to fit her body. Meanwhile, Nadia had to wiggle into her dress. Was that a torn seam on her butt? *I really need to start doing squats again.* Her hair was frizzy and her skin blotching with freckles. Eva, on the other hand, looked like she walked right off the runway with her perfect hair and pale Nordic skin.

People glanced at them as they walked by. They hadn't left Eva's building for five minutes before some middle-aged man openly gawked at them. Probably wondering if they were sisters, gal pals… or, who knew? Maybe they were his porn fantasy come to life. The blonde and the redhead. How much money could they make per view?

Disgusting! Why did Nadia always do this to herself? Few people actually made crass comments in public. Probably helped that she was traditionally femme looking and Eva's aura screamed *I have a billion fucking dollars. Back off. I've got a Daddy who owns the company you work for!*

Eva had a million suggestions of what they could do. Shopping! Wait, Nadia didn't have any money, and she didn't feel comfortable having Eva spoil her in that capacity… yet. How about coffee at this quaint restaurant? Oh, shit, they were closed! Um, well, there was the park. Didn't Nadia say something about the park? She totally said something about the park. Time to go to the park!

What did one do at the park on the most awkward date ever? *We should have stayed at her place.* Yet Nadia was hesitant to stay only at Eva's apartment. Oh, on her way over she didn't think it would be so bad. It looked a little drizzly, so maybe they could watch.

Then she stepped into Eva's supposed studio apartment and declared it *waaaay* too uncomfortable. How many square feet did it have, anyway? The place was bigger than the whole first floor of her rental house! *I know it's her downtown residence, but don't tell me it's a studio apartment.* She was expecting a thousand square feet at the most. After all, Eva was a rich heiress. Of course she would have a big and nice apartment, even if it was a studio. That wasn't a thousand square feet, though. That was a fucking mansion decorated to look like a studio apartment. The bedroom area was cordoned off with half-walls and sheer white curtains. Not to mention how pristine the place was. *I could have eaten right off the counter.* How much did Eva pay for her cleaning service? No. Nadia didn't want to know.

So now they were stuck on a park bench watching people jog and walk their dogs. This was the kind of neighborhood where families felt comfortable and secure going out. So was the neighborhood Nadia lived in, but that was a different class of family. Working families, stealing away a few precious minutes to play catch or teach a kid how to ride a bike. Families did that here too. But the dads wore collared shirts, and the moms strutted around in heels and were permanently glued to their cell phones. They weren't calling their oldest kids to find out where they were or how they were doing, either. They were scheduling Botox appointments and chatting to Lucy from the *club* about that fake-ass bitch Wanda. "*Who does that fucking tramp think she is? Stealing Josie's husband… they've barely been married six months! Isn't there at least a one-year moratorium on these things?*"

At least now Nadia knew what the people coming into Mr. Cole's office talked about when they went home. Not that she ever wanted to know.

"Shame you're wearing those shoes," Eva said, crossing arms and legs as she watched a game of ultimate Frisbee spark in the middle of the grass.

Nadia shifted where she sat. Was it the breeze going by? Her sweater wasn't good enough. "You're sporty, huh?"

"Guess so. Look at me, a big ol' lesbian stereotype."

"You're not a stereotype." If anything, Nadia envied her. *When I attempted to look and act more stereotypically lesbian, it completely backfired.* Nadia couldn't pull off short hair. Or boyish clothes. Or any of the other shit she was "supposed" to wear now that she identified as gay. Choosing to stick with the more comfortable, conventionally feminine look was all well and good until she tried dating, however. *Nobody recognizes that I'm gay.* Were lesbians still using handkerchiefs to communicate their preferences? Yes? No?

Eva knows I'm gay. Eva knew she was really, really, hella gay.

"Cold?" Eva gestured to how Nadia shivered every time a cool breeze blew by. Even though Nadia shook her head, Eva still removed her blazer and offered it. When Nadia didn't immediately take it, Eva draped the jacket across her date's shoulders without another word. She recrossed her now bare arms.

Wow. The jacket smelled so strongly of some different perfume that Nadia briefly wondered if the scent came from a different woman. How many women did Eva see? One a month? Two? Three? Was she super into one-night stands? Didn't matter if they were supposed to be dating now. Or was this still a trial date? Yes, a trial date. That was the best way to look at things.

"Ah, there they are." Eva covertly pointed to a female couple walking a Pekingese dog up the bike path. "The only other lesbos who show their faces around here."

Nadia glanced at the two thirty-something women holding hands as they crossed the park. The taller woman sported a thin pony-tail through the back of her ball cap, red tank top pressed against braless breasts and khaki shorts tapering off toward thick calves and Converse shoes. A blue sweater was tied around her waist, and a thick Rolex watch glistening on her skinny wrist. The woman whose hand she held? Wearing a sweet daisy-patterned sundress and running her fingers through thick brown curls. They didn't have to be holding hands for Nadia to get the message that they were gay. The diamond rings glistening on their left hands helped, though.

The dog caught the scent of the other couple sitting on the bench and pulled against its leash. The woman with the red tank top barked at the pup to mind his manners, but the puppy continued to pull, *pull* against its owner's hand.

"Excuse us," the woman in the sundress said as they passed Nadia and Eva. "Pug is all about female strangers."

"'Cause she's a real bitch," her partner said. "Er, yeah, excuse us."

They continued on the way, the woman in the sundress looking at the other couple over her shoulder. "You're a cute couple!" she called.

Nadia froze beneath Eva's jacket. Eva, on the other hand, was quick to respond. "Thanks! Big fans of you guys!"

Once they were gone, Eva turned to Nadia.

"As much fun as I'm having here, I think it's time we got some coffee. Come *on.*"

With Eva's blazer still draped around her shoulders, Nadia was dragged to the nearest chain coffee shop, where sizes weren't *small, medium,* and *large* and everyone asked for things made out of chocolate or peppermint. Didn't help that this particular store was decked out with fancy accent lighting and signs covered in someone's expert cursive handwriting. Instead of the usual tables and chairs Nadia saw at her local chain café, this store had wrought iron bistro sets with votive candle centerpieces. Not a single person wore something more casual than designer jeans and a nice shirt. Eva's T-shirt didn't count.

"What's your poison?" Eva asked, taking out her wallet before Nadia could protest. "The coffee's decent here. Tea might be better. I make better lattes." She snorted. "That says a lot."

"I liked your latte…"

Eva grinned as they reached the register. "Let's share a pot of tea."

"They have that here?" She must have been thinking of another chain.

"This one does. They know how to appeal to their neighborhood."

Eva purchased a French breakfast blend as well as some scones to share. Nadia knew better than to chow down on scones. She wasn't athletic like Eva. *I'm not going to burn that fat and calories quite as easily.*

"So!" Eva was already slapping the bistro table as soon as they sat down next to a hedge growing outside the wide windows. "No more of this quiet stuff. We're on a date, damnit. Shouldn't we be talking?"

"Well…" Nadia shed the blazer and let it hang on the back of her chair. "It is more comfortable and conducive to doing that here." The park felt a bit exposed. People also felt more inclined to make comments, Nadia noticed. "I'm not sure what we would talk about, though."

Eva folded her arms on the table and leaned forward. "You thought we were only going to fool around in my apartment, huh?" Her wicked grin went straight to Nadia's heart. "Now you're finding out that I'm more three-dimensional than you took me for."

"I never thought you were…"

"It's fine." Eva poured the tea with the grace of a girl who went to finishing school. "We all have our first impressions of people."

Steam drifted off the tea in Nadia's cup. "What was your first impression of me?"

"Oh, besides thinking you're one of the most beautiful women I ever laid my eyes on?" Eva put the teapot back down. "That you're no different from me, really. It's one of the reasons I was so attracted to you from the get-go."

Nadia bristled. "How so?" How could they possibly be alike? Besides the female and gay parts.

"We're both trying to blend into a world that demands certain things from us." Eva shrugged, as if that was all she had to say. "We're just doing it in separate ways."

When Nadia was not forthcoming with an answer, Eva was pressed to continue.

"Look. My parents – and the nannies, true – did their best to raise me to be the perfect heiress. So few girls turn out to be perfect heiresses. They thought their biggest threat regarding me would be premarital sex, with boys, of course. Or that I would be an ill-mannered, spoiled brat." She grinned again. "Okay, so maybe that last one sort of came true. But can you really raise any girl in that kind of life and *not* spoil her. And why don't we talk about all the spoiled boys?" Her animated hands almost knocked over her tea. "Sorry." Her sheepish smile was more endearing than off-putting. *She has beautiful cheekbones.* Those Warren genes were unreal.

"So what you're saying is that you got back by being gay?"

"By being outrageously gay. I sometimes think about nature vs. nurture, you know? I don't think anyone could have stopped me from lusting after Rebecca Lewis in seventh grade and having my gay-as-hell epiphany the moment I entered high school. I think that's totally nature in that regard. Trust me, I tried liking boys, to make life easier. Didn't work."

"I see."

"But I wasn't always so tomboyish. Not that I was given much choice until puberty. I used to look the typical Sunday school girl. Long hair and frilly dresses for days."

Nadia giggled. "I can't imagine it."

"Oh, I was cute. Henry says that even his teenage boy ass thought I was adorable. Then one day I went to the salon and cut off my hair. When my mother had a heart attack, I told her it was to make playing sports easier. You would have thought I presented her with my shorn locks and dumped them in her lap."

Dare I ever meet her family? Didn't sound like a good idea. Nadia had "met" Henry plenty of times in the office, and he seemed nice enough, but that didn't speak of his more conservative parents. "Maybe you were rebelling at the time. But it works for you. Not me. I can't pull off your look."

"You didn't look so bad in my blazer."

Nadia blushed. "How am I blending in?" Not that Eva explained how she was doing it.

"You're really feminine. Like, *really* feminine. I bet you have trouble dating, yeah?"

"If you mean I have trouble meeting girls, I suppose." It was true. All of it was true. Nadia had the best luck with online dating, where her profile said GAY GAY LADIES ONLY GAY and even then dates were usually a mix of "You look so different from your profile picture" and "That's you? Really?" because she blended in so well with her heteronormative surroundings. There was a reason she and Jasmine were able to fill any given room with strong feminine vibes. Between the two of them, the world was liable to be stuffed with frilly dresses and fuzzier hair.

Could Nadia help that she felt most comfortable that way, as opposed to Eva, who felt the most comfortable cutting off her hair and having a closet full of tailored pants?

"That works to your advantage, I'm sure," Eva said. "Society loves to reward women who fit that status quo. I'm not saying that to be mean or to make you feel bad. You should own how you want to be. But you've gotta admit that I would be treated better if I grew out my hair and wore dresses more often."

I can't even imagine it. "Perhaps so. I won't pretend to know what it's like at your level."

Eva cocked her head. "You make a lot of assumptions about me."

The teacup shook in Nadia's hand. "What do you mean?" *I've been caught!*

Eva shrugged. "Whether it's because I'm rich or because I'm aggressive as I am, you make a lot of off-based assumptions. I'm used to that, though."

"I'm sorry." Nadia stared into her tea. The scones were still untouched. "I didn't mean to make you uncomfortable."

"I'm not uncomfortable. I'd just like you to take the chance to get to know who I really am." Before Nadia could cover her mouth in embarrassment, Eva burst in laughter. "Listen, it should say a lot about me if some uptight snob like Kathryn Alison is my BFF."

Nadia removed her hand. "Or maybe it says a lot about her?"

"Both. Says more about us than you being good friends with Jasmine Bliss."

"That'll be Jasmine Cole soon." Nadia didn't want to spend the day thinking about bridesmaid business, but here she was, wondering what monstrosity of a purple dress Jasmine would try shoving her into.

"Trust me. I haven't forgotten. Besides the baby and work, that wedding is all my sister-in-law will talk about."

"So let's talk about something else!" Was the ice broken? *I think it is.* "Time for me to talk about myself." When Eva raised her eyebrows in curiosity, Nadia couldn't help but grab a scone and shove it in her mouth. "Hope you don't mind some pastry spray," she garbled.

Eva motioned to the whole plate of scones. "Please. Help yourself. I'm greatly amused."

Nadia *would* help herself. She was willing to take one for the carb and sugar team. Damn! Who knew this chain made such good scones?

***

By the time the tea was completely drained from the pot and cups, Eva had heard Nadia's entire life story. Or at least it definitely felt like that.

Eva's object of affection was a small town girl from a middle class family. Of course, in a small town, middle class was living like a king. *No wonder everyone buys real estate out there.* Nadia had done everything right growing up. The right classes. The right wholesome boyfriends. The right clubs. The right career pursuits when she went off to a state school to study English and accounting. The accounting degree hadn't panned out. Apparently it required too much *math.*

Instead, Nadia switched focus to administrative deeds. A friend of a friend told her about making good money being a receptionist for the big offices in the city. Thanks to this connection, Nadia's first job out of college was working as the second assistant to a small company's CEO. Within three years, she had graduated to being Ethan Cole's executive receptionist.

"I applied to that job on a lark," she said halfway through a third scone. "The guy I worked for last was moving to Europe and I wasn't keen to follow. So I heard that Mr. Cole was hiring, and I applied, not thinking I would even get a call back. I had no idea he was going to interview me himself!"

Eva didn't have to heart to tell her "*It's because you're hot.*" Cole was a lot of positive things, Eva supposed, but transparently a horndog was not one them. She wasn't at all surprised to hear that he had openly flirted with Nadia before she made it clear it was never happening.

While it was all well and good to find out her biography, Eva was more interested in Nadia's hobbies. What did she do on the weekends? Wait, she didn't actually own her home? Why not? Renting was such a waste of money, not that Eva couldn't afford to rent her apartment and most of the furniture in it. *I would never lease a car, though. That's a real waste of money!*

"One of my favorite things to do is curl up on the couch with a blanket and watch old black and white movies, especially if it's raining outside. Maybe make some tea and pop some popcorn." Nadia covered her face with her empty teacup. "You ever do something like that?"

Eva knew what she was implying. "*You wanna do that together sometime?*" Yes. Yes she did. She wanted to do it right now. Why were they still here?

They should be in her apartment making love! Or cuddling. That was fair game too.

This whole date had been nice, but Eva knew she would crack soon. *You want me to hang out with this beautiful woman and* not *spend half my time thinking about banging her?* Sometimes Eva embarrassed herself. Couldn't she enjoy a sweet date without going into sexual overdrive? That wasn't the basis of a good relationship. And for the first time in a hell of a long time? She was interested in seeing how far she could take this relationship.

If she didn't get caught not listening and staring at cleavage instead.

"I appreciate a good rainy day at home," she said, averting her eyes. The more animated Nadia became, the more her breasts tried to pop out of her bust. "Don't watch many black and white movies, though. I usually binge watch TV shows. I just got done catching up with *Orange Is the New Black*. Thinking about rewatching *Firefly* soon."

"Oh my God, you watch *Firefly?*"

"The greatest transgression in TV history was the canceling of that show." Eva scoffed. "That and not making Dana Sculley a lesbian. What were they thinking? I bet Gillian Anderson would've been up for it."

Nadia slammed her cup down. "I watch all her shows!"

How about that?

Since Nadia ate all the scones, Eva was left with a growling stomach early in the evening. Unfortunately, the Greek place she wanted to go to was packed with guests, and it was one of the few restaurants Eva *couldn't* pay her way into.

Her backup plan, however, was a family Mexican restaurant at the end of the block. Since Nadia had already blown her calories for the day on scones, she went ahead and ate all the tortilla chips too. Eva ordered them a huge plate of fajitas to share. *I picked well.* Juices ran down Nadia's face, neck, and chest. She laughed every time it happened, and Eva played up being a good date by tossing napkins in her potential girlfriend's direction.

"I had fun today," Nadia said in front of Eva's apartment building. The sun was as good as gone, but that didn't stop the city lights illuminating the whole sidewalk. "Maybe we could do it again some other time?"

Huh? What? Was she leaving already? "You're not going to come up?"

Eva must have looked so distraught, for Nadia began to laugh at the face in front of her.

"I was wondering how you would react."

"Hey!" Eva gently shoved Nadia's shoulder. "That's not nice. Don't play with a girl's heart like that."

"You have a heart?"

Time to shove the other shoulder!

"I've got some time to spare." Coquettish Nadia kicked one of her heels behind her, puffy cheek digging against her sweater. "You got a nightcap for me?"

I've got a million nightcaps. If nightcap was code for orgasm? Hell yeah!

As Nadia turned toward the front door, Eva caught a flash of light from across the street.

Fuck. Eva completely shielded Nadia and hurried her past the doorman. "There's a rat," she murmured to the man. "Get rid of him."

"Yes, Ms. Warren." The doorman pulled out his work cell phone and made a call.

"What's wrong?" Nadia hesitated in the lobby.

Eva hooked their arms together and directed her toward the elevator. "No worries. Wine or champagne?" *Get her mind off the pap across the street!*

Eva was one of those heiresses the paparazzi loved to hate. They loved that she was an unapologetic lesbian ready-made for high society drama. They hated that she hid most of her dates from the world. What? Why wouldn't she? *Not best form to parade my gay dates in front of the paps.* If straight women didn't like being front page with their love lives, it was doubly worse for those not-so-straight women trying to keep things private until they were ready to make their own announcements to the world. Which might never happen.

The last time Eva was papped with a date was in Rio. That bikini model really enjoyed going down on a girl's pussy, but hated having the whole world know about it. Not to mention the call Isabella made to her daughter after *The Daily Social* picked it up and posted those gross photos on their blog. It still made Eva's skin burn to think about. *Went to a lawyer about it, was laughed out of his office.* Nobody wanted to help her. It took Henry's smug face and a few phone calls to get those pictures taken off the internet. By then the damage was done. That model fell off the face of the earth. Eva may not have been pursuing something more serious with her, but it was still a shitty way to end things.

With any luck, Nadia's beautiful features would not make their way into the press.

Eva pulled her into a side-embrace as they rode the elevator. Nadia pretended to be busy gussying up, but the red on her cheeks betrayed how totally not *blasé* she felt.

Someone finally mentioned that she preferred wine over champagne. "Red, if you have it." Nadia took off her sweater and hung it up on the hook by Eva's door. Like Eva wouldn't have red wine! *It's the superior color, so of course I have it.* She practically sniffed as she thought it.

For the second time that day Nadia looked completely lost in the middle of Eva's apartment. "Have a seat on the couch," Eva said, pulling out two wineglasses from an antique hutch Kathryn bequeathed her as a housewarming gift. "1925 or 1945?"

"Depends. From where?"

"I've got Napa Valley and Tuscany."

Nadia sat on the couch. "I actually don't know about any of that."

"I recommend the Napa Valley. When in doubt, go Californian."

"I'll take your word on it."

Eva brought over both glasses. "You ever been to California?"

"Once or twice. Why?"

"After my semester is done, I'm thinking of going to San Diego for a weekend." Eva sniffed the wine before taking the first sip. Nadia took her cue to do the same, her face espousing bitterness. *Not much of a wine drinker, I see.* "You should come with me."

"Don't know about that…"

"I love to travel." Eva leaned back, her posture terrible enough to give her mother a stroke. "Around America, around the world… doesn't matter to me. My family has a personal jet I can use when no one else is. One time I went to Omaha for two days simply to say I did."

"What was in Omaha?"

Eva let the alcohol settle. "Absolutely nothing. Exactly what I wanted."

"I see." Nadia was slow to drink more of her wine.

"To be frank," Eva continued, although she was already hating herself for this, "I'm going to be super busy starting this next week. I've got a ton of papers to write and research data to present. Then I have to fit a trip to Montana in there somewhere, because if I don't make an appearance at my parents' anniversary party they probably *will* disown me. So what I'm trying to say is… this might be the last time I can see you for a while. If you wanted to have another date, it would be nice to go somewhere, yeah?"

Nadia wouldn't meet her heated gaze. "Maybe. I'll think about it. I've never been whisked away like that before."

She wasn't going to drink the wine. She must not have liked it… whatever. Eva knew how to bridge the gap between relaxing with wine and making the most out of a night.

"Ah…" Eva placing their glasses on the coffee table and attacking her date's throat with tender kisses was the best. "I was wondering when this would happen."

Eva was almost too lost in the feel of Nadia's skin beneath her lips. "You kept me from it all day. You gonna say no now too?"

"What would you do if I did?"

Eva pulled Nadia's head toward her, offering a kiss where it mattered most. "Be really, really sad."

"And horny?"

"Duh." Eva grinned against Nadia's skin. "But that's a given. I think that might be my natural state. Horny 24/7. Is that a bad thing?"

Nadia looped her arms around Eva's shoulders. "Only if you're not going to get any."

"You think I'm gonna get some tonight?" She couldn't help it. She had to kiss those freckled cheeks and touch those thighs poking out from this lovely blue dress. *Should be on my floor, damnit!* "What's the forecast?"

Skin tingled beneath Eva's touch. *Uh oh, her thighs are quivering!* Fantastic. As nature intended.

"Sunny with a chance of naked and writhing," Nadia muttered, hands now all over Eva as well. *Why am I wearing so many clothes? Wow. I'm dumb.* Yet when she tried to take off her T-shirt, Nadia was adamant she keep it on. "I like the way you look in it," she explained. "I think you might be sexier in these plainer clothes than in the stuff you wear to the office."

That almost wounded Eva's pride. Almost.

"I'll have you know that *you're* gorgeous no matter what you wear." Bless her for never wearing pants, though. That would be terrible for these situations that required Eva to part legs and sneak her hand between them. She wanted to feel nothing but skin. Not denim. Not cotton. Bad enough the crotch of her pants was already irritating her. Funny how that happened when she started to have sex. "It's like you dress to entice me. You could wear long-johns and I'd be all over you like water on a lake."

"That so?" Nadia's voice was already capturing that dreamy quality that said she was retreating into the hedonistic part of her mind. "Keep talking to me like that and you might convince me."

"What do I have to do to convince you that I think you're the hottest woman in this city?" Maybe the world. Who knew?

Nadia bit her lip, her body sinking farther into the couch as Eva overpowered her. *My couch has never been so awesome.* They didn't even have to take this to the bed! "Make me feel like it," Nadia said.

There were a million ways to do that. And as much as Eva wanted to bury her face in tits and suck on some nipples, there were other, *better* ways to give Nadia what she wanted. Ways that Eva had yet to bestow and were long overdue.

"Oh my God," Nadia muttered once she realized what Eva kneeling before the couch meant. "At least you bought me dinner first this time."

"At least you *let* me buy you dinner first this time." Eva kissed her knee. "Even I have a script that I don't mind following once in a while."

"So?" Did Nadia realize how hard she was massaging her own breasts? Whoops. There popped one out now. Damnit. Just when Eva was getting ready to smash her face into some pussy! "What are you waiting for? You want an invitation?"

"Maybe." Eva was going to leave a full trail of kisses up Nadia's thigh. "Ask nicely."

Nadia had to consider that a moment. What? Was she shy? *Now?* "Don't suppose you'd be willing to go down on a poor ol' girl, would you?"

That was the nicest, most roundabout way any woman had ever asked Eva to eat her out. *And I am so ready to do it.* Nadia's scent called to her like a Siren out at sea. Eva was ready to crash right into this woman's abode, come hell or high water.

There were a million ways to tease her before getting right to it. Should Eva nibble on her thighs, maintaining flirtatious eye contact? Or should she rub her nose against the wide breadth of Nadia's lingerie, getting drunk on a woman's scent and the promises of what it heralded? *If I could do both at once, I totally would.* She decided to let Nadia's reactions guide her. Nothing better than making an already happy woman even happier.

"Well," Nadia sighed, her determination to not sound like she was about to pass out in pleasure only making her sexier, "I should have anticipated you were this good, Ms. Warren, and yet even your reputation hasn't… um… preceded… shit, *shit!*"

Words? What were words? Useless, really. Eva had no use for Nadia's words, unless she had something really important to say. *One day I'll tie some silk around her mouth and make her speak only in grunts and moans.* Eva was getting ahead of herself. Nothing indicated that Nadia would be interested in that… yet.

Besides, Eva was too preoccupied pulling off Nadia's lingerie and going for the goods that she didn't have time to listen to any words that weren't "yes" or "no."

Once she started, she couldn't see herself stopping. Nadia wasn't merely soft, sweet, and silky. She held the power to conk Eva right in the head; slap her right across the face. Unlike any woman before. Did any of them feel this good against Eva's face, though? Hell no! They didn't have thighs that were the perfect thickness for pressing against high cheekbones. They didn't utter the greatest sound ever breathed: a mixture of soft moans and hedonistic whimpers. They didn't drip a lovely nectar that only a wonderful woman like Nadia could spoil her partner with. Those other women, if Eva was being generous, only did the bare minimum. *The bare minimum!* Even if they were totally into it and thought Eva was the best lay ever, they didn't make her feel like *this*. Eva wasn't even entwined with Nadia, yet… she was ready to declare this so good that she could forget half of the other women she had ever been with.

I need to make her come. I need to do it now. Point of pride, or a display of prowess? Eva didn't care what it said about her. From the moment Nadia first shuddered against Eva's face and grabbed her hand to hold, it was already over. Eva was going to give her the greatest evening of her life. The night up in the mountains didn't count!

"Oh, fuck." Nadia's breathy whispers were almost hotter than the heat hitting Eva in the face. Almost. Eva had her lips wrapped tightly around her partner's clit, tongue taking precarious dives into warm reaches unknown. *So I don't know which is better. I want it all.* One hand dug into Nadia's thigh while the other clenched the woman's hand so tightly she thought they would bruise. Eva was not physically climaxing, but her pride and her heart were about to have an orgasm of their own. "I'm coming…"

Her words slipped into incoherent moans that echoed in Eva's apartment. Nadia wasn't the first woman to achieve such a feat, but she *was* the first one to make Eva so famished for more that she almost suffocated.

The world went from warm to scorching hot as the sweetest taste in the world hit Eva's tongue ten-fold. She wanted to see Nadia writhe on the couch, but such a thing was impossible in this position. No matter. *I can feel it.* Hands grabbed Eva's hair and tugged, fingers absentmindedly massaging her scalp. Finally, Eva had to come up for air, but not before covering Nadia's mound with heavy kisses.

"Hoooly shit." Sweet laughter rang from Nadia's throat. Eva remained kneeling on the floor, drawing lines of disbelieving attention with her nose down Nadia's calf. "Yeah. That was definitely good." Eva barely had time to start gathering her bearings again before Nadia leaned forward on the couch, pulling down the rest of her bust. Those lithe and tender fingers moved effortlessly from her breasts to Eva's chin. "Don't think you're the only one with skill here."

Eva's eyes widened. "Why, Ms. Gaines, are you insinuating something?"

"Only that I'm going to rock your world as well as you rock mine, Ms. Warren. But not before you kiss me with those lips of yours. I want to know what I taste like on your tongue."

Eva may be able to acquiesce to that!

Chapter 15

Nadia had never so eagerly fallen into bed with someone before. Yet after the day they had together, the memories they had already created, and the way Eva had taken her to a place of pleasure on the *couch*… well, what could Nadia say? She was ready!

Ready to make love. Ready to show Eva how good *she* could be in bed too. Ready to completely forget who she was and where she was. Already, the barriers crumbled. It helped that she saw Eva in these plain(er) clothes and in this somewhat humble abode. She felt like she was a real person. *I know she's a real person, obviously, but this makes it so much easier.* Nadia was able to forget the thousands of dollars Eva may wear at any moment… and the vast mansion she lived in on the outskirts of town. Those things intimidated Nadia, even if she didn't want to admit them. But here? Like this? They were two women falling in love and exploring each other's bodies.

Having way, way too much fun.

What excited Nadia the most was how good Eva felt in her arms. Whether the other woman rolled on top, fell to the side, or occasionally slipped beneath Nadia's body, she never stopped feeling good. There were muscles hidden beneath those expensive jeans and that cotton shirt. More curves hiding from the world beneath carefully crafted lingerie. Nadia couldn't help herself. She wanted to know what tailor-made panties felt like in her mouth.

"Hey!" Eva cried with a start, while Nadia tackled her and covered her with giggly kisses. Her teeth snapped at the single string beneath them. "Kinky little devil over here."

"Shut up and take it," Nadia muttered with silk in her mouth – and her chin dragging across Eva's firm and naked ass. She pulled the underwear down with her teeth all the way to Eva's thighs before sitting back up again. "You could probably stand to lie on your stomach for once, hm?" She massaged her partner's flesh with two eager hands. *Should I spank her? I feel like I should spank her.* Probably not the best thing to do to a self-professed Domme the second time they had full-blown sex. "You look good from this angle. Just saying."

"I am so getting you back for this!" Could Eva look any more beautiful when she was incredulous? "Some other time, of course. I'll let it slide this once. Carry on."

"Uh huh." Nadia didn't doubt that her real time with Eva would happen soon enough. Maybe not tonight, but sometime… *Hello, tingles.* Was it wrong to start fantasizing about another future encounter that hadn't even been decided upon yet?

Sheesh. Who had time to think about that?

Nadia knew the sex was good when everything became a crazy blur. One minute she was truly tasting Eva for the first time – and damn, was the subtle flavor of her body unexpected – and the next she was beneath her date's body, where God probably intended her to be.

"Fuck me," Nadia begged between kisses. Her body undulated against Eva's, their naked bodies eschewing bed covers, because who had time for that bullshit? "Don't stop 'til I come."

Had someone ever been so obliged to give her what she wanted?

Sometimes it felt so one-sided. Sometimes Nadia also felt a little guilty about that. Shouldn't she be doing more for this woman who was so into her? Should she be content to stay on the bottom with this crazy woman rutting between her legs like a fucking stallion? *Who am I kidding? I couldn't even if I was selfless enough to!*

She knew the sex was more than good when she became nothing more than a conduit for quick, bursting motions and the type of pleasure that's born from sweat and a great, pounding need to make physical contact with someone. The most amazing thing wasn't how awesome it felt, however, or how long they could go – although time was probably more than askew at the moment. Hell no. The most amazing thing was how safe and free she felt expressing her sexuality with someone like Eva. Outside of this bed, they were from different worlds. In it? One would never guess that one was the privileged princess of New England royalty and the other a humble small town girl whose parents still pretended she wasn't gay.

It was *really* easy to forget their trappings when Eva was always 100% all right with coming first. And when she came? The surge of her hips and the look of pure ecstasy on her feminine face couldn't be matched. Nadia hated herself for missing a single second of it – even when she wasn't far behind. For who could witness, let alone be on the other end of, something like this and not be completely captivated?

"You were right," Eva said, breathless. She collapsed on top of Nadia, their bodies warm from lovemaking and too tired to move. "Holy shit is the only way to describe that."

Nadia didn't want her to roll off anyway. Didn't help that her limbs' positions were currently dependent on Eva's. One wrong move and Nadia had to face how cramped she was. "You weren't so bad either."

Kisses covered her collarbone. Lazy, happy kisses. "Takes two."

"All right, hold on." Nadia playfully pushed against Eva's face, rolling her over onto the other side of the bed. "Give a girl a few minutes before she's ready to go again."

"Again? We're going again?" Eva was up, or at least sitting up against her headboard. She pulled a light blanket over her thighs. Why so shy all of a sudden? Not like Nadia had never seen those pretty blond hairs on her mound before. "Can I take a shower first?"

Nadia rubbed her lover's leg. "Only if I take one with you. What kind of shower you got in this place, anyway? How many jets?"

"Two. Don't you have two jets in your shower? It's like... the bare minimum to be civilized."

Rolling her eyes, Nadia flopped back against the nearest pillow and shook her head. "You're too much. Next time, we're hooking up at my place."

"Next time, hm?" Eva waggled her brows. "Don't tempt me with things I don't get to have for a while."

"What do you mean?"

Eva slowly fell over right into Nadia's naked lap. "I told you. Outside of a couple of late evenings, this is the most fun I'm going to have before I take the summer off."

"Oh." *No time for me, then?* Nadia supposed that was to be expected. Eva may have been a privileged git at times, but she was still busy with her schooling. *At least she takes it seriously?* If Nadia stood a chance with someone like Eva, then she had to be serious about what she did instead of resting on her golden laurels.

"Trust me, sweet, I'm going to miss the fuck out of you." Eva reiterated this point with more kisses to Nadia's stomach and breasts. "I'm going to think about you every day. Promise you won't block my number again?"

"Okay. Guess not." Nadia giggled. "How are you going to make it up to me? You can't seduce a girl, fuck her hard, and leave her hanging. What kind of monster are you?"

"Tell you what. I'll take you somewhere fun after I'm done. You and me, on the other side of the country or beyond. Call your shitty boss and tell him you're phoning in gay."

"He'd probably like that," Nadia mumbled.

"So do it! If I know I'm taking a woman like you out for all sorts of fun, I'll be a lot more chipper these next few weeks."

"Aw, really?"

Eva's wandering hand was going to be the death of her. She kept slipping it between Nadia's thighs, as if that's where it eternally belonged. "Definitely."

"All right." Nadia sighed. "Guess I won't block your number again. For now."

"And when we get back together?" Eva continued. "Let's talk about you being my girlfriend."

Nadia leaned into Eva's embrace. "Only if we can talk about you being mine too."

The kiss they shared said that such things were implied.

Chapter 16

Nadia spent the next few weeks swinging like a pendulum between two equally dominating thoughts. The first was how much she had enjoyed her last date with Eva. After they parted the following morning, it was with an understanding that they may not be able to see each other for a while… but they would certainly stay in contact.

No one anticipated that Nadia would be drowning in hot, lingering thoughts of the way Eva was fond of making love. She would relax in the bath – naked, of course – imagining the other woman there with her, drinking wine and making bawdy jokes until they inevitably started having sex. When Nadia went to bed? Didn't matter if she wore clothes. Her thoughts and dreams always went to Eva tearing them off her lover's body and making unrelenting love to her.

At first, these thoughts remained safely at home. Then they followed Nadia to work, where she was forced to face the other dominating thought: that she couldn't tell anyone about her recent dating fortune.

I seriously haven't told anyone. Not even Jasmine, who stopped by the office more often than not to have lunch with Nadia and go over wedding details. One time Nadia had the great misfortune of suffering through this with her *boss* in tow! They sat in the restaurant on the bottom floor of the building, Nadia half-listening to the bickering between fiancés about what foods to serve at their wedding. Not exactly the best time to say, "*By the way, I'm boning the Warren woman again. You ever get your pearl polished like it's the most precious gem in the world? Yeah? Gross.*"

It wasn't that Nadia thought her friends would make fun of her. If anything, her non-rich friends would have shat themselves to know Nadia was officially dating one of the biggest catches in Lesbian Town. Perhaps that was part of the problem. Nadia was not looking for a high-profile relationship. If she were dating someone from a more humble background? Hell yeah, she would be posting about it on Facebook and posting pics on her Instagram! As it was, she already had a sinking feeling about what it would mean to publicly date Eva Warren.

Shortly after agreeing to date her, Nadia set up a Google alert for the hot heiress. *That's not creepy, right?* She wanted to know for sure what she was getting into, after all. It totally wasn't stalking if it was public information. Eva didn't have a Wikipedia page or social media accounts. Nadia had to get third party information from somewhere!

The day after she set up that Google alert? Eva popped up on a blog.

It was me. On the date. With her. Eva had looked straight at the cameraman and covered Nadia up by the time the pictures were snapped. *She saw them, but she didn't say anything.* Hadn't she mentioned something about rats to the doorman? Were paps what she meant? Would the paparazzi really care about Eva's dating life? Her only claim to fame was being the lesbian daughter of a rich and influential family! *Sigh.*

Nadia was grateful that nobody had recognized her. That didn't mean they would be so lucky in the future.

And it definitely did not help when Nadia discovered that Eva had her own tag on this tabloid… and clicking on it took her down a dark and dirty rabbit hole.

Half the pics were gratuitous pap shots of Eva minding her own business on her college campus, in restaurants, walking down the street, and even at functions like galas and fundraisers. The other half? Down and dirty date photos going as far back as six or seven years.

So. Many. Women.

Nadia's head spun counting the different women Eva had been romantically seen with over the past several years. Some were other heiresses, trying to hide their identities and then later spurned by the press and their families for daring to hold hands with a woman like Eva (or any woman for that matter.) Others were supermodels, actresses, even the occasional rock or pop singer who now declared themselves a proud member of the LGBT community or put out official statements saying "*She was helping me across the street. That's why she was holding my hand. By the way, have I told you about my boyfriend?*"

None of these pics were as bad as the ones from the year before. Rio. A supermodel who was never mentioned again.

The scumbag photographers had done nothing to blur out what was going on between two consenting adults.

It wasn't simple jealousy blazing in Nadia's blood as she threw her phone across her bed. It was fear.

What if that had been her? What if a pap had used a high-powered camera from hell to catch Eva going down on Nadia? The other way around? Riding a damn strap-on? *Whoa, where did that image come from?* They hadn't gotten that far. Yet.

Besides, it was entirely possible that she and Eva had nothing going on between them aside from lust. Nadia didn't want to deal with the public analysis if this was only a fling that lasted a few months. A year from now, Nadia wanted to enjoy a possible single life as Mr. Cole's receptionist. She didn't need to cause her boss any problems – let alone her *job.*

Easy enough to say when she had time to daydream in the afternoon.

Sometimes she held her chin in her hands and stared at the office doors, imagining Eva strutting through them with a wink in her eyes and a smile on her lips. What better way to mix up the monotony than being flirted with by a gorgeous, confidant woman? *Sheesh. We've come a long way from a few months ago.* Why had Nadia dreaded Eva's visits? Because she flirted with her? Quell horror!

But Eva didn't stop by anymore. Her brother did, the only person taller than his sister – and as blond.

They carry themselves the same exact way. That wasn't to say Henry had a feminine gait or Eva a masculine one. More like they transcended mere mortals when it came to drawing all the attention in the room. They had generations' worth of finishing school and the right to call themselves charming beneath their gold and silver belts. Suffice to say, there was more than one occasion of Henry Warren entering the office and getting Nadia's hopes up for the briefest second. *Oh. Not Eva.*

Did her brother even know Eva was dating this receptionist? If he did, he never implied. He was polite to Nadia every time they interacted, but Henry Warren was polite to *everyone.*

Nadia's thoughts constantly lingered on this shit until she finally burst during lunch with Jasmine one sunny May afternoon.

"Do you get tired of being papped all the time?

Jasmine was big news lately. Before the wedding announcement, the paps loved her already. Ever since it was found out Jasmine Bliss was having the wedding of the summer? She was constantly papped having lunch (not with Nadia, thank God,) shopping, and riding in her car. Things were especially dicey when she and Mr. Cole spent nights in their downtown apartment instead of going to their house up in the Hills. Paps loved to stake out downtown apartments, as Nadia had come to find out. Less security.

"It freaked me out at first," Jasmine began, picking at her apple and almond salad. "But I got used to it. It's not that big of a deal anymore."

"Really? I can't imagine…"

Jasmine shrugged. She was fresh from her hair stylist, a man so in-demand that it took a recommendation from someone of influence to even get an appointment with him. Let alone how much he cost… *Then again, if I could get my hair as bouncy as hers, I would go too!*

"What did I show up in this time?" Jasmine laughed. "Last week I was looking at wedding dresses through a shop window and ended up with captions that said I was going to buy them all. Can you imagine? I'm struggling to find one dress that matches me, let alone five!"

"You can afford it now."

"Yeah, I guess."

What would I want to get married in? Nadia was always partial to flowy dresses. Nothing too princessey or ballroomy. Lots of lace. A garland of daisies for her hair.

Wouldn't that be lovely?

"I haven't seen you in anything particular lately," Nadia said. "Was wondering."

"Hmm." Sometimes Jasmine was more clever than she let on. "Still thinking about dating Eva Warren?"

"What makes you say that?" Nadia couldn't make eye contact. Her first mistake.

"You keep asking me about dating billionaires and how to deal with instant fame. You're not the type to fantasize about that kind of life. So… you must have another reason to be curious." Great. Now she was grinning. "I have it on good authority that she's still single."

"Whose authority?"

"You know I'm good friends with her sister-in-law, don't you?"

Of course Nadia knew that. Everyone knew about the unlikely alliance between Jasmine and her fiancé's ex-girlfriend, now the wife of Henry Warren. *Always a small world.* "I have a hard time believing that you two spend a lot of time discussing lesbian gossip."

Jasmine laughed. "We don't. But last time I saw Monica, she said that Eva was moping around acting like a lovelorn… what did she say? Banshee?"

Banshee! Now that Nadia could believe. Eva wasn't the type to weep softly. She'd make a big show out of it and ensure that the whole house heard her. Banshee it was, then.

"Wonder who she could be lovesick over?"

"Don't know," Nadia said. "None of my business, either."

"Uh. Huh."

Nadia couldn't deny that she was smitten at the thought of Eva being *lovesick* over her. How true that was, however, could not be determined.

Until she received a phone call a few days later.

"You. Me. San Diego. Next weekend."

Nadia was on break at work. The breakroom was empty, save for a cleaning man sweeping up lunch crumbs. He was not paying attention to Nadia as she sat at one of the tables and crunched on chips. "Excuse me?" she sputtered through sweet and smoky barbecue.

"Come on! You heard me! I told you I was breaking this dry spell with a trip to San Diego, and let me tell you, I'm so worn out that I am likely to fly out *tonight* if you don't promise you'll meet me at the airport next weekend."

"Next weekend?" Nadia had to quickly think of what her plans were. *Haha! Nothing!* Unless sitting around her house watching TV and swinging on the porch counted as plans. In no universe – aside from the universe belonging to eighty-year-old women – was that a viable existence for someone as young and ready to go as Nadia.

"Hey." Eva's voice lowered to a sultry croon that hit Nadia right in the heart and loins. *Oh, right. She's hot, isn't she? We haven't had sex in like three weeks.* Nadia did not count the several occasions she touched herself to memories of the way Eva made her come. "I want to whisk you away to a fun weekend getaway full of some of the best food you've ever had. And some of the best *sex* you've ever had. What? Got another girlfriend while I was busy?"

Nadia shook her head, not that Eva could hear it. "Nope. I am available."

"Then let me text you the travel details so we can get out of here."

Before Nadia's imagination could run away from her, she stopped Eva from abruptly hanging up on her to ask, "This will be discreet, yeah?"

Was the other woman incredulously sputtering over the line? "Of course? What? You think I'm going to rent a skywriter to announce to the world that I'm fucking you on the other side of the country? What kind of girl do you take me for?"

Nadia laughed, albeit awkwardly. "You're right. Sorry. I'm still not used to dating someone like you."

"Someone like… oh, shut up! Ain't I as human beneath these clothes as you are?"

Asks the woman with a perfectly flat stomach. Sure. Human. "Maybe I don't want to date a human. Maybe I want to date a sex demon. Or at least for one weekend. I haven't gotten any since the last time you saw me."

"That's good! Because you're my girlfriend, and you sleeping with someone else would make me awfully sad."

Her girlfriend, huh? Nadia would see about that. Next weekend.

***

"Knock, knock."

Eva heard her brother's voice before he actually knocked on her bedroom door. "Yeah?" she called, stuffing a sweater into her suitcase. On one hand her brother coming all this way to talk to her said something, and on the other, she really needed to get this sweater into the corner of her suitcase. *Is it cold in San Diego this year?* With the air conditioners going full blast? Yeah.

Henry strolled into her chambers, hands in pockets and sleeves rolled up to show off his lean and blond forearms. When her brother wasn't dressing like some country club prick, he looked his damn age. *Stop telling me we're related.* Eva shot her brother a sly look. Good. He was a healthy thirty-five. A completely different generation from his little sister.

"Finished with your semester?"

Eva slammed her suitcase down and began the arduous task of clasping it shut. *Some people have assistants to do this for them.* Eva hated using assistants. Maybe when she started working for the family business she would cosign to have one – a woman, of course – but until then? She could do things like this on her own.

"Yup. Finished. *Finito. Fertig.*" That German always poked up its head at weird times. "Going to blow off some steam in San Diego this weekend. Sorry, you can't come. Girls' time."

"So I saw when I checked your itinerary. Taking a new friend with you?"

Eva pivoted on her right foot. *What a smarmy asshole.* The only time Henry gave her shit for her sexuality was when he thought he was making playful digs at her dating life. Because that's what Eva needed. "Maybe. Nothing serious. Seeing a girl… told her I would make up my absence by taking her to San Diego with me. Why? Got a problem with that?"

"Certainly not."

"Then why are you here?"

Henry held up his palms in defense against his sister's tone. "Caught you at a bad time, did I?"

"Maybe." Eva put her hands on her hips. "Depends on how this conversation goes."

"Very well. I came all this way for two reasons. One, I wanted to wish you a fun and safe trip this weekend. I don't make a habit of stalking your travel itineraries, but when you're using the family jet…"

"Yeah, yeah, you technically own it so you have to sign off on everything." Big deal. Like Eva didn't know. That itinerary said how long she would be gone, where she would be touching down, and any other passengers aside from staff she would be traveling with. Nadia's name hadn't been written down yet. They weren't a public couple, and Henry went by Cole's office enough. *Awkward for everyone.* "What's the other reason?"

"Before I knew you would be out of town this weekend, I was going to ask if you could spot me a favor. Now I have to ask you to do it when you get back. Requires some rescheduling, but I think we can swing it."

"Do I even want to know?"

"It's business related." Henry grinned. "Thought you might be interested, since you're one semester away from finishing your degree."

Okay, so that made Eva grin back at him. "Anything!"

"Thought that would make you happy." Henry stared at a family photo on Eva's dresser. *Speaking of awkward…* that photo was at least ten years old and sported the last time Eva had long hair. The only reason she kept it was because all the other family photos gave her shivers. And, well, a girl had to keep up appearances for when family trolled through her room. Not having any photo there was sacrilegious, after all. "When you get back from San Diego, I'll have a business meeting set up for you. Details later. I'm not even sure about them myself."

"Why not?" *This is Henry we're talking about. Want a man who knows what he's doing next Tuesday at 10 AM? Henry's your man!* No one spent more time *planning* than Henry Warren. No wonder he was the golden of golden children around those parts.

Sometimes Eva's brother was capable of being bemused. This was one of those times, apparently. "This request is actually coming from Mother and Father. They specifically asked me to have you go to this meeting."

"…Huh."

"That's sort of what I said."

"Well!" Eva plopped down on the nearest couch. "I'm your girl. Er, woman. Whatever you need for the family business, I will do my best to procure."

Henry nodded in acknowledgment before taking his silent leave. "Oh," he said, stopping in the doorway. "If things go well with this young lady, you should bring her by for dinner sometime." He stopped himself from going through the doorway again. "Weekends are best if you're trying to avoid my wife."

Eva had to do her best to not laugh. Nope, Henry had no idea who his sister was dating. Nadia had no reason to avoid Monica when she knew her well enough already.

As soon as the door closed, Eva was up again, grabbing her phone and texting her excitement to her hot date of the weekend. *San Diego, here we come!* And come, and come…

Part 2

HARD TO KEEP

Chapter 17

Eva had every intention of keeping her cool when she met Nadia at the private airport that Friday evening. After all, the poor dear had gotten off work and hopped an Uber straight to the address Eva provided. It help that Nadia was already aware of the private airport of the elite and famous. Her boss flew out of there regularly.

Oh, Eva had so many intentions. And those intentions went right out the window when she saw Nadia at the airport.

It was their first time meeting in weeks. Too many long, stressful weeks in which Eva Warren often swore she was going to lose her damn mind if she didn't get laid soon. Every time she thought about sex? Nadia immediately entered her fantasies, ready to do more than a little kissing and cuddling. *Don't get me started on when I was ovulating.* Right in the middle of her end of term presentation in front of a panel of stuffy old men who were on a first name basis with her father. Blech!

"Hey! How are…"

Nadia was unceremoniously cut short when Eva pulled her into a surprise kiss. Well, it wasn't a surprise to Eva. A surprise to Nadia? Those muffled moans and the flailing hands implied so!

"You. Me. Plane. Now." Eva took Nadia by the hand and hauled her toward the Warren family jet warming up on the runway. A male flight attendant waited at the top of the stairs, his scarf more fabulous than the female pilot's. *Good ol' Richie.* Eva gave a brusque greeting as she pulled Nadia in behind her. Down on the tarmac, another flight attendant loaded Nadia's one suitcase. *Good ol' Richie who will save the sex comments until my date is gone.* For some reason Eva's parents didn't like flying with Richie. Eva definitely didn't have a problem with an attendant who had a Pride tattoo hiding beneath his uniform sleeve. Henry didn't either. Henry was *way* too chill to give a shit about something like that. As long as Richie could mix Mr. Warren's favorite cocktails without complaint, then Henry *loved* him.

Nadia barely had time to take in her new surroundings before Eva had her on a couch, sampling what good perfume tasted like. *It tastes like ass and alcohol, and I don't give a shit!* Beneath that rosy perfume was Nadia's real taste. Eva had gone without it for weeks. How could she go without it for another hour?

"Ahem," Richie said behind them. Nadia squeaked against Eva's lips, her body turning limp against the couch. Eva rounded on the flight attendant. "Captain wants to know if you're ready to leave. We've got, um, weather coming in tonight…"

"Yes! For the love of God, get us to San Diego."

"Yes *ma'am.*"

Richie popped into the cockpit. Nadia popped off the couch so she could fix up her hair.

"Sorry," Eva said, flopping down where Nadia had been two seconds ago. "I was overcome. With needs."

Nadia cleared her throat. "Can safely say I've never ended a work day like that before."

Eva leaned forward, taking her girlfriend's – she was her girlfriend, right? – curvy hips into her hands. "You should be ending every work day like that." Damn, was her ass great or what? Would it be uncouth if Eva buried her face in it right now? This blue dress Nadia wore was too much. Could Eva take it off and *then* bury her face in every part of Nadia it could find? Maybe they should wait until they were in the air…

"Your eagerness is refreshing, Ms. Warren."

Oh my God, she said Ms. Warren. Because Eva needed a bigger aphrodisiac? "But?"

"But I would like to catch my breath before you steal all of it again."

How could Eva say no to those beautiful eyes staring down into hers? "Fine. Drinks and canoodling until we're three thousand feet in the air."

"Drinks?"

Eva flagged Richie down once he emerged from the cockpit. "Oh, yeah, we keep this thing stashed with liquor. My mother needs her medication whenever she flies." That sounded funnier in her head. Not so much when she spat out that her mother was a borderline alcoholic.

Thankfully, Nadia did not say anything about it. All she would say was, "Do you have any rum? I don't want a lot. Just a bit to take the edge of the work week off."

"Do we have… I think the question is, do you want Captain Morgan or Bacardi?"

"Throw the Captain into some Coke and we'll call it good."

Eva did her one better. As soon as Richie brought the drink over and suggested they buckle up for takeoff, Eva wrapped her arm around Nadia's shoulders and insisted they share the drink. After all, she didn't want her date too tipsy during the flight. Eva had plans. And needs.

Those plans manifested somewhere over Nebraska. There was a reason it was called flyover country. What better way to chase the sunset across America than to enjoy the company of a beautiful lady on a leather couch? When Eva shooed Richie into the cockpit to talk to the pilot about whatever it was staff talked about, the flight attendant rolled his eyes and asked that Eva keep the body fluids away from the furniture. He was the one who had to clean them up.

***

Nadia should have expected nothing less than a five-star hotel suite overlooking the beach. This was San Diego, and she was with a gorgeous heiress who had millions of dollars at her disposal. Couple that with Eva already looking California-ready in her white pantsuit, and Nadia was both in love and way out of her element.

Pretend you won a trip of a lifetime. Pretend you saved up all year to do something like this. Easy enough to think when she pressed her face against the floor-to-ceiling windows overlooking the hotel's private beach, already populated with revelers dancing on a wooden platform. *I wonder what they're listening to.*

Whatever self-serving fantasy she came up with, however, was quickly busted when Eva came up behind her and asked what she wanted for dinner. Restaurant or room service?

At least she's not jumping my bones anymore. Nadia kind of missed it already. Granted, it was a bit much when they hadn't even exchanged greetings yet and Eva was already smothering her, but damn if it wasn't surprising!

The only reason Eva got it out of her system was because she managed to seduce Nadia somewhere over Kansas. Or was it Nebraska? Oklahoma? Nadia couldn't say she was paying attention once Eva's fingers were inside of her and the kisses got so hot and heavy that they almost suffocated on each other.

"I'm a bit tired," Nadia admitted. "Let's stay in tonight."

Eva flashed that dazzling smile at her. *Crap. Gonna fall into bed with her again at this rate.* "That's what I was hoping you would say. Hang on. I know what to order."

Their first evening in was the sort of relaxing fare Nadia needed at the end of her week. Eva concurred with the same sentiments as they ate and talked about what happened while they were apart. Nadia could not compete with Eva's schoolwork, but she had dealt with her share of demanding rich people coming into Mr. Cole's office all week. Ever since the company merged with another, there had been a lot of uptight people throwing their weight around.

"Sounds dreadful," Eva said, sitting as close to Nadia as she could. A clipped nail tickled her arm. "So glad my family doesn't bother with corporate offices. What we can't do at home gets taken to someone else's office."

"That doesn't sound practical."

"Eh, it somehow works." Eva poured herself more wine. Nadia declined another glass. "Better than dealing with all that drama in your office on a daily basis."

"I guess so." Drama was one way to put it. For the past few weeks Nadia had seen her fair share of drama, particularly between Adrienne Thomas and Amber. They had gone from buddy-buddy to sneering at one another whenever they were in the same room together. Since Amber was Mr. Cole's assistant… that was almost every day. Sometimes multiple times a day. The worst part was how they kept trying to drag Nadia into their mess. Nadia was inclined to take Amber's side, simply because she knew her better and also knew that Ms. Thomas could be her own special mess, but Amber wasn't an innocent party either. She had more or less told Nadia that she would pursue a mutually beneficial relationship with anyone if she thought it would up her standing in the world. "You'd be amazed at how much lesbian drama there is."

"Pft. No I wouldn't. Everyone knows that Adrienne Thomas is a bisexual cougar."

"Everyone?" Nadia had assumed a few things, but she knew better than to imply them in front of present company. "Sounds like a stretch."

"I mean everyone in our… I guess I mean my sphere." Eva finished cleaning her plate and shoved it across the table. "Lots of rumors about her. Only problem is that she won't own up to it. She's closeted even to herself. Which is hilarious, because she's already banged one of my friends. Female friends, that is."

"Huh. Interesting."

"So how is she creating drama?"

"I think there's something going on between her and Amber, Mr. Cole's assistant."

"Don't really know her, no. Not surprised he would hire some queer hottie with a stripper name, though. Isn't he marrying one, too?"

Nadia almost choked on her food.

Although they had decided to stay in for the night, Nadia found herself pulled to the window again. Night had fully fallen by now. Moonlight sparkled on the Pacific Ocean, but it was the torches and the flashes of partygoers down at the beachside club that attracted most of Nadia's attention. More people had shown up in the hour since she last looked out there.

"They have those parties every weekend," Eva said behind her. "Do you wanna go?"

"Huh?" Nadia laughed uneasily. "A dance club on the beach? Never done something like that before…"

"So you wanna go?"

Nadia did not commit to an answer.

"Come on," Eva said with a wink. "Let me change clothes. You're already perfect in that pretty dress of yours."

Nadia looked down while Eva opened her suitcase on the other side of the room. "Really?" She didn't usually wear cotton to work in a billionaire's executive office, but knowing she was flying right after work meant she chanced wearing a cheaper fabric. That wasn't to say her blue sweetheart dress with little white and green flowers was anything less than nice. *I suppose I could go to a dance on the beach in this.* Nadia raced to her bag and pulled out her hairbrush. Probably a pointless endeavor when it would soon be absorbing sea breezes, but at least she would look fabulous when they got there!

Eva wore jeans and a loose black peasant top that hung so nicely on her frame that Nadia once again felt like a train wreck compared to her lover. Yet when Eva took her by the hand and led her down to the lobby, also filled with casually dressed Californians and their equally casual tourist friends, Nadia felt more at ease. This wasn't back home. This was a new frontier, so to speak, where nobody knew who they were and almost no one cared that they looked gay enough to fill the room with rainbows.

The late May night was nice and balmy, with a cool breeze licking Nadia's bare legs and tickling her cheeks. Eva looped one arm around Nadia's shoulders and sent daggers at any man who approached them with drinks.

Music grew louder as they approached the wooden platform. Electronic beats with a Latin flare blasted from a DJ's speakers. Eva diverted Nadia away from the platform, however, and went straight to the populated bar. She ordered them both tequilas to set the mood.

"We already had rum and wine today!" Nadia exclaimed, a glass shoved into her hand.

"And we already had sex too. So what?"

So what!

Nadia wasn't shy about partying. She had spent her fair share of time in college partying with the best of them. *Never got so sick I was in trouble, but I may have gone to a few midterms hungover or still slightly drunk…* That felt like an age ago, though. Nadia wasn't quite close to thirty yet, but she definitely wasn't in her early 20s anymore. After the rum and Coke and the wine at dinner, she was ready to call it quits on the alcohol for the night. *I haven't been drunk in months.* Yet how could she turn down a free tequila at a beach party in San Diego?

"All right. One drink, and then we dance!"

One drink quickly turned into two. Then three. A possible fourth was in there too. (Not all tequila, of course. That would be absurd!)

But suffice to say, Nadia was ready to party by the time that second drink hit her. And if she thought she was drinking a lot? Eva beat her by at least one extra drink. *Are we going to die? We might die tonight.* What did it mean if they weren't even the drunkest couple at the club? Bouncers and security surrounded the platform, waiting for people to stumble, start fights, and get into so much trouble that they had to be escorted away from the premises. Nadia and Eva didn't reach that level of drunk, but they did almost fall against the bar at the end of the night.

The dancing, though. That was what Nadia would remember for years to come.

It was impossible to tell how good they were when the night was fuzzy and everyone else couldn't dance either, but Nadia instantly melted against Eva once they were on the dancefloor. *Is it the alcohol, or is it me really wanting to touch her?* Nadia definitely got touchier when she was intoxicated. Apparently Eva did too. She wasn't shy about groping and dirty dancing once the drinks were in her. Probably when they weren't in her, too. At first Nadia was worried that they had too much of a height difference to make this type of dancing worth it, but Eva was such a natural that it was like dancing with someone Nadia had been with for years. *That's the drink making you think that, girl.*

"You are the hottest woman here," Eva whispered in Nadia's ear during their third dance. They existed within each other's arms, swaying to a slower song and taking in the scent of alcohol, the ocean, and the sweat gathering between them. "Do you know how many of these people have been stealing glances at you? They want you as much as I do."

"You're full of it." Nadia couldn't say a damn thing without laughing. And she couldn't put her hands on Eva without *oopsie-daisy* grabbing her breasts beneath her blouse. "They're all looking at you. You're the blond Amazonian who wants to fuck her way through the room."

Something flashed in Eva's eyes. What was that? A trick on Nadia? *I'm too drunk. Fuck.* "Only if it's you I'm fucking."

They kissed long enough to stop dancing and catch the attention of the dancers around them. Whistles and cheers blew up over the music. Nadia was too drunk to care.

She knew it was time to leave the club when she could no longer feel the beat of the music. Only the beating of her heart, pumping roaring blood through her veins that commanded her to do foolish things. Perhaps fooling around with the woman she came here with wasn't *foolish,* per se, but it took a concerted effort on both of their parts to actually get back up to their suite and fall into bed together.

Nadia didn't remember much more after that. It wasn't about what they did in bed, really. It was about how she fell asleep feeling more at peace than she had in a long time.

Chapter 18

"What do you mean you're in San Diego?" Jasmine couldn't shrill over the phone more if she tried. "What the hell is in San Diego?"

"Quite the night life, actually." Nadia ignored the slight throbbing in her head. At least her hangover was finally starting to abate. Did not help that Jasmine rang her not once, but thrice, the first two calls going to Nadia's voicemail as she attempted to sleep off her hangover – in Eva's arms, of course. *She snores when she's hungover.* Nadia was so smashed the night before she didn't give a shit if a bear came tearing through the suite roaring its fucking head off. "Sorry I missed your thing. I didn't know I was coming to San Diego until yesterday." Yeah, Nadia was still stretching truths wherever she could. *I knew far enough ahead of time to ask for a day or two off.* How funny. Ethan Cole knew about Nadia's vacation before his own fiancée did.

Now the woman's indignant disposition was making itself known on the other side of the country. "How the hell does that work?"

No time like the present to come a *little* clean. "You're minding your own business one minute, and then the next you're joining the mile-high club over Nebraska. Or maybe it was Colorado. I have no idea." It all looked the same until they hit the Rockies.

"What!"

Nadia scoffed into her phone. Five feet away, a lifeguard made some rounds at the hotel pool. His California tan and those damn washboard abs both distracted Nadia and made her feel ill again. "You're marrying a billionaire, you know how it works." Nadia had a feeling that if she kept dating Eva she would be whisked away to all sorts of destinations around the world.

"What billionaire are *you* marrying?"

"Nobody! I'm not marrying anyone!" *Good job, Nadia.*

"Oh, but you're jet-setting across the country to party near Tijuana and get your pussy fingered over Omaha. Got it."

"You're turning into Bridezilla over there." To be fair, the whole reason for this call was because Nadia was supposed to go to a wedding planning meeting with her friend. *I, uh, may have forgotten about that after Eva asked me out.*

"Excuse me," Jasmine continued, "but you're coming out of left field here and I'm not sure what's going on."

"Me neither!"

"Who the fuck are you with?"

"If I told you, I would have to kill you. For my own honor."

"You are not there with Eva Warren."

"Bye!" Nadia turned off her phone and stuffed it in her purse for good measure.

The chair next to her squeaked as Eva sat back, sunglasses flashing a horrendous glare in Nadia's direction. "Have a good conversation with your friend?"

Nadia pretended to be nonplussed by the prying tone. She stretched her arms above her head, the towel she kept draped over her bare midsection riding up toward her navy blue bikini top. *I'm nowhere near as hot as she is.* Nadia had considered her bikini purchase a score months ago. She had bought it at the cutest midscale boutique when she had just lost the Christmas weight. Now she had alcohol bloat. And had her breasts gotten bigger? They wanted to pop out of this top.

Eva, on the other hand, came sauntering out of the hotel suite wearing a black bikini that showed off her athletic body in ways that both aroused Nadia and made her insanely jealous. *Jealous that I don't look like that… jealous that other people are staring at her… jealous that we're not in bed right now.* Nadia hated how much she wanted to smother Eva and at least make out with her. *I think we had sex last night?* Too hard to remember. If they did have sex, it probably wasn't awesome. Nadia was not allowing any alcohol today.

"That was Jasmine. Apparently I forgot about a meeting with the wedding planner."

"How are you going to survive? Sounds like you're missing out!"

Nadia laughed. Her natural laugh, too. None of the controlled giggles or sarcastic chuckles she used when she thought about it. This was the guffaw that burst from her whenever someone's humor caught her by total surprise. The way Eva drolly said what she did? Nadia couldn't help but snort all over her tanning arm.

"Seriously." Eva took a sip of her iced tea and leaned back against her chair. She was mostly in the shadows of an awning, her fair Scandinavian skin under no immediate threat of burning to a crisp. Not like Nadia's Irish hue that was likely to burst in both freckles and flames at any moment. Had she applied enough sunscreen? *Yes, because Eva offered to rub it in in front of all these people.* There were a few teens and children at their end of the pool, but for the most part it was beautiful adults and some not-so-beautiful companions. No celebrities, but Nadia definitely recognized some socialites from the way they acted and primped in front of their compacts. Eva couldn't be bothered to care about the makeup she wasn't even wearing that day. "I can't imagine getting roped into that bullshit. I was a bridesmaid at my brother's wedding, but I managed to get out of most of that. I showed up for the rehearsal and got the hell out."

"Jasmine's a little frazzled over the whole thing."

"I bet." Eva's tone implied she was done talking about Jasmine specifically. "So you haven't told anyone about us, huh?"

Nadia blushed. She didn't think it had to do with the California heat. "You figured that out, huh?"

"Whatever. Hope you're not embarrassed by me or something."

Really! They were having this conversation in public? Granted, when Nadia looked around, she didn't notice anyone looking in their direction… except maybe that muscular, tanned lifeguard who glanced at them.

"I'm not embarrassed," Nadia mumbled. She didn't know if Eva could hear her over the poolside conversations and the fervent splashing of water. "I wanna take things slow, you know. You're not a conventional woman for me to date. Even Jasmine knowing would cause some grief." Nadia scoffed. "Sometimes I'm not sure she can actually keep a secret. I tell her, and the next thing you know…"

"Your boss suddenly has renewed interest in you?"

Nadia wasn't going to deign that with an answer. She would lean back in her lounge chair and stare at the back of her sunglasses.

Until some masculine figure blocked her line of sight, anyway.

"Ladies," said the lifeguard, posing with hands on hips and knee cocked to one side. *Oh my God. Is that his cock?* Nadia couldn't help it. She lifted her sunglasses and stared at the hefty bulge in the man's swim trunks. *The fuck!* Was this thing flaccid? "Enjoying your day?"

"Let me guess," Eva called from her seat. "You're on break, stud?"

The young man had a million dollar Californian smile. *God. If this were a year ago, I might actually go for him.* Nadia hadn't always loved herself. "A man takes a break when he can."

"Yes. To come flirt with a couple of young hot women. Got it."

His smile faltered. To think, Eva was being *gentle* with him. If she really wanted him out of the picture, she would've bitten with an expensive smile of her own. "So anyway," he said, focusing all of his attention on Nadia. "The name's Dali. Like Salvador."

Da… li… Nadia needed to mind her laughter. First this guy was sloshing his flaccid dick in her direction, and now he was trying to impress her with a name like that. "Hi," Nadia said, for a lack of anything else to converse with. She wasn't as good as Eva when it came to brushing off men. *Blame my past.* Her ex-boyfriend was smiling right now. When he found out his bisexual ex-girlfriend had changed her sexuality on Facebook to *Raging Lesbian*, he sent her a lovely nastygram that implied she was a few foul things. *Why am I thinking of that loser?*

"Your first time in San Diego?"

Eva ignored them both. Nadia, on the other hand, was stuck with this mess. "Yeah. I'm here with my… friend." She gestured to Eva, who raised both blond eyebrows at being called a friend. *I don't know how this guy would react otherwise.* Nadia didn't like taking her chances when it came to strange men. "Weekend vacation. You must work here, huh?"

"Oh, yeah. Full time. It's a good gig." Was he ever going to stop looking at her? Nadia was starting to feel a little uncomfortable. Didn't help that her towel kept slipping off her midriff. Did this guy need to see her cleavage? Apparently. *Why do I have to be even a little curvy? Makes men drool. Ugh!* Made Eva drool too, but that was beside the point. "You, ah… here with a boyfriend?"

Not "*Do you have a boyfriend?*" but implying that she may or may not have a man keeping track of her. This guy wasn't looking for a serious girlfriend. He was looking for a fling, and probably spent a good amount of his work time hitting on pretty guests for the sole purpose of getting into their pants. "Nope. Can't say I have a boyfriend."

Eva jerked up. Nadia jerked up too, already anticipating that her girlfriend was about to tear this guy a new asshole. *No, no, don't cause a scene please…* Nadia hated scenes. She was a Libra! She couldn't handle scenes!

But Eva was not looking to chew off heads or rip new assholes. Her eyes were on the pool – and her body was off the lounge chair so quickly that she looked like a pale blur racing into the water with a large splash.

"Oh my God!" Was that Nadia? Some random woman? Dali the hung lifeguard? Whoever it was, that cry echoed across the pool as Eva Warren dove in to grab some unsupervised toddler who fell in only seconds before.

Nadia had seen it. Kinda. Out of the corner of her eye. She was distracted by this hunk of man-meat making a fool of himself because she had wide hips, big breasts, and fluffy red hair. *I'm cursed.* Cursed enough that she distracted lifeguards from their duties.

There was no time to ask "*Where are the parents?*" Once that boy was in the water, so was Eva, because Dali wasn't going to do his fucking job.

Everyone, save some harried dad, was frozen where they sat or stood. Even the people who were already in the pool stopped swimming so they could stare at the svelte body yanking a tinier one out of the water. Eva's blond head broke the surface with a gasp, the kid shortly following. He immediately started crying.

Dali abandoned Nadia's side the moment everyone burst out in either cries or applause. Eva slapped her hand on the side of the pool and pulled herself out once the kid was out of her grasp. The harried dad clutched his son and began profusely thanking the wet and bedraggled Warren heiress. Eva held up her hand to eschew his thanks. It took another person running up with the sunglasses she had still been wearing when she jumped into the pool to get her to even acknowledge anyone.

"Do your fucking job," she snapped at the hapless lifeguard. "I should report you, but I'll leave that to the dad."

Eva sat on her chair, towel cast over her head as she attempted to dry herself off. No good. Chlorinated water dripped everywhere. Nadia sat on the edge of her own chair and debated whether or not to help Eva dry off – but the heiress was still fuming over incompetent lifeguards who almost got a little kid killed.

"You all right?" Nadia finally asked. "That was something else." Truth be told, Nadia was in shock. One moment she was being flirted with, and the next? Her girlfriend was saving some toddler from drowning!

"I'm fine." Dang. Why was she snapping at Nadia? "Let me calm down a bit. Didn't think I would be playing lifeguard on my fucking vacation."

Nadia got up and bought her girlfriend another iced tea. For herself she got a Diet Coke. She exchanged sheepish glances with Dali, who was busy reporting what happened to his supervisor and the hotel manager. No one was happy with the situation, and it was only a matter of time before someone wanted to talk to Eva. The dad was already trying to rain praises upon Ms. Warren, who only wanted to be left alone now.

"Thanks." Eva took the Diet Coke instead of the tea. *Okay, then.*

"Do you wanna go back to the room?" Nadia asked.

Diet Coke disappeared down Eva's long throat. "Sure. Why not. This place isn't fun anymore. Too many incompetent males."

As soon as their drinks were finished, the pair scuttled away from the pool, Nadia wrapped in her towel and Eva wearing a white T-shirt to cover her figure. The manager tried to stop them to shake Eva's hand. She brushed him off, took Nadia by the arm, and yanked her into the elevator.

Once their hotel suite door closed, Nadia found out what was wrong. It had little to do with that kid. That was only the tipping point for Eva Warren.

"Can you believe that asshole?" Eva tossed her wet sunglasses onto the bed and turned toward Nadia. Her T-shirt was wet now too, clinging to her lean figure and horrendously distracting Nadia. "Flirting with us instead of doing his fucking job!"

"He said that he was on break…"

"He probably says that all the time. You think a guy like that cares about his job enough when he's got a million hot women there every day?" Eva scoffed. "And of course he had to flirt with us. Of course. Can't have one damn vacation where some muscle-bound psychopath doesn't try to get in my pants. It's like they can smell my money from miles away."

Nadia held her towel tighter to her body. "You're also hot."

Yeah, that was the wrong thing to say.

"Don't even remind me that men think I'm hot!" Ironically, Eva yanked her T-shirt over her head at that moment, tossing it onto a chair before running her hand through her slick hair. "What about you? You were flirting with him too!"

"What?" Nadia shook her head. "What did you want me to do? Tell him to buzz off?"

"Yeah!"

"What if he got weird?"

"He was already getting weird. *Tsch.* This is the problem with dating hot girls. Everywhere we go we're a pair of commodities. One thing when it's straight friends…"

"Hey, now." Nadia took one step toward her. "That's not fair. I don't do well with men flirting with me. It actually makes me uncomfortable, okay? I don't like it any more than you do."

"Oh, yeah? Then why were you more than happy to stare at his cock? Please. Like I didn't see it too. Guy was practically shoving it in our mouths."

"You don't have to be so crude!" Nadia may be shit at confrontations, but she wasn't a doormat, either. If someone actually started some shit with her? All bets were off. She could extend her claws too. Eva had the tough skin to take it. "So what if that guy thought I was hot and was flirting with me? What do you think you had been doing before I finally said yes?"

"Don't you compare me to some Neanderthal like that!"

Nadia turned away. *I can't do this.* Not the confrontation – although that sucked too – but the accusations that she was openly flirting with some dumbass like Dali. Was it awful that he was foregoing work and putting people in danger? Of course it was! How was it Nadia's fault? Or did this go deeper? Had something cracked inside Eva?

"You can't have it both ways," Nadia finally said. She still refused to look Eva in the eye. "You can't want all the women you know to think I'm hot and be jealous of you while ignoring men. I've been dealing with advances from men as long as you have."

"Yes, but which of us have actually *dated* men?"

"Oh, fuck no." That was it. Eva had pushed the wrong damn button! "You're not dragging my dating history into this. I *don't* date men anymore! I never should have to begin with! Sorry if that makes me not gay enough for you." Nadia may not identify as bisexual any longer, but she was not going to put up with any biphobia from the women she dated. *I remember too well how it feels to hate my sexuality.* She also hated it when bisexual women gave her shit about lesbians. When would both sides stop attacking each other… and why was she always trapped in the middle? "We can't all be Queen of the Dykes."

"Fuck off," Eva snapped. "I don't think that at all."

She had stopped yelling. If anything, that was hurt in her voice. The crestfallen countenance added to the sorry display Nadia turned around to.

Eva was fighting back tears. If she were wearing makeup, it would be running – Nadia didn't care how good the makeup supposedly was. "I'm sorry," Eva choked. Now it was her turn to avoid eye contact. "I got jealous. I own up to that."

Nadia couldn't stay upset. She went to Eva, pulling her into a hug. *She's not just jealous. There's something deeper going on.* "What's wrong? You can't just be jealous."

"No… it's nothing."

Yet she was shuddering in Nadia's embrace. How could that be nothing? "I have no interest in men anymore. You don't have to worry about me getting bored with you in favor of a man or breaking up with you so I can be with men."

Eva nodded, but she seemed so far away that Nadia wasn't sure she got through to her. "I'm not a man-hater, I swear."

Where did that come from? "Do people think that about you?"

"Of course they do."

"Who cares if you are? What have men done for you lately?"

Nope. Not even that could get a smile out of Eva.

"Hey, what's wrong?" Nadia put her hands on Eva's cheeks and forced her to make eye contact. "You can tell me. I mean, we don't know each other super well yet, but… you've got something you need to talk about."

"I'm fine," Eva attempted to insist. "It's nothing."

They may have been dressed in their (wet) bathing suits, but Nadia didn't think twice about leading Eva over to the bed and sitting on the edge. "Tell me. I ain't gonna laugh at you or think it's nothing." Nadia knew what it was like for people, let alone lovers, to not take her concerns seriously. "If you can't tell me, then who can you tell?"

Eva snuffed her words. "My girlfriend, for one."

"Fine." Nadia clasped her hands on top of Eva's. *They're still wet.* "I'm your girlfriend. Now tell me what's going on with you."

Her face lit up a little "It's not recent. It's something that happened a long time ago."

"Some girl dump you for a guy?"

"Man, I wish that was the worst of it." Eva took a deep breath. The short story she told had Nadia wanting to give her more than a hug.

Chapter 19

"I used to be really into soccer," Eva began, wondering how the fuck she was going to recount this bullshit without a full-blown panic attack. "When I wasn't studying, it was my life. Going to a place like my school," The Winchester Academy, the closest thing to a "normal school" the rich sent their children to, "I had to have something to take my mind off the pettiness. Friendships were so fake you didn't know who was selling your secrets and who was only being nice to you because they wanted to meet your brother or, worse, your father. My only 'friends' were on the team." *I met Kathryn at Winchester, but she was older than me.* By the time Eva was an upperclassman, Kathryn was already at college kicking ass. *Must be nice being straight and having everyone throw themselves at you.* "They were more like my family than my real family."

Nadia stayed close but did not interrupt. "Go on."

"I was really good," Eva said. "Coach said I could make captain my senior year if I continued to work hard. I had a rivalry with some other heiress named Jenny Myers who wanted the captainship so she could put it on her résumé. She wanted to go to Yale, but her family wasn't prestigious enough to automatically get her in. But she wasn't as good or as popular on the team as I was. Honestly, if she hadn't pulled her stupid stunt, I would've totally been captain."

"So what happened?" There was a tenuous quality to Nadia's voice that Eva appreciated. *Guess that means she's really listening.* "She Tonya Harding you?" Or maybe not.

"No. Worse. Jenny went to her boyfriend, a real fuckhead from a shifty family. She convinced them to help her out. I don't want to know how."

"Oh."

"Yeah. Oh."

Nadia's eyes lit up in disbelief. "Oh my God… they didn't…"

"I wanna say right now that I was *not* assaulted." Eva couldn't stand the thought of her girlfriend thinking she had been… when she was seventeen… by a group of losers who… *I'm gonna barf. Right here. On this bed and all over the floor. All over my half-naked girlfriend.* "Okay? I wasn't. I didn't let them touch me."

Nadia took her by the shoulders. Her touch sure was nice. "I wasn't going to assume so. But something happened, huh?"

"They threatened me. A whole group of them. Boys' team shitfucks." It pissed Eva off that she couldn't even relive her glory days on the Winchester Girls' Soccer Squad with her best friend's boyfriend, who had been captain of that shitty boys' team back in his day. *He graduated even before Kathryn, though.* The guys who were upperclassmen with Eva were barely out of middle school when her friend's boyfriend would've had power to do something. *Like he would've helped. By that time he was in some shitty frat being a frat boy.* Eva didn't want to think about it. She tried not to judge the people closest to her too harshly. That way led to more madness than she could stand. *I get enough of it with my family.*

"I'm sorry, Eva."

"I always stayed after practice, partly because I didn't want to go home. They knew they could break into the girls' locker room and find me there alone. Not even the coach was there at that time. So I guess I shouldn't have been too shocked to turn around when changing my fucking bra and see those wastes of sperm gathering around me."

"Jesus, Eva."

"Like I said, they didn't touch me!"

"They left an impact on you, though."

"You think?" Eva wanted to laugh. Laughing was the only way to make peace with those traumatizing memories. "They sure did threaten me, though. They wanted to make sure I knew that they could gang me up any time they wanted. I believed them, too. Knowing how some of them turned out? Fuck, I believe it." Three of those guys were charged with rape at their colleges. *Of course they got away with it. They always do.*

Nadia squeezed Eva's shoulders. She wanted to hold her girlfriend, didn't she? Eva wasn't used to that. "I'm sorry."

"But like… nothing happened, right?" God, why couldn't Eva get over it? Not that it haunted her every day of her life, but there were times when she would close her eyes to take a nap and suddenly see that bunch of boys in the girls' locker room. *My overactive imagination loves to think about what could have happened.* The only thing really protecting Eva was her status as one of the richest heiresses around. Her father would have been good for something for once, and that would have been taking out every one of those fuckers… if not in the courtroom, then at least in the boardroom. "I should be over it. I don't have to see any of those people anymore. Who gives a fuck!"

"That's awful, though." Nadia wiped something off Eva's cheek? *Fuck, am I crying?* Eva hadn't even noticed. "What they did to you was absolutely awful. It doesn't matter if they touched you or not. They meant to intimidate you and used their gender as their weapon. How could anyone expect you to *not* be affected by that?"

"You might be surprised," Eva mumbled. The only person in her family who knew about that incident was Henry, and Eva didn't tell her brother until a few years after the fact. *I only told him because I had this random breakdown at home.* He refused to leave her room until she confessed something, and that was the first thing on the tip of her tongue. To say he was livid was an understatement, but what could he do?

Nadia, so far, was more than sympathetic. Eva also wasn't used to that. *I've never told a girlfriend about that before.* A girlfriend who wasn't platonic, anyway. Kathryn knew about it. The incident was Eva's favorite thing to drunkenly rant about, either on the phone or in person. *I ain't sleeping with Kathryn, though.* Platonic sleepovers didn't count, even if they were both naked in bed after a long night of partying.

"I don't wanna say that day made me fear men or something…" Yeah, right. Eva already knew that few men would do anything to help her, unless it was to protect their honor as well. *My father right there.* "I was already gay as hell by then. But it didn't do either side any favors. And they got what they wanted. I was too shaken up to go for captain my senior year. I told the coach I wanted to focus more on my studies and play on the side. I ended up getting so distracted during one practice that I twisted my ankle and had to sit out the remainder of the season anyway. Fuck. They really got what they wanted. That bitch got to be captain, *and* I flopped out." Joke was on that girl. The team did so badly without Eva that they were knocked out of the regional playoffs.

"No, I understand." Nadia sat back and gave Eva some much-needed breathing room. "If something like that happened to me, I would've died."

"I felt like I was going to die. I had no idea what they would actually do to me."

"I'm sorry," Nadia said again.

"Don't be. It's my issue."

Nadia looked away. "I've got issues too."

"Oh?" Eva sniffed. *Stop. Crying.* Not that the tears were pouring, but Eva was tired of the wetness on her face. "Dare I ask?"

Nadia gave a half-hearted shrug. "Until over a year ago, I identified as bisexual. That was a mistake."

"I see."

"I say it was a mistake because for one, I realized that men were never going to give me the emotional satisfaction that women could give me.

Also… I got really tired of dating them. Like really, really tired. They either wanted me for my body or to control me."

She didn't offer more information than that. "But you're actually attracted to women too, yeah?" God, here came Eva's insecurities to the surface. "Sexually, I mean."

"Of course I am." Nadia took her girlfriend's hands. "You think I could have dirty, messy sex with you and *not* be into women?"

"Messy, huh?"

"Do you not remember last night?"

"Uh, no. Not really. I was plastered."

"Me too."

We probably fell asleep making out. Eva woke up naked, but she often woke up unexplainably naked. "You're really hot in this bikini of yours." She chuckled through her next round of sniffing. "I was mostly jealous about that guy. I've been burned a lot."

"What do you mean?"

"Hm… the kind of women who date me tend to treat me as a novelty in their love lives, or because they think I'm a quick cash ticket. A lot of them are either closeted and can't come out, so it doesn't work out, or they're not really gay to begin with. I'm an experiment made extra attractive because of my money and lifestyle. I know that's what's going on when I go on dates and sleep with them. That doesn't mean it doesn't hurt when they're seen with a guy the following week." Nothing said Eva was a rock star like watching most of the women she dated end up with men as soon as possible. One would think she was going out of her way to turn every woman around her straight. *It shouldn't hurt me as much as it does.* But it did. It was a reminder that she was different, that she wasn't someone people treated seriously.

Nadia sympathetically shook her head. "Dating men is really convenient when you're open to it. But like I said, I can't do it anymore. I only found them tenuously attractive to begin with. Now I don't want to ever bother again. Way too controlling."

Eva had to hold back more laughter.

"What is it?"

"You know I can get pretty controlling too? Or did you forget one of the reasons you didn't want to date me to begin with?"

"You said that you weren't into lifestyle type stuff."

"I'm not, but you have to understand. I don't dabble in BDSM because it's fun and hot. I do it because…" Eva's brain was already on another planet. No, she didn't indulge in a lot of Domme play, or at least not as often as people assumed. Mostly because it was hard finding willing partners, and because it took a lot out of her.

Nadia caressed the space between Eva's knuckles. "Because it lets you take control."

"Yeah. Pretty much." Eva wouldn't deny it. She was sure there was some psychological bullfuckery at play there, but wasn't that true for everyone who dabbled in it? *Not to mention the ones who make a lifestyle out of it.* Her brother's face was front and center in her mind. Henry was probably one of the most unlikely men to be a lifestyle Dom, going on appearances alone. Nobody was surprised when Eva seemingly followed in his footsteps. *"Oh, those Warrens. So classy and kinky! Do you think Gerald and Isabella are into it too?"* Eva shivered to think of it. Her mother was definitely submissive, but not *that* way.

But Eva didn't want a lifestyle like that. She had a dominating personality, but that didn't mean she was into throwing it around and making others constantly bow to her. The only reason she started exploring BDSM was because it was one of the first times she allowed herself to take complete control, even with other women. *If I could walk into a situation with a woman actually looking for another to dominate her, even for a night, then it felt better.* Lesbian dating in everyday life was already hard enough as it was.

Then there was Nadia, who said she wasn't into that… but now gave Eva such sympathetic eyes that she couldn't help but want her even more.

Eva had had girlfriends before. Sometimes even serious ones. But she never had a girlfriend who stung her like Nadia did.

"Guess I look like a stereotype now," Eva said. "Of course the rich bitch with a gay chip on her shoulder wants to Top. Why wouldn't she?"

"I don't think you're stereotypical at all." Nadia tucked some of Eva's drying hair behind her ear. *I need a haircut. Once it's past my ears, it's too long!* "I think you're trying to find what works for you so you can be happy."

"Know what would make me happy right now?" Here came another stereotype.

Nadia leaned back. Did she know she was giving Eva a great view of her breasts like that? *God bless bikini tops.* Eva didn't look half as hot in her bikini. She didn't have the same amount of curves to fill it out. Nadia, though? *Whoa. Victoria's Secret is missing out over here.*

"I've got a good idea. It probably involves me on my back."

Eva couldn't deny that either. "Maybe. A little."

"You sound like I should be annoyed with how much you want to have sex. Come on. It's 2016. Women have dirty sex with each other. Not as often as they *should,* I'll grant you, but you're not the only one who gets horny at least once a day." Nadia grinned. "Sometimes more, if around the right person."

"Once a day, huh?"

"At certain times of the month it's that high, for sure."

"How about right now?" Eva touched her girlfriend's thigh. She was not pushed away. *God bless these heavenly thighs!* Curvy, but firm. This woman worked the hell out. Shit, walking around in her office heels probably gave her calves of steel too. "What time of the month is it for you now?"

Nadia shrugged. Great. Now her tits were jiggling. Was she doing this on purpose? "I'd tell you, but that look in your eye says you're not thinking of conventional sex."

Oops. Caught.

Eva had thought a lot of things about Nadia even before they started dating. She couldn't with a good conscience say that she thought of anything but sex the first time they met. That wasn't unusual. Nor was it unusual for Eva to see women she found particularly attractive and immediately think of them in more… how did Nadia put it? Unconventional ways? *I ain't green when it comes to bondage.* There was almost nothing hotter than a woman tied up and awaiting Eva's way of loving.

Eva wasn't green to a lot of other things, though. But Nadia was, and that was a block between them.

"Man, I knew this day was coming." Nadia kicked her legs up on the bed and pretended to be distracted by her own hair. "Only a matter of time before you took me over your knee and flogged me."

"That's, um, not how it usually works… and we don't have to do anything like that." *Can we, though? Can we please?* Eva may have gotten into kinkier shit because it appealed to her psychologically, but she stayed because of how much she ended up enjoying it.

"But you want to."

"I…"

Nadia plopped down onto the bed, supporting herself on her elbows and spreading her legs wide open. *Holy shit!* Nadia's important parts may have been covered by pieces of bathing suit, but Eva knew what was beneath that material: the hottest breasts and the most hypnotic, headiest scent to ever smack Eva in the face.

"I'd say do your worst, but I don't think that's what I'm supposed to say. Besides, it's my first time. You should give me like… half your best."

"I…"

A bare foot covered in the scent of chlorinated water landed on Eva's shoulder. "Let's start more from the beginning. Tell me one thing you want to do to me… and I'll tell you one thing that I want you to do to me."

Eva didn't know if this was a trap or if she had drowned in that pool and gone to Heaven.

Chapter 20

What has gotten into me? Nadia enjoyed spending her time beneath another woman's body as much as any other lesbian, but this was on a different level. *Is this who I am now?* Who? A girl who enjoyed sex in all of its forms? For shame!

"You sure this is what you want?" Eva held her girlfriend's hands above her head, her grip so tight that Nadia had to bite her lip. "I'd love for you to tell me yes, by the way."

"Yes," Nadia said. "I want it. With you."

Were those the magical words? They must have been, for Eva hit her with a kiss so hard that Nadia drowned beneath the pressure. *I always knew she was holding so much back.* Not just from what she knew about Eva from before they started going out, either. Nadia could tell from the way Eva made love, especially that first time. *Especially* that first time! Eva was about two seconds away from taking total and complete control back in that winter mansion. *I didn't realize how much she needed that control.* A scary tale like

Eva's wasn't unusual, unfortunately. But she was the first lesbian Nadia knew who decided to work through her problems with kinky scenes.

Now she wanted to share those explorations with Nadia? The time had finally come, one would suspect.

"With me, huh?" Those words hit Nadia's lips the moment they left Eva's. "All right."

Her grip lessened, but only so Eva could secure Nadia's wrists together with a handkerchief. When Nadia kept accidentally lowering her arms whenever she moved, Eva took the extra measure of using the one necktie she brought to San Diego – to tie Nadia to the headboard, of course.

"Now you're all mine." Hands meandered with intent down Nadia's body, grabbing her breasts through her bikini top, massaging her abdomen, and teasing her thighs still clamped together. "I get to do whatever I want to you." They had discussed a safe word before beginning, but Nadia had no intention of using it yet. With any luck, there wouldn't be a need for it during her first real encounter like this. "Fuck you, mostly."

"Go on," Nadia urged. "Fuck me." She raised her hips, in case there was any room for miscommunication. Nadia grazed Eva's straddled thighs.

"Hmph. You know I like begging by now." Hungry lips took their fill of Nadia's cleavage, teeth pulling on her bikini top. "But you're overestimating your role right now. Just let me do my thing. You can beg soon enough."

"Yes *ma'am.*"

"That sounds so stuffy. What do I look like? Somebody's mother? You can do better."

"Yes, Ms. Warren." Nadia bit her lip. "And you don't look like anyone's mother."

"Good. Because I'm *not.* I'm your lover, darling, and I'm going to make sure I earn that title over and over again."

She did not disappoint.

Nadia was helpless to move her hands, which felt like a crime against the great, sexual need blossoming between her and Eva. She wanted to touch that soft blond hair. She wanted to grab those shoulders and brace herself for the thrusts she knew were coming. She wanted to grab ass and pinch nipples. Touching herself? Oh, she definitely wanted that too! As luck would have it, though, Eva wanted her lover to be touched too. Deeply. Intimately.

"Fuck!" Nadia wasn't forbidden from saying anything, right? Right? She could exclaim her surprise every time Eva licked her folds and sucked on her clit, right? She could thrust her hips against that angular face and cover it in her arousal, *right?* Because Eva was busy earning her title as Nadia's lover, and she started with a frisky tongue that couldn't stop darting into Nadia's body as if it wanted to make its home there. *Pull on up and move on in, damnit!* Nadia really started to lose it when Eva's thumb dug into her partner's inner thigh. "*Fuck!*"

"If that's what you really want…" Two fingers slipped right in, creating that *come hither* motion so quickly that Nadia didn't even need her clit tended to. She was ready to come now!

But that would've been too boring for someone of Eva Warren's caliber. She wasn't going to let Nadia come until someone's mouth was on her breasts, teeth pulling away the bathing suit material until Nadia was dressed appropriately only for a poolside porn party.

With her wrists bound to the headboard, Nadia could safely say that she had never felt so… consumed, before. And if there was one thing Eva was good at, it was consuming a girl until she came so hard that the explosion rocked them both.

"Tell me you want to come," Eva grunted into Nadia's ear. "Beg for it. Beg until you don't have any more breath."

Nadia did her one better. She wailed as orgasm went ahead and crashed against her, every inch of her body trembling from the waves claiming her, inside out. Oh, there may have been some begging in there, not that Nadia could remember it. Her brain was toast.

The crazy thing? An orgasm like that – the kind clenching Eva's fingers so deep within that she couldn't have pulled them out even if she wanted – didn't abate Nadia's sexual needs. If anything, it only gave her a momentary reprieve, long enough for her to catch her breath and appreciate how damn hot Eva *(I'm sorry, Ms. Warren)* was. She was still in her black bikini, the glittery stones holding the straps up making her look like the most sophisticated dominatrix to cross Nadia's path.

"More?" Eva said. "You better want more, because I've got more to give you."

Her wet fingers pushed between Nadia's lips, forcing her to lick them clean. *That's what I taste like, all right.* With her legs still spread, she could safely say that's what she *felt* like too. Eva better appreciate how wet her lover was right now. "Yes, please," Nadia muttered on those dirty fingers. "I want more."

Eva got up from the bed, and with a lingering gaze that took in the sordid sight of Nadia's body, went to her suitcase.

Nadia shouldn't have been surprised that her girlfriend always went on her fuckbuddy holidays more than a little prepared. One section of her suitcase was dedicated to everything a girl could need to enjoy another woman's company… or her own, if it came down to it. Nadia wouldn't be caught dead with half that shit in her suitcase! *Then again, I usually fly commercial, with TSA breathing down my neck.* Eva didn't deal with that shit. She could load a whole luggage set stuffed with dildos and nipple clamps and no one would ever know – or at least bring it up to the spoiled heiress who was used to having no one challenge her.

When they briefly discussed what they wanted to do and have done to each other, they both came to the same happy conclusion. Eva wanted to Top beautiful women and all that entailed. Nadia… liked her definition of Topping, to say the least.

They could get into the implications later. For right now, it was enough to know that Eva could put on a cock that was already bigger than most of the men Nadia had been with. *So this is what everyone raves about, huh?* Nadia always thought she should have realized that she wasn't into men when even mediocre dick didn't do anything for her, no matter how good the guy was with it. It also wasn't Nadia's first rodeo on the other end of a strap-on. Unfortunately, that last woman who used one on her didn't really know what she was doing. Too bad, considering the biggest pros to using a fake cock was that it not only stayed hard, damnit, but the woman on the other end had a pretty good idea what made it feel good for the one on the receiving end.

Eva knew exactly what she was doing. This was not her first rodeo, either.

"God, look at this angel you have given me." Eva taunted her lover by sitting on the edge of the bed and not doing a damn thing with the body anticipating her a few inches away. "What have I done to deserve such a blessing?" One hand slapped down on Nadia's breast, squeezing it until she closed her eyes and gasped. "Better take advantage of it before it's yanked away."

If Nadia thought Eva was insatiable *without* the kink…

Having her hands bound took this experience to another level. Nadia was completely at Eva's mercy, a tool to be used, an object to be desired. In ordinary circumstances, this would have appalled her. Perhaps with a man, it still would have. But this was not so right now, with Eva, a woman of never-ending surprises and complexities. Nadia found not only sexual satisfaction submitting in the here and now to Eva, but she was able to let go, to focus only on the pleasure she felt instead of what she had to give in return. *My pleasure is hers when we're like this.* Was this the first time in Nadia's life she ever felt so comfortable during sex? Even when she initially struggled to take the size of the thing entering her? (Not to say it was *huge,* but it had been a while since Nadia saw something like that.) Even when Eva growled against her lover's cheek, uttering the filthiest shit to ever delight Nadia's ears? *Yes, call me that again…*

She belonged to Eva. Eva belonged to her too, if Nadia believed that this was a binding spell placed upon the heiress. Eva may have been with other women like this before, but did she make these sounds? Those faces? Did she get this excited, eyes glazing over, mouth agape, sweat pouring from her skin as she fucked the breath out of Nadia's tied-up body?

Eva never stopped kissing her. Never stopped worshiping her body. Never relented from the control expressed between them. Never, ever stopped exuding an aura of complete and utter happiness. It was as good as saying that she loved Nadia. Or perhaps that was Nadia's foolish heart willing it to be so right now.

"*Fuck,* I'm going to come." Eva angled her hips to both of their benefits. Nadia got deeper penetration that made her want to come *so damn hard* and Eva got a view to definitely die for. How much could Nadia arch her back before it became painful? She was about to find out. "You better come with me."

Nadia thought she would never ask.

Maybe it was the object between them. Maybe it was the sharing of their hearts earlier that day. Maybe it was seeing the more human side of the heiress that made Nadia swear that this was the most intimate sex she had ever had.

And now she was addicted to it.

When she came, it was right after Eva, who threw back her head and thanked God for granting her this moment. Her eyes opened and locked onto Nadia's. Together they rode through the last seconds of their mutual orgasm, Nadia's heart bursting into a million little awestruck pieces. She hoped Eva felt the same thing. If she didn't, then Nadia wouldn't be able to bear it.

Chapter 21

Eva had barely started to unpack before someone knocked.

I know that knock. She glanced over her shoulder and saw her brother's tall and lean figure taking up the doorway. "Evening," he greeted, "heard you got back from San Diego."

"Indeed I did." Eva finished refolding a T-shirt before shoving it into a dresser. "Surprised to see you in my neck of the woods." Monday and Tuesday nights were Henry's main times to be with his wife, who went away to work the rest of the week. Usually Henry shut himself up in his chambers with her. *I never want to think about what they're doing.* Besides making her little nieces and nephews, apparently. "Monica let you slum it out over here, huh?"

"She's not feeling too well." Henry entered the room, hands in pockets.

"Send her my sympathies."

"Eva," her brother began, "remember that business meeting I told you about? The one our parents requested you go to?"

She dropped the bra in her hand. Henry was polite enough to not stare at it. "Yeah?"

"I hate to interrupt your settling, but it's tonight. Last minute, I know."

"Tonight!" Eva let out a pent-up whistle. "Wasting no time, huh? Who's it with?"

"Yes, I finished making the arrangements. If you get ready right now, a family car will be waiting for you out front." Henry stopped talking.

Eva picked her bra up off the floor. "Aaaaand who's it with?"

Henry's cheeks puffed, a tell that Eva long ago learned meant he was anticipating some blowback from what he was about to reveal. *Oh, get on with it!* Eva didn't care if she had to go have a business meeting with a dictator if it meant proving herself to her family. "Now, before I say anything…"

"Tell me!"

Getting that name out of him was like pulling one of his teeth. "Damon Monroe."

Eva dropped her bra again. "*What?*"

"Right? I was shocked they asked for you to do it too. Even I've barely talked to the man. My wife has talked to him more than I have."

I bet. Monica and Damon Monroe were in the same line of business… when it came to sex. *Damon owns the nightclub I go to.* And the one Henry went to. A lot. "What could they possibly want me to talk to him about?"

"I honestly have no idea, Eva. But I suggest you get ready now. The meeting's at eight."

"Eight o…" Eva glanced at the clock. *Fuck!* It was already six! Assuming they were supposed to meet downtown, Eva had about half an hour to get ready. For a meeting with one of the biggest bastards in the business? Eva needed at least an hour to get ready!

Henry vacated the room so his sister could take a quick shower and change. Within a record thirty-five minutes, she was in the back of a family car, heading back into town.

"Hey," she said into Nadia's voicemail. "Letting you know I got back home all right. Some business stuff came up so if you try to text or call I may not be able to reply for a while. I…" Eva choked. Nope. Now was not the time. "I hope you have a good night. I'll try to call you in the next couple of weeks."

She turned off the phone as the car rounded a large curve. Eva pulled out a compact and made sure her hair and makeup were up to par. She knew what Damon Monroe was like… and how he liked his women.

Gag.

What in the world did the Monroes want with them, though? The two families had a long, albeit somewhat friendly rivalry that lasted generations. *We're two of the oldest high-society families in the city.* Rumor had it some great-grandparents had an affair. Ever since, the papers loved to speculate some other forms of cross-pollination between the Warrens and Monroes.

Fat chance. Damon was only a few years older than Eva, but he was notoriously standoffish and a bigger womanizer than most. *Glad I'm out and proud.* Someone couldn't stand the thought of someone like Monroe hitting on her. He was the type of man who was used to getting any woman he wanted… if he tried something with Eva, yikes.

Then again, this was a machination of her parents. God only knew what they were up to. A meeting with someone as big as Monroe usually commanded Henry's necessity. *Stop freaking out.* Eva had this. She hadn't spent so much time at school and shadowing some of her brother's business meetings to choke in front of Damon Fucking Monroe.

***

"Ms. Warren." Monroe stood from the table, hand extending to her. "How lovely to see you outside of the club for once."

Eva would not even smile at that. "Yes," she sweetly said, giving his hand a firm shake. *And I thought I had big hands.* At least his weren't sweaty. That was usually what happened whenever Eva shook hands with a man. "Pleasure to see you too, Mr. Monroe." Although they had seen and even cordially greeted one another plenty of times over the years, they never had a real conversation. Until now, perhaps. Good thing they were both fluent in ass-kissing.

"Please, have a seat."

Eva sat across from him at the table. A waiter brought Eva a glass of water and asked if she wanted anything else to drink. She decided to forego ordering something for now.

"So, catch me up to speed," Eva said, folding her hands on the table. Her black suit jacket felt so constricting after a weekend of bikinis and jeans and T-shirts. *Nadia's rubbing off on me. She doesn't fall for the flashy shit.* Eva had to curb a smile before it took over her face and embarrassed her in front of Damon Monroe. "I found out about this meeting at the last minute. Unfortunately, neither my parents nor my brother were forthcoming with information. I'm looking forward to speaking with you about business matters, but I'm afraid to admit that I do not know what those matters are."

Monroe sat back in his seat. *Damn, this guy has a commanding presence.* From the distance he looked like another capable heir in a suit. Up close? In these dim lights that cast shadows across his face? Even Eva was a little intimidated. "Your guess is as good as mine, Ms. Warren. I was hoping that you could tell me, since I wasn't given much information either."

"But… didn't you arrange this meeting?"

"Actually, no. My father did."

"Your father."

"He was very adamant that I come meet you tonight. I had other plans, but he was insistent. Said it could very well change my life."

"I… see…"

Both Eva and Monroe made a sour face at the same time.

"Excuse me," the host of the restaurant said behind Eva. "Two more guests have arrived. Mrs. Warren and Mr. Monroe. Er, that is to say… the other Ms. Warren and Mr. Monroe."

Eva knew she was in big trouble when the senior Mr. Monroe walked through the door. The person behind him?

Isabella.

"Mother!" Eva stood, the makeup on her face the only thing keeping it from paling as bright as the moon. "What are you doing here? Since when are you in town?"

Isabella stopped in front of her daughter. "I come and go as I please, don't I? And you're one to talk. I intended to take the family jet here earlier today, but *someone* was already using it. Where the hell were you?"

Eva narrowed her eyes at her mother. "Taking some personal time. I just finished my semester, not that I believe you're too interested in that."

"Don't be so rude." Isabella flashed the men at the table a smile. Eva couldn't bring herself to do it. When she looked at the Monroes? Russell Monroe, a man past sixty and with nary a black hair remaining on his head, leered right at her. Damon, on the other hand, looked so uncomfortable that he must have been having the same revelations as Eva.

No. This isn't happening… they wouldn't…

"Eva, I'm sure you know the Monroes, Russell and his son Damon." Isabella gestured to them. "Have a seat. We have a lot to talk about."

Eva did not want to sit down. She feared the moment she planted her ass back in that chair, she would sorely regret it. After such a great weekend, too…

"You know the Warrens, of course," Russell said to his son.

"Of course. Eva and I almost had a pleasant conversation before you walked in. Although we weren't sure what we were here to talk about. I'm guessing you're about to tell us."

The only people not cringing at the table were over the age of fifty.

"Eva," Isabella hissed into her daughter's ear. "Why are you wearing this ridiculous outfit?"

"What?" Ridiculous? Did she even want to know? *I dressed for a business meeting!* Or were business suits no longer suitable for meetings? The Monroes weren't the only ones who could show up in tailored Italian suits. Like any other billionaire businessperson, Eva had her favorite tailor in the world who made sure every piece flawlessly fit her feminine frame. *I bet if Nadia saw me she would jump my bones.* Why not? She had jumped Eva's bones twice that day. Once when they woke up, and once when they were in the air. Someone had become addicted to getting laid at three thousand feet in the air. Damn Richie wouldn't stop laughing when they departed the airport.

"You could at least pretend to care about your appearance," Isabella said with another sniff. "These are the Monroes, for God's sake."

"Mother…"

Whatever Russell muttered into his son's ear wasn't making Damon happy either. They shared a mutual look of "*Fuck our parents*" before Russell took the reins of this ill-fated meeting. "She's not too bad to look at, really."

Eva sat up with a start. Damon Monroe looked like he was either going to snap at his father or crawl beneath the table, whichever one would get him in the most trouble. Even thirty-year-old men could be massively embarrassed by their fathers.

"No way." Eva would be the first one to say it. "You two have to be nuts. This is *not* a betrothal banquet!"

Eva hadn't uttered that phrase in years. It was the type of term that was bandied about certain circles of friends, but Eva thought she was long past listening to teenage girls giggle about their parents attempting to set up fortuitous betrothals. *Some things haven't changed in 2016.* Eva should have seen this coming the moment she heard she was meeting with the Monroes, a family that had utilized arranged marriages going back generations. *Even my family isn't that stuffy.* Until now, it seemed.

"Does this look like a banquet to you?" Isabella asked with fluttering eyelashes. "It's a dinner between families, dear."

"Father," Damon said to the man on his left, "please do not tell me you are wasting my time with this."

"Wasting your time? Why, son…"

Damon cleared his throat. There was a huge elephant in the room, and her name was Eva Warren. *You know, the one so gay she has cropped hair and is wearing a suit? Fuck me.* She had felt plenty comfortable before she was made out a possible fuck trophy for a man. Not any man, either! A Monroe! *I'm gonna vomit.*

"Fine!" Isabella exclaimed. "There's no sense hiding it, Russell. These kids are too quick for us. Let's be blunt about it."

Oh, no.

"Yes, Eva. *Yes* this is a business arrangement. What, do you think either Russell or I expect you and the younger Mr. Monroe to fall in love? Please. This isn't about love. This is what is best for our families."

Eva was speechless. Damon looked like he needed a few hard drinks. *So much for that badass façade of his!* Eva's was crumbling too. To think… the two of them came here tonight to talk real business.

"You want to be a part of the family business?" Isabella continued. "The first thing you can do to improve our family's standing is to marry into an equally great family." Wow. That was the smuggest demeanor ever. The way Isabella Warren and Russell Monroe looked at one another, Eva was game to believe her father was dead and these senior citizens were going to forge their *own* empire. "Jesus Christ, Eva, why do you have to be so difficult?"

"*Me?*" Eva swung her arm across the table. "Is that a face of a man who is happy with this arrangement?"

"Hardly," Damon muttered. "Father, I respect what you're trying to do here, but you can't actually be serious. Ms. Warren is about as interested in me as I am in her." That was to say, not at all. *He likes me okay as long as I keep pumping money into his sex club, but that's where it ends.* And Eva only cared about him as long as he left her alone. "It would never work."

"Can you believe these children?" Russell asked Isabella. "They have no idea how easy they have it these days. I was betrothed before I could form coherent memories of my childhood."

Isabella forced a smile through lips caked in dark pink lipstick. "My husband and I were a love match, I suppose, but we were certainly introduced by our parents and encouraged to date, shall we say." Her visage turned icy when it looked toward Eva again. "You know very little has ever been expected of you, Eva. Having a good marriage is the easiest thing you could do. You can take up the issue of heirs with the Monroes. I'm sure they'll be… understanding."

"Oh my God." Yup. She was gonna vomit. Eva grabbed her bag and stood without any further words. *The thought of me and… him!* Was her mother nuts? She knew her daughter was gay, didn't she? These people all knew she was gay. Of course they did! But they either didn't respect it or probably thought she would take one for the team long enough to produce some babies. *Kill me! I'd rather die!* Yes, Eva was that dramatic about it. She figured most women in her position would be.

There was also the fact she couldn't stand this awkward situation any longer.

"Have a nice life. Good luck finding your new Mrs. Monroe. I ain't her." Eva took her bag and shot through the restaurant. She couldn't wait to get in that elevator and get the fuck home! *I should go to my apartment. What if my mother ends up at the family house?*

Eva thought she would have the elevator to herself. A large hand stopped the doors before they could close all the way.

"May I?" Damon Monroe helped himself in before Eva could give permission. *I don't care.* She kept her head down, wondering why they had to be on top of a thirty-story building downtown. Did restaurants really need views like that… when they didn't even have real windows? "I need to make an escape as well."

He hit the ground floor button. Eva refused to make eye contact.

"I'm sorry about that," Damon began, when they had barely gone down a single floor. "I honestly had no idea that was going to happen. We were ambushed."

"Uh huh." She didn't want to be near him. Not because she thought he was complicit to that humiliation, but because he represented everything she *didn't* want in life. She didn't want a husband and kids, let alone a husband who was as uptight and domineering as Damon Monroe… and kids she would have little control over because their lives were planned out from the moment they were conceived. Eva knew most of her old Winchester classmates would've been beyond honored to even be considered for the position of Monroe matriarch, but she was not one of them.

They rode in silence. For the most part.

"I would never," Eva spat into the mirrored-doors staring back at them. "I'd rather die."

"For what's it worth, I would never either." Was that a droll smile fighting at the corners of the man's mouth? Gross. "You're not really my type. I don't think I'm yours, either."

"Too butch for you?" Eva shot back. "Too blond? Take your pick."

"Oh, now, there's no such thing as too blond. I hear you blondes have the most fun."

"Great. He's a kidder, too." Eva snorted. "Tell you what. My best friend is a blond heiress, richer than me. I'll call her up for you and you can fuck her. She likes men." Could this elevator go any slower? "Kathryn Alison. I'm sure you've heard of her."

"Oh, Ms. Warren." The elevator was finally reaching the ground floor. "What makes you think I haven't sampled the Alison heritage yet? Cheers."

The doors opened. Before Damon could step out and leave Eva behind, she said, "Good luck finding the blonde of your dreams, Monroe. May she be feminine and heterosexual."

He flashed her a dastardly smile before heading toward the main entrance. Eva forced the doors closed and continued her descent to the parking garage, where her car and driver awaited.

***

"Henry!" Eva called, infiltrating the East Wing of Warren Estate at a late hour. "*Henry!*"

The one night maid on duty squeaked as Eva marched by. "He's in his office, ma'am. Please… please be careful. The Lady is not feeling well."

"Fuck her." Monica could wake up in labor for all Eva cared. Henry was in his office? All the better. Eva could bypass her brother and sister-in-law's personal chambers in favor of ransacking his office. "Henry!"

Sure enough, he was at his desk, one lamp on as he wrote out a missive by hand. None of the Warrens fancied using assistants, or at least not at eleven in the evening. *I took a long time getting back home.* Eva was originally going to crash at her apartment to make sure her mother couldn't access her for more embarrassment, but something was bothering her. Something beyond what her shitty mother had done.

She had to go home and clear this air with her brother. The fact she didn't even have to wake him up? A bonus.

"What the hell is the matter?" Henry jerked up from his desk, dropping his fountain pen. "What happened? You look like you've been chased by someone!"

Good to know I look super fresh. Eva stood before him in nothing but her trousers and white silk dress shirt. She had tossed her suit jacket at the main hall coat closet so she could race up here as quickly as possible. "Yeah, by our fuckin' mother! Did you know she was in town?"

Henry was probably debating whether or not he was dreaming. After all, Eva was talking utter nonsense. "What are you talking about? Why would our mother be in town and not tell us?"

"Because she and Russell Monroe ambushed my dinner to try to arrange a marriage!"

"What?" Was that the only word he knew? Or was Henry that dumbfounded alongside his sister? "You're kidding. Start from the beginning."

Eva spilled as many words as she could in a few minutes. How Damon Monroe didn't know what they were doing there either. How Isabella and Russell showed up to start their own crazy party. The implications Lady Warren made about her daughter. "*What's the big deal, Eva? You have one purpose. Get married and have babies. It's not like it requires any work! What are you waiting for? You're almost ancient. Sheesh.*"

"Wow," Henry said, sitting back in his office chair. "Wow."

"Did you know anything about that?"

"Most certainly not. I should have suspected something, though."

"Why's that?"

Whenever Henry made that incredulous face, Eva could bet on hearing something she didn't want to acknowledge. "When we were in Montana,

Mother approached me inquiring what I thought about your future prospects. I told her you seemed perfectly capable of determining your own romantic destiny. Honestly, I daresay she was going to arrange a gay marriage for you."

"Oh, yeah, *that* would be the day!" As if that would ever happen. The thought of Isabella Warren stooping so far as to try to arrange a fortuitous *lesbian* match for her daughter was as plausible as her accepting her daughter's lesbianism to begin with. It was never happening. "Are you kidding me, Henry? Why now, though? She's been obsessed with my sexuality all year!"

"I hate to break it to you, but you're at that ripe old age of twenty-five. In our mother's day, if a young lady didn't have a match by then, she was…"

"Don't remind me." Hooray for misogyny. "This goes beyond that. You know what? This started right when you got married." How had Eva not seen it before? "God, she even said it herself tonight! She wasn't making *me* a match… she was making one for the family!"

"Yes." Henry folded his hands on his desk. Sometimes Eva really hated that soft expression he used on her when she was on the verge of having a fit. *I can't tell if it's big-brotherly or fatherly. Either way, I hate it.* She hated that sometimes she thought of her big brother as more of a father than her own father. God knew Henry was already a better father than their own… and his baby wasn't even born yet! "Our parents have made it known since the day I announced my engagement that they did not approve of my wife. Little they could do about it though. It was my wife who helped bail them out of their debt." Like Eva needed reminding. "When we actually married and she announced her pregnancy? I'm sure that sent Mother into a tailspin. You're the only other child in our family. Our mother is old-fashioned. She sees a daughter as a bartering chip. You only got away with not hearing about it for so long because there was hope that I would make a better perceived match… and because, well…"

Eva hadn't wanted to do it, but after the emotional exposure she suffered in front of Nadia during their San Diego weekend? She was especially vulnerable now. *Don't cry… don't cry…* But before Nadia, there were only two other people Eva felt comfortable crying in front of. Since Kathryn wasn't returning calls that night, that left Henry.

He let her cry, turning away in his chair so she would have more privacy. *Yeah, don't touch me. Don't.* Eva grabbed some tissues from a box on his desk and hurried to wipe away the tears bursting from her eyes. "Fuck me," she muttered. "I hate her, Henry. I honestly do."

"I'd tell you that you're not allowed to hate our mother, but I can't say I'm too fond of her either. She has a tendency to make everyone's life hell. It's a wonder she wasn't the reason we were in massive debt for so long."

"So I hate her. There. I got it out." She also got some tears and snot out too. Lovely. At least she didn't need to maintain her makeup any longer.

Henry finally rounded his desk, although he did not move to touch his sister. Some may have seen this as cold, but Eva had always preferred initiating intimacy in her family. *If he touches me without me moving first, he can kiss his face goodbye.* Would her sister-in-law still love her husband as much if he didn't have a face? Eva had short nails, but she knew how to claw in any cat fight.

"I know that you have been through a lot," Henry began, fingers gripping the edge of his desk. "Our parents have always been hard people. They've never been happy, and they often took it out on us. Believe me. I had my share of issues growing up. It wasn't easy watching them do that to you too."

"Please," Eva muttered. "You were their golden boy." She glanced at his head of blond hair. "Literally and figuratively."

Henry crossed his khaki-clad legs. He was the only person in the family taller than Eva. "Not always. I haven't been their favorite person this past year."

"They give you shit, but they didn't do anything to stop you from getting married. Bitching about it doesn't count." Eva blew her nose into a fresh handkerchief. "You're married to a wealthy woman with a successful business patronized by some of the richest men in the world. You're having a baby. Those two things will always trump everything else. At the end of the day that's all they've wanted from you." Eva corrected herself. "That and being somewhat competent at the family business, anyway."

"And what have they wanted from you?"

Eva winced. "Until tonight? I didn't think they wanted anything from me, besides to not fuck up so badly that our family's image was irreparably damaged." Sometimes the elder Warrens thought Eva was fucking shit up with the whole gay thing. But how could she prevent that? It was who she was. Trying to hide her lesbianism would've been like trying to hide her Warren genetics: dying her hair black and walking with a forced hobble so she wasn't over six feet tall. "Tonight I find out that they want me to marry rich and have babies too."

"So they want the same thing from you that they want from me."

"I..." Eva scoffed. "It's different, and you know it." She wasn't in the mood to school him in feminism. That was his wife's job now.

"It is different, yes, but it's important to keep in mind. What they *want* is for you to marry a rich hotshot from a prestigious family. Like Damon Monroe." Was Henry shuddering at the thought as well? *Yeah, that would be a helluva family dinner.* Both families would call the paps to get it covered. "What you might end up doing is marrying a rich hotshot woman from a prestigious family." Oh, no. Was that a dad joke coming on? Already? "I hear that's legal now."

"Oh my God." Eva couldn't look at him. Not with that smug, clever look on his face. *Good job following Supreme Court decisions, I guess.* "I don't want to even think about it." She couldn't prevent it, though. She thought of Nadia. In a wedding dress. A sexy one, of course. Could Eva get away with thinking of her girlfriend in anything but a sexy wedding dress? "The odds of me marrying a rich girl are slim to none anyway."

"By the way," Henry said, smoothly switching topics. "How was San Diego? I know I asked earlier, but we didn't have much time to chat."

"It was good. Saved a kid's life from drowning." Eva glanced at her brother. "I'm serious. Some kid fell in the pool and the lifeguard was too busy flirting to get his job done."

"Wow."

"So don't let anyone tell you that I don't have a heart."

"I would never, anyway."

Embarrassment burst from Eva in the form of her lightly punching her brother in the arm. When he gave her a *What did you do that for?* look, Eva said, "I kinda have a girlfriend now."

"Really? A serious one?"

More embarrassment. "I guess. We're exclusive, at least."

He didn't punch her, but Henry *did* clap her on the shoulder with that big, sturdy hand of his. Eva lost half the breath in her lungs. *Holy shit, he's strong!* So not fair. Why couldn't she be that strong?

"Good for you. You should invite her to dinner sometime. I'm sure Monica would love to meet her too."

Stop saying that! Every time Henry brought up meeting Nadia, Eva got a bout of hives. He still didn't know that his sister was dating his wife's ex-boyfriend's secretary. A woman he now saw at least once a month.

The only reason Eva wasn't forthcoming with information about Nadia was to protect her, really. Eva wanted to take things slowly, due to her status and her ability to show up in the papers without even realizing it. *I can't believe she saw those pictures of me and the model in Brazil.* That was an awkward conversation to have at Sunday breakfast after a night of intimate cuddling and even more intimate, uh, intercourse. *We're both insatiable when we get down to it.* Heh. Talk about a problem Eva loved to have.

"Maybe," she finally said to her brother. "We're taking things slowly. She's not as enamored with my lifestyle as some women would be."

"That probably means she's a keeper, then."

"You'd think so, but…" Eva sighed. "Never mind. I'm tired. I should go to bed and let you get back to finishing up your work."

His hand did not leave her shoulder. "Are you going to be okay?"

"No," Eva admitted. "Not right now. Tonight was too wild for me to handle, especially after traveling. Do me a favor. If Mother comes home, tell her I'm not feeling well. I only came here tonight because I wanted to… I dunno… yell at you?"

"Do you feel better having yelled at me?"

"Sure. You feel better having me yell at you?"

"Eva, my dearest sister," no, no, not another stupid grin, "like you, I'm not into being the one yelled at."

Sometimes Eva didn't know how she stood being in this damn family.

Chapter 22

Was it possible to be too giddy to work? Because Nadia was quickly becoming too giddy to work.

Tuesday was a damn mess. After having missed two days of work, Nadia had a tough time getting back into the flow. It didn't help that some drama had erupted between Amber and Adrienne over the weekend.

"We are going *out,*" Adrienne announced, sashaying out of Mr. Cole's office with him not far behind. Her Christian Dior dress was simple and not the most stylish for someone like Adrienne. Nadia had noticed things like this before, but having dated Eva was beginning to see them more often. For one, Adrienne Thomas was not the best at switching up her wardrobe. She relied too much on the same designers. *So does Eva, but they're designers that work so well on her.* Adrienne didn't make her clothes her own. She wore them as if they were supposed to make *her.*

"You hear that?" Mr. Cole said to Nadia. "We are going *out.*" He mouthed the last word so Adrienne wouldn't hear.

"And we're not taking that tramp with us."

"And we're not taking Ms. Mayview with us," Mr. Cole confirmed.

Nadia had no idea what to say to that, other than, "Yes, Mr. Cole. You and Ms. Thomas have a good afternoon. Will you be back before five?"

"I'll try to be," Mr. Cole said. "If not, don't wait up for me."

"Will do."

Nadia put a hold on all calls and appointments. Luckily, Mr. Cole had already cleared his schedule, and now Nadia knew why. Wherever they were going, it was going to take all day. Not that Nadia cared. Her job was a lot easier without the bosses around. The worst she had to deal with was prickly business associates who wanted to see one of the partners *right now.*

It also meant a lot less drama. Theoretically.

"Fine. Leave me in the dust." Amber stood to the side of Nadia's desk and crossed her arms. "Spent a good chunk of my time working that bitter clit, but whatever."

Nadia looked around the executive office. None of the other workers heard that, did they? Only two other people were there, but this wasn't something Amber and Adrienne needed getting around. "So you did it?"

"Honey, I've done that cunt six ways to Sunday by now. What a pillow biting power bottom. I swear to you." Amber waggled her blond eyebrows. Not blond like Eva's. Eva was a bright, almost platinum blond while her brother was a sandier blond. Amber, on the other hand, had hair that verged on a dirty brown at times. Sometimes Nadia wondered if that was Amber's natural color. If it wasn't, she needed to find a new dye. "Meet me in the break room and I'll tell you all about it."

Nadia hurried to log out of her computer before following Amber into the breakroom. It was coffee time anyway.

"So!" Amber poured Nadia a cup of coffee but left her to put in the amount of cream she wanted. "Bet you want to know all the details about me and that insufferable mess of a woman."

Yes, but Nadia wasn't going to go digging for those while still technically at work. "You don't need to go into that much detail. Give me the notes."

Amber slid into the plastic chair next to hers. Coffee cooled between them while Mr. Cole's assistant made sure the door was closed and then lowered her voice. "I've been pumping money out of that wallet for a couple of weeks now. Since right before Mr. Cole's engagement party that Adrienne threw him."

"Really?"

"Hell yeah. We boned in the bathroom there."

I've boned in a bathroom too… A couple of them now. Or did hotels not count? "Is it serious? Are you like her secret girlfriend or something?"

"I have no fucking clue. Adrienne is scared shitless about being exposed as bi, though. And let me tell you, that woman is *bi!*"

"I'll take your word for it." Nadia would have never guessed. All she knew about Adrienne Thomas's personal life was that she once was involved with Mr. Cole, long before they started working together. "Why would she want to hide it, though?"

"Why would anyone want to hide it? Afraid it will hurt her image."

"Is that why you two are bitter right now?"

"Kinda. I didn't do anything. I'm not even pushing her to make us public, because then my job could be in jeopardy and, honestly, I'm not even that interested in being the future Mrs. Thomas." Amber sipped her coffee. "I'm having some fun right now. Though, I gotta tell you, after she and I are officially done, I might want to move on to a woman with more gumption and directive in the sack. Or a guy. I'll take whatever."

Nadia had no idea what to say.

"She's paranoid right now. Convinced that everyone is gonna find out about us and that will be the end of her. She forgets we're living in 2016 now. People don't care as much. I tried telling her that but it blew up into a shitstorm over the weekend. I went from naked in her bed to taking the quietest cab ride home. She didn't even pay for it!"

The coffee in front of Nadia grew cold. "That's quite the tale."

"How about you? Taking two days off to go on a last minute vacation." Amber was grinning even though she told a story like that? "Tell me the pussy was great."

Oh, good. Nadia could use her coffee to cover her flushed face.

"You slut. I'm jealous."

"I certainly like being with her more than I would like being with Ms. Thomas, I think." More like Nadia was 100% sure about that.

"Eva Warren, right?"

Coffee stagnated in Nadia's throat. "You can't tell anyone," she hastily said. "Seriously. We're taking things slow. I haven't even told Jasmine about it yet."

Amber mimed zipping up her lips. "You've got it good," she then said. "A rich heiress who is out and hot? Tell me she fucks like a champion."

When she put it that crudely… "She is more than all right in bed." Eva was a damn queen who made Nadia also feel like a queen in turn. They had spent most of their time in San Diego making love of some kind. *I couldn't get enough of her body.* Whether she was beneath it, grinding on top of it, or burying her face in its depths, Nadia was team Eva Warren's body all the damn way. "I have no real complaints."

"Damn." Amber kicked back in her seat. "I need to get me an Eva Warren. Let me know if you two break up."

Nadia couldn't tell if she was joking or not. *Probably not.* "Think it would be easier for you to find a boyfriend than another rich girlfriend."

"Hmm. When you get a renewed taste of the female form…"

Nadia couldn't argue that. She was the woman who had sworn off guys for good. Right in time too, apparently.

The rest of her work day was uneventful. A few testy calls from people demanding to be put through to Mr. Cole, but for the most part, it wasn't anything Nadia couldn't diplomatically handle. She spent more of her mental energy thinking of Amber's drama and her own life.

Right at five, when people were packing up early and going home – Amber included – Nadia received a text from Eva.

"You off work yet? I want to see you."

Her heart fluttered. Her thumb shook as she carefully typed out a reply. *"Already need more of me? It's only been a day, Ms. Warren."* The goofiest grin covered Nadia's face. Calling her Ms. Warren made her think of Saturday after the incident at the pool. *I kinda want her to tie me up again.* Nadia never thought she would be into that. Maybe handcuffs for the occasional night at most. Actual bondage? Whoa.

"*I need you. Where can I meet you?*"

"*What's wrong with your place?*"

"*Don't feel like being there. Can we meet at your place?*"

Her… place?

Nadia stared at that message as if it were going to bite her. Lights turned off in the office. One of the male employees sputtered a goodnight to her on his way out the door. Nadia was the only one left by ten after, meaning she had the honors of locking the place up. "*I don't live anywhere near downtown.*"

"*I don't care. Where do you live? I'll meet you there. I'll even bring dinner. Chinese?*"

This was only a little unexpected. What should Nadia do? Invite Eva over? Normally she wouldn't have a problem allowing a woman she considered as good as her girlfriend into her home. This, though? Eva came from such a different background. Nadia had seen her apartment and what she considered the bare minimum for hotel standards. There was no way she would be okay with a little house in the suburbs.

"*Okay. I'll send you the address.*"

"*I'm driving my Jaguar today. I'll wait for you.*"

"*How far away are you from my home?*"

"*Two minutes.*"

Nadia sat back from her desk. Whoa, indeed.

***

Eva sat on a swing on a semi-enclosed porch, watching the mid-spring sunlight stream through the foliage lining the street. *I've never been on a porch swing before…* She had seen them before, of course. In movies. In books. Even at friends' houses growing up, not that she stayed friends with those girls for long. Never long enough to take a ride on a porch swing.

Come to think of it, Eva had never really been in a neighborhood like this before.

It looked like small town America. The kind parents like hers lamented, even though they were never a part of it. Was this town really a part of her sprawling metropolis? How had she never seen it before? *Savant's Town* it was called on her map. Upper middleclass all the way. The Warrens considered upper middleclass respectable. Yet Eva had never seen this street or the midrange cars driving up and down it before.

What had Nadia been so shy about showing her? Not even the black Jaguar looked out of place in the driveway. Did Nadia have a roommate? Was it nosy neighbors? Eva canvassed the neighborhood earlier, making sure no paps tailed her to Savant's Town. If Nadia was concerned about her privacy? Then so was Eva.

I don't look too audacious, do I? When she decided to come meet Nadia on her own turf, she decided to keep her outfit casual. If Eva wasn't careful, people would start thinking she always wore jeans and a T-shirt. Her blazer, however, was audaciously designer. *The first one I grabbed out of my apartment closet.* She looked sexy, hm? Would Nadia think she was hot in this getup? It seemed to work on their first real date.

Eva whipped out her phone again. It was almost six. The Chinese food at her feet was going to get cold soon. Where the hell was Nadia?

She got a text. No one could check that text faster than Eva.

"*What are you doing tonight? Girl's night?*" Kathryn's name flashed above the words.

"*Sorry, got plans.*"

"*Oh? With whom? That lucky girl of yours?*"

"*Shut up. You spend most of your time with your boyfriend. You should move in with him. Or him in with you.*"

"*When you move in with your girl, I'll consider it.*"

"*Why, you…*"

An engine rattled enough to make Eva jerk in her seat.

A city bus rumbled down the street, stopping first about a mile away on the long road, and then a few houses down from Nadia's. A beautiful head of red hair descended the back steps and rushed in Eva's direction. She stood up and crossed her fingers that it was Nadia.

Of course it was. Who else would it be?

Eva's girlfriend stopped on the pathway leading up to the porch. What was she gawking at? The fact that Eva was there? Or that she was wearing those clothes? Could Eva really stop Nadia in her tracks this late into their relationship?

"What?" That was the first thing Eva said to her.

Nadia put her hands on her hips. "No overnight bag? I've seriously underestimated you, Ms. Warren."

Damn. Take me to church, why don't you? For the first time in over a day, Eva grinned. "It's in the car. I always keep an overnight bag in the car."

Nadia ascended the front steps. Her flowery perfume had Eva shining a bigger grin on her face. "In case one of your girlfriends asks you to stay the night, of course."

Eva grabbed her by the arm. Softly, of course, but it was enough to make Nadia drop her keys and gape at Eva. "You're the only woman I'm staying any nights with."

The key was off the wood beneath their feet and in the rusty keyhole. "For now, anyway."

Why did she talk that way? Nadia always made it sound like Eva was going to dump her for a newer model at any moment. *Is that what she thinks of me?*

Eva didn't know what she was expecting from Nadia's abode. When she found out her girlfriend had a house, she immediately imagined the type of house she was accustomed to. Sleek. Modern. A veritable mansion, even if it only had a few bedrooms. Of course, Eva knew that most houses in the world were small. This one didn't look huge from the outside, anyway. Chipped navy blue paint with faded white trim. Gutters stuffed with flower blossoms that had whipped around in the spring wind. A yard that needed some weeding and trimming. Eva didn't care about that. She saw those types of places from the outside all the time. Theoretically.

Inside? Inside was a completely new world.

The place was so dim. And musty! Hadn't a window been opened in the past few years? Oh, it was clean, Eva supposed. But that was carpet all over the floor. Not good carpet, either. The kind of carpet that desperately needed to be pulled up and thrown into a dumpster. The furniture didn't match. Were the pieces from separate sets? Leather and cloth together? So many types of woods thrown together in some foresty hodgepodge? Good God. Nadia had maple furniture crammed with oak in the corner. Didn't she know that like hues should go together? Was that china in the glass case? Was it even real?

She wouldn't touch on the hideous lampshade. Or the other one. Or the *other* one.

"Sorry it's not the Hilton," Nadia said dryly. "I don't have control over most of the stuff in here. I'm renting it all." She gave Eva a wry look as she locked the door behind them. "Even I can admit that the old woman has some questionable taste."

"It's fine." Eva didn't want to look at any of that stuff anyway. She wanted to look at Nadia, her gorgeous, sweet girlfriend who knew how to make Eva's body tingle in ways it often didn't get to experience.

She really needed those tingles right now. God, did she need them!

"Come here." Instead of making Nadia come to her, however, Eva went to her, slamming her against the door and ravaging her lips with tumultuous kisses.

It had only been two days since they last saw each other, but damn if Eva's need wasn't overflowing like a broken dam right now!

Nadia never said no. Nor did she push Eva away. If anything, her readiness to kiss Eva back was greatly welcomed. Chinese? What Chinese? How could they think about dinner when they needed each other *right now?*

Nadia really had no idea. How could she? Eva hadn't shared what had happened since returning. All Nadia could have known was that Eva was so horny she couldn't wait for bedtime to get beneath someone's skirt.

"Holy fucking moly," Nadia gasped, her dress doing unnatural things as it slowly came off her body. "I've never fucked in the living room before."

"You ready to try it?" Eva was ready to try some things. Like smacking that curvy ass spilling from Nadia's flirtatious *thong.* A thong! *Come on!*

Nadia grasped her girlfriend's face and brought her in for another kiss. "You're going to make me become addicted to you."

"Is that a bad thing? I want you in my life every single day. Every time I see you? I feel so much better." That wasn't a lie. Nadia was the best medicine to ever walk into Eva's life. *If I thought she was hot before we started going out… God, am I a fool or what?*

Nadia has no protests to give when someone's mouth lowered to her exposed nipple. "You're going to kill me at this rate."

"With orgasms. I'm going to kill you with orgasms."

"If you insist, Ms. Warren."

Eva turned her around, Nadia's yelp of surprise slicing through the air with the weapon of femininity. "Call me that again. If you dare."

The switch was flipped now. The reason Eva needed to see Nadia so badly? She had lost control. Monday night was such a shitfest of her mother's machinations that Eva needed to find someone to take out her frustrations on. Before Nadia? She would have either gone to the club (the one that Damon Monroe owned, no less) or flipped through her shortlist of submissive women she knew were down to beg. When Eva Warren lost control? Someone had to pay.

Why not Nadia?

Nadia shot her a penetrating glare. "Ms. Warren, do your worst."

Right now, Eva's worst was lifting that skirt and smacking that ass as hard as she could. *Even my hand stings.* The snap of flesh on flesh dominated the dimly lit living room. Nadia's cry of erotic pain was delayed. She was probably in shock that something like that felt so good.

"That's what you wanted, right?" Eva sucked on the earlobe taunting her lips. Heat hit her hand the moment she grazed Nadia's spreading thighs. It didn't take long for wetness to join it. "You wanted me to spank your ass."

"Y… yes."

"Yes, what?"

"Yes, Ms. Warren."

That got her other cheek a smack to match the first. The woman's whole body quivered beneath Eva's touch. "You're so hot. You know that, Ms. Gaines? You drive me crazy with how irresistible you are." It was true. Every curve, every inch of skin, every lock of gorgeous red hair was an aphrodisiac to Eva Warren. What could be more satisfying than taking out her control issues on this woman? Especially if she was game to take it?

Nadia's eyes glazed over. "You're not so bad yourself, Ms. Warren."

That was it. No turning back now.

"Your room or on the couch? Pick now."

Nadia craned her head back. "The bedroom's upstairs. You wanna wait that long?"

No. No, Eva did not want to wait that long.

While it was not their first time making love on a couch, it was their first time doing it on Nadia's couch – and throwing in a helping of kink. Eva only held back what she ultimately wanted to unleash because her girlfriend was still too fresh to the scene. Even in her quest to regain control in her life, she was still able to consider that. *The one thing that would make me want to get an experienced sub looking for punishment.* Eva didn't care what the punishment was for. She just wanted to administer it.

As soon as Nadia's ass was as red as her hair and she moaned in an unexpected orgasm, Eva knew her job was done. She didn't need to be touched in turn. Not yet. They could make slow love later that night. This served a different purpose, and they both got a lot out of it.

***

"Are you staying the night?" Nadia asked, finger tracing the outline of Eva's lips. They lay beneath Nadia's thick comforter, enjoying one another's naked bodies after that slow and sweet love Eva eschewed earlier. *I don't need the control anymore.* God knew she hadn't claimed it when they finally made it to bed after Chinese food and some television. By the time they actually had sex, Eva had calmed down enough to enjoy it for what it was. *Sensual.* They had made love side-by-side, their limbs entwined while Eva took her time bringing herself to orgasm on Nadia's body. It had been worth it, too.

Now she took in that lovely glow emanating from her girlfriend. The one that said she had been thoroughly loved on by Eva. "Do you want me to stay the night?"

"You did pack an overnight bag."

"Doesn't mean I have to stay."

"Why wouldn't I want you to stay? You brought me Chinese. And many orgasms."

"I did, didn't I?" Eva ran her fingers through tufts of wavy red hair. *Her hair is so unreal.* The color, the texture, the sheer volume. Did Nadia know and appreciate how hot she was? Maybe to an extent. Like most women, however, Nadia had bouts of self-doubt. Even Eva had those, and she had the money and genetics to have whatever kind of body she wanted. *Even a man's body, if I so desired.* There were times during her adolescence when she considered it.

Nadia rolled against her girlfriend, smothering her own face in Eva's breasts. "You should stay the night if you want. Only thing is that I have to get up at six for work."

"I'll drive you to work. No need to take the bus." Eva snorted. "Why do you take the bus, anyway? Don't have your license?"

"I have my license, but I can't afford a car."

"Really?"

That was definitely an eye roll if Eva ever saw one. "Not all of us can keep a Jaguar and a Lambo on hand, Ms. Warren. Some of us can barely afford the roofs over our heads."

Eva propped herself up on her elbow. "You have trouble paying rent?" This place? All the way out here in the city boonies? Sure, Nadia rented a whole house… but she was the receptionist to one of the richest men around. Surely, she was paid well!

"I wouldn't say trouble… but I do have to watch my spending. Taking public transit is the easiest way to do that. It's inconvenient, but not terrible. I have one of the nicer bus lines. And it's some of the only time I get to read any books. Once I come home, I want to vegetate and eat. Maybe shower and…"

"And?"

Nadia giggled. *I love this giggle.* So feminine and sweet. "Have some fun with myself."

"Thatta girl." Eva was big on women touching themselves all they could. Every day. "But yeah, I'll drive you to work tomorrow. Might as well if you're letting me stay the night in your comfy bed." It wasn't a Waldorf-Astoria bed, but it was well broken-in and comfy. Eva could get used to this quiet house and the pretty girlfriend helping her keep this bed warm.

"You brought me free Chinese food. That counts for something."

Eva kissed her. "When do we get to tell the world that you're my girlfriend?"

"Maybe soon. If we get more serious."

"How much more serious can we get aside from getting engaged? Besides, don't people like Jasmine Bliss know by now? Come on."

"Uh… no, she doesn't. She has an idea, but I may or may not have told her someone is absconding with me to San Diego… and Hong Kong?"

"Hong Kong! What the hell?" Eva was pretty sure they didn't actually go to Hong Kong. It had been a good two years since Eva was last in Hong Kong. Nadia wasn't even on her radar back then.

"I've noticed I say some shit when put on the spot by Jasmine."

"Apparently!"

Nadia was already getting sleepy. Her eyes fluttered, and when they were open, her look was so glazed over that Eva wondered why Nadia didn't put her head down and sleep. Not like it was too early to go to bed if she was getting up at six in the morning. After the fun they had all evening? It was a wonder Eva wasn't crashing too.

She probably wasn't crashing because she smelled. Like sex, of course, but also that wonderful body odor that haunted a woman after a long day.

"Mind if I take a shower?" Eva was already kicking back the covers. "Together?"

"Mmm." Nadia curled around Eva's pillow. "You go ahead. I'll take one in the morning."

Eva located the upstairs bathroom with little issue. *Not like there are many rooms to get lost in around here.* The small house only had two bedrooms. All Eva risked barging in on were dust mites copulating or old linens falling out of a closet. The bathroom? She knew which one it was right away due to a cute – if not old-fashioned – wooden sign on the door that could be flipped to say *Available* or *Occupied.* Eva was of the opinion that Nadia's bathroom was always available for anyone to enter at any time.

Ain't this quaint? Eva put her hands on her hips after turning on the light. An exposed lightbulb flickered above her head. The bathroom was so drafty that Eva couldn't wait to turn on the hot water and start steaming things up. Unlike any of her bathrooms, however, she didn't have to pass into another room to find the shower. Or the tub. Because in these types of dwellings, they were one in the same, and often the focal point of the room.

A shower in the tub. That was something, all right. *I have to hand it to people. It sure is a good use of space.* Eva already missed sliding glass doors, exquisite tiles, and benches to laze about on as hot water poured from powerful jets. The acrylic tub did not foster any confidence for Eva to step into. Nor did that bath mat look like it came from this year. Or the year before. Was that mold? Oh, fuck, was that *rust* all over the fixtures? Rust? Was that healthy? Eva Warren had never seen rust in a bathroom before!

These conditions are deplorable. Should she say something? Should she call someone to come clean this shit up on Nadia's behalf? Wait. She rented. Should Eva call the owner? Who was the owner making Eva's girlfriend live like this?

She whipped out her cell phone and took some pictures. She sent them to the first person she could think of who would know what to do in this situation: the woman who spent half her time fighting for the rights of the poor and oppressed.

"*Why the fuck are you sending me pics of a crusty bathroom?*" Kathryn texted back not a minute later. Eva leaned against the counter. Dubiously. She didn't know what was living beneath the trim. "*Is there a dead body I should be seeing? Where the hell are you?*"

"*I'm at my girlfriend's. Should I be concerned that this is how she lives?*"

"*Oh for fuck's sake.*"

"*What?*"

"*You dumbass, that's what NORMAL bathrooms look like. That place looks pretty damn clean for a really old house. There might be some structural issues but… I know a lot of people who would kill to have a place like that.*"

"*Really???*"

"*You're unbelievable. I hope you didn't embarrass the poor girl.*"

"*I haven't said anything.*"

"*You better not, then.*"

Eva put her phone back in her pocket and crossed her arms. She could forego taking a shower and deal with the BO for now, but she wouldn't want to leave the house smelling like this. On one hand she was grateful that she didn't drag Nadia into the bathroom to inadvertently embarrass her. On the other? Would've been great to watch how she interacted with her own bathroom!

Sure, Eva knew that was being ridiculous. She got that. Was even embarrassed by the fact that her privilege wasn't only showing, it was broadcasting throughout the neighborhood.

Didn't mean she was comfortable!

It's just a shower. I will be clean and smell better afterward. Eva undressed and stood naked in the middle of the bathroom.

Now, how did one work the damn shower? The plastic handle didn't want to budge one way or the other. Why wasn't there water coming out of it? Shit! This was what those jokes about using other people's showers were about, weren't they? Eva started jiggling things around until water finally spurt from the showerhead – it was frigid. Absolutely frigid.

Her poor billionaire heiress heart couldn't handle this!

Once Eva finally got the water temperature under control, she got in and waited to feel clean. Didn't help that she had forgotten her overnight materials and now stared down what her girlfriend used in the shower.

Eva rarely had troubles with using her friends' or girlfriends' products. How many times had she stolen a shower in Kathryn's apartment and happily bathed herself in elegant body washes and marveled over certain razors enough to go out and ask for a recommendation? Not that Eva shaved that much. She preferred a little fuzz in certain areas, and everything else could be professionally waxed or electrocuted out of her body…

What the hell was this stuff that Nadia owned? Nadia always had the smoothest skin and smelled like the millions of dollars in Eva's personal bank account. Was she really using this stuff? It didn't look safe. What the hell were these ingredients? Was this company the kind that tested on animals? Oh, hell no. Eva was oblivious to some issues in the world, but animal testing was a no-go in her life.

Also, those were totally disposable razors. Disposable. Razors.

She cut the shower short as much as she could while still retaining some semblance of propriety. Life was much better cuddling up next to Nadia in bed, anyway. Eva was quickly becoming addicted to the way Nadia sweetly breathed whenever she dozed. It was the kind of addiction that both terrified and thrilled her.

First this house she should have known how to navigate but was as foreign to her as Greek. Now she was harboring the kinds of feelings that made her want to curl up in a ball and search for that control slipping from her fingers.

"Hey," Eva said, nudging Nadia awake. "You wanna go to Hong Kong? I can make an honest woman out of you."

Chapter 23

Nadia had to hand it to Hong Kong. It probably had the most gorgeous nighttime skyline.

"Isn't it beautiful?" she asked, peering at the harbor through large hotel windows. "I feel like I could stay here forever."

It wasn't just the colorful lights illuminating the skyline that made her want to stay in Hong Kong for more than the one night she could afford. *Last weekend, San Diego. This weekend? Hong Kong!* It was also the frisky woman covering her bare back in kisses.

They had already made extensive love that night, but a second round readied to mount in Nadia's loins. Eva would have to wait, however. Right now Nadia wanted to lie on her stomach, arms folded beneath her head as she gazed out the window.

"You're beautiful," Eva muttered into the curve of her lover's spine. "Seriously. How have I gotten so lucky?"

"You can't take me all around the world every weekend," Nadia admonished her. "At some point we're going to have to stay in for one weekend."

"Nonsense. I'll take you wherever I want." Eva encouraged Nadia to roll over onto her back with a strong, commanding hand. *Oh, my. This again?* Somebody stop the tingles! "I'll also do whatever I want to you."

When she had that look in her eye, Nadia knew to go along with it. *I know my limits.* Eva hadn't done much to push them, so what was there to worry about? The fact Nadia was so comfortable with her now made this almost feel like fate. *Beautiful, rich girlfriend who is a total tiger in the sack? What god did I please to make this happen?* Nadia would have to make sure to keep praising that deity.

"You're right. You do get to do whatever you want to me. Particularly if it's hot."

"How's three fingers sound?"

"*Three?* What, you think I've got the Grand Canyon carved out in there?"

"Only if the Grand Canyon can constrict me like a damn python."

"That's your favorite part, isn't it?"

"Gee, I wonder." Eva thrust her hips against Nadia's opened thighs, the impact making them both smile. "Some hot woman's pussy snapping off my fingers because it's having an orgasm that good. Pft. Is it my favorite part…"

Eva looped her arms around her lover's neck. "Come down here and fuck me."

"Thought you'd never ask, darling."

Sort of a shame, really. Her first and only night in Hong Kong, and Nadia never left the hotel room. It was almost like she assumed there would be more trips in the future.

***

"Know how you always give me crap about my boyfriend?" Kathryn asked, stretching her arms above her head. "Now I get to give you crap about your girlfriend. Because she's turned you into a total nut."

The lovely June weather found them having a late lunch at one of the only outdoor eateries downtown they could make an appearance at. While ass-sniffing paps could be hiding anywhere among the other diners, women of their standing made a point of sitting in the back or against the building wall, sunglasses down and hats pulled against their scalps. Kathryn and Eva both sported matching Prada sunglasses, although they forewent the hats. Their delicate pale skin would have to deal with sunlight. *Besides, when you're as tall and blond as we are, we're going to turn heads anyway.* Might as well show theirs off.

"I don't know what you're talking about." Eva yawned into her orange juice. "I'm the same as always. And I'm always ready to take you to task over that boyfriend of yours."

"Be that as it may, there's something different about you. This girl is making you less cynical." Kathryn forced a frown. "Darn. Who am I going to be cynical with if you're turning into Ever-After Eva?"

"It's not like that. We're dating right now."

"Please. You don't get this giddy over any other girl."

"Who says I'm giddy?"

Kathryn glanced at the foot constantly bobbing beneath the table. "Uh huh."

"I'm caffeinated! Besides," Eva stuffed her feet behind the legs of her chair to keep them still. "after the Monday night I had last week, I needed to get out of the country with someone I wanted to be with. You heard what happened." Only took multiple voicemails for Kathryn to finally get clued in on what Isabella Warren was up to.

"Half the world would have heard if those voicemails were hacked." Kathryn shuddered. "Imagining you and Damon Monroe… vomit."

"How do you think I feel? And like you're one to talk. He wasn't shy about insinuating something between you and him."

A shrug. "That was a long time ago. A one-night stand. Who cares?"

"Hope it was worth it."

Kathryn distracted herself with her phone while Eva turned her body toward the street. "Never said it wasn't."

"Bet your boyfriend loves that."

"He doesn't know." Kathryn peered over her phone. "Not going to."

"How juicy."

"I hear that's not the only juicy thing going on."

"Ohoho." Eva slammed her now empty glass back down onto the bistro table. "Did you just make a lesbian sex joke?"

"As if that's out of character for me?"

Eva leaned back in her chair. The tables at this place were so crammed together that she struggled to not smack the person behind her in the head. "All right. You caught me. Things are going well with my object of affection. About time, too. She gave me the run-around for months."

"Good. Was starting to wonder if I would have to stage an intervention." Kathryn knew plenty enough about Eva and Nadia making sweet love whenever they could now. *What? Nadia may not want to kiss and tell, but I have to tell somebody!* Eva couldn't hold all the details in anymore. Besides, what was the point of having a best friend if she couldn't gab about love and sex with her? Eva was one of the first to find out about Kathryn going out with a playboy like Ian Mathers. Seemed only fair.

"She wants to take it slow, though." Eva's phone buzzed in her jacket pocket. She ignored it. "Hasn't even told Jasmine Bliss about it yet. You know those two are BFFs."

"Like a regular ol' Kathryn and Eva."

"What are you trying to say?"

"Absolutely nothing." Whatever Kathryn was doing on her phone better be important. "But if she doesn't want to fuck around with you out in the open, you better respect that."

"Why wouldn't I respect it?"

Kathryn glanced up at her. "I know how you can get. Once you've got a girlfriend, you want to spoil her until she either starts taking advantage of you or suffocates."

"Hey…" Eva's phone buzzed again. She was still ignoring it. "That's not true. Is it?"

"Really? You need to ask? What happened with the last few girlfriends?"

"I never really had any like this."

"Even so?"

Eva had to think about that. What *had* happened in those relationship? Besides frivolous dating and sex around the wor… oh.

"It's not only my smothering that gets to them," Eva admitted. "Some managed to not get turned off by that *or* take advantage of me. But they broke it off because of the BDSM thing."

"And this girl?"

"So far she kinda likes it."

"God, she has to, working for Ethan Cole and being friends with his sub."

The phone buzzed yet again. "Fuck." Eva pulled it out of her pocket. "Guess I should check this. Sorry."

She didn't instantly recognize the number. She did, however, recognize the business name accompanying it. *My PR adviser?*

"Ms. Warren, please contact us at your convenience. Sooner rather than later."

Eva sighed, throwing a few dollars down on the table, "I'll either be right back or abandoning you depending on how this phone call goes."

It did not go well.

***

"Are you fucking *kidding* me?" Eva paced in front of her PR adviser's desk, so deep in disbelief that she refused to acknowledge the pictures in front of her. "Hong Kong?"

"Ms. Warren," said the female adviser, her stuffy black-rimmed glasses glaring in Eva's direction, "this is serious. The publication has threatened that if you don't pay up, they will post these pictures uncensored to the internet."

"They can't do that!"

"Unfortunately, they can."

Eva didn't want to look at them anymore. *That was supposed to be personal… how dare they… how dare they steal something so fucking intimate!* The worst part was that she didn't feel ill seeing her own orgasmic face. She felt ill seeing Nadia's.

God, this was a disaster.

"How much are they asking for?"

The woman clasped her hands on top of the desk. "Two million."

"Two… two million? What? Pesos?"

"Dollars."

"Of course it's in fucking dollars! You think I'm funny? The fuck!" Eva really wanted to kick a chair over. She didn't, but she *really* wanted to. "What makes them think they can ask for two million of my own dollars for something like this? They're the ones being perverts!"

"Unfortunately," Eva really hated that word, "the Chinese media would love to spin it as *you* being the pervert. As well as this young lady you are with in these pictures."

Because of course this woman had seen the pics! They were right there, weren't they? "Who else has seen these?"

"So far, only myself, the photographer, and the editor."

"Both men, I'm sure."

"To be sure."

"God! Of course I'll pay. I *can't* have these pictures out there! Not only is it mortifying for my family… after last time something like this happened… shit. It would totally destroy her." Eva gestured to Nadia's bold and red hair in the pictures. Anyone who had ever seen her before would instantly know that it was Nadia Gaines beneath Eva Warren's eager body. People would have a field day. People who hated Eva would continue to get their kicks, and Nadia? She would never be able to show her face at Thomas-Cole again. Not at the receptionist's desk, anyway.

The PR adviser wrote something down. "I'll call them back and inform them that you are willing to pay to have these photos destroyed. They're going to call *me* back and say they want another million to ensure that. So, expect a bill of three million."

"Fuck you."

"Take it out on me all you want." The adviser's expression never changed. "But let me give you some free advice, Ms. Warren. If this girlfriend of yours is really serious about her privacy for whatever reason, you need to use some more discretion. Having sex in front of windows like that is not going to end well for either of you. I'm sorry, but you are a media target due to your… preferences."

"Did I say fuck you? I meant fuck you with a rusty screwdriver."

"I suggest you two lay low for a while. Maybe take a break. Right now this publisher and any of its affiliates are going to be watching you. We're only paying to have these photos taken care of. Don't give them more."

Eva didn't want to hear it. She picked up one of the pictures and tore it in half.

Chapter 24

Nadia was tired of looking at her phone.

It did not help that her phone held none of the answers she was searching for. No matter how many buttons she pressed, texts she sent, or emails she opened, Nadia was still as lost as she had been when she vacated her shower and curled up in bed.

Where the fuck is this party happening? Nadia had not been selected as Jasmine's maid of honor at her wedding – which was later that month, Christ – and thus had nothing to do with the bachelorette party going on that weekend. That was left to some other woman Nadia barely knew. Apparently this woman didn't know much about communication. Because the directions she sent about where to meet for Jasmine's bachelorette party? Made. No. Sense.

"It's a literal parking lot!" Nadia shouted at her phone. "We're partying in a parking lot?" The press would love to get shots of a billionaire's fiancée getting drunk and dirty in some undisclosed parking lot. Not that Nadia was raring to go there either.

The other source of Nadia's ire was the fact that Eva hadn't talked to her in days.

Days!

The last text Nadia received from her girlfriend was a short and clippy, "*Something's come up and we need to lay low for a while. I'll call you when I get a chance.*" It had been a while, not that Nadia had any idea what they were laying low for. The least Eva could do was acknowledge somebody's texts asking if she was okay.

Not that Eva had been completely silent in other ways. Two days ago Nadia received a bouquet of red roses at the office. Unmarked, of course, but everyone had their ideas about who had sent them. To her chagrin, the person in the lead was none other than Eva. The sad part? The only one who was serious was Amber.

When Nadia got home, however, she had another gift waiting for her. A shipping company had left a package full of expensive, lush beauty products made by companies even Nadia had never heard of.

This basket had come with a note, at least. "*My girlfriend deserves to be pampered in ways she doesn't yet know.*" This included notices that some spa days had been paid for ahead of time. Solo spa days.

Nadia thought it terribly romantic until she started going through the basket and found ridiculously fancy razors and… waxing… products…

It wasn't that Nadia took this to mean she had too much body hair. Even if that's what Eva meant, it was stupid. The only hair on Nadia's body was on her head, arms, and the carpet-matching drapes she let cover her mound. Everything else was shaved once or twice a week, *especially* on days she knew she was meeting someone. No, what made Nadia sigh and roll her eyes was realizing that this basket came to her after Eva had been in her girlfriend's shower and scoped things out.

Nadia hated her cheap razors, but they were what she could get. How was it Eva's place to decide to upgrade them all without consultation?

Although Nadia was over that annoyance, she wasn't over the fact that Eva was ignoring her calls and texts. What a turn of events. From being pursued to being the pursuer.

Finally, Nadia received a text… from Amber.

"*You see this mess of directions?*" She must have been referring to the bachelorette party. "*You got any idea what they mean? I'm afraid I'll end up down at the wharf, crashing some gang's card game! That's not how I want to go down, Nadia. Help a girl out?*"

Nadia told her that it was all a mess on that end too. "*Wanna go together?*"

"*Sure. Thought you would be going with your girlfriend, though. Isn't she invited?*"

"*Probably. Dunno. She's not talking to me right now.*"

"*Whaaat? Something happen?*"

"*I have no idea. Things were going good, then she stops communicating.*"

"*She break up with you???*"

"*I don't think so…*" Nadia so did not want to consider that. Just when she was getting comfortable with having Eva as her girlfriend, too. Did she have a commitment problem? She seemed so gung-ho about them being together and had made such a big deal about them hanging out and going on dates through the summer break. "*But she won't answer my questions, so I guess I'm not sure.*"

Amber suggested they meet up for Jasmine's bachelorette party and go together. Nadia tentatively agreed, but didn't say she would cancel if Eva decided to go too. In a way, Nadia saw it as a good opportunity to make their relationship public. With all the focus on Jasmine, nobody would give a shit about the two lesbians cuddling in the corner and sharing drinks. Er, assuming that would even be a thing at this party… Nadia couldn't even tell where the hell it would be.

***

"Wow," both Nadia and Amber said in unison, as a guy with a huge erection walked by carrying a tray of cocktails. "Either we're at the wrong party, or the right one," Nadia finished.

"I'll take one of those," Amber said. She gestured rudely to the Speedo-clad server who winked at them. "And that one." What, there was another one? "Oh, somebody triple team me in the corner…"

Nadia coughed, and not because her "date" for the night was being silly. After being lost for fifteen minutes, the pair finally found the location of Jasmine's bachelorette party. As it turned out, it was in the middle of a huge parking lot – but sometime in the past two days, a giant party pod had been constructed, and inside? The boldest display of a heterosexual woman's wet dream. Or half of a bisexual woman's one, if Amber was anything to go by.

"There certainly are a lot of nice looking men here, I'll give it that." Nadia wasn't *interested,* but she was definitely staring at another crazy boner ambling by. Did these guys fluff themselves up in the bathroom before making their alcoholic rounds? Or were they naturally hard 24/7? Okay, so Nadia didn't actually want to know.

They located Jasmine, already tipsy on some drinks and more than generous with the hugs. She expressed surprise that the pair came together. Had she forgotten that they worked in the same office? *She should try stopping by more often.* Jasmine was so far up her own ass with wedding planning and dealing with other personal matters that she never had time to come by the office… for anything but shoving wedding things into Mr. Cole's face. More and more, Amber was becoming Nadia's closest friend. And apparently Nadia was Amber's, because she made no secret that there was still a ton of drama between her and Adrienne Thomas. *Sex, alcohol, and more sex.* Amber openly admitted that she was being used to sate Adrienne's bisexual philandering like some terrible stereotype everyone wanted to let die. But on the other, Amber admitted she really, really loved the money thrown at her. "Makes it worth it," Amber had said more than once. "I don't let my emotions, um, happen." Sounded oh so healthy to Nadia.

The bachelorette party was already in full swing by the time the pair got their bearings. Perhaps Amber had her bearings first. She was slapping her hand on the nearest bar and getting loaded on alcohol so she could enjoy the view wherever she turned. Men in Speedos. Men in open suits. Men with body hair and men as slick as the few days after they were born. Maybe slicker! Nadia was mildly amused, since she certainly had an appreciation for good looking men, but she would be the first to admit that they didn't do anything for her anymore. All she could really do was laugh when some young twenty-something guy slathered in baby oil came up to her with the drink she ordered.

"You! I'm dancing with you, sexy!" Amber dragged one particular stud off to the cordoned off dance area and instantly started grinding against him. Good for her. If Nadia were dating Adrienne Thomas, she would probably need a polar opposite palate cleanser too.

Nadia was content to settle down with a drink and watch the shenanigans going on. Maybe she would catch a show in the VIP room or find someone of a like mind to talk to – Jasmine was probably out of it for the night. Didn't matter. Nadia needed some relaxation after her work week.

That was a great plan that could have come into fruition if it weren't for the parade of high-society princesses sashaying into the party, a fashionable half hour late – Eva leading the way.

***

"Holy fucking balls, this is a lot of cock!"

Eva knew this was a bachelorette party she was storming in on, but, like… *damn!* Who invited the Thunder From Down Under? The in real life *Magic Mike* team? Chippendale's? Had every male stripper or escort been bought up for Jasmine Bliss's bachelorette party? *I have to hand it to her… she's ejecting herself from the single life with absolute style.* Not that Eva was prepared for the amount of stiff masts pointing their way through the crowds of partying, drunk as hell women who were all falling over themselves every time some hottie walked by them. *If I ever have a bachelorette party, it better be like this, but with tits.*

"She wasn't kidding," Kathryn mumbled, already shoved against the wall by a gyrating guy whose tan may or may *not* have been real. "I'm kinda scared, though." She looked to Eva for help. What? Like Eva was going to slam herself into some fake-tan douche and declare Kathryn her girlfriend for the night? *If I ain't careful, this will be Miami all over again.* What happened the last time they were in Miami together? Kathryn may or may not have drunkenly called Eva her wife to scare off some douchebags.

Whatever. Kathryn was fine. She was already flinging her arms around that guy's shoulders.

"Sorry we're late." Eva said to Jasmine as she grabbed a complimentary martini off a passing tray. "When we saw 'that one plaza downtown' on our notes, it took some trial and error to figure out… there are like… five plazas around your boyfriend's office alone." Seriously, who had written those directions?

Eva not so covertly looked around the room in search of a special someone. Nadia would be there, right? Eva was the first to admit that she had been a jackass that past week. She didn't think twice about RSVPing to the party invite, but then she remembered that a certain someone was Jasmine's best friend. Oops. *Good job, Eva.* If she did see Nadia, however, she was going to start explaining herself. Like why she hadn't been responding to those calls and texts. As much as Eva appreciated her girlfriend's concern, there was never a good time to fully explain keeping the paps off their asses. Kinda literally, too.

"Thanks for coming," Jasmine said from her seat. "As you can see, it's a giant dick orgy with lots of booze."

"Hot. Wait, do you mean the orgy is huge, or the dicks?"

"Both!" Someone squealed.

Jasmine glanced at Eva and then toward an open door. "She's in the other room. I'm assuming you're looking for someone."

"Oh, who?" Eva asked sweetly. "I have no idea who you're talking about."

Mumbling, Jasmine slipped from her seat, told her new guests to have all the fun they wanted, and went into another room. Eva turned to find her own best friend flirting with yet another guy with an erection the size of his head.

"Hey!" Eva was going to have to be a babysitter tonight, wasn't she? "She's got a boyfriend. Captain of the ol' soccer team, if you catch my drift." She stared right at his bulge. "He kicks good, is what I'm trying to say."

"That's it." Kathryn grabbed another martini drifting by. "I've got a mission tonight. Bag me some dicks."

"And they say we gays are the promiscuous cheaters."

"I ain't cheating if I don't actually do anything!"

Eva knew her friend could get like this when she was intoxicated, but she did not expect to be Team Ian that night. Every five minutes Kathryn was giggling around some other man who either had an ass from God or a cock that could *not* be real. It was a good thing that Eva was not disgusted by the male form. If anything, she found them greatly amusing. Cocks, right? What were up – *up* – with those things, anyway? Eva would've been a terrible experimenter. If she ever grew the gumption to lose her gold star status, she would end up embarrassing the guy by laughing at the physics of a penis. One time, when she was as drunk as Kathryn, they talked about what it was like to have sex with their respective preferences. Kathryn was shocked that quivering pussies were an actual thing, and Eva was a mixture of horrified and scandalized that cocks could be used like balloon animals if the guy was relaxed enough.

Didn't mean she wanted to spend a straight woman's bachelorette party running around after drunk Kathryn, though. While Kathryn didn't need *endless* supervision, she got smashed enough on Bacardi that she would've been the easiest pickings in the world for any guy here looking to make some quick cash off a billionaire. Eva couldn't even go to the bathroom without coming back to find Kathryn surrounded by six half-naked men pretending she was the most interesting woman in the world. Oh, and the hottest, of course. Funny thing was that Eva totally guessed that at least half of those men were gayer than gay. Their sheepish grins in her butchy direction sort of sealed that.

"You lost me another one!" Kathryn shouted after Eva broke up that little party with some stiff glares of her own. "I swear to God, Eva!"

"You've got a boyfriend!" How many times did Kathryn need reminding of this? She was always going on about how *bomb* her sex life was with that schmuck.

"I *knooow,* that's why you've gotta take a selfie of me grinding with some dude so we can send it to him!"

"Hon, it ain't a selfie if I'm taking it for you!"

"Hey! Hey you!" Kathryn was stumbling toward the bar again. "Get over here and let me rub up against you! I've got money!" Here they fucking went again.

This bullshit meant Eva had little time to search for Nadia, although she caught the occasional glimpse of her curve-hugging red dress and the more extravagant red of her hair. The one time they made eye contact was so brief that Eva questioned whether it happened or not. She even went so far as to text Nadia and ask to meet her in a quiet corner so they could briefly catch up and plan a more intimate date to really go over things. *I'll have to come clean eventually.* Tonight was not the night, however. Nadia was looking pretty tipsy, too. Poor Eva was designated driver after her minimum drinks.

Which meant she was going to remember a lot of embarrassing things.

There was a sex toy presentation going on in the VIP room. So many women having sloppy, drunken sex with boy-toys who probably didn't even get it in. Women Eva didn't recognize throwing up in the bathrooms. And women she *did* recognize making complete asses out of themselves.

The killer was when Adrienne Thomas showed up at nine-thirty, probably fresh from some business function since she was way overdressed in a body-hugging cocktail dress. That wasn't mentioning how damn out of place she looked surrounded by drunk-as-fuck women and their deflating boyfriends of the evening. By nine-forty-five, the party was on another planet, and both Eva and Adrienne looked like they were ready for it to end, and one of them had just arrived!

"If you like dick," Eva said, leaning against one of many dark walls. "Then you came to the right place." She jerked her thumb toward Kathryn, who was sitting in a chair and getting her tenth lap dance of the night.

"I… see…" Damn, Adrienne Thomas sure did have an awkward smile. *That's right. I hear she's playing for the home team recently.* How interesting. "Looks like a girl could really cause some trouble, huh?"

Eva rolled her eyes toward Kathryn again. "I'll say. Excuse me. Someone is dangerously close to blacking out and cheating on her boyfriend. If I let her, I'll never hear the end of it when she's sober and crying." Eva kicked herself off the wall and batted yet another man away from her friend. She doubted it would be the last one for a while.

***

"Oh my God. Look who's here."

Nadia, who kept close to Amber through the evening, turned her head and saw Adrienne stumbling through the party like a lost lamb in Chanel. "Wow. I knew she was invited, but I thought she would stay away." Jasmine was probably shocked too, although last Nadia saw the bride she was in a drunken stupor in the VIP room. *I've been a good girl. Only a few drinks.* Spaced well enough apart with plenty of water in between. Amber had drunk more, but she also claimed to have a high tolerance. The only other woman there that night who didn't seem too inebriated was Eva.

Sigh. Eva.

Nadia kept her distance. She thought about texting Eva, but 1) she didn't want to seem desperate, and 2) she forgot to charge her phone earlier that day and wanted to make sure it stayed alive long enough to get her home, in case there was an emergency. Should she go right up to Eva and say hello? Or should she wait for her to come over? With Amber around?

So she didn't think about it. She enjoyed the shows and the company she currently had. Oh, and the delicious daiquiris helped too. Amber could have been a better conversationalist, but as soon as Adrienne arrived, things got interesting again.

"You still seeing her?"

Amber shrugged. "Fucked her a couple of days ago. Dunno if that means I'm seeing her, though. We're not a serious couple." Did the alcohol bring out the tension in her voice, or what? That was also a sneer in Adrienne's direction. "You still seeing Eva Warren?"

Nadia needed one last drink for the night. Would a rum and Coke be too much? "I thought we were doing well. We were getting exclusive. Calling each other girlfriends. She took me to San Diego one weekend and Hong Kong the next."

"Wow." Amber finished her current drink. "Adrienne hasn't taken me anywhere. She takes me to her place or a hotel, if we even make it that far. Then she makes me do all the work."

Nadia snorted. "I haven't had to do much work, if you know what I mean."

"God, you've got it good. So what happened?"

"No idea. She said something came up and we had to lay low or some bullshit."

"Oh, no. That's not good."

"It's not?"

The music changed to an annoying remix of a Top 40 hit. Both women grimaced as a shrill voice entered their ears and the beat became so erratic that chairs wobbled. Amber had to lean in closer so Nadia could hear her. "She's weaning you off of her. She might call you for a couple booty encounters of the sexy kind, but she's going to cut you totally off soon. You might end up in her black book for when she's bored and feels a little Irish, but other than that…"

"No way. You're being mean."

"I'm not. Girl, I've been looking for my meal ticket for a while now. You think I wanna be an assistant for the rest of my life? Fuck that. I wanna marry big, and I wanna marry hella rich. Man, woman, I don't care which. Even if we divorce I want to at least be assured that I could live a life of luxury. Or at least until I find my next spouse. God bless the Supreme Court for granting me the right to marry a rich bitch and take her money too."

Nadia didn't know what to say. Disgusting? Harrowing? "You've sure got goals."

"Hey, I'm not above love. If I fall in love, that's cool. But they better be rich. I have expensive tastes."

"So you're basically using your job as a way to fish for a spouse and keeping that slutty omnivore of a bisexual trope alive?"

"We all have our life goals, honey. Besides…" Amber advertised her modest but perky breasts to Adrienne as she slipped by. "What's wrong with being a slutty bisexual? It's the best of both worlds! Both can also fuck like champions. One of these days I'll get that stuck-up executive to slam a strap-on in me." Amber gave Nadia a sly look. "Bet Eva Warren knows how to use one."

Nadia was blushing too hard to comment.

"Ah, jeez. You're making me so jealous over here, Nads." Amber only called her that when she was getting *drunk*. "You've got a hot, rich girlfriend who's confident, knows how to screw, and spoils you super silly? You've got it all."

"Not sure we're really going out right now. Not even sure she's my girlfriend."

Eva briefly crossed their radar, chasing down Kathryn as she drunkenly stumbled toward a group of half-naked men. "Too bad for you then. Go to the bathroom with me? We'll get one more round of drinks on the way back, and then I'm probably calling it a night. I'm not interested in any of the guys here."

"Not rich enough for you?"

"Bingo."

They stood in line for the bathroom for about fifteen minutes, and then had to wait another five while someone cleaned up the most recent vomit mess. *Are we at a bachelorette party or the club?* Nadia seriously thought about going home. Jasmine was out of commission, and Amber was going to go home after another drink, so…

"Shit! Forgot my watch back where we were sitting!" Amber's brief heart attack ended when she jumped out of line. "Keep my place for me, would you? I'll be right back!"

Nadia sighed. What was the difference to her?

***

Kathryn was finally sedated after a huge glass of water. Eva didn't know how the hell that worked, but she got the breather she desperately wanted when her friend started snoring in one of the huge chairs near the VIP area.

"Watch her, huh?" Eva gestured to one of their mutual friends who was sitting down for a rest. "I need a break from playing babysitter."

She was barely halfway across one of the rooms when she bumped into a blond blur.

"Sorry!" Ethan Cole's assistant bowed her head in apology, her eyes focused on a spot beyond Eva… and then on her. "Oh, hi…"

"Hello." *Is she drunk? Can't tell.* Possible that this young lady was good at holding her liquor. Wait. Wasn't this the girl Nadia worked with? Hmm. "You're in a big hurry, huh?"

"I, uh, forgot my watch somewhere. Sort of my favorite piece, you know?"

At least it was a fun mystery to solve. "Where did you leave it?"

Amber wasn't forthcoming with an answer. She was too busy leering at Eva, and Eva knew what a *leer* was. *That's it. Drink in my breasts, my hips. Enjoy my hair and nails while you're at it. Yes, that's an expensive scent you can't afford. No, I won't buy you any tonight.* All Eva really remembered about Amber was that she was receptive to lesbian flirtation. It was fun to flirt with her in front of Nadia… back then. Now? Not so much. Eva had what she wanted.

"I think I left it in the VIP room."

"Need some help looking for it?"

Amber grinned. "Sure. Could always use an extra pair of eyes."

It was definitely more fun to look for a missing watch than to look at more people having sex. Sheesh.

It was also more fun to see women like Jasmine Bliss so inebriated that she was left alone in the VIP room to wallow in her own drunkenness. They found her slumped over in a chair, still visibly breathing, but definitely, *definitely* partied out.

"Aw, someone is passing out." Eva approached her with Amber right behind. "Here I was hoping this place would be empty. Oh well, I'll take you home with me later." She said that with a wink to Amber. She giggled. *I should probably cool it on the flirting, even though it's second nature to me.* Whatever. Not like Jasmine would remember and tell on her.

Eva went to Jasmine's side. "Help me get her up. She needs to get in a cab."

Jasmine was hoisted off the couch, one arm swinging around each woman's shoulders. One was considerably taller than the other and had to bend down to help.

"She's fun," Eva said as Jasmine's weight sagged. "If I ever get married, make sure she's invited. Don't know if I want the gal who put this together throwing my bachelorette party though. Might be *too* wild."

"Especially if it's women instead of men, right?" Amber made sure she had a decent grip on Jasmine before helping her toward the nearest door.

"Oh, yeah, especially then." Eva could imagine it now. What she needed was naked women everywhere at her bachelorette party.

Both she and Amber managed to get drunken Jasmine to the next room. Supposedly, this place should have been empty too. Not so.

"Whoa!"

They came upon a man and a woman going at it in a dark corner, in some poor chair that squeaked every time the woman slammed her hips down into the man's lap. *Would you look at that?* Good thing Eva was used to seeing straight couples mid-coitus. Going to the sex club had that effect on one's life. Even so, even Eva was a little scandalized to see Adrienne Thomas riding some young stud. They both remained oblivious even when three women entered.

"Good… good for her," Jasmine said. "She got a nice ass, huh?"

Amber lost her grip for a moment, her face set in an exceptional grimace. "That is a big one," she muttered. Eva hoped she meant Adrienne's ass, because that dick? Not so big. Or at least Gold Star Eva had seen *way* bigger… and not only at the club, either. This party was a nice example of exquisitely large cock.

So Eva didn't know how else to react, other than to scoff. "This is the most beautiful, pristine display of heterosexual affection I have ever seen." Eva spoke too soon. Adrienne cried out in orgasm, throwing her head back while the stud started making noises too. "Okay, we gotta go. If I see sperm, I dry heave."

Amber was not quick to help. "Only if you promise to do that to me later."

Whoa. Who did she think she was? Eva had no idea what to think.

They dragged Jasmine through the front room, where they collected her mother (of all people) and paid their respects to the hostess. "Do you need help?" Jasmine's maid of honor asked, pulling out a cell phone.

"No, no, we'll get her a cab and then be going ourselves. Thanks for the party."

Meanwhile, Jasmine's mother was sober enough to help her daughter into the back of a cab. "Thank you, girls, for helping us out here," the mother said to Eva, who leaned through the open window. "I can take it from here."

Eva waved before backing away. Jasmine waved back. "Bye, Jasmine!" Amber yelled as the cab began to pull away. "Give Mr. Cole my regards!"

As soon as they were back in the party room, Amber's happy demeanor disappeared and was promptly replaced with disdain. "What a fucking whore," she muttered.

"Uh." What had Eva walked back into? "I know you're not talking about Jasmine Bliss. Unless you have some juicy gossip to share."

Amber huffed. "I don't give a shit about her. You don't know who I'm talking about?" She jerked her head toward the room they dragged Jasmine through. "There's a hint for you."

"I see." Oh, this was good. The young assistant had a problem with Adrienne Thomas getting her dicking on? "So about that juicy gossip…"

"Help me find my watch and buy me a drink and I'll tell you about it."

Eva shrugged. As soon as this was taken care of, she was finding Nadia, but all right.

They found the watch over by the bar anyway. Amber squealed in delight as she slipped it back on her thin wrist. Eva should have known something else was up when the young woman pulled her hair back and stuck her chest out before asking for a gin and tonic. Eva pushed some bills across the bar and asked for a Coke.

"You want some juicy gossip?" Amber asked, hopping onto the stool right beside Eva. "Adrienne Thomas is a slut. There you go."

"That… doesn't tell me anything." It also wasn't any of her business.

"You don't get it. She goes for anyone. Man, woman, she'll bite all of their heads and dicks off."

Oh, so that's what this was about? Eva could sniff out lesbian drama from a mile away, no alcohol required. "Sounds like someone protests too much. How often has she banged you to make you this bitter?"

That got Eva the exact reaction she wanted. Amber almost fell off her stool, trying to regain her composure as she was caught Sapphic-minded.

"I'm not bitter."

"You're so bitter I want to order a black coffee just to put the cream in it myself."

"I'm not bitter!"

"I've had two conversations with you so far in my life, and even I can tell you're bitter."

"All right." Amber quickly grabbed her drink as soon as it was in front of her. "You'd be bitter too if she kept stringing you along…"

Eva sipped her Coke before putting it back down again. "A woman like that is going through a phase. She's fucking anything that moves because she's trying to validate herself. Last I heard, her ex-boyfriend who once proposed to her is getting married to some other brunette." Eva shrugged. "That sucks she's leading you on, though. You should cut her off before she hurts you anymore. That's my advice, anyway."

"Don't recall asking you for it."

"Ouch." Did Amber need more alcohol? *How does Nadia put up with this attitude?* A woman like Amber was so high maintenance that even Eva didn't want to touch her. Good thing they never exchanged numbers. "If you don't want my advice, then stop acting like you want it."

Amber nursed her drink, never once looking up at Eva. When she did put her drink back down, it was with an air of finality that not even Eva could replicate. "Are you and Nadia a thing?"

"Hm? She tell you about that?"

"Yeah, she told me about that."

"We may have a thing."

"How serious is it?"

Aw, how sweet. Nadia's little friend was looking out for her. No doubt Nadia had whined about Eva's lack of communication recently. *Can't blame her for that.* It only reminded Eva that she needed to go find her girlfriend sooner rather than later. "Depends. How serious is she telling you it is?" If Eva had learned one thing so far, it was that she should let Nadia dictate these things to the public. So far, the only people Eva had given more than the bare minimum information to were her brother and best friend. And Kathryn was busy snoring in some corner, waiting to be driven home so she could wake up to the worst hangover in the comfort of her bed.

Amber hopped off her stool and came closer to Eva. She could smell some kind of peppery perfume. Department store, definitely. High-end department store, but department store nonetheless. This was the kind of woman who begged to be spoiled. She wore this perfume knowing that Eva would recognize it for what it was… and offer something better. In exchange for sex, of course. *In another life, this gold digger was an escort.* She had all the markings. Maybe Amber didn't do it as a full time gig, but Eva would hazard a guess that she put in a few months doing the odd gig here and there to make ends meet – and to find Mr. Richly Right.

"Not so serious," Amber purred. *Great. She's flirting with me.* "She made it sound like you two had broken it off."

"Huh?"

A lean hand grazed her leg. "So are you two still going out? Or are you looking for someone new?"

"If you're rebounding from Adrienne like this," Eva growled in warning, "you might regret it." And Eva immediately regretted saying that. Stuff like that would only make Amber more self-righteous. "No good will come from it."

"Oh, come on." The stench of alcohol was strong now. Amber may hold her liquor well, but she had reached the tipping point with that gin and tonic. "I've heard about what you're like. They say you're the biggest playgirl around these parts."

Speaking of parts… Amber was getting dangerously close to certain parts of Eva's. "Whoa." Eva pulled away the hand getting frisky with her groin. "I don't think so."

"Why not!"

"For one? I'm sort of seeing someone. Exclusively." Like Eva would jeopardize that for some drunken sex with someone who was too bitter to function at the moment. Eva Warren was *not* a rebound, even when she was single and looking. "For another? You're obviously drunk now. I ain't into that." *I mean, it's kinda illegal and ethically unsound. Gross.* Eva wasn't drunk enough in turn.

"I'm not drunk." Amber stumbled against the bar. "You… you're scared I'm so good you'll leave that stick in the mud Nadia."

"See? You're drunk. You're talking shit about your friend."

"She's not my friend! You think I'm friends with someone so boring? She doesn't even realize how good she has it with you. I… I would be a much better girlfriend for you. I'd make you feel like the fuckin' queen you are. I'd take such good care of you that…"

Eva raised one unimpressed eyebrow. "That I'd be spurred to throw money and gifts at you? Honey, I know all about your type. Maybe if I wasn't perfectly happy with the woman I've got now. I'd string you along for a weekend or two." Amber smiled to hear that. "Yeah, I'd fuck you. I wouldn't give you any reason to complain, either. You want me to make you think about nothing but how female I am? I could do that. Want me to give you the *boyfriend* experience, strap-on and all? I'm a God damn pro at this point. I'd take you to Rome, Thailand, Mexico… wherever you fancied going and fucking. I'd buy you awesome local food and get you so many souvenirs you wouldn't know where to store them. I'd pay some of your bills and buy you a high-ticket item you've been slobbering over for months. You look like a designer bag kind of girl. Please. I personally know a few. I'd get you shit for *free*."

Amber was going to embarrass herself if she kept grinning like that.

"Then one of two things would happen. Either I dumped you because I grew bored with you already, or you dumped me because you found someone more to your tastes, physically. Woman or man, it really wouldn't matter. You want a rich partner, yeah? I'm filthy stinking rich, and I still have yet to start my career that will make me even more money. But I don't think for two minutes it means you would stay with me. I'm not your type. You think I'm fun for a weekend or a month, but then you pine after a manly man or a woman so soft and feminine that she makes you think of Adrienne Thomas."

There went that smile! About time, too.

"What do you fucking know?" Amber spat. "You know nothing about me and Adrienne."

"Nope. And I don't really want to. One thing's for sure, though. You're coming for me because you see that meal ticket slipping away. You'll even risk your friendship with your own coworker to get me to make you feel better about yourself and to give you the payday you're looking for. Why the hell would I want to deal with that? Even for a night? I'm sure you're nice when you're sober and not hurting. But…"

Ah, shit. Eva should have seen it coming. Amber was either going to smack her…

Or kiss her.

There was nothing sweet or sultry in that kiss that lasted about three seconds, enough time for Eva to realize what was happening and pull away. The only things she felt on Amber's end were anger, betrayal, and such a deep, unnerving sadness that the last thing this girl needed was more alcohol, or even a one night stand.

The last thing Eva needed? Was what happened right after she pulled away from Amber's angry kiss of shame and betrayal.

"What the fuck!" Nadia, as beautiful as she was dangerous with that visage, marched up and practically shoved Amber away from the bar. "The hell do you think you're doing? The fuck is wrong with you!"

Amber didn't fight back. She was a defeated dog, wiping her pink lips with French-tipped nails and glaring at the floor. Amber wasn't even on this planet anymore. She had retreated into some dark corner that was occupied with darker thoughts.

Not that Nadia cared. She knew what she had seen. Amber would take a hard, righteous *smack!* to the cheek and like it.

Yes. Eva really had a knack for the lesbian drama, didn't she?

"Get out of here. Take your own cab home, bitch."

Amber grabbed her handbag and skittered off, her knees making her drunken ass hobble toward the entrance. There were probably tears of embarrassment in her eyes.

"You!"

Eva braced herself. For a smack of her own, anyway.

She didn't get smacked. She got a terrible look that told her she and Nadia were *done.* Or at least that's what Eva saw before Nadia also ran off.

"Hey," Eva languidly said to the bartender. "You see that shit?"

He was already making her a complimentary cocktail. "I'm so glad I'm not into women," he muttered, sliding the glass across the bar. Eva caught it with a shaky hand.

The only thing missing from this scene was a dazed and sex-drunk Adrienne Thomas, making her grand exit from the other room with her skirt still tucked high and her hair in such disarray that it didn't take a worldly woman to know what she had been up to. However, Eva *was* a pretty worldly woman, even with her level of privilege. She had a server deliver a drink to Adrienne, complete with a note. "*Thanks to you, I lost my girlfriend. Go get yours back, hussy. Sort your shit out while you're at it. EW.*"

Eva then went off to collect Kathryn so they could go home. Eva didn't bother going back to her own apartment. Once Kathryn was snoring in bed, Eva joined her, staring at her friend's ceiling and wondering how the *fuck* she was going to fix this mess.

Chapter 25

I should have known.

Nadia should have known a lot of things. Like how Amber was going to jump on Eva as soon as it was most convenient. Or how Eva was going to dump Nadia as soon as she became bored, like she became bored with so many other women. *I thought we had something, but I should have known.*

The weekend was not kind to Nadia, aside from the fact she had Monday off because the office was being fumigated. That meant she got another day off from Amber. Fucking. Amber. That. Asshole.

Nadia knew they weren't real friends. They almost never hung out, except for in the office and at business functions they were both required to be at. They only went to the bachelorette party together because it was convenient. They weren't... *friends.*

I should have known.

She went straight home and crashed into a stupor before a single tear could be shed. What alcohol she had consumed made sure she didn't feel too much. Thank God for that, too. Nadia was so emotionally vulnerable that she doubted she would stop crying once she started.

So she waited until Sunday to cry.

Didn't help that she had a clear head. A clear enough head that made her replay those seconds over and over. Amber getting cozy with Eva. Eva not bothering to push her away. Amber kissing Eva.

Eva kissing Amber.

She had been totally kissing Amber back. Nadia saw it with her own eyes. Their lips were locked and things looked pretty cozy.

Fuck me to hell and back. They were totally going to hook up. Then what? Eva would nonchalantly call Nadia for a date, as if nothing happened with another woman? How many other women had Eva been with since they started going out? Was that bullshit about them being apart for weeks while Eva finished her semester just that? Bullshit? So she could see other women or at least get them out of the way?

How long would that have continued? Nadia couldn't stand to think about being strung along for the wild ride that was dating a playgirl like Eva Warren. She was young and rich. In the end, she was like all those men Nadia saw coming in and out of the executive office. She should have followed her gut. It hadn't led her astray for so long. Then she stopped listening to it. Why? Because Eva was hot, with charm Nadia couldn't walk away from? *I fell for it. I fell for it like so many women before me.* What bullshit.

Nadia needed someone to talk to. On Monday morning, she woke up, wondering what the fuck to do with her day off. *I wanted to spend it with Eva.* Either on a trip somewhere or at home. She wanted to be all over Eva Warren like she was a second skin.

Because I'm in love with her.

Nadia had been pushing that thought down until dating Eva turned into something more serious. *Then* Nadia could face the L word. When the time was right. When they had been together for a while and knew each other's quirks like they knew their own. When Eva began scuffing her feet and muttering things about how deeply she felt for Nadia. How they never just had sex – they always made love.

Idiot. I'm an idiot. Idiots in love were always the worst idiots. For fuck's sake.

Nadia didn't know where else to go or who else to call. No. She couldn't call someone. This wasn't something to be told over the phone. When she got in the cab summoned to her driveway, she only knew of one place to go – and considering the cost of the cab, she really, really hoped someone would be home.

She also knew that Jasmine had been so tanked at her bachelorette party that it was entirely possible she was indisposed. Too bad. Nadia had been a shoulder to cry on for Jasmine more than once. Time to return the favor.

It was her first time going back to the manor in the Hills since the bridal shower back in February. Now that it was almost summer, the greenery was ripe and the flowers were in full bloom. One thing Nadia could say about her boss was that he had the most exquisite flower garden. Guests always proclaimed it the best, too, and they would know. Nadia had to admit, as the cab rolled down Mr. Cole's driveway, that it was calming to look at. So many colors. So many varieties… everything woven together into distinct patterns that evoked emotions she desperately needed to cling to right now.

Nadia paid the cab driver and walked up the front steps to Mr. Cole's manor. The security guards had all recognized her, but now she had to deal with the maid coming to inspect who had pulled up.

"Hi… is Jasmine home?" Wow. Was this Nadia's first time speaking in two days? Rough. "I understand if she isn't."

"Miss Bliss is home." The maid stood back and glanced at the grand staircase. "I don't know if she's available, though. I can go check for you. Wait here."

Nadia slumped down onto a chaise lounge lining the front hall. It wasn't long before Jasmine descended the front staircase, wearing a springtime pink shift hanging loosely on her figure. Was she glowing? Wow. For someone who was so trashed two nights ago, Jasmine wasn't doing too bad. Must have been that bridal glow before her wedding. *Don't remind me.* Nadia's bridesmaid's dress was currently wrapped up in her bedroom closet.

Jasmine took one look at her friend's face and suggested they go for a walk in the gardens. If the front foliage was gorgeous, then the gardens were so otherworldly that Nadia felt like she was strolling through a slice of paradise. Too bad she was too down on herself to fully appreciate it.

"Spill," Jasmine said, the moment they sat on a bench overlooking a prism of orchids.

Nadia asked if she could pluck a tulip from the garden. Jasmine opened her arms wide, telling her friend that she was more than welcome to pluck every bulb from the garden behind them. She returned with a single red tulip, sniffing it… and plucking one of the petals.

"I hate Amber." God, it felt good to say that.

"Uh huh."

Nadia tossed the petal onto the ground. "I'm serious. She wants to make my life hard." That was an understatement. *More like ruin my damn life.*

"You gonna expand on that?"

"Nope."

Another petal hit the ground. Jasmine crossed her legs. "So whatever happened between you and…"

"Don't know what you're talking about."

"I haven't even finished."

"I know who you mean."

"You said that you didn't know what I was talking about."

Caught, Nadia crumpled a third petal in her hand. "Whatever. That's behind me now." It had to be. Eva had fucked up. Would she admit she had fucked up? Nadia certainly wasn't going to keep dating a philanderer of that caliber. Even a smaller caliber. Fuck that.

"You can't leave it at that," Jasmine continued. "Last I heard you and her were tearing it up in San Diego. And Hong Kong. *Hong Kong.*"

Nadia scoffed. *Says the woman who travels the world like it's nothing now.* "You've been all over the world. Hong Kong isn't that special." Oh, it had been absolutely magical. What little she saw of it, anyway.

"Would you come off it? You came here for a reason. If it wasn't to rant about her, then what was it?"

Nadia sighed. What could she talk about that wasn't directly about Eva? *How about the shit that's going on at work?* "There is *so much drama* at the office right now!"

Jasmine sat back at such exasperated words. "How's that? Ethan hasn't said anything about drama."

"Because *Ethan* spends his days doing important billionaire business while I run the front lines. Of course there's always drama, but… it's so bad recently. Pretty much ever since Ms. Thomas joined the office." And Amber. Nobody could forget that hussy who showed up mere weeks before Adrienne.

"Oh?" That piqued Jasmine's interest like nothing else. "Ethan said something about tearing her a new asshole because she missed a meeting. Was it because of her assistant?"

Whoa, Nadia had almost forgotten about that submissive little whelp. He had long been fired. Shortly before Amber and Adrienne became a thing, Nadia would hazard to guess. "That guy was an ass and nobody was sorry when she fired him. I mean broke up with him. I mean whatever." Nadia crossed her arms and legs at the same time. "But yeah, that's the tip of the iceberg. She comes in late a lot, but she never missed a meeting again. I think one time she came in drunk, but don't quote me on that." *Quote me on that.* Adrienne Thomas was such a functional mess that it would've been hilarious if it wasn't so *sad* too.

"What's her deal?" Jasmine didn't know? Weird, considering she was marrying the woman's business partner… and ex-boyfriend.

"Amber says she's going through a lot."

"Why the fuck would Amber know that?" Jasmine leaned closer to Nadia. "Hey, I thought you guys were buddies. Now you're saying you hate her. Either it's high school, or she did something to really piss you off."

One thing at a time! "Amber sees her a lot because she takes notes at meetings and sometimes overhears things between her and Mr. Cole. Personal things." That was a safe thing to say, right?

"Go on," Jasmine said.

Nadia stared at the petals she had strewn on the brick walkway. They made her think of the flowers Eva had sent to the office not too long ago. *I was tickled that she had thought of me, even if it was an inconvenience.* Something burned in Nadia's eye. She wiped it away before it could become a bigger nuisance. "It doesn't matter. It was a fling."

"With Amber?"

Nadia blanched in disgust. "No! I really shouldn't say it." It wasn't Nadia's place to talk about the relationship between two other women.

"You wouldn't have come out all this way when you don't even have a car unless you wanted to say it."

"Fine." Nadia would square her shoulders and dump her own drama on her friend's. "Eva wasn't really interested in me unless I was playing 'hard to get.' I was a notch on her bedpost." That was the only real explanation Nadia would allow herself. Hadn't she seen it coming from a mile away, anyway? It was half the reason she didn't want to date Eva to begin with! *She would use me. Treat me fine for a few weeks. Then move on to some other woman.* The sooner Nadia made peace with that, the better. She didn't doubt that she would be seeing pictures of Eva and some other supermodel honey soon.

Jasmine wrinkled her nose. "Did she tell you this? Or dump you?"

"No. Not technically." Nadia's sighs couldn't possibly get more dramatic than they already were. *What do I say? Do I make something up again?* It wasn't healthy to come up with stories, let alone to one of her best friends. But what could she say? The truth? *I don't want to. I don't want to mention what happened at the bachelorette party.* Jasmine didn't need that hanging over her fun. Perhaps it was best to truncate the facts a bit. "I sort of broke it off with her after we got back from Hong Kong. Went back to giving her the cold shoulder and blocking her number." That may have happened months ago, but who was keeping track? Besides, as soon as Nadia worked up the nerve, she was blocking Eva's number again. She didn't need that in her life. "I mean… that wasn't very mature of me, but she's not someone I want to confront. She's used to getting her way, you know?"

"I highly doubt she would *hurt* you."

"I didn't say that! You know how I am with confrontation."

"Yeah, Captain Passive Aggressive. How's that working out for you?"

Nadia wanted to fling herself off the bench and into some rose thorns. "So let's say I'm not seeing her anymore. The bachelorette party was really awkward. I don't think she cared anymore." That was not a look of *caring* on Eva's face when Nadia caught her and Amber in that situation. "Between you and me… it's not me she's interested in anymore." Nadia didn't say anything beyond that.

Jasmine pointed her crestfallen countenance toward the brick walkway. "I'm sorry this is happening. Do you want me to talk to Ethan?"

"What good would that do me?" Frustration mounted between Nadia and Jasmine. "Last thing I need is the boss actually being *aware* of all the lesbian drama exploding around him!" Oh, God, that would've been the worst! Bad enough the boss had a habit of sauntering into the break room to stretch his legs while Nadia and Amber gabbed about lesbian dating politics. For him to know what was going on beneath his nose? Even if he did already know, he better *know* to not say anything.

"He's probably more aware than you think he is."

Nadia rolled her eyes toward Jasmine so hard that it was a wonder they didn't fall out of their sockets.

"Fine. He doesn't know a damn thing."

"That's more like it."

"I'm sorry you're dealing with all of this," Jasmine said in the end. "Is there anything I can do? You wanna stay and have dinner? Belinda's making enchiladas, and they're pretty out of this world."

Nadia shrugged. Was Belinda that maid? "I'm down for anything that doesn't make me think about drama. Wait, Amber isn't here, is she?"

"No…"

"Good. I didn't know if she would be up here helping Mr. Cole work."

"I think everyone but him has the day off."

"Does he *ever* stop working?"

This time Jasmine took up the mantle of eye rolling. "He's been better since Adrienne joined his company. But no. When you've made your own billions, you've made them in a very specific way. Mostly by working yourself to death."

"Won't that suck for you?" Jasmine already complained that she and Mr. Cole didn't spend enough time together, due to his job. *Is that what I would sign up for if I decided to be serious with Eva? Not that it's happening now…*

"I know what I'm getting into, at least." Jasmine stood, brushing debris from her shift. "It's not like he doesn't make time for me. He is busy a lot of the time. Certainly busier than some of the other men I know around here…"

Nadia agreed to stay for dinner. Jasmine had no idea, but enchiladas were once a comfort food Nadia relied on to get through college. Perhaps it was a sign. A delicious but probably not nutritious sign.

***

Jasmine was nice enough to send Nadia home in a complimentary car. The driver didn't say anything as he weaved through the skinny streets of Savant's Town and dropped Nadia off in front of her little house. She gave him her thanks before approaching the front porch, head pointed down.

"Hey."

Nadia jerked back. Someone was on her porch, and it wasn't Eva.

It was some other tawdry blonde who Nadia had no intention of being around for a while. Even at work tomorrow.

"What are you doing here?" Nadia spat. She refused to take the first step up to the porch.

Amber leaned against a column. *I don't think I've ever seen her in jeans and a sweatshirt before…* With her hair pulled up in a sloppy bun, Amber almost looked… normal, as opposed to a self-professed gold-digger. "I came by to apologize about what happened Saturday night. Can I come in? I've got some shit to spill."

"I'm sure anything coming out of your mouth right now *is* shit."

"Ouch. I deserved that."

Nadia finally walked up to the porch. "Whatever. Guess we should hash this out now before we're too awkward to deal with at work tomorrow." She pulled out her house key.

Amber watched her fumble with the lock. "Eva didn't kiss me. She didn't even kiss me back. I swear…"

The door opened. Nadia hauled herself in, almost tempted to slam the door in Amber's face. She didn't, though. She let it stay open, inviting Amber in, if only tentatively. *Let's get this over with.* Whatever Amber had to say, it couldn't be good. It couldn't make Nadia feel better. Even if she admitted to jumping Eva and immediately getting shoved off, Nadia *still* wouldn't feel better. Her issues with dating someone like Eva were still too deep and fragile. If only she hadn't come to the insane conclusion that she was falling for the playgirl heiress that every woman with even the slightest gay inclination wanted to score for herself.

Chapter 26

Another hand of Old Maid lost. Eva slapped the Joker onto the dining table and sneered toward the kitchen. "This game is rigged."

Kathryn finished wiping something off her counter while the scent of baked chicken filled the air. "When it's only two people playing, yeah, the odds aren't in your favor." She grabbed a towel and opened the oven. That chicken smell was more enticing now. Shit. Eva had hardly consumed a thing that week. Her stomach growled so loudly that someone laughed on the other side of the table.

"I think someone is ready for dinner, hon." Ian Mathers picked up the cards and shuffled them in the middle of the table. The *thwaaapppt* of every card smacking another forced Eva out of her chair. "And it ain't me. I know how you cook."

"She almost fucked like ten dudes at Jasmine's bachelorette party, and you're criticizing her cooking skills?" Eva marched into her friend's kitchen, instantly smacked in the face with *Chicken! Lemon sauce! Grilled greens! Fresh bread warming!* Kathryn didn't often cook like this, but Eva could get used to it.

Ian shrugged. "I saw the blurry cell phone pics she sent me. If I were her, I definitely would've drunkenly fucked those dudes."

"For God's sake, both of you." Exasperated, Kathryn slammed the oven door closed again, hands on her filling-out hips. *Someone's getting older.* Thirty was creeping on Kathryn like men creeped on Eva whenever she went to the wrong conventions and they found out how much money she had. "I'm still recovering from that hangover. Can we not?" She waved at Eva. "Besides, you're one to give me crap. How many girlfriends have you lost now because you can't keep your clit in your pants?"

"Oooh." A masculine hairline appeared above the counter's edge. "Dirty lesbian drama. Tell me more."

Last thing I want is this guy knowing my drama. Eva ignored Kathryn's boyfriend. This was some sort of anniversary dinner – anniversary of what, exactly, Eva had no idea – that she had crashed, but Kathryn was kind enough to invite her best friend after finding out what level of depression she had sunk into over the past week. "I didn't do anything. That woman kissed *me* and at the worst moment."

"And have you done anything to explain yourself?"

"No…" What the fuck could Eva say? She was back to being blocked by Nadia. Seemed like that happened every time they had even the slightest disagreement. Eva was used to emotionally charged relationships with other women, but this was ridiculous. Was Nadia going to run every single time? *There's gotta be something deeper going on than that Amber brat kissing me in front of her.* Granted, Eva hadn't been in a hurry to explain herself. She was tired of explaining herself.

"Then how can you expect things to sort themselves out?"

"She blocked my number, and I'm not in the mood to go up to Ethan Cole's office to explain myself in front of him and half his office."

That hairline still had yet to go the fuck away. "Who the hell are we talking about?" We? What *we?* "Who are you dating in Ethan Cole's office?

Oh my God. Please tell me it's that Thomas woman. She's got so many sticks up her ass I'm hearing rumors that she likes it."

"Ew. No."

Kathryn chewed on her words before spitting them out. "She's talking about Nadia."

"Hey!"

"Who?"

"Shut up! It's none of his business."

That traitorous asshole stole a glance at her boyfriend. "Ethan Cole's receptionist."

"Oooh. Her. She's a hottie."

"Jesus," Eva muttered, unabashedly stealing some of the fresh bread still wrapped in foil. "Tell him my whole history, why don't you?"

"Come on, Eva." If Kathryn kept dressing in red pants and pink blouses, people would start thinking she was a fashionable mom. With the messy bun and a makeup-less face that definitely did still look hungover from days ago? She was not a fashionable mom. *She feels like my mom right now.* Only two years separated them, but Kathryn's ascent to a new decade in her life was pulling her farther away from Eva. "Why the big secret still? Not like she's in the closet."

"This is true." That man never shut up, did he? "I barely know who you're talking about, and I still know she's gay."

"Gee. Thanks." Eva was going to steal a chunk of bread every time someone got on her nerves. "Dissect my love life. Go on. Do it some more."

Kathryn sighed, one hand on her hip and the other leaning against the counter. "You're a mess." She looked to her boyfriend. "I went to her place this morning to find her wearing the same clothes for the third day."

"Did not." Eva huffed. "Two days in a row." She had no reason to change lately. What was the point, when she wasn't going out? "Kiss my ass while you're at it."

"Don't be such a petulant child." That definitely got Ian turning back around and ignoring the row brewing behind him. Not the way Eva wanted it to happen, but… "You spent how many months flirting with that woman in the hopes she would go out with you? Then you get her, and you drop her at first convenience?"

"I didn't drop her! She's the one who keeps blocking me!" Eva slammed her hand against the counter. "What do you want me to do? Stalk her down and beg her to listen to me? Fuck that! I ain't got time for that."

"You would only say that if you truly didn't care about her. I've known you for how many years now? Even back at Winchester you were dating and dropping as soon as things got too inconvenient, or Heaven forbid, you got bored. You weren't bored with this woman. Grow a fucking pair and go make things right with her. You didn't even mess up! But you *are* messing up by letting this fester and making yourself so damn embarrassing to look at."

"Excuse you." Eva shifted uncomfortably between both feet. "I'm not the one who looks like a first grade teacher at the end of her rope."

"Don't turn this back on me. You were happy with her, yeah? Fix it."

"*How?*"

"Isn't she going to be a bridesmaid at the Cole wedding next weekend?"

"Uh huh."

"And you were invited?"

"Uh huh…"

"Finally, something to liven up a wedding." Ian stopped shuffling the cards and stacked them in the middle of Kathryn's dining table. "And knowing Ethan Cole, he'll be excited if you bring your A+ lesbian drama to his wedding. Make it memorable. For all of us."

Eva crossed the kitchen, grabbed an abandoned towel, and threw it at Ian.

"That's the spirit," Kathryn said. "Fight the patriarchy, hon. With any luck, at this time in two weeks you'll be happily engaged to the receptionist of your dreams."

Was the room hot from all that cooking? The room felt really hot from all the cooking. Or maybe that was Eva's face baking in embarrassment.

Me and her, engaged? Yeah, right. Eva wasn't in the market to get married anytime soon. She was definitely not dragging Nadia into something like that. Not for a good… few years, at least.

"Aw, look at her, honey." Kathryn smiled. "Our little baby's in love."

"Am not!"

"Then I'm not in love either. Sorry, Ian. It's over."

"Damnit. Now I have to find someone else to cook me chicken."

Eva had half a mind to march out of there to make some stupid point, but Ian had said the magic word, and now all she could think about was how hungry she was. Hungry for chicken? Yes, but she was also hungry for something more emotionally satisfying. Like love? Like love.

***

Those pesky emotions were nothing but a yo-yo yanking Eva in two different directions. *Of all the times to not have schoolwork to distract me.* This summer was supposed to be fun. It was supposed to be full of spoiling a woman like Nadia rotten and opening her mind to the idea of making this a more serious thing come fall and winter. *Oh, who am I kidding? We'd have gone on break again so I can finish up my degree.* That fall semester was shaping up to be a total fucking mess. Eva needed to get all the partying in that she could.

Didn't help that her PR agent called her Friday to talk about the Hong Kong press that had those awful pictures. "*It appears that the press went out of business. Whole office is closed up and all the workers were laid off. I have no idea what happened to those photos after the money was transferred. I'll keep you informed.*"

Informed! Sounded like a good reason to pack up and get the fuck out of the country for a while. So she went to her family's Caribbean island, a place she had taken many lovers before, but decided now was the perfect destination to decompress and think about what she wanted.

Eva didn't listen to any music as she sat by the bedroom window, letting in the Caribbean air and appreciating the kind of warmth on her skin that she couldn't get back home. The year-round staff people who lived and worked on the island didn't care that she was alone. For most of them, who came off as rather conservative, they were probably grateful that she wasn't flaunting some lesbian lover in front of them. When she was by herself, Eva was quiet and had few demands. Being asked to be left alone for a day or two aside from bringing her food was one of those demands everyone was more than happy to obey.

While the sun began to descend behind the horizon her second evening there, Eva wrote out by hand what she expected from her life.

1. *A cemented role in my family, preferably on the business front.*
2. *A hot and sweet girlfriend. (Maybe wife one day???)*
3. *The respect of my parents.*
4. *Maybe my own business? Dunno doing what.*
5. *Some good friends who accept me for who I am.*
6. *The freedom to do as I please and spend my money as I see fit.*
7. *Cats, I guess.*

Eva picked up a red pen and struck through the things she knew she would probably never have… like her parents' respect. *That's a venture not worth pursuing, unfortunately.* Eva would have more luck watching her whole family die off and taking over as the sole member of the Warren legacy. *Don't do that to me, Henry. I swear to God…*

She had some good friends who accepted her for who she was, but she also realized that she was in her mid-20s, and things were going to change. A lot. People she were close to now may not be around by the time she was 30. Other people would come into her life, and as she cut back on the partying and milling about, they would probably be cut from a better cloth than the fly-by-the-night friends she had now.

Business was another matter. Eva would have her Master's by the end of the year, and then it was up to her brother to find her a place in the business. To cut her out of that would be as good as telling her to pack her bags and get out of the mansion. Eva could start her business any time, but she didn't know what she wanted to focus on. Until then, her own income came from trusts and the smart investments she made so far in her life. *That's not how I want to live, though.* Eva wouldn't be happy sitting back and letting the passive income roll in indefinitely. She wanted to *earn* some money. Life was too uncertain to leave it up to investments.

Cats aside, that left matters of love.

Eva stared at that point for a good fifteen minutes, unable to write anything else down or focus on, well, anything else. Was this what it meant to reach a certain age? Eva was far from *old,* but she wasn't a kid anymore, either. She was finishing up grad school and setting her sights on a piece of the family business pie. That didn't mean she couldn't date around, but perhaps it was time to start considering a more solid relationship outside of *So this one time I took a German model and banged her in a Seoul hotel?*

Girlfriends had come and gone in her life, some more serious than others. When she was finishing up her undergraduate degree, she had her most serious girlfriend thus far. Unfortunately, Sandra decided that Eva's need for certain forms of control were too much to deal with. She then conveniently took a job offer in Japan. Eva was rich enough to fly wherever she wanted at a moment's notice, but a long-distance relationship wasn't what she wanted.

So what did she want?

Eva pushed aside the list and pulled forward a fresh sheet of paper. Outside, one of the live-in employees did his evening sweep of the shore, looking for anything that was out of place – or anything that could conveniently go into the dinner pot. Security wasn't a huge issue on that private island. There was the occasional lost sailor who was grateful for access to a shower, some food, and a phone, but for the most part the only people who stopped by unannounced were supply boats. Now, the man doing his sweep glanced up and briefly made eye contact with Eva as she gazed out her window. They exchanged polite smiles before he moved on, walking stick pressing into the sand with every step. His basketball shorts were stuffed with shells.

Eva's fingers searched for the cotton curtain and pulled it across the window.

"*The perfect woman,*" she wrote on top of the fresh page. "*Or at least the most realistic perfect woman.*" Eva scratched that part out. No excuses. No mistakes. She was going to paint herself a picture of the woman she wanted to spend the rest of her life with.

1. *Someone who is beautiful. Someone who is aesthetically pleasing and gets me going. Someone who has a shine to her that exudes in the most gorgeous of auras. Someone who is confident in her appearance.*

Eva knew it wasn't the best way to start out her "perfect woman" composition. Focusing on appearances? Really? That was something horny teenager and college student Eva would be all about. One hot girl after another, with big tits and hips to grab during every crazed thrust. *I'm still a kid, I guess.* Only now Eva didn't mean superficial beauty. Of course it was important that she was sexually attracted to the woman of her dreams. That didn't mean she had to adhere to certain beauty standards. Eva had been attracted to all types of women. Mostly feminine ones, but beyond that? Body types, hair color, race and ethnicities… her favorite partners ran the gamut. There were even a few gender nonconforming women in there. *I learned a lot from them. Ahem.* That confidence, though, was one of the most important aspects. Eva didn't want to spend the rest of her life paying for her girlfriend's numerous plastic surgeries and dealing with endless insecurity. Insecurity was natural to a point, but Eva had a limit.

2. *Someone I can have a lot of fun with. We don't have to like all the same things, but someone who wants to travel around the world and is ready for adventures. But also someone who wants to stay home with me and relax.*
3. *Someone who understands me, and is someone I can understand. I'm a mess. I need a woman who will deal with my family history and expectations put upon me. Someone who is compatible with me, in that she understands I need to exert control in the bedroom most of the time.*
    a. *But someone who I can trust so completely that maybe I'm up for letting go of control too…*

Eva tapped her pencil against the table. "That'll be the day." She had experimented with being the pillow biter a time or two. Beneath a domineering woman, that is. *It was fun. Wasn't in a hurry to do it again.* The perfect woman would make her think about doing it again.

4. Someone I want to build a home with. Someone I want to talk to every day, even if it's to rant about my day or hear her thoughts about what's going on in the world. She doesn't have to be a homemaker. I can provide that for her. But she could be at home or she could be working with me, I don't care.

5. Someone who is intelligent and witty. I want to laugh every day. I want to be intellectually challenged. I never want to feel like we're stale.

6. Someone who thinks I'm as hot as I think she is!

7. Someone who is down for staying unmarried partners for years or maybe getting married next year. Whatever feels right. Just not someone who is in a hurry to get married and nothing else.

Kind. Funny. Assertive. Loving. Smart & Witty. Gorgeous. Sexy. Adventurous In and Out Of The Bedroom. Confident. Puts Up With My Bullshit. Laughs At My Jokes. Makes Jokes I Think Are Funny.

Eva erased something and wiped the shavings away.

"*Someone I'm inspired to love forever.*"

No time to waste. If she stopped to think too hard about her list, she would freeze up and make the wrong decisions. Nope. Eva was picking up her red pen and jotting down the women she had been with who fit in every category. She wanted to create the image of the perfect woman, or perhaps a Frankenstein version of all the women she had dated, depending on how often they showed up on her list.

Sandra fit a good chunk of these requirements. Everything but the sexual ones. Unfortunately, that was a huge deal breaker for Eva. She wanted to have sex. She wanted to have a lot of sex. Damnit, she was in her mid-20s. She was horny and ready for some fun. The kicker? She didn't care if it was with multiple women or the one. *Actually, only one might be nice.*

Get to know someone so well that you know their every inch and what they like about that inch!

Eva started to see the pattern halfway down the list. But she forced herself to finish it. Sandra. Cathy. Lilith. Maria. Aria. Olivia. Penny. Natalia. Simone. Hilary.

Nadia.

One of those names appeared in every category. Only that one.

Eva got up and buzzed one of the servants in the main house. She asked for a bottle of whatever rum was handiest, because she was going to need it. Rum was absolutely necessary when stuck on a private Caribbean island. Rum was also absolutely necessary when a lesbian was formulating a plan on how to get – and keep! – the perfect woman who had been under her nose and now needed some serious convincing to stay with her rich bitch heiress ass.

With any luck, she wouldn't pass out drunk before having her breakthrough!

Chapter 27

Until now, Nadia had been completely indifferent about weddings. Some were nice. Some were boring. Usually there was booze and dancing, so that was good. It was a nice excuse to dress up super pretty and feel nice for a day, whether as part of the bridal party or a guest eating cake and making DJ requests.

Then she was one of three bridesmaids at a billion dollar wedding.

While Jasmine's wedding was one of the greatest well-oiled machines to ever grace the planet, Nadia was still pulled into a whirlwind of stress, anxiety, and a lot of yelling from a wedding planner permanently attached to her headset. By the time the vows between her boss and her best friend were said, Nadia was already game to get into a cab and go home. Instead, she had to get into a shuttle limo and be taken to the reception farther up in the Hills.

It didn't help that she saw Eva every time she turned around.

Of course she had come. Why wouldn't she have been invited? Even if Jasmine didn't like her, she was a member of a family considered close to the groom. *I suppose I had hoped she wouldn't come at all.*

But she *had* come. Eva Warren strutted up to a seat of honor alongside her brother and sister-in-law. If that wasn't insulting to Nadia's senses enough, she was wearing a black Dolce & Gabbana suit that was tailored to every line and subtle curve of her body. Her blond hair was sufficiently feathered by both a competent stylist and the early summer breeze blowing through Mr. Cole's flower garden. When Nadia was forced to walk by her, she made a point of keeping her face pointed forward. She had to, anyway. There were a hundred photographers getting shots of Nadia carrying her flowers and walking in purple stiletto heels.

By the time she was at the reception, she knew her time was limited. The formalities of the ceremony could only protect her for so long. At some point, Eva was going to try something.

This was assuming, of course, that Nadia didn't try talking to her first.

She thought about it a dozen times. Eva hadn't brought a +1 and was only seen with her family and a couple of friends. *I wish she had brought a date. It would've hurt, but then I would know I could move on.* Jasmine had been right. Nadia was too passive-aggressive for her own good. Funny. She was raised to think that passive-aggression was the pinnacle of politeness. "*Why would anyone give you shit if you never even said or did anything, sweetie?*" That was Mrs. Gaines's opinion on the matter. Now Nadia knew how cruel it was to go radio silent.

However, Nadia did not approach Eva. The bridesmaid was either too busy dealing with Jasmine's wardrobe malfunctions and temperament, or she was glued to her chair at the banquet table because her feet ached and she was sore all over.

It was inevitable. They could not be at the same function for this long and not have a confrontation. If Nadia wasn't going to initiate it? Someone else had to.

The more aggressive, domineering one of the pair.

Eva pounded her heels against the ballroom floor, en route to the bridal banquet table. It looked like she was heading straight for the bride and groom – but at the last moment she veered to her left, her glare almost knocking Nadia out of her seat.

"You're killing me," Eva hissed across the table. That tone, the passion shooting fire from her teeth made Nadia sit back with a start. "What are we even arguing about? I *so* did not flirt with that boring-ass girl… on purpose. I swear!"

Nadia gripped her wineglass, eyes boring into Eva's fragile visage. *Don't toss it in her face. This is your best friend's wedding. Don't toss wine into an heiress's face…* It was so tempting, though. Give Eva a taste of how it felt to walk up to her and Amber kissing like horny lovers. *I thought I was over it.* Nope! Apparently not! The moment Eva was here, acting like Nadia owed her something? Wine. Face. Imminent. Better than the other thing Nadia wanted to do to that face… which was kiss it.

Jasmine's maid of honor, Selena, jumped up and slammed a hand onto Nadia's shoulder. "Let's go have a dance! We've got these pretty dresses on and it would be the perfect opportunity to attract some bigshots…"

"Sure," Nadia said, outright ignoring Eva's frazzled expression. "Wouldn't mind attracting some *big*shots. I hear there's a Saudi prince here." Nadia took Selena's hand and went with her to the dancefloor. Where was the nearest single guy to dance with? Ah, the thought of Eva's face when she saw Nadia dancing with a man…

She glanced over her shoulder. Eva was nowhere to be seen. *Oh.*

"What's that about, huh?" Selena asked. She swayed back and forth on the dancefloor with Nadia only somewhat joining her. Even when they took off their shoes and attempted more vigorous movements, Nadia's feet were still too sore to deal with. "That woman giving you problems? I could get my brother to scare her off."

"No, no problems." Nadia sighed. "I think we might be broken up."

"Oh, I…"

Someone interrupted them. Nadia was half-afraid to turn around and see Eva asking for a dance, but she did not see a feminine face at all. She saw the same one Selena did. Yeah, Selena, the one who was apparently trawling for a rich husband at her friend's wedding. The young, rich-looking man interrupting their gal-pal dance pinged Selena's radar. Hard.

However, he did not address her. He addressed *Nadia.*

"Would you care to dance with me?" he asked, holding out a hand. "Um, don't ask questions. Yes or no is good. But if you say no, I've got a girlfriend to go back to who will kick my ass for not dancing with another woman… er… that came out wrong."

"Whelp," Selena said, stepping away. "I'm relieved from this duty. Good luck, girl."

Nadia stared at the hand still extended in her direction. She vaguely recognized this man, although couldn't remember his name – he definitely didn't stop by Mr. Cole's office often, if at all. *He said he has a girlfriend? Why is he asking me to dance, then?* Nadia gingerly took his hand and was pleasantly surprised to find it so soft.

Hazel eyes glanced around the ballroom. A slight breath of relief shot from the man's mouth. "All right. I'll make this quick. I'm supposed to tell you to go to some room in ten minutes… fuck, I forgot which one. Hang on." He pulled out his cell phone and sent a quick text.

"Who… are you?" He wasn't asking Nadia to walk into some dangerous situation, was he? *I know how these billionaires are. They're probably arranging a drug-filled orgy in one of the back rooms.* Nadia was game to make Eva a little jealous, but she wasn't *join an orgy full of dudes and maybe get gangbanged* game. (But if Eva asked, she was.)

"Oh, sorry! Ian Mathers." Their precarious dance position turned into a firm handshake. "Kathryn Alison's boyfriend. I'm not flirting with you, honest. I don't have a death wish."

"Kathryn… oh my God, this is about Eva, isn't it?"

"Er… guilty. A little. But before you run off, I'm supposed to tell you that she's *really sorry* about everything that's happened and she wants to speak with you in private. And if you ask me," Nadia hadn't, "that woman has got it really, really bad for you. Trust me. I know what it's like to play around for years and then suddenly fall for someone you see all the time. If she's asking *me* to come get you, then she's got it bad. That woman doesn't talk to me unless it's to threaten to castrate me. For fun."

Nadia stepped back. "Excuse me."

"Room 2, wherever that is!" Ian's voice called after her. "Ten minutes! Did my part…"

Nadia sat down in the nearest chair, massaging her feet and keeping her head down. *Don't look for Eva. Don't do it. Don't succumb.* Nadia wanted to be strong. She didn't want to give in to that woman's demands. *If I decide I want to talk, she'll know, damnit.* Someone needed to lose some control for a while.

This time it was a feminine figure shadowing her.

"God," Nadia muttered, not even bothering to look up. This person she knew *just* from the posture. "Your boyfriend didn't work, so you've come to fetch me, huh?"

Kathryn barred Nadia from getting up. Like Nadia couldn't take down this tall stick of a woman! "Normally I would tell that dumbass to fix her own relationship problems, but I'm tired of seeing her mope around and I'm *really* tired of the midnight phone calls from the Caribbean. I'm not saying get back together with her, but you need to at least give her some closure. She has no idea if you two are broken up or not. Trust me, you're not going to ruin this heterosexual marriage party for her by telling her to stay away forever. But she's gotta hear it. From you."

Nadia leaned back in the chair. "Do you know what she did?"

"Yes, she told me all about Ethan Cole's assistant throwing herself at her. You've gotta be looking for reasons to dump her, though, if you really think it was mutual.

"I know it wasn't mutual."

"For the love of… go talk to her! Please! For all our sake's!"

"Fine!" Nadia stood up, wobbling on her bare and aching feet. "If you two promise to leave me alone, I will."

"Thank God. I'll take care of any damage you inflict. Get it done."

One thing was for sure: even Kathryn wasn't sure if Nadia and Eva should be together. *Granted, Kathryn doesn't know me.* Not that it made any difference to Nadia. If Eva's best friend of how many years was saying *get it done,* then that said a lot more than what was offered at face value.

Nadia had to ask where Room 2 was before departing the dancefloor – and then going back to grab her shoes, because some people found it uncouth to walk around a wedding barefoot.

The reception hall boasted a few private rooms far in the back, beyond the main ballroom, restrooms, and liquor parlor. *Should get a drink before doing this.* Although Nadia had rehearsed a litany of breakup lines in the past several days, she still knew she would be thrown for a loop when she walked in and saw Eva waiting for her.

Sure enough, there she was, body draped across a couch, drumming fingers on her thigh while the other hand held a glass of something brown and iced. Nadia wasn't the only one with thoughts of alcohol, apparently.

Shit. I knew this would happen. The moment Nadia got a good look at her, all she could think about was the fastest way to get those clothes off Eva's body. *What the hell is it about suits that make a girl both want to appreciate them* and *destroy them? Get a grip, Nadia.* She squared her shoulders and clicked the door shut behind her.

"All right, I'm here." Nadia inhaled deeply. "What do you want?"

Eva was halfway off the couch when she spoke with such conviction that Nadia had to take a step back. "You. I want you."

Don't. Fall. For. It. "You don't get me. Not that easily."

"No fucking shit." The glass of liquor clinked against the nearest coffee table. "You've been yo-yoing me for months now. This is the cruelest game of hard to get I've ever played. Congratulations, I guess."

Nadia scoffed. "I'm not playing 'hard to get.' If you think such a game exists, then you're a bigger idiot than I ever thought. I'm not a fucking trophy you can win and mount on your wall."

"When have I ever made you feel like that? Huh?" Was that desperation in Eva's voice? *Of course it is.* Didn't mean it left Nadia unaffected, though. "If I've ever made you feel like you're nothing more than some prize, then I'm sorry. That was my failure. I never wanted you to feel anything but good around me."

"I did," Nadia said softly. This was not going the way she thought it would. "For a while."

"So what happened? Is this about Amber? You can't seriously believe that she and I had something going on. I only openly flirted with her that one time, before we started dating."

"I know." Nadia broke eye contact. Looking into those troubled blues was too much to deal with right now. "She told me."

"Great! What's the problem? Think you could drop my number without explanation?"

"This isn't going to work, Eva. You know that. We're not compatible."

"Says who?"

"Come on!" Why did she have to be so damn difficult? Was Eva crammed so far up her own ass that she was incapable of seeing that writing on the wall since their first supposed date? "Why do you think I never said yes to going out with you, Eva? You think I wasn't attracted to you for all that time? Is that what you wanted to hear? That every time you walked into that office my panties got wet and I dreamed of you pounding me until I couldn't walk anymore?"

Eva's eyes widened. "Uh, no, that's not what I had in mind. But go ahead and say that again if you want..."

"Fuck off, perv." Nadia grabbed the door handle.

"Hey!" Eva slammed her hand against the door above Nadia's head. *Why does she have to be so tall!* Why did she have to wear such stunning perfume? Why did she have to have such warm breath against Nadia's cheek? Why did she have to have such a strong presence that encircled Nadia and made her want to curl up in the embrace of this rough and ready woman? *I hate it. I spent the entirety of my last relationship wishing for this kind of woman in my life, and now that she's here, I can't let her go...* "You owe me an explanation."

Right... Kathryn said the word closure, hadn't she? Eva would keep chasing Nadia until some damn closure was offered. Nadia supposed she did owe a bit of an explanation... but did Eva have to be so *on top* of her right now?

Nadia released the door handle. Neither of them backed away. "I don't think I'm cut out for being in a relationship with someone at your level."

Eva relaxed her stance. "What does that mean? My family?"

"Yeah… and the money. I'm sorry. It's too much."

They were quiet for a minute, although they still remained crammed together by the door. Every breath was another shot of Eva's perfume in Nadia's mind. *No, don't commit it to memory. That's dangerous.* The last thing Nadia needed was night after night of going to sleep thinking of this scent. "You're breaking up with me because I'm rich," Eva finally said, with a hint of disbelief. "Are you kidding?"

"I'm sure you're not used to hearing that. I bet most girls fall over to get to your money."

"Nadia… I never once thought you were taking advantage of me."

"How could you? I never asked for anything." Nadia had made a point of not letting Eva pay for everything, even though it was her second nature to flash her credit card wherever they went. *She didn't even have to think about it.* She never had to count pennies in her life.

"Yeah, I noticed." Eva sighed. "There's gotta be something else. If it were discomfort with how much money I have, you would have mentioned it instead of… letting what happened at the bachelorette party be a convenient excuse to stop talking to me."

"To be fair, you're the one who went quiet first."

"I told you we had to lay low!"

"But why?" Nadia turned, pressed against the door with Eva looming over her. *I hate it. I love it. I hate that I love having her on me like this.* "You never told me what happened. Something with your family?" *That's another thing. I can't deal with your homophobic parents.* Nadia had never even met them. She didn't want to.

Another sigh, this one heavier than all the others combined. Eva pressed herself against the wall and closed her eyes. "We got papped in Hong Kong. Badly."

Breath left Nadia's lungs. "What does that mean? The badly part… and I don't remember us being in the press. Someone would have mentioned it." A lot of someones would have gone crazy to see photographic evidence of Eva and Nadia.

Eva averted her eyes, wetted her lips, and balled her hands into protective fists. "They got pics of us having sex."

Nadia gasped. "No!"

"Yup. The whole shebang. Literally. She-banging. You and me, our bodies bare and faces as clear as your pretty skin." Even now she was being flirtatious? "My PR manager called me to say the paper was offering me a deal. They wanted millions of dollars to keep from publishing those photos. So I paid it, and agreed with my PR manager that you and I shouldn't be seen together for a while."

"Oh my God." Nadia wanted to vomit! *Someone not only watched us having sex… but took pictures?* She remembered what went on beneath those sheets in Hong Kong pretty clearly. To say it was deliciously raunchy was an understatement. Apparently raunchy enough to end up on some Cantonese blog, too!

"I couldn't tell you about it. You made it clear in the beginning that you didn't want to be public for now. For us to be outed like that? I was already embarrassed to hell and back, but I knew it would absolutely destroy you."

Nadia was still trying to process that. *What? What happened? Pics of us having sex?* "And that only happened because of who you are."

Eva shuddered. "Seems that way. They've been glomming pictures of me in sexual situations since the day I turned 18. I'm hot, I'm rich, and I'm *gay*. You think they're not as aware of that as everyone else?"

"You deal with it?"

"The fuck am I supposed to do? Anyone with any celebrity has to deal with the sharks. We used to have classes about public relations and the media when I was at Winchester. It's fucking mandatory teaching."

"That's messed up!"

"That's life. You're right. You were always right. This is *my* life, and by dating me, you're signing up for all the bullshit that comes with me. My bullshit parents, the bullshit media, my bullshit studies… but I want to think that there are good things too?"

"Like *what?*"

"Like this."

Nadia knew it was coming. She was given plenty of time to push Eva away, to run, to say no. *I can't. I want this too. Why am I such a mess around this fool?* Nadia's arms were as quick to go around Eva as Eva's were quick to go around Nadia. The famished kiss that erupted between them was unprecedented in their relationship thus far. This wasn't testing tepid waters. This wasn't giving in to tingles that hounded Nadia whenever Eva was in the same room as her. This wasn't mere desire quenched by steaming passion.

This was something far more dangerous.

Now, desperation? There was plenty of that on both of their ends. Nadia was desperate to be given a reason to stay with Eva. And Eva? She was definitely desperate for *something.*

Nadia. She was desperate for Nadia. The woman could feel that when her lover pushed her against the wall and covered her in heavy kisses.

"You're killing me, you know that?" Eva wasn't choking, was she? No way. This was a woman always so composed, so put together. She exuded confidence with the best of them – *them* being the billionaire brutes coming in and out of Mr. Cole's office on a daily basis. Eva was on that level, right?

And now she was choking back tears over *Nadia?*

"How dare you…" Eva's hands were tangled in Nadia's loose hair, pulling her head back even though they couldn't bear to make eye contact. *Don't cry. Please.* Nadia wouldn't be able to stand that. "How dare you make me fall for you? Of all the heartbreaking lesbians in the world, it would be the one who doesn't even want me."

"It's not that!" Damn choking was contagious! Nadia grabbed Eva's jacket and brought her closer. *Don't go. Don't leave. Don't run away.* "I want you. I always have. You drive me crazy because of how much I want you, even though I know it's only going to hurt us in the end!"

"What are you talking about?" Eva regained her composure with a snap. Probably because Nadia was full-blown crying now, her tears of frustration mounting the room. *I want you, Eva Warren. I want you so much that I can't stand the thought of you being with anyone else!* If she said that out loud, she would be done for. "It doesn't matter who I'm with, Nadia! It's the same problems! Maybe even worse, because I don't get along or feel a connection with anyone else like I do with you! You think I've shared the things I've shared with you… with anyone else? Fuck no! You're the only one I've trusted enough with that shit!"

"Don't worry." Nadia finally opened the door, determined to get away from this mess. "I'm not going to tell anyone. Your secrets are safe with me."

"Where are you going?"

"I need to get back to the wedding." Nadia paused long enough in the open doorway to send her ex-girlfriend one last look. "I'm sorry, Eva. You know it's not going to work." She shut the door in Eva's face before running to the nearest bathroom. Unfortunately, Nadia could not run away from that sweet scent following her. Eva always had a way of haunting her.

Chapter 28

Eva sat at the bar, knocking back hard drinks while the wedding wrapped up around her. *I hate straight people weddings.* She wasn't big on gay weddings either, but damn if she didn't feel as much like shit at those. Two men, two women… who gave a shit. Two straight people trading nuptials? Fuck it. More Jack Daniels, please.

"Rough day, huh?" Kathryn slipped onto the stool beside her. "I'm sorry."

"Whatever." Eva rolled the ice around in her glass. "This time next week I'll be rebounding in San Francisco."

Kathryn didn't reply to that. "You wanna bail and go back to my place? I hear someone hasn't seen *Titanic* in a good long while. Watch Leo die again. That always cheers you up."

"No thanks. Wouldn't want to ruin your romantic night with your boyfriend."

"Who the hell says we're having a romantic night? We're going to Paris soon. That can wait. Whatever."

"Please." Eva snorted into her glass. "You guys are at a wedding. You're going to go home with him and make love with thoughts of how much you two love each other."

Kathryn shifted on her stool. *Made you uncomfortable, huh?* "What makes you say that?"

"Because that's what I would do if I had my girlfriend."

Before Kathryn could attempt to assuage Eva's bad mood, the announcement for the bouquet and garter toss was made. *Gag.* Eva stared forward as it was decided to go against tradition and do the garter toss first.

"Oh, for fuck's sake," Kathryn moaned. "Ian's in the bunch."

"That man wants to marry you so badly that he'll punch out every other man here for Jasmine Bliss's garter."

"Don't remind me." If Kathryn and Eva could agree on one thing, it was that neither was big on getting married anytime soon. *I'm definitely not getting married soon.* Not without an eligible woman at her side. "Oh… oh no."

Male voices roared in laughter and good humor behind Eva.

"Get me out of here, Eva."

She didn't have to turn around to see who had caught the garter. "Fuck you, Kathryn."

"Tequila, please."

The bartender grabbed a bottle while Kathryn slammed her head against the counter. Eva clapped her on the back…

…And caught sight of Nadia gliding by, standing off to the side for the bouquet toss.

Jasmine stood at the front of the room, bouquet high in the air while every eligible woman – beside Kathryn and Eva, apparently – grouped up to try their hand at destiny.

Nadia never once extended her hands for the bouquet. It sailed over her head, batting some other woman's hand. This created a rowdy volley, petals fluttering to the ground while more than one woman fought for control of the bouquet. *It's like a fucking war in here.* Eva would have laughed if she had any good humor left in her.

Someone smacked the bouquet so hard it landed right in Nadia's hands.

Eva missed the commotion erupting among all the women who lost out. Nadia shrieked, dropping the bouquet and turning away from the cursed thing.

Her eyes met Eva's only a few yards away.

While Jasmine Bliss gave some sassy sendoff before hopping in the limo that would take her and her new husband away on their honeymoon, Nadia and Eva continued to stare each other down, both refusing to take a single step toward the other. Yet they found themselves unable to look away. Would this be the last time? For what reason? Because Nadia deemed it too hard to be in a relationship with someone like Eva?

With someone who…

Who…

Maybe it was good ol' Jack Daniels who gave Eva the impetus she needed to get off her stool and approach Nadia. Nobody was watching – well, nobody except for maybe Kathryn, but she didn't count – since there were much more interesting things to watch aside from two women staring each other down.

"I didn't do that on purpose," Nadia insisted. Someone had grabbed the bouquet off the ground. Maybe they thought it still counted.

Eva dared to lift her hand and pull a flower petal from Nadia's hair. "Yet it happened anyway. Story of our lives."

Nadia caught Eva's hand on its way down to her side. "I'm sorry," she said. "For being such an ass. I should've been direct with you instead of a passive-aggressive bitch."

"Yeah, well…" Eva wasn't blushing. Nope. *I am so not blushing. Fuck that!* Was Eva the one who took charge around there or not? Was she going to let this final chance slip through her fingers? Hell no! She was going to take Nadia by the hand and attempt to haul her out of the reception hall like a real woman should! "Come on. You're going home with me."

"What!" Nadia struggled in Eva's grip. Obviously not hard enough, though. Not like Eva had the firmest grip in the world on her. "Excuse you! Give me one good reason I should go home with you."

"Because I fucking love you." Eva yanked Nadia into her embrace. "How's that for a damn good reason?"

***

They reached Eva's Jaguar in record time. But before Eva could hurry to whip out her keys and get in the driver's seat, she glanced up at Nadia waiting by the passenger's side.

"I'm… I'm too tipsy to drive," Eva admitted.

"Oh?" Nadia held out her hand. "Good thing I have my license and know where you live downtown."

"You can't drive my car!"

"Who says?"

"I do! It's my car!"

Nadia rounded the front of the Jaguar, her dark purple dress brushing against the black finish. "Give me the keys, please." She nuzzled close to Eva, batting long, dark eyelashes and pushing her chest up. "I want to get home and fuck you."

Eva slammed her keys into Nadia's hand. She slid into the passenger's seat without a second thought. Or without any thoughts besides *get us home quick because I wanna fuck too!*

Nadia was a million shining dollars behind the steering wheel of Eva's black Jaguar. In fact, she looked like she was born to drive a damn Jaguar. The way she tossed her hair behind her, the top coming down and Eva's sunglasses adorning her cute face… shit! Eva really was inebriated enough right now to start fooling around in front of God and billionaire country. *This drive home better sober me up some. Because I. Want. Some.* Her need for Nadia was like needing to breathe, to drink, to sleep and eat. Such a base desire that she couldn't even decide what she wanted to do first.

"You know how to drive a stick?" Eva called over the motor.

"Do I… excuse me, Ms. Warren, but unlike you I've *driven* some *sticks* before."

"Hey!"

"What?" Nadia blew her a kiss. "Jealous?"

Hell yes I get jealous every time I think about you with a guy. Or another girl. Eva got jealous, period. "If it's a stick you wanna ride," Eva purred into Nadia's ear. "Then you'll be happy to know I keep a collection at home."

"Ooooh, such a flirt." Nadia shifted gears before pulling out of the parking space. "You're as smooth as this ride, Ms. Warren."

"Call me Ms. Warren one more time."

"Ms. Warren."

Nadia had better know how to drive while a crazy woman nibbled her earlobe, because that's what she had to deal with as they drove down the reception hall driveway and toward the main road. *I'll have my hand up her skirt before we get into town.* Truer words had never been thought. May not be the best idea in the world, but Eva didn't care. She wanted to rock Nadia's world until it couldn't be rocked any more.

"Whoa!" Nadia slammed on the brakes. The Jaguar jerked forward, throwing Eva forward enough to make her grateful that she was wearing her seatbelt. "Get a load of that!"

Eva looked to where Nadia was pointing. There, against a finely trimmed hedge, were two women who were *way* ahead of the other gays at the straightest wedding of the year.

"Good for them. They made up." Wasn't that Amber's ass? And that was Adrienne Thomas losing her shit all over another woman's body, right? "I'll do you better, though," Eva said directly into Nadia's ear. "Get us home and we'll put those losers to shame."

Another car honked behind them. Nadia ignored it, choosing to instead slowly turn her head and grin right into Eva's giddy face. "If you promise."

"I always make good on my promises."

"In that case." Nadia switched gears again. "I'll get us home just under the speed limit. Then we're going to ignore the speed limit in bed."

"There are speed limits in bed?"

"Not with you."

"Damn straight. Er, I mean…"

The car continued down the driveway. "Don't worry, Ms. Warren. I feel plenty gay today. Somehow you always make me feel plenty gay whenever you're around me."

"I do what I can for the lesbian cause."

They turned right, weaving down from the Hills and toward the massive, sprawling city. Somewhere in that mess of high-rises was Eva's apartment, and somewhere in that apartment was a bed waiting for these two star-crossed lovers to make the fuck up.

***

Nadia stumbled into Eva's apartment right behind her, the hardwoods making her stilettos echo as if they walked in a cavernous room. *No, just Eva's huge studio apartment.* It didn't seem so huge now. Cozy, really. Pretty, powdery blue on the walls and accented on the couches and bed. It went well with the sleek, black electronics and the white trim of the windows.

"Come here." Eva's soft – if not sobered – voice called to Nadia as she took in the femininity of her girlfriend's apartment. *Time to forget it already?* What else could she possibly think of as they kissed like the silly lovers they were. "You're back in my home, sweetie. I'm not letting you go until I'm well and done with you."

As into this as Nadia was, she was even more into the idea of alleviating her poor feet. She slipped out of her stilettos, losing half an inch on Eva and making her work more for that kiss.

"Do you really love me?" Nadia whispered on those perfectly pink lips. "Or were you saying that to get me to come home with you?" *Don't tell me it was a lie.* Did she want those words to have been true? What woman wouldn't?

"I wouldn't lie about something like that." Eva pulled her closer, letting Nadia feel all the heat emanating between them. *Have we ever been this close before? Even while making love?* "I would die before leading you on about something as important and critical as that. If I said I loved you, then I love you. Don't you believe me?" The next kiss was the softest, inviting Nadia to reply even through these sweet kisses.

"I believe you." Nadia tugged on the suit jacket adorning her girlfriend's long and lean torso. *Can I take this off?* "I think I love you too."

"You think?"

"You haven't given me much time to think about it. How do you know that you love me?"

Eva chuckled. "What if I told you that I realized you're basically my perfect woman?"

"I'd say that there's no such thing as a perfect woman." Nadia pulled back the jacket and revealed the white silk dress shirt beneath. "Er, almost. You might be up there. Damn." Wasn't it kosher to run her hands up and down those glass buttons? To feel up those breasts in what was sure to be a lacy bra?

"You like that, huh?" Eva shrugged out of her jacket and let it plummet to the floor. "There's more where this came from. Allow me to direct you to my big, comfortable bed."

Nadia allowed it. The only way this could have been better was if Eva picked her up and carried her to the bed in the far corner of the room. Barring that, however, she would be perfectly turned on by being corralled.

She landed on Eva's bed with a graceful plop. The spring of the mattress was enough to turn Nadia around and give her a lovely view of the woman leaning one knee against the edge of the bed and slowly unbuttoning her shirt. Eva did it with such precision that each button popped open at perfectly timed intervals. *Pop.* Collarbone. *Pop.* Cleavage. *Pop.* Black bra. *Pop.* Stomach. *Pop.* Bellybutton. *Pop, pop, pop.*

"Like what you see, Ms. Gaines?" Eva wasn't in a hurry to take off her shirt after that. She was, however, into giving Nadia a scorching gaze. *I've seen smoldering looks before… this is so beyond that.* Nadia was going to melt into a puddle of aroused mush at this rate. "Because I really, really like what I see from here."

"Oh, this old thing?" The dress on Nadia's body cost at least five thousand dollars. *Jasmine paid for it.* Wait, Jasmine who? Oh. Her. Pft. "I barely fit into it. See?" She gestured to the way her breasts spilled from the bust when she languished in this position. "I'm bursting at the seams." Nadia pulled up her skirt, revealing her thighs. "Oh, no."

It had the desired effect. Eva was on top of her, attempting to devour every bit of her flesh as it emerged from the blasted dress.

"Yes, yes…" Nadia thought of a million ways to encourage her lover to keep going. Was there a sensitive place not being touched? *Touch it. Now.* A spot in need of some tender – or not so tender – loving? *Worship it.* Sounds that needed appreciating? *Listen to every sound I make.* Nadia did not hold back. Every word, every moan passing her lips was meant for Eva to hear and use as inspiration. It so happened that Nadia's whole body quivered to be caressed, grabbed, and *handled.* "Make love to me, baby." How strange and yet so natural to call her that. *I never call anyone baby.* Nadia never even called her ex-boyfriends baby, and they threw that word at her so lazily that it was fair game. "Fuck me."

"I will." Eva climbed onto the bed and pushed Nadia beneath her. "Until you feel how much I love you."

They had indulged in passionate sex before. There were times they were so wrapped up in each other, kissing, caressing, thrusting until they couldn't anymore that Nadia swore she had never been so close to someone before. *And this was before I realized I loved her.* Now? Those previous notions were shattered as she and Eva made love with an understanding that this was it, this was probably as close to forever as they had ever been in their lives.

For once, Nadia was willing to throw out her fears and apprehensions about dating someone like Eva. *She loves me. She wants me. That's all that matters.* Did Nadia feel it? Holy shit, yes! That wasn't mere lust pushing them toward ecstasy. A hundred layers of emotions built up and were torn away every time they kissed and came together in a bed shaking embrace. They still hadn't taken off all their clothing yet. Eva's trousers disappeared. Nadia's dress came off, leaving her in subtly colored yet daring lingerie.

Somehow, though, the two of them still managed to feel like one even with some clothing still existing between them.

"Do you love me?" Eva gasped into Nadia's ear, their legs entwining. Nadia's lips were attached to her girlfriend's throat, furiously determined to leave a hot red mark there for days to come. *I want me all over her. When she leaves my side, the world will know she's mine because of how I've claimed her body.* Her lip prints. Her scratch marks. Her scent. Her name on Eva's tongue. "I want you to love me, babe."

"Yes." Nadia freed her legs from Eva's and opened them wide. *I want her in me five minutes ago!* "How could I not love someone like you?"

"I should be asking you that."

"Don't." Nadia kissed her so hard it almost hurt. "Just do it."

She loved how so many walls came down between them whenever they made love like this. No longer was one the privileged heiress of an old and prestigious family. No longer was the other constantly comparing herself to every supermodel and other daughter of privilege to come before her. *She's choosing me. Eva Warren wants me to be her girlfriend.* But they weren't Nadia and Eva any longer, were they? The women currently fighting to express their innermost feelings and desires for one another on that bed were just that: two women sharing that insane chemical that brought down whole bloodlines.

They were naked now. Aside from expensive makeup on their faces and products in their hair, they were exactly the same in mind and body.

I don't want to let her go. I don't want her to be anywhere but on top of me. Eva wasn't letting Nadia go anywhere. Not that Nadia wanted to go anywhere. As far as she was concerned, her mission in life was to stay right there, taking those fingers, those lips, those feminine moans and absorbing them into her body until there was no telling where Nadia ended and Eva began. *Isn't this what it's supposed to be about?*

The only way it could have been sweeter was if they came together. But Nadia shattered the orgasmic silence by being the first one to give in, her sweat boiling on her skin as her spine strained so hard to arch beneath Eva's body.

For another hour they explored what it meant to be in love with one another and how best to physically express that. Nadia gave herself over, a willing woman ready to do what she was bade and eager to please. She was pleased in turn, whether it was from receiving a delectable kiss to her nether lips or darting her own tongue into the tangy recesses of Eva's body. Nadia didn't care if she was on her back, on her stomach with ass down or in the air, arms pressed behind her back and legs spread wide. It all felt equally good and inspired her to give in turn.

"Tell me you love me." Eva still couldn't keep her hands off Nadia's slick and pleasured body even as she attempted to pull out what she declared to be the only boyfriend she ever needed. "I want to hear you say it again."

Nadia ran her fingers up and down Eva's toned leg. She didn't have many curves, but she was athletic enough to court firm muscles beneath her skin. *More than I do, anyway.* Yet Eva's softness was in the silkiness of her skin and that loving look in her eye. "I love you. Let me be the one you need so you can unleash everything troubling you."

Eva snapped the buckled straps and rolled on top of Nadia with more fervent kisses. "Likewise, babe."

Ah, the way she said that wasn't cheesy at all. So soft and full of the adoration Nadia craved in her relationships.

There were other things she craved too. Like unrelenting sexual satisfaction.

That was certainly not wanting in her life. Not with someone as skilled and determined as Eva, who fucked Nadia with a level of carnality that no man could achieve. *She's so deep!* Nadia emitted one endless moan of pleasure from beginning to end. How could she make any other sound when Eva filled her and gave her a sense of wholeness that was missing from her life? Whether Nadia clutched her girlfriend's shoulders and took it between the legs like a seasoned lover or was flipped over and taken from behind, she didn't care! There was such finesse and an understanding of what made Nadia go mad with pleasure that one could not even compare Eva Warren to men – or other women, for that matter. She was on another level. Another planet. Another celestial body that only she could command.

Hearing, feeling her climax was the most satisfying part of all.

She sucked in her breath first, stilling her hips, folding her hands into fists and letting her fingers tremble in Nadia's pillow. *She's so fucking beautiful.* That was pure ecstasy on Eva's face as orgasm consumed her. The same face Nadia saw the first time they had sex six months ago. Was that the moment Eva first realized she had real feelings for Nadia? No. No way. They had barely known each other.

And yet…

"Oh my God." Eva collapsed, half on Nadia, half threatening to fall off the bed. "I can't. Not anymore. Fuck."

Nadia had come so many times already that another two or three didn't seem like anything. *I'm past the point where I'm limited.* But that was her physiology. Eva was the type to save it all up for one or two explosive orgasms that took all the wind out of her. That made her easy to please now.

"That was the best." Nadia curled against her. Fingers languidly touched Eva's wet thighs.

"You say that every time." The woman was still breathless.

Nadia kissed her girlfriend's chest, working her way down stomach and abdomen. "I'll keep saying it as long as it's true." Her own intense scent hit her as soon as she made it to the straps around Eva's waist. "For now, you should relax. Let me pleasure you for a while."

"Don't even know how… oh, well, I suppose you could do that… wow… that is hot…"

Nadia couldn't reply. Her mouth was a bit preoccupied. The rest of her? Thinking up more devious ways to show this woman how much her girlfriend loved her.

Part 3

HARD TO STAY

Chapter 29

For two weeks Eva and Nadia lived in contented bliss. Lazy summer days were in full-force in the region, granting long, hot afternoons and evenings that considerably cooled off to allow for more crazy lovemaking.

Eva didn't often allow herself flights of crazy fancy. But the longer she spent with Nadia, the more she became convinced that this could possibly be *forever.* No matter how much she reminded herself that this was a honeymoon phase and that true colors would show themselves eventually… Eva didn't care. This was already the best summer ever. Better than the summer she spent in Greece with that supposed girlfriend Hilary. *Who was that again? I've totally forgotten.* No one was as memorable as Nadia was.

With no obligations on her end, Eva was able to spend most of her time thinking up ways to spoil her girlfriend. Every day she had a new bouquet of flowers delivered to Ethan Cole's office, until Nadia sent her a picture of five bouquets lining her desk, each one in a different stage of wilting. In fact, Eva got a lot of pictures since the boss was out of town on his honeymoon and life in the office was extremely slow.

Not just pictures of flowers and daily *How does my outfit look?* texts, either. One day Eva was minding her own business, having lunch with a friend, and opened her texts to see a gratuitous shot of Nadia's cleavage waiting for her.

Was that how it was going to be? *Did I mention this was the best summer ever yet?*

They spent most of their nights together, either at Nadia's house or Eva's downtown studio apartment. As much as Eva enjoyed having Nadia to liven her place up – not to mention make it *sexier* – she had to admit Nadia's house was cozy as hell. What was better than getting naked beneath those covers, windows open and admitting the sweet summer night sounds of trees rustling and birds chirping? The one night Eva went home to the family estate and went to bed alone was almost miserable. Didn't help Nadia had already gone to sleep and wasn't answering any texts until morning.

"Someone's having a good day," Henry said as they passed one another in the main hall of the house. "Don't mean myself."

He was dressed to take a spin in his Rolls-Royce convertible, probably to head up to Monica's place of business to either visit her or bring her home for her weekend. *And they say I dress funny.* Eva made fashion statements by wearing outlandish pantsuits that turned heads before her own head of blond could. Henry? He wasn't happy unless he looked like some douche straight from the '30s. Or was it the '40s? Anything from before 1980 gave Eva hives.

"There may or may not be some butterflies fluttering in the air this summer." Eva checked her hair and makeup in a large mirror before turning to her brother. His own reflection was good enough to talk to before then. "You're not the only one with summer romances to tend to, Henry."

He grinned, probably in remembrance of his own summer fling that turned into a happy marriage – one year ago, no less. *This time last year he was deeply in love with Monica and carrying on a relationship right beneath everyone's noses.* "So did you make up with that lady you were seeing? I seem to recall a little scenario at Cole's wedding."

Eva did her best to not shudder in embarrassment. "It was effective. Ahem."

"Good to hear that. If you're feeling serious with her, you should bring her to dinner tomorrow night. Now that her ex-boyfriend is married off, Monica has been turning her matchmaking sights on you, dear sister."

"Oh, please!" Pregnancy hormones had turned Eva's sister-in-law into a Cupid-like terror. And not the cute, cherub Cupid either. *I mean the crazy one who fucked up Psyche.* "I would love to be spared from that. First of all, what the hell does she know about lesbian attraction and love?" Eva held up her hand before her brother could say something *surely* witty. "Don't tell me. Don't wanna know."

"So bring your girlfriend by for dinner tomorrow to preemptively shut her up." Henry shrugged. "It's not like we don't know the young woman."

That might be part of the problem. Eva didn't care, but Nadia had implied she was self-conscious about re-meeting the Warrens under such circumstances. "I'll ask her about it. Sheesh. Only in this family do we get excited about Monday night dinners." They had Monica's work schedule to thank for that.

***

"Dinner with your family?" Nadia froze next to Eva. The air conditioner wasn't that powerful, was it? *Maybe we should cover these breasts up.* Eva pulled her bed covers up all the way – until they reached Nadia's fantastic tits, anyway. She couldn't bring herself to do it. Some sort of spiritual transgression would occur if Eva covered up those beautifully round breasts… with their firm pink nipples… little red hairs… *fuck!* Horny again. "I don't know about that."

Eva headed off the trepidation coming in her direction. "My parents aren't going to be there. Just my brother and his wife." That was all the family Eva needed. Even her parents barely got the honor since they made it clear she was barely a daughter of theirs. "I know it's awkward for you, but they know we're seriously dating now." Lots of people had received the message after the wedding. There were already rumors swimming around, but without people like Kathryn or Jasmine denying it, rumor turned into fervently accepted truth. *People can't stay out of others' business.* Didn't Eva know it! She was as bad sometimes. "I might as well bring you home to the folks, so to speak."

Nadia absentmindedly played with her hair as it splayed across one of Eva's pillows. What should have been a paradisiacal Sunday evening together was turning into discomfort. And Eva started it. "I'm not saying no," Nadia began. "But I'm also not readily saying yes."

"Babe," Eva said, wrapping her arms around her girlfriend. She dreaded the winter, when it might be too cold to be so naked together, even with the heater on. "It would mean a lot to me. They're hilariously old-fashioned in a lot of ways, but nice." Nicer than her parents, anyway.

"Okay, okay." Nadia laughed, uneasily. "I've got work, though."

"I'll come pick you up." Not like Eva had anything else going on a summery Monday.

"I'll have to change for something like that."

"Please. Whatever you're wearing to work in a billionaire's executive office is damn well good enough for dinner with my brother and his wife. Besides, they usually eat earlier, so we'll need to go right over."

Nadia looked the other way when Eva attempted to make eye contact. *Oh, give me a break.* Eva lowered her face – and planted it right between Nadia's breasts. *Yup. This is it. This is where I am meant to be for all eternity.*

"What the hell." At least Nadia was genuinely laughing now. "You're such a lesbian."

Was that a challenge? Eva grabbed both breasts, and with her face still planted firmly against Nadia's chest, shook them with enough vigor to cause an earthquake.

"Oh my God!" Eva almost got knocked off the bed for that. "You're killing me. Who knew you were this silly all along?"

Eva released her girlfriend's breasts and lifted her head. "What are you talking about? You think I'm cool and suave 24/7? Please. I get as ridiculous as anyone else when it comes to a pair of titties. As far as I'm concerned, it's the greatest part about being gay. I want to die from suffocating in tits." To prove her point, she pushed her face between them again. *What is she? A 36D?* Eva needed to find out so she could send her beloved more than flowers – how about some lingerie?

"Is that so? How about this?" Containing her giggles, Nadia grabbed one of her own breasts… and promptly smacked Eva's cheek with it.

"Hey! That was kinda hot."

"Oh, really? And the other one?" *Bap!*

"I dare you to do this at the dinner table tomorrow." *Don't. My sister-in-law will find it hilariously delightful.* "I would be so happy and horrified."

"Both good markers of a good dinner with the family." Nadia smooshed both of her breasts against Eva's face." *I mean, this is pretty great. Now can I figure out how to drown between her thighs?* Some of Nadia's orgasms made Eva feel like that was going to happen anyway. There was nothing like meeting that heat and wetness with nothing but her nose and tongue to experience it.

Neither of them were laughing when Eva caught her girlfriend's hand and sucked on one of those hard nipples. Good thing they had all the time in the world that night. Nadia may have work in the morning, but who cared? There was always more love to make.

***

Although her girlfriend said that whatever she wore to work would be good enough for dinner with the Warrens, Nadia was still critical of herself in the women's restroom mirror.

This can't be good enough, can it? Nadia had very little in the way of designers in her wardrobe. The few designer looks she did have were usually saved for extremely formal situations, like the few times she had to accompany said boss to one of his shindigs.

She tugged on the black dress she wore that day. Did it make her look fat? Eva always went on about Nadia's curves, but someone was bloated from PMS lately. Shit. Why did that pudge have to be there? It wasn't there that morning when Nadia got dressed at home! *Why did I eat that sodium bomb soup for lunch?* Sodium always made her pooch for a few hours.

She had too much cleavage. The skirt was too short. The designer was two seasons ago, not just one. Her makeup was overdone. Her hair needed to be washed. Holy shit! Where did this massive ass come from? Nadia distracted herself by opening her purse and pulling out her travel hairbrush. Least she could do was brush this shit one last time before answering Eva's texts saying she was waiting downstairs.

Something thumped in the handicap stall.

Nadia inhaled a deep breath. She slammed her hairbrush into her purse and pulled out a lipstick tube next. "Having fun in there, you two?" She reapplied her lipstick, leaning forward to make sure it was even – and that her cleavage wasn't *too* much for meeting family.

"Shit," someone hissed from the stall.

"Like you're the only ones who've gotten hinky in the stall before." Nadia could look back in fondness on that time in The Crimson Dove. "Having fun, Amber? Ms. Thomas?"

"Would you leave please?" Amber called. "Don't you have your own fuck date to get to?" Poor dear was so exasperated. *Can't imagine why. Is Adrienne really that good?* "Some of us are in the middle of ours and wouldn't mind getting rid of some overdue sexual tension."

"Oh my God!" Adrienne moaned. "Don't say that!"

"Come off it, girl. Like she doesn't know what we're doing in here."

Nadia finished her makeup and grabbed her phone. "*Be right down,*" she texted Eva. "*Juicy lesbian sex happening in the women's restroom. Guess who.*"

"*It better be between you and the women at work, because I need a hot image.*"

Nadia snorted as she turned off her phone and tossed it into her bag. "Wish me luck, ladies!" she cheerily called to the busy women in the handicap stall. "I'm off to meet my girlfriend's family. And then get laid."

"Have fun!"

"Oh my God. Shut up."

Nadia was grateful to get out of there and hop in the elevator. *At least my relationship isn't that messy.* Amber took the first week of Mr. Cole's honeymoon off, but that didn't mean the office was totally empty. Adrienne picked up the business slack while her partner was off honeymooning. At first, it was awkward between her and Nadia, as if Adrienne knew what Amber was spouting to her lesbian friend. Then things got worse when Amber returned from vacation that day. After all, a girl had a backlog of work for Mr. Cole to finish before he returned.

Although Nadia had seen the embarrassing shit they were up to at the wedding, she hadn't assumed that Amber and Adrienne were back together. Apparently they were, though. If so, celebrating in the bathroom was a weird way to do it. Not that Nadia had any room to judge.

"Aren't you the most gorgeous girl to come out of that building?" Eva leaned back in her driver's seat the moment Nadia approached. The warm summer evening made Nadia's dress stick even closer to her body, but what could she do? *Damn. Was hoping the Jaguar top would be up and the air conditioner on.* Nope. Eva had the top down and leaned back in a burgundy pantsuit, black silk tank top tucked into her trousers. Those sunglasses clashed fantastically with the amber and black onyx earrings dangling from her ears. Did she get a haircut? It looked shorter. "Get in here so I can take you home and rip that dress off you. I'll buy you a new one when we're done."

Nadia opened the door and slid into the comfortable passenger seat. Her seatbelt was barely on before Eva forced her way into traffic. "I thought we were having dinner first?"

"Oh, whatever. After that text you sent me a few minutes ago? I've got sex on the brain."

"You've always got sex on the brain." Eva was one entendre after another.

"Like you don't?" Nadia's girlfriend flashed her a dazzling smile before hitting the gas at a green light. "How many times have you called me saying you miss my amazing bed skills?"

"That was one time!" The only reason Nadia called her up to complain about how ornery she felt was because she had unfortunately come across some lesbian erotica on late night TV. It was awful, but it put the ideas in her head. *I wanted my girlfriend, okay?* She hoped this wasn't a honeymoon phase. Nadia was ready to have mind-blowing sex every day for the rest of her life. *Okay, don't get ahead of yourself here…*

Eva pulled off onto a side street the first chance she got. "One time is enough, sweetie. Puts certain expectations in my head."

"Says the girl wearing that sexy outfit."

"*I'm* in the sexy outfit? And what are you wearing? A burlap sack?"

Nadia giggled. "How far is it to your estate?"

"With traffic the way it is now? Uh, half an hour. At best."

That was being generous. The Warren Estate was still in city limits, but also on the outskirts of said city limits. Old money like these people wanted to stay close to the business happenings while having an air of country living. This was especially true for the Warrens who, as Nadia gathered from plenty of eavesdropping and a little digging of her own, once had a family big enough to command a formidable French-styled compound. The herd had thinned considerably since those early 20th century days, however. The only one living there full time was Henry Warren, and even with his child on the way, that was still a mere four Warrens to occupy the huge mansion as opposed to the fifteen or so a hundred years ago.

There were pictures of the premises online, and Eva had a few hanging around her apartment. None of those prepared Nadia for the grandeur surrounding her once they pulled onto the private lane and passed through security.

Wow. Nadia slipped farther down into her seat. Eva kept her eyes on the road, but only one hand on the steering wheel. This was a lane she had driven – with this car, no less – a thousand times. If it was kept this immaculate and clear? She could probably drive it blindfolded. *How much does it cost to keep this place running?* Evergreen trees lining the lane needed constant pruning. Flowers needed watering and weeding. The lawn? The lawn needed to be mowed at least once a week. That didn't account for the house itself!

"This side right here," Eva said, parking in a little alcove on the west side of the front property, "is all mine. Believe it or not, there are three addresses at this house. The West Wing is my address and will one day be my property."

"That's a thing?"

"What? Three addresses in one building? We get what we want. Makes inheritance so much easier. Brother gets the East Wing, I get the West."

"What about the middle?" The imposing U of this horseshoe made Nadia nervous. Eva barely showed any emotion as she came around and opened her girlfriend's door for her.

"That's where the staff lives."

Staff! Of course they had live-in staff. This place probably counted as a village. "No, I mean… who owns it? When your parents pass on, that is."

"Oh." Eva took her hand and helped her up. "Dunno. I'm assuming my brother, since he's the golden heir and all that bullshit."

Eva said this was to make inheritance easier, but it sounded like a mess to Nadia.

They walked hand-in-hand up to the main entrance in the middle of the U. *You know, where the staff lives.* Eva said hello to the butler awaiting them. A brief introduction made the man's eyebrows go up. *She doesn't introduce her girlfriend to the staff often, huh?* Nadia gave a small how-do-you-do before following Eva into the cool and open main hall.

Cold sweat covered her hand. From Eva.

"Baby?" Nadia asked, turning to her girlfriend. Eva was hard as stone as she gaped at the scene before her. When Nadia turned her head again, she was treated to a pair of older Warrens – she knew they were Warrens because of their ridiculous height and the commanding way they swept through their property. "Who are they?" Nadia knew. With that look on Eva's face? The way she grabbed Nadia's hand and refused to let it go?

"Eva!" the older woman greeted, approaching in a green sundress and ballet flats. Her long hair settled on her shoulders when she stopped, forcing a grin – and then letting that grin disappear when she saw the connection between Eva and Nadia. "Who is… this…"

Eva cleared her throat. "This is my girlfriend, Nadia." To Nadia, she grumbled, "This is my mother. Pretend she's not here."

Chapter 30

Nadia had been to a lot of awkward family dinners, but this one won without any contest.

The Warrens were an eclectic bunch, especially if Nadia threw herself in there for consideration. First, there was the mix of hair colors that made them look like they did it on purpose. The two blondes, Henry and Eva, were alike and yet so different. They had the same body type – gender aside – and hair representing different ends of the blond spectrum. Henry's sandy-colored hair blended seamlessly in with his white collared shirt and khaki trousers. Eva's hair almost looked platinum in comparison. When their mother, the esteemed Isabella Warren, sat down with her brown locks, Nadia turned to Gerald, a man with hair so white that Nadia did not doubt he was the one carrying the strong and Nordic genes.

Throw in Monica's silky dark hair and Nadia's red fluff, and they were all asking themselves the same superficial question: *what* color would the grandchildren's' hair be, anyway?

That was where the fun ended, however. Monica and Nadia also shared shorter statures – although Monica wasn't anywhere near as curvy as Nadia, pregnancy bump aside – but that didn't mean anything when the original Warrens were all over six feet tall. Eva clearly received her tastes in fashion from her mother. Both women preferred to wear colorful outfits that were the center of attention above their own feminine looks. The men? Everything they wore blended together in perfect unison.

It didn't matter how these people dressed, however. Their auras and body language brought out the awkwardness and ill feelings blooming between them.

Everything started at the head of the six-person table, where Henry sat, supposedly earning the right to usurp the patriarch because he now ran the house and business. His father, Gerald, sat at the other end, both men almost identical in their superficial mannerisms: they ate the same way, idled in their seats identically, and were masters at sparing glances without really looking like they were interested in what someone had to say. But where Gerald's actions were peppered with an air of sobriety so intense that it cleared up Nadia's acute allergies, Henry was downright casual. His wife Monica sat next to him and across from Nadia. The newest member of the Warren clan didn't have a bad look for anyone, including her mother-in-law on the other side of her, who never missed a chance to tell Monica that she was so *swollen.* What was wrong with that baby? She wasn't contaminating the gene pool, was she? *Oh my God. Kill me.* Eva had said her mother didn't approve of Monica as Henry's wife and mother of the next generation of Warrens, and now it was awful to watch Monica politely brush off her mother-in-law.

Isabella Warren, the once great Lady of the Warren Estate – before she lost that title to her daughter-in-law – was from another planet.

So was Gerald, but at least the patriarch kept to himself and let his wife do all the conniving and sniveling on both of their behalves. *Eva says he completely embarrassed himself to the family by getting into massive debt that his children had to bail him out of.* Gerald never looked happy with his new (non) station in the family, but he seemed to have made peace with it. He casually dismissed his daughter and her date, and they in turn paid him no attention either.

Isabella had to pick up the slack.

"So, *Evangeline,*" she said halfway through the appetizer. Eva stiffened beside Nadia. *So much for a simple family dinner.* Eva's discomfort was so tangible that Nadia could stroke it with the back of her hand. "I hear you went to the Governor's Ball a few weeks ago."

"Yes." Eva kept her eyes on her plate. Her posture became more rigid than before. "Henry couldn't go, so I went on the family's behalf. Was dreadfully boring, before you ask."

"Good thing I wasn't going to, then. Those events aren't supposed to be fun, unless you're a masochist." Wasn't that a lovely sneer? "Last I heard, there was only one masochist in this family." Her slitted eyes glared in Monica's direction. Nadia thought she was off the hook until she met Isabella's dire look. The moment it happened, Eva's hand rounded Nadia's bare knee and squeezed. "Unless you have something to share, Eva."

Stop squeezing me so hard! That pressure was transferring to Nadia's utensils. The servant arrived with a tray full of entrees. *It had to be pot roast, huh?* The same meal they ate the night Nadia and Eva first made love.

It was as if Eva had the same thought. "The only thing I had to share today was my girlfriend. Henry insisted I bring her to dinner."

Her brother dropped his knife and fork and gave her an exasperated look. *Good to know that even with the age difference they're still siblings.* With Nadia sitting between them, she got the brunt of the dirty looks shooting between Henry and Eva. "*Oh, sure, blame me for this." "You didn't tell me Mother and Father were going to be here! I would have rescheduled. And stayed far away." "I didn't know they would be here until the last minute. There wasn't enough time to let you know. I'm as shocked as you." "Fuck off, Henry."*

"Wasn't that sweet of your brother?" Isabella's mouth continued to twitch. "Always looking out for the young and beautiful women. He certainly has a type, doesn't he?"

Was there a faker laugh in the universe? Nadia shifted in her seat, uncomfortable. Eva, on the other hand, scoffed in disgust. "Henry has a reputation for being quite the gentleman, yes." Eva turned the attention to another poor victim. "Doesn't he, Monica?"

Better Monica than Nadia. At least Monica knew how to handle her mother-in-law by now, even if they didn't get along. "Yes." A poker face erupted at the table. *Damn.* Nadia had seen Monica's fake demeanor before, but it wasn't usually this intense. She stroked her husband's arm while they shared a sweet, matrimonial look. "Henry is a perfect gentleman."

"Which begs to question why you have not met a fine young gentleman of your own yet," Isabella continued. The smiles – even the fake ones – fell off everyone else's faces. "That goes to the both of you. Surely, two lovely young ladies like you must be dripping eligible suitors." Oh. Oh no. That treacherous face was now pointed at Nadia. *I've known this woman for one hour and I both fear and loathe her.* "Eva I can understand, though. Look at my poor daughter. Tries to dress like a man. She always did idolize her big brother a little too much…"

Eva's utensils clattered against her plate. Nadia put her hand on her girlfriend's arm, right in front of Isabel. "I think Eva is beautiful. I know I'm not the only one. Man or woman." That was more for Isabel's benefit, but Eva flinched to hear that men might think she was beautiful. *I know, I know, you don't want male attention at all.* Neither did Nadia most of the time, but she handled it better than Eva did. Because of how they were socialized growing up? Because of what Eva had been through? Who knew what the real reason was. "She works so hard and yet manages to look so fashionable. You see her in the papers all the time." Eva hadn't been kidding when she said she was a bit of style icon in the papers. If they couldn't get pics of her having lesbian love affairs with women who had no business being outed, then they took large, close-up glamour photos of her. Two weeks ago Nadia opened a paper to see a small spread of Eva in different colored outfits, the article writer commenting favorably on her flawless sense of style. "*A bit more bold colors and patterns than most closets should boast, but when has Eva Warren not managed to pull of the more gauche styles? Givenchy should start paying her to be their unofficial spokes model. Mark my words, this time two months from now young heiresses with power on the mind will be dressing like Eva again."* Nadia had read that caption fondly back then. Now she worried for her girlfriend. What other things were people saying about Eva – both in front of her and behind her back?

"My daughter has always had more unconventional tastes. She used to wear such beautiful dresses. We had an old family seamstress who made them all. Absolutely delightful. Then again, she also used to have the prettiest hair."

"It's still pretty."

Isabella tensed. "If you like the shorn look. Which I do not care for. A woman should appreciate her head of hair while she still has her natural coloring. Take yourself, for instance, Ms. Gaines. You're one of the most stunning redheads I have ever seen."

"Um," Nadia began, not sure where to look. To Isabella, who was possibly complimenting her? Or to Eva, who was shooting daggers of warning in her direction? *Don't look at Monica.* Her poker face was faltering. That couldn't have been a good sign. "Thank you."

"What are you? Irish?"

Both Eva and Monica dropped their utensils again. Butterfingers was now an official Warren trait.

"I… yes. Some Irish." Should Nadia have been entertaining these thoughts? "I'm a bit of this and that. My family didn't really keep track. I think we are a bit German and Slavic too."

"German… and Slavic…" Now the smile was totally gone. "Don't suppose your mother's maiden name is Goldstein or Epstein?"

"Mother!"

"All right, Mother," Henry gently said. "This is Nadia's first time visiting. She's not on to you yet. If you want to ask if she's Jewish, just ask."

"I…"

"Don't answer that," Eva hissed.

Nadia had a feeling nothing good came from her being both Irish and Jewish. *I don't know if I'm Jewish!* She also didn't know how that culturally worked. Something about her mother being the one who counted… would Isabella be more pleased to know any Jewish heritage came from Nadia's father? Her mother's side was as Irish as it got. (And not Jewish-Irish, either. Staunchly Catholic to a fault.)

"Why, you two make me sound like a racist or something." Isabella sniffed. "Not sure how I feel about that. Why does it matter, anyway? Not like even if you two get married this young woman's genes will be entering our pool." That cold look was not reserved for Nadia. It went straight into Monica, who bore it well.

"It's too early to be talking about that anyway," Eva insisted. "Nadia and I have only been dating for a short time."

"Now, Eva…" Gerald's voice was so rarely heard that everyone at the table looked at him. "Let's not by hasty about our fads."

"Oh, for the love of…" Eva put her elbows on the table and pushed her forehead against her hands. "I'm *gay,* okay? That's not changing. Ever. I date women. Get over it."

"This is hardly appropriate dinner conversation."

"Henry, control your dinner table. What kind of man are you?"

"Now, Bella, that's not necessary. Our son is taking care of our business well."

"Business, yes, but what about this?" Isabella gestured to Monica as if she weren't there. "Business is great! His personal life is a mess. Look at what he lets our daughter get away with."

"I'm twenty-fucking-five."

"Eva! Do not swear at the table! At least be that much of a lady."

"For the love of… son, control your table."

"Funny, Father. You always make it feel like *your* table when you come home."

"Well…"

Nadia cut them off after that. *This pot roast is delicious.* This dysfunctional family was a mess, or at least when the parents came home. The way both Eva and Henry quietly dealt with their parents' bullshit was both mature and unfortunate. Henry was mature. Eva was unfortunate.

The tension built up in Eva until she had to excuse herself. She came back five minutes later to a much more subdued table now that the topic had changed to the latest goings-on in the bustling region of western Montana, where Isabella and Gerald now lived, but the damage had been done. All Henry and Monica could say after dinner adjourned was, "You survived that. Things can only get better from here."

***

"I'll take you home," Eva insisted after dinner. The sun was still out, although it threatened to descend behind the trees even at seven in the middle of summer. "You shouldn't have to deal with these people."

"No, it's fine." Nadia took her hand, the two of them standing outside the dining room. Much to Eva's relief, her parents followed Henry and his wife into the East Wing, barraging them with names they had picked. "You invited me to the stay the night. So I will."

"You don't understand. My parents stay in my part of the house when they visit. Which means they'll be all up in my business until I go to bed."

Nadia wrapped her arms around Eva's midsection. *Damn, she is so tense.* Not that Nadia blamed her. "So go to bed early. With me."

Finally, Eva softened. "And get up early so I can take you to work." Neither of them mentioned Nadia's overnight bag which had been dropped off in Eva's room. *I can't believe my girlfriend has her own servants to wait on her when she's here. How crazy is that?* "All right, but I preemptively apologize for anything they might say or do. They are not pleasant. You saw them at dinner."

"Yes, I was there. Nobody was happy with them."

"No. Monica doesn't say anything because she's a people-pleaser and wants to keep the in-laws placated considering how much they disapprove of Henry marrying her. I…" Eva stopped. Nadia turned, facing one very pregnant woman, arms crossed on top of her bulge.

"Monica doesn't say anything because she's long learned to pick her battles." Monica shrugged. "And the last thing I need right now is stress.

No offense, Eva, but your parents aren't worth the stress. I can deal with them."

She stepped forward, warm smile radiating and hands extending to Nadia. *Are we happy now? Have things settled down?* Nadia took Monica's small hands. She guessed this was their first time touching, although they had known each other for as long as Nadia had been working for Mr. Cole.

"It's so lovely to have you finally visit us as Eva's girlfriend, Ms. Gaines." Monica had a firm touch that courted a greater strength than even Nadia had given her credit for. "She's been pining after you for so long that I almost thought she had lost her mind."

Was that a compliment? It was totally a compliment, yeah?

"Thank you." Nadia released Monica's hands. "It took some convincing, I admit. I don't think I'm as readily available to this lifestyle as you are." Monica had an extensive history dating billionaires. Not to mention the business she ran catering to them. What did Nadia have going for her? *I work for her ex-boyfriend, one of those other billionaires.* Nadia had never courted dreams of dating above her station. Hadn't she spent many months turning down Eva's advances for that reason? *That and other reasons, I suppose.*

"Oh, it's not so bad if you have someone on your side. Eva's probably the least spoiled out of all of us. Why, she's almost normal!"

"Thanks, Monica."

"My pleasure." Monica turned, her gait pointing her straight toward the entrance of the East Wing. "Now please excuse me. Part of knowing my battles is pretending to go along with Isabella's ridiculous name suggestions. She's under the impression that I am naming my child Esther after her grandmother. I think she might be disappointed, but she doesn't have to know."

A maid came up to Eva the moment Monica disappeared down another hallway. "If it pleases you, Miss, your room is ready."

"*Yes,* it pleases me." Eva swung her arm around Nadia's shoulders. "I need a hard drink, and you need to see what it's like to live in true Warren luxury, my dear."

Nadia was equal parts dreading and looking forward to this. As someone who loved watching those house buying shows on TV, Nadia was eternally curious about how these types of homes were laid out and what they looked like up close. However, that was purely from an observational point of view. She didn't want to be immersed in them like Eva was. One thing to enjoy such surroundings from afar, from the comfort of her middle class home and on her medium-sized TV with spotty reception during rainy days. Quite another to traipse through them herself and pretend to be a part of that world.

Indeed, Eva's personal wing of this large manor was a bit… much.

It truly was another home within a home. They went down a long hallway, paneled in white wood and lined with soft burgundy carpets that almost matched the color of Eva's suit. Paintings of landscapes hung on the wall. A few floral pictures. Large windows let in the evening sunlight and illuminated the details of the early 20th century architecture. *It's lovely. Like walking through the country club or a hotel.* Not exactly Eva's house.

Doors led to various rooms one would find in any other home. A large chef's kitchen, currently stocked with Eva's favorite foods but otherwise devoid of life. A dining room that was completely clean aside from a coffee table stacked with business textbooks. *Does she spend a lot of evenings here eating dinner and studying?* Nadia glanced at her girlfriend as they continued down the hall. Summer had been good to Eva. She was a lot mellower compared to some of the anxiety she boasted during the school term.

"That's the living area. Den. Whatever." Eva leaned against the doorway. Nadia peeked in. *Wow. That is a white room.* Definitely made it brighter and more cheerful than other rooms. "One of the only rooms I've actually remodeled to my tastes. Besides my bedroom, anyway."

Nadia took her hand again. "I'd like to see your bedroom."

Eva stopped them in the hallway so she could waggle her eyebrows at her girlfriend. "Would you, now? The evening is still young. I was thinking some cocktails out on my balcony and enjoying the sunset. I have a fantastic view of the mountains to the west. This time of year it's great to sit out there and enjoy the warmth."

"All right."

They did that, detouring through another small living quarter (that didn't look like it had been used much aside from the occasional guest) and trekking up a private staircase to Eva's bed chambers. *This is the size of her studio apartment downtown. Sheesh.* Nadia couldn't be surprised anymore. Of course Eva had another living area and master bath enclosed next to her huge bedroom. Because of course she did!

The only thing that shocked Nadia was the view. First, the balcony was gigantic, running the entire length of Eva's private quarters. Outdoor furniture speckled the stone flooring and railing. Eva mixed them their cocktails while Nadia gazed at the summer sunset descending the lavender mountains in the distance. Bright evergreen trees clustered together on the edge of the property. Wildflowers bloomed in a variety of yellows and oranges. The air was so warm, the breeze so refreshing that Nadia needed neither a sweater nor a fan to maintain perfect temperature. Eva removed her jacket before she sat down with two margaritas, one glass passing to Nadia the moment she whipped out her phone to take some pictures.

"This is so going on Instagram." Nadia sipped her margarita and took pictures at the same time. "Obviously I won't turn my GPS tracking on."

"Take all the pics you want. Told you it was a great view."

Nadia put her phone down. Eva contemplated the scenery while she drank her margarita, legs crossed on her lounge chair. "You all right?"

Eva forced a smile. She didn't have the same poker face that Monica Warren did, that was for sure. "I'm fine as long as you're here."

That should've been something sweet to hear at the end of a long day. *How many people get to spend their Monday evenings like this?* Nadia still had four more days of work that week, but this was not a bad way to start things off. *Is now a good time to ask if I can stay at her place all week?* Nadia had been entertaining that idea for a while. No, she wasn't in a huge hurry to move in with Eva – quite the opposite. *One thing at a time!* But she did like the idea of spending every night that week curled up in Eva's bed. *Or I guess we could keep switching locations.* Someone had to watch that house Nadia was renting, she supposed.

"Be right back, love." Eva stood and bestowed a kiss upon Nadia's brow. "Gonna get another drink. One wasn't enough. You want another?"

"No, thanks." There had been wine at dinner. Enough for Nadia. "I'll wait for you here."

Wait Nadia did.

For a long while.

How much time passed before Nadia got up to investigate where her girlfriend was? Fifteen minutes? Twenty minutes? Plenty of time to relax. Almost too much time. When Nadia realized that the sun was going down incredibly quickly, she also noticed that Eva should've been back long before now. *Is she okay?* Nadia left her empty glass on her chair and, bypassing Eva's burgundy jacket left on *her* chair, went into the West Wing to locate her girlfriend.

She found her in the private living area. With her mother.

"It's not appropriate!" Isabella insisted. "I don't care what that girl does with her life. You know why I don't care? Because she's not a part of this family and never will be. I've made one concession for your brother. You think you're going to be pardoned, Eva? Especially after how you *embarrassed* us in front of the Monroes? Fat chance in hell of that!"

Nadia steeled herself where she stood. Nobody had seen her yet. Least of all Eva, who kept her eyes down and her demeanor grim. "This might shock you, Mother, but you don't get to decide who I do or do not marry… including their gender. First of all, Nadia and I aren't serious. You could look forward to us breaking up for good. I bet you'd like that."

"Don't be impertinent."

"Or maybe I *will* marry her one day. Did you hear? That's legal now. In every state. Including this one, and even fucking Montana before you think about dragging me there to marry some billionaire cow hand."

"Why are you so disagreeable? Why won't you listen to me for once?"

"Is this why you randomly showed up today? To lecture me about my future? *Again?* Save it for voicemail next time."

"Your father and I dropped by because our grandchild is about to be born. You think I want to miss that?"

"You hate Monica!"

"Oh, for Pete's sake, I don't hate her! I don't *approve* of her. How can I when she has the past that she has? That doesn't mean I'm going to hold it against my grandchild. That baby is going to be your brother's heir. It's my duty to make sure it's born healthy and raised well."

"You mean raised the way you want it to be."

"Why does that have to go against your brother's wishes?"

"What about Monica's? Or did you forget she's the baby's mother?"

"Don't make this about Monica. I came here to talk to you. Look at me! For God's sake, why can you never look me in the eye? Did I give birth to a doormat?"

"If you think I'm a doormat, then you haven't been seeing what I've been up to for the past ten years."

"Of course, Eva. I've had a front row seat to your rebellion since the day you decided to be a teenager… and never stop."

"Would you please *leave?* I've got a guest and don't want to be rude."

"Fine." Isabella turned toward the nearest door. "We'll discuss this later. And don't worry. Last I heard Mr. Damon Monroe had himself a new squeeze, so you're off the hook with him. Hmph. All that money lost, though."

"Good night, Mother."

"Yes, dear. Good night."

Isabella left her daughter's chambers. Eva went to her liquor cabinet with a huff. It was only then she spotted Nadia at the far end of the room.

"How much of that did you hear?"

Nadia wrung her hands together. "Enough, probably."

"Fuck." Eva stopped pouring – and then kept pouring. "I always hope nobody hears that shit. My mother's such a homophobic mess." She took a shot and then poured herself another.

Nadia approached. "From the sounds of it, she approves of no one, male or female."

"But there are males she approves of. She'll never approve of me marrying a woman."

"Too bad there's nothing she can do about that, huh?"

Time to pour another shot.

"Eva," Nadia said softly. She put her hand over the top of the shot glass. "I'm sorry she treats you that way. Nobody deserves that."

"Whatever. It's the price I pay for being born privileged."

"I said nobody deserves that. Not even as a price to pay."

Eva put her bottle away. "I'm sorry. She fucks me up."

"I'm sure she does." Nadia forced herself into one of Eva's hugs. The arms wrapping around her, however, were limp. *She's a million miles away right now.* Thinking about her mother's stinging words? Wishing she was back in San Diego or Hong Kong? Wishing she was alone? *Should I go?* No. That would be a bad day. Eva would turn back to that bottle so quickly that Nadia would be kicking herself to hear the hungover voicemail the next day. *Assuming she doesn't end up in the hospital to begin with.* "But you don't answer to her. You have your own life. She probably hates that. She's lost a lot of control in your family and will do anything to glom on to a bit of it." Nadia garnered that based on what she heard and observed. *Billionaires. It's how they are.*

"She's been trying to control me since the day I was born." Eva sat down on the nearest couch. Her black tank top lost its sheen the more she pouted. Nadia stood behind her and ran fingers through gelled blond hair. "I know they were disappointed when I was born a girl. I told you I was a spare?"

"Yeah. You've mentioned it." Nadia knew about those politics too. *An heir and a spare and as many as you can bear.*

"It's true, okay? They've never hidden it. But I know they wish I were a boy. When I was born a girl, the sexism kicked in. I was still a spare, but my main role in life was to grow up a good girl who would be married off to some family like the Monroes. My mother says she and my father were a love match, but I know they were introduced. Besides. Those people? In love?"

"It can happen. I'm sure you've seen it. I've seen it too."

Eva scoffed. "What do *you* know?"

Angry fingers dug into Eva's scalp. "I know and see a lot, baby. I hear people's conversations when they think I'm not listening. You think I've been at my job for this long and don't notice things people are talking about? I've seen marriages come and go in as little as two years." One case in particular stood out in Nadia's memory. *The Klines.* Magda and Stewart Kline. They had just married when Nadia started working for Mr. Cole. In the two years she had worked there, Magda had gone from sweet and in love to the most irritable wretch in the world. Stewart? He was on his third mistress in six months. Apparently trying to have their own heirs took a toll on their love. Not that Nadia thought it excused the yelling and the cheating, but she had seen it happen to one billionaire couple… so why couldn't it happen to another? Eva's parents were not exempt, especially if they felt pressured to have a second child long after Isabella probably thought she was done with childbearing. Mothers had taken out issues on their daughters for a lot less.

"Be that as it may," Eva grumbled, leaning away from Nadia's touch. "It didn't give her or my father the right to treat me like they did. I've never felt love from them. Only expectations and subsequent disappointments. The only time they made a public showing of caring for me was because I was an investment."

"I'm sorry."

"Yeah," Eva said with a sigh. "Me too. Trust me. There isn't enough money in the world to make up for my mother petting my hair when I was eight and calling me her precious porcelain doll."

Nadia felt a million shudders tear through Eva, even though she could not see them. *Oh, no.* Nadia certainly couldn't relate. Not only had she been conventionally feminine from the time she could remember, but her mother was always laissez-faire about how her daughter lived (within moderation, of course.) Nadia was tentatively out to her parents, but only because it was an awkward conversation to have with them. Neither her mother nor her father seemed to care for the most part. Nadia hadn't mentioned Eva yet, but she didn't doubt they would be excited to know how rich she was. *Money would definitely buy their happiness in that regard.*

"Do you think… that's part of the reason you're butch now?"

"Who are you? My shrink?" Eva leaned back in the couch again. She welcomed Nadia's hands on her face. "I've wondered that sometimes, but the inclination has always been there. I think I would've ended up like this even if my parents were supportive of it. I only went along with the hair and dresses growing up because I had to. As soon as I had more control over my life, I cut that shit out. Literally." She pointed to her short hair. "I haven't let it get past my ears since high school."

"But you've worn some dresses."

"Only when pertinent, like my brother's wedding. I don't hate dresses. I prefer to not wear them. Unlike you." Eva rolled her eyes. "Still can't get over that time you wore pants in front of me."

"First of all, I was at home." Nadia left a soft kiss between Eva's eyes. "And second of all, guess what?"

"What?"

"I love you."

Eva lifted her head. "You mean that, huh?"

"Yeah, I do." Maybe it was a tenuous love early in a relationship, but it was definitely love of some kind. Nadia cared for this woman who was more silly kid than super serious adult, even though Eva could certainly be serious when she put her mind to it. She enjoyed spending time with Eva. She wanted to get to know her more and maybe explore a more serious relationship later on. It may not be deep romantic love yet, but it could certainly turn into it sooner rather than later. "Do you love me?"

"Absolutely." Eva reached up and brought down Nadia's head for a kiss. Their lips grazed before meeting again. "You're one of my favorite things about life right now."

Nadia blushed to hear something like that said so candidly. "What can I do to take your mind off the bullshit of your parents showing up to make your life hell?"

Eva flung herself across her couch. "What do you think? Take off that dress, babe. Nothing makes me happier than seeing you prance around in your underwear."

"Hmph." Nadia walked away, sure to sashay her hips so her ass did nothing but entice her girlfriend to follow her into the bedroom. "Think you get to order me around like that?" *I kinda like it when you order me around.* There were a lot of things pushing Nadia away early on in their relationship. This, however, was one of the things pulling her *toward* Eva. *Maybe she'll spank me. Ooh.* Nadia lingered in the bedroom doorway. Without looking back at Eva, she pulled down her zipper, showing off the strap of her black bra beneath. "Let me give *you* a little order, Ms. Warren. Do me hard and good so I don't regret coming to your mansion on an otherwise nondescript Monday night."

Eva was off that couch before Nadia could scurry into the bedroom and scurry *out* of that dress. By the time Eva entered, kicking and locking the door behind her, Nadia was in nothing but her underwear, posing like a Victoria's Secret model.

The way Eva stared at her made Nadia feel like a model, that was for sure.

"Oh, no, what am I going to do? There's a gorgeous girl here. In her *underwear.*"

Nadia sat on the end of the bed. Usually she hated how everything jiggled when she moved that quickly in her underwear. In Eva's bedroom, though? She knew that every little vibration got her closer to an earth-shattering orgasm.

Seeing herself through another woman's eyes was always a great trip.

"Come on, Ms. Warren." Nadia crossed her legs and shook her hair behind her shoulders. "Come and take control of me. Whatever you want."

"Whatever *I* want? How about you?" Eva's eyes were already glazing over from the many possibilities entering her mind. "What do you want, babe?"

"I want whatever you're offering." What did Nadia have to do? Unsnap the front of her bra and let her breasts pop out? Oh. Okay. She could do that.

"God. You have no idea what you're getting yourself into." Eva loomed over her girlfriend, her demeanor going from soft to hard as fuck in fewer than five seconds. "One of these days I'll show you what it's really like to be beneath me."

"Hopefully sooner rather than later." Nadia shook off her bra. So this was what it felt like to be mostly naked on a billionaire's mansion bed? Huh. She should've tried it out sooner. Felt pretty… powerful. Especially when the billionaire was a woman as hot as she was cold at times.

"Lay back. I'm taking these panties off with my teeth, and then fucking you until you can't come anymore."

What Eva promised, she often delivered. Nadia was particularly impressed with how her girlfriend could maintain control even when *someone* was thrashing around like a wannabe porn star. *I refuse to believe that anything we do is pornographic.* Eva was the worst of them. Nadia may have the porn star ready body, but Eva was the one who knew how to make the bed hit the wall and make her girlfriend moan so loudly that more than one servant appeared outside the door wondering if everyone was all right.

Nadia knew, because she was at the edge of the bed, watching their shadows dance on the other side of the door while Eva rammed her from behind. Normally Nadia didn't like exhibitionism, but there was definitely something to be said for half the household knowing she was having some of the best fucking sex ever. Nadia didn't care if Eva used her fingers, her tongue, or a plethora of fancy sex toys that made a girl's G-spot throb in pleasure. All she knew was that it felt good and she was happy to help her girlfriend feel better for a little while.

Not like it didn't make her feel better too!

Chapter 31

Nadia finished applying her makeup in Eva's bathroom mirror early Tuesday morning. "Hey," she greeted her girlfriend, accepting a kiss to her cheek. Eva dumped two sex toys into the sink before stumbling to the adjacent water closet. Nadia had woken up an hour ago to shower and get ready for work, but Eva was content to now roll out of bed and take her own shower before driving Nadia to her job downtown. "Trying to make a statement Ms. Warren?"

Eva mumbled something before suddenly becoming coherent. "I'll clean 'em up! Even though that's your cum all over them…"

At least she didn't leave it for the servants to do. Nadia politely ignored the eight-inch purple strap-on (ribbed for her pleasure, no less) and the glass dildo clattering next to it. *Can't believe she actually let me use one on her.* Nadia was used to her more butch lovers preferring to keep the penetration focused on her. Eva, on the other hand, was practically begging for it by the time Nadia had already come three times. *She still had all the control, though.* Telling Nadia what to do, how to do it, when to stop, when to pull out, when to fuck her again… Eva was totally a power bottom in another life.

I'm a fool for her bossing me around in the bedroom. Who knew?

Nadia put her makeup away and dragged her purse back into the bedroom. Did she smell breakfast waiting for her out in the living area? Time to investigate.

Indeed, she did find hot coffee, bagels, and healthy spreads waiting for her on a small coffee table. She also found Isabella Warren, sitting on a couch and sparing Nadia an exasperated look.

"You," she snapped, fingers included. "Come over here, would you? Ahem. Please."

Nadia froze where she stood. "Um."

"Are you daft or deaf? I don't have all morning. Trust me, dear, if you're dating my daughter, you don't want to piss me off."

And you want to piss me off? Nadia went, anyway, against her best judgment. Was Eva already in the shower? Shit. At least her girlfriend could fend off the monster-in-law.

"My," Isabella said, almost approvingly. "Aren't you a pretty thing?" She gestured to the blue cinch dress adorning Nadia's body. "You are gorgeous, dear, I'll give you that. Would've killed for a body like yours back in my prime. Those are some very nice childbearing hips you have. Too bad you're not a woman of means looking for a husband. I've got a son, you know."

Nadia stepped back. How was she supposed to respond to *that?*

"So. I may not understand my daughter's sexual interests, but I'll have to hand it to her – she always picks pretty women for her playthings." Isabella drank her morning coffee as if she hadn't insulted poor Nadia. "Which begs the question. What *am* I going to do about you?"

"Hopefully nothing." Nadia checked the time on her phone. Eva better hurry up and get her out of this mess. *Tonight we're sleeping at my place.*

"Now, now, I can't do *nothing.* You see, I only have two children, and the oldest has gone and married a woman I can't in good conscience condone. Do you know anything about her history? Her present, for Pete's sake? That woman is used goods on the market. Not to mention how she embarrasses us all with that… business… of hers." Apparently, Isabella Warren did not appreciate a good brothel catering to rich clientele into BDSM. "Let me tell you one thing if nothing else, Ms. Nadia. At some point Eva will have to do her familial duty if she wants to stay in it. Perhaps she won't be marrying a Monroe anytime soon, but she *will* marry a man of particular means if she would like to remain a member of good standing in this family."

Nadia squared her shoulders. *What bullshit.* "Last I checked she was about to get her Master's in Business."

"And? Won't mean a thing if nobody will hire her." Isabella sent her a dour look. "Including her brother."

"What are you talking about?"

"Henry hasn't committed anything to Eva yet. He won't, either. He screwed up badly enough marrying that woman. He's interested in making amends to secure his inheritance for his supposed family. That means obeying us when we ask him to fall in line on this matter."

"Why are you telling me this?"

"*Because,* dearie, I thought it was good to give you fair warning. Your time with my daughter is fleeting. I don't care what she does behind closed doors even though I find it disgusting. No offense."

"Oh, none taken." Nadia rolled her eyes.

"But when Eva marries, she'll need to keep up appearances. That means keeping a pretty thing like you in the shadows until she's old and gray. Now, if I may say so, you are *far* too pretty to be kept in any shadows. You'd be better off moving on and finding someone new. Someone who can appreciate you. Someone who…"

"Mother."

Eva stood behind Nadia, dressed in a college T-shirt and jeans. "Ah, good morning," Isabella greeted. "Was having a chat with this lovely young woman here."

"I bet you were. Unfortunately for you, I need to get her to work."

"Right, right. I believe I heard mention that she works at Ethan Cole's office?"

"She's his receptionist."

"Isn't that the ex-boyfriend of…"

"Your daughter-in-law. Yes. It's a small world, isn't it?" Eva grabbed Nadia's arm and pulled her toward the door. *Ow!* While Nadia understood her girlfriend was in a hurry to get the fuck out of there, was this really the way to make it happen? "We've really gotta get going."

"You two have fun!" Isabella called after them. "But not too much fun. Remember that we have an image to maintain. Try to keep the homo out of the press for once, would you, Eva?"

Isabella had said a lot of shit over the past twelve hours. Certainly she had said a lot to humiliate Eva. But something about that last line… *The press. The homo. Eva. An image to maintain.*

By the time they were in the Jaguar, Nadia exploded.

"That woman is horrible!"

The engine remained idle. Eva's hands were on her legs. "My father isn't much better. She's just their mouth."

"I knew she didn't like me, but the way she was… the way she was commenting on my body and talking about our sex life."

Eva took her hand. "I'm sorry. I really didn't think they would be here. I think it's best if you don't come back to this house until they finally go back to Montana."

That wasn't the point. That hadn't been the point since the beginning of their relationship.

I need to own up to it. I need to face the fact I'm dating a billionaire heiress. Eva could dress up in a T-shirt and jeans, but this was a Jaguar they were sitting in, and *that* was a fucking mansion-compound-palace! Eva had a mountain of pressure on her that she often kept hidden from the world, let alone her girlfriends. Shit! She was usually dating supermodels! Her best friend was fighting with Adrienne Thomas for the title of richest woman in the city! Eva was going to have a career like most people Nadia knew, but she would not be working beneath anyone… not even her brother. She was vying for an equal share in the family business, even if she had to work her way up to it. *Get me out of here.* Nadia had half a mind to exit the car. But what would she do? Call an Uber and wait for it to show up at the Warren Estate? Ha! They wouldn't make it through the three lines of security!

"Is there anything I can do to make you feel better?" Now it was Eva's turn to throw that back at Nadia. Except she didn't mean sex. Sex was not going to save Nadia's sanity right now.

What had Jasmine told her long ago? "*For one, you don't have to worry about money. Ever. That's the craziest thing to get used to.*" Nadia had never gotten used to it. She didn't like it when Eva made a show out of spending money on her. She hadn't even let her heiress girlfriend buy her something beyond dinner. Oh, and trips around the world, but that didn't count. Not in the way Nadia thought about spending money.

"Don't know," she muttered. "Take me to work."

They made it to the office in record time, although not fast enough. Half the office was already there, and Nadia barely had time to kiss her girlfriend goodbye and get to her desk. There may not have been any appointments that morning since Mr. Cole was still on his honeymoon, but there were phone calls to answer. Mr. Cole would have a very full schedule to come back to.

"Did I see you escorted in here by Eva Warren?" Amber asked, hopping on Nadia's desk. "Because that's what it looked like. Naughty girl. You two make up again?"

"Yup. Spent the night at her place." Nadia finished logging into her computer. "And by her place, I mean the Warren Estate."

"Wow. That place is nice. I've been there for work."

"Not as nice as Adrienne's place, I'm sure."

"Granted, she's got a swank apartment a few blocks from here. But I prefer when she takes me *out* of her apartment, if you know what I mean."

"No, I don't." Nadia glanced up at her supposed friend. *Are we friends again?* "Is she going public with you?"

"Huh? No. But she makes sure I'm good and spoiled. See this?" Amber showed off a shiny tennis bracelet. "Bought it for me this weekend in New York City. She took me there for some fun. Guess we're back on now too."

"You're over her fucking that guy at the bachelorette party?"

"Like I didn't fuck a guy that weekend too."

"You two…"

"Are such stereotypes. I know. We deserve each other, yadda yadda."

Nadia didn't pretend to understand bisexual drama. She barely understood lesbian drama. *When the two collide… yikes.* "Do you like her? Like… *like* her, like her."

"If you mean do I wanna marry her… eh. Dunno. She's fun, but high maintenance. Everything has to be her way and she gets frustrated with me easily. She's still pissed about being bi, if you ask me. Girl has a lot of issues to work through. Me? I made my peace long ago."

"You follow the money, yeah?"

"I guess. Adrienne makes sure I have nothing to want for. She's paying my rent so I could move closer to her."

"Wow."

"What's your honey buying for you?"

Nadia looked at her desktop and then back at Amber.

She picked up the phone and called HR.

"Hi, sorry, Nadia Gaines here. I made it to work but I feel like *death*. Think I have the flu. Amber's gonna take over for me today, okay? Cough. Cough."

"I am, huh?"

Nadia hung up. Then she picked up her phone and called Eva, hoping she had caught her before she left.

"Hey, baby," she said in a sing-song voice. Amber made a gagging motion in front of her. "I called in sick. You're going to come get me and take me out for the day. I want the works. You're sparing no expense."

"Thatta girl," Amber said when Nadia hung up on her girlfriend. "Get that money before she slips through your dexterous lesbian fingers."

Oh, Nadia was going to make sure that happened. First stop? Ensuring she never had to take the bus again.

Chapter 32

"Does it have to be Italian, though?" Eva whined, standing in the middle of a damn car dealership. "You are so transparent right now."

Nadia was ignoring her. She was all about ignoring Eva right now.

See, there was this Fiat Nadia had her eyes on the moment they walked into the dealership. A Fiat. A perfectly fine car, Eva was sure, but it was not what she had in mind when Nadia outrageously asked for a *car*. For one, Eva now associated all things Italian (particularly automobile) with Ethan Cole, a man who owned every kind of Italian sports car there was. Eva may have owned a Lambo, but there reached a point in a woman's life where she had to back away from so much Italian anything.

"I love it," Nadia exclaimed, keeping her hands on her face so she wouldn't put her prints all over the black Fiat. "Look at the red trim, Eva."

"I see the red trim." And the red interior. It wasn't the same red as Nadia's hair, but it was definitely very *her*. Even the shape of the car fit the short and curvy frame Nadia ran around with. *That's not the point.* When

Nadia called her back that morning, telling her she was taking a sick day and wanted to spend the day together… well, this wasn't what Eva had in mind.

Not that she had a problem with buying her girlfriend expensive items. In fact, Eva had tried multiple times to spoil Nadia silly with shopping trips. So far, though, Eva's girlfriend was uncomfortable with things bigger than a dinner and a night in a hotel. *Basically, she doesn't want tangible things from me.* Until now, anyway. Nadia was cashing in her "dating a billionaire heiress" chips and this was how she decided to start things off with?

Whatever, right?

The salesman had instantly recognized Eva, much to her detriment. Oh, as a couple of women coming into a car dealership, Eva knew they were at a disadvantage. Hilariously enough, being recognized only made things worse for them. This man knew exactly how much money Eva had at her disposal. (Which was a lot. A cool billion if all her investments and such were added up.) What was the cost of a new car to her? They were going to give her the female *and* rich bitch markup!

Eva was already adding it up in her head by the time Nadia was allowed to get into the driver's seat and squeal in excitement. *God, guess it's worth it.* Nadia almost never looked that happy. Not even with Eva.

"Would you look at that?" Eva quipped, coming closer to the car. "Red wheels. That's cute."

Nadia pulled down her sunglasses. "How do I look? Ready to go to work?"

Eva leaned through the window. "Ready to go anywhere. Except for on a date with me. I get to drive you around for those."

Giggling, Nadia checked herself in the rearview mirror. The salesman stood before the hood, grinning in the knowledge that he could make a super easy sale here.

"You want this car, huh?"

Nadia slammed her hand against the horn. Both Eva and the salesman jumped back with separate heart attacks. "Fuck yeah I want this car!" Nadia cried over the obnoxious sound.

Eva had two choices. She could go down with a fight against the salesman, or she could accept the markups at face value. Normally, she would spend at least half an hour schmoozing the manager, namedropping her family and friends, and witling the price down to a more reasonable number. But when she turned and beheld her feminine girlfriend pretending to drive the Italian car, Eva realized she would rather spend her time making her darling happy as opposed to haggling over a car she wouldn't ever drive.

She arranged for the car to be delivered to Nadia's house later that day. The way Nadia looked at her as Eva signed the agreement to pay full price was full of awe. It would have been adorable if it weren't for the fact… Eva had seen that look plenty of times before.

Women get excited by how much money I have. Granted, Eva had never bought a car for a girlfriend before, but she told herself that Nadia was different. Nadia was a more serious relationship than anyone else Eva had ever been with. *Yup. That's what I'm going with.*

"I didn't think you would actually buy me a car," Nadia admitted when they were back in Eva's. "Like… I knew you *could*… but actually doing it?"

Eva shrugged, keys hanging from the ignition. "I like spoiling my lady." She leaned over and kissed Nadia on the cheek. "What should we get you next? Your own downtown apartment."

"You're joking, surely."

Well, I was… "The house you're renting is really cozy. Would be a shame to see you lose it before I even have the chance to convince you to move in with me."

"Eva!"

"What? Too soon?"

Nadia blushed. "How would that even work? I couldn't live at your estate. No way. And your apartment is much too small for the both of us."

Only because it's stuffed with my things. "I would buy us a new apartment and sell that one. Would two bedrooms be enough?"

"Would two… you're too much, Eva. We can't even talk about this yet."

"Why not?" Eva took her girlfriend's hand. "When's your lease up on that house? I'll pay it off for you and we'll start looking for an apartment tomorrow. All I ask is that you let me design the living room. I'm rather partial to my whites and baby blues. Helps calm me after a long and stressful day." She squeezed that hand in her grip. "So does sex, though. With you letting me fuck you the way you do? Mmhmm."

"Eva!"

"What? It's the truth. Where do you want to live? Right in the heart of downtown near where you work? Or somewhere a little more… natural? I hear the central park is prime real estate right now. Doesn't have to be a penthouse. I just need good security and concierge."

"We can't move in together yet!"

"Why not?"

Nadia pulled her hand out of Eva's. "We haven't been together long enough yet."

"Is there a minimum amount of time we have to be dating? Technically, it's been a few months. We are well within our right to move in together without incurring U-Haul jokes." Eva was only half serious about this joke. If Nadia were gung-ho about moving in together, Eva might be game. As it was? She mostly wanted to test the waters lapping at their feet.

"We don't know each other well enough yet."

"Do you love me?" Eva's fingers grazed Nadia's cheek. "That's all I care about."

"Of course I love you. Do you think I've been lying to you all this time? I should be asking you if *you* love me."

"Didn't I buy you a damn car? You think I do that for anyone I'm dating?"

"No, but…"

Eva's fingers slipped from Nadia's cheek to her chin, tugging it around so their eyes met in the front seat of the Jaguar. "Exactly. You're special to me. You turn me on in ways I've never experienced before. Honest!"

"Really? I can't believe that."

"It's true. I've never loved someone like I love you, Nadia. Maybe it's to my detriment, but there it is. I just dropped thousands of dollars on the car of your dreams because you asked for it."

"I promise I'm not taking advantage of you." Her countenance was more than a little crestfallen when she said that. "Okay, maybe a bit. I don't know what came over me. One moment I was thinking about what's happened in the past twenty-four hours, and the next I was wondering why I kept fighting the fact I'm dating an heiress."

"I've never hidden it, you know. You're welcome to mooch money off me anytime. Well, in some form of moderation, I suppose. But I never got the impression you're into me for my money. If anything, that's your least favorite thing about me."

"I don't dislike that you have money!"

"It comes between us, though. I'm not complaining. Maybe it's a good thing that I'm dating someone who isn't impressed by my funds."

Nadia gazed out the window. "I'm impressed, but I don't want anything to do with it."

"Babe," Eva said putting both hands on the steering wheel again. "I've got a fuckton of money. I don't spend it indiscriminately, no, but it means we could have a helluva life together. I'm glad you don't love me because of my money. But you don't have to be afraid to acknowledge it either. I'd rather you ask me for things that you want and need than be embarrassed to."

Nadia snorted. "'Cause I totally needed a *Fiat*."

"You need a car. You picked the most practical one that you happened to like." Eva shrugged. "My cars both cost way more. It's not a big deal."

"No… no I shouldn't have done that. I shouldn't…"

"Hey." Eva put her hand on Nadia's leg. "Pandora's Box has been opened, babe. I'm going to spoil you so hard today that my accountant is going to get whiplash looking at my receipts."

Was that a smile on Nadia's face? It better be, because Eva was definitely smiling back at her. *She really has no idea.* Did Nadia think she was going to be calling the shots today? Ha. It was her idea to buy a car, but

Eva could think of a few dozen things her girlfriend desperately needed to be showered in. Like expensive perfume. And clothes. Lots and lots of clothes.

***

Fuck her accountant! I'm the one with whiplash!

Nadia had no idea what the fuck to do with so many shopping bags. They were stuffed with dresses, skirts, blouses, and yes, even pants. Eva had insisted on taking Nadia to so many places and covering her in material affection that one would think she was going to sustain herself for the rest of her life on designer wear. *How much will this go for when it's considered vintage?* The only reason Nadia knew how to pronounce most of these designer names was because she had been working for Mr. Cole for so long. When one got a piece from The Crimson Dove every time someone *else* got a new assistant…

What blew out the candles on her cake though was one of the final places they went to that afternoon. Eva pulled up in front of a nondescript shop showcasing a single piece of lingerie in the store window. *Oh. Oh no…*

Oh, yes.

Did Nadia think she was going to get away with all-day shopping and *not* go to a lingerie boutique? Haha! *I'm such a naïve dumbass sometimes.*

Eva made sure their shopping bags were secured in the back of her car. "Come on, babe. We've got an arousing game of dress up to play."

Could anyone else in the world say that and *not* embarrass Nadia? Because even Eva embarrassed her. Not enough to make her refuse to go inside, but enough to make her freeze up in the car before someone forced it open for her.

"I bet you'd look super sexy in dark purple lace."

Nadia got out with a grunt. "If I'm trying on lingerie, then so are you."

"What makes you think I'm not?" Eva put a gentle hand on her girlfriend's shoulder. "I want to make sure I look good for you too."

"I can't imagine you looking bad in *anything*." This was Eva they were talking about. She could show up in a red and pink plaid suit and make the "fashion hits" list in the papers. Some women could pull off anything. Nadia was not one of them, no matter what Eva tried to say.

"News flash, babe." Eva opened the boutique door and waited for Nadia to step in first. "You look great in anything too. Or out of anything. I like to think of lingerie as the… in between temptation. Remember last night when you enticed me into bed with that sexy black bra and panty set? Yeah. Like that. Times infinity."

For a brief moment, Nadia truly felt like the sexiest girl in the world. Easy to do when one's hot girlfriend was taking her lingerie shopping – and smacking her ass when she thought nobody else was looking.

***

Taking women lingerie shopping was always a trip and a half.
This was not Eva's first time at this particular rodeo. *I've even stayed on a few bulls during the process. How about that?* Not even at this particular boutique, which happened to be one of the nicest in the city. Better than even some of New York's lingerie departments… although France and various cities around East Asia were, in Eva's opinion, the crème de la crème. *Unfortunately, the Asian stores don't have shit that fits my voluptuous girlfriend, and the French ones are too snobby for even me to deal with.* So it was the local boutique.

Even with *her* working there.

Her name was Terry, a thirty-something conservative who was too professional to say something to Eva's face, but always ready to share a sneer or some other derisive look whenever Eva brought in a honey – or came in by herself! Sure enough, Terry was working at the boutique that day. Terry, who had no business being a Judgmental Judy when it came to her core clientele: the wives, daughters, and girlfriends of rich juggernauts.

Think of all the premarital relations you're promoting, Terry! Eva had to get her kicks somehow. And smiling at that thought made it easier for her to play it cool in front of Nadia, who pranced around in one piece of lingerie after another for her girlfriend's great amusement. *Or is it only gross when it's two women doing it?* Nadia dressing up in purple, red, blue, and even green was definitely not gross. It was the best damn shit in the world, and Eva found new ways to titter every time Nadia popped out of the changing room wearing a new lacy style that hugged every curve and made her look like the greatest model in the world. *I may be a bit biased, though.*

"Do another turn for me, love," Eva said, sitting on the back of a leather couch with her shoes scattered on the floor. "Ah! So airy. White really is your color. Or non-color, I suppose."

Nadia had a habit of fluffing her hair every time she stood in front of the mirror. This particular piece of lingerie was entirely white, with solid silk covering her breasts and gauze (not so) covering everything else. Those black panties were the ones Nadia walked in wearing beneath her dress. *Get her a white thong to wear with that and I am thinking anniversary dinner over here.* When was their anniversary, again? Might not be a bad idea to figure that out.

"You think so? I don't wear a lot of white. Sort of washes out my skin. Last time I wore a white dress I swear I sprouted freckles when I hadn't had them in years."

Eva turned to Terry, who stood to the side with the most practiced smile a woman could get away with. "What do you think? Doesn't my girlfriend look great in white? With that hair?"

Terry bristled, smile faltering. "White is a good color on you, Miss."

"Really?" Nadia considered the look some more. Eva, meanwhile, glanced at Terry and hid a childish snicker. "I mean, you're buying, so…"

"Yes, I am, and you're free to keep that in my place if you don't have room in your closet."

"Where else would I keep all the stuff you've bought me so far today?"

"I mean, I hope you're not planning on keeping the Fiat in my apartment…"

"Ms. Warren has a good eye," Terry continued. "I don't think anyone ever disputes that."

You play this game so well. Terry could not be goaded into outright homophobia, even though it boiled so deeply within those veins. So many twitches. So many sighs. So many callous looks in Eva's direction when she thought nobody was looking.

"In fact, she has such a good eye, that many women seem to come to her for her opinions on lingerie."

Eva's cheeks flushed red for a hot second. Once the blip of anger died down, Eva cleared her throat and said, "I do like to think that I am an authority on all things women and lingerie. You know. Being a woman myself."

Nadia disappeared into the changing room again. Terry released her façade and faced Eva.

"Should I have the items bagged up for you, Ms. Warren?"

"The ones hanging up there, yes. I think the others are in the reject pile." Nadia could not be convinced to wear canary yellow. Not that Eva understood that… "Thank you."

"Oh, it's my pleasure, Ms. Warren. You're one of our biggest customers. I daresay half the women in this city have you to thank for their nighttime sleepwear."

"I do what I can to make women both comfortable and fashionable when they go to bed."

"I'm sure their boyfriends and husbands appreciate it as much as we do. Or am I thinking of someone else? No, I don't think so. I do believe the last woman you brought in here is now dating that soccer player. She came back in here once asking for the next size up in a piece you once bought her. Turns out she's pregnant. How about that?"

"Yes," Eva said through gritted teeth. "How about that. Some women are bisexual." She knew Lisa was bisexual, and didn't care. Why did it matter? After they broke up, Lisa went on to date that soccer player. Who. Cared?

Really, who cared? Eva hadn't cared, although she had to roll her eyes sometimes. *Like he gives it to you better than I do. Yeah, right, Lisa.* Most of the women who dated Eva told her that she was "surprisingly" better than most of the boyfriends of the past. It was almost like Eva listened to them and paid attention to what they liked and wanted. The kicker? Some women were *so* floored that sex could be pleasurable without a cock involved. Eva was usually too drunk on lust or spending money to care about these asinine comments. But that didn't mean it felt good to have someone like Terry the Lingerie Saleslady try to put her in her place.

My gay place. My gay and will never fit in anywhere place.

Lisa could do what she wanted, like Eva could do what she wanted. It hadn't been romantic love of any kind, anyway.

Nadia popped out, dressed in her tantalizing outfit that had been making Eva horny all day. Almost hornier than any of those lingerie pieces, if one could believe it. *I can barely believe it.* As lovely as the lingerie had been, though, there was something about Nadia wearing her everyday clothes that turned Eva on even more.

Eva swallowed, hard, before getting up to slip her shoes back on and go to the register with her credit card in hand. For some reason, the thought of Nadia breaking up with her and going on to be with a soccer player hurt more than Lisa actually doing it.

"Thank you," Nadia said, taking Eva's hand as they exited the boutique. "I've never had someone buy me lingerie before."

"My plea…" Something moved in the corner of Eva's eyes. A fucking flash. *Carnivores!* She swung around, blocking Nadia from the pap crawling around a neighboring park. "Fuck. Quick." She reached into one of the bags and pulled out her sweater. The charcoal color engulfed Nadia's red hair as it flung over her head. "Come on!"

Nadia didn't ask what was going on. She held the sweater to her head and rushed to the Jaguar still parked by the curb. Once they were in, Eva took off, not even sure where they were going next.

"Paparazzi?" Nadia didn't take the sweater off her head. Nor did she look out the window. "When are there no paparazzi following me around?" Eva stopped at a red light. "Bastards. I think the rumor is out that you and I are dating, and they're going the extra mile to catch us together."

"What? What rumors?"

Eva leaned her elbow out the window and chewed her cuticle. "You're not famous, but you're a person of media interest because of who you work for. Not to mention you're drop-dead gorgeous, and the media loves the idea of a high-society woman like me dating a beautiful woman like you. It's a fetishist's playground." Sometimes Eva dated women who were both unknown and considered unconventionally attractive. *That means they didn't conform to gender norms enough. Still hot to me.* Those dates were almost never papped or reported on. Not sexy enough. Not pornographic enough, because Eva lived to be reminded that her mere existence as a "hot" lesbian was for straight male consumption.

"Fetishists…"

"Unfortunately. We're a good looking couple. People want to see us, especially since we're not public yet."

Nadia shifted in her seat. "Do you want to be public?"

"You're asking me if I want the whole world to know that I'm dating a smoking hot woman who makes me laugh and gets me excited to see her every day." Eva could smile as drolly as the next billionaire. "Of course I want to be public, but I know you don't like the attention, so…"

"If we're more serious now, maybe it's not a bad idea to come out of the relationship closet."

"Might as well. We're both out of the other one."

"I bet your mother would love that, too."

Eva also knew how to bristle as well as Terry did. "My mother will open a bottle of *whine.*"

"Why don't we go somewhere we can be really open, then?"

"Don't know where that would be." Eva's stomach growled. "But apparently I am hungry for dinner."

"That gay bar is only a few blocks away from here."

"I haven't been therc in forever."

"Really?"

"Yeah. I went a couple of times in undergrad, but I was a bit… overdressed for that crowd, if you catch my drift."

"You're not overdressed now."

"Guess not."

"So let's go. Think you might be surprised how out of my element I can be there too."

Finally, the light turned green. *Damn, I hate this intersection.* "Two out of their element lesbians. What could possibly go wrong?"

Chapter 33

Nadia had never been to the gay bar before… with a girlfriend, anyway. Let alone a girlfriend everyone would instantly recognize, whether they personally knew her or not. Most of them probably were in the "or not" category, since most of the women who frequented Les Are Mis were blue collar or in college.

Or, if they didn't belong to either category, they still blended in very well. Which Nadia did not, with her vibrantly red hair and (more so than usual) expensive clothing. Even Eva looked more down to Earth that night, although her clothes were certainly more expensive than her girlfriend's!

Les Are Mis was not a popular place on Tuesday nights. It wasn't popular most nights, when Nadia thought about it. Lesbian bars were on the wan across America. To think that a city as big as that one could boast multiple bars for men but barely this one for women! When the bar wasn't functioning as a would-be weekend hotspot for every woman-loving-woman in the region, it was a low-key eatery full of fried dishes and sides for the health obsessed. *Lesbians love their quinoa.*

Most of the social interaction, regardless of consuming food or drink, was happening at the front counter, where a woman with purple hair and gauges in her ears mixed drinks and brought out food from the back. She barely glanced at Nadia and Eva when they entered. Then she did a double-take, and the look in her eye did not inspire any confidence.

"What's good on tap?" Eva asked nobody in particular as she sat down. Nadia slipped onto the stool next to her and grabbed a food menu. *Do I go crazy with the health food or say fuck it and get the greasiest French fries on the planet?* "Do you guys have Greenwich?"

"Er… no." The bartender tossed a towel over her black Ramones T-shirt and crossed her arms. "Unfortunately. We've got the usual. If you want craft, there's Blue City and Riverwatch, but that's not on tap."

"I'm fine with a cocktail," Nadia said. "Rum and Coke."

Eva paid for their drinks and stole the menu from her. "Hell yeah, burgers and fries night."

"It's not fancy, that's for sure," the bartender said.

"That's fine. Don't need fancy when it comes to burgers and fries."

The bartender wandered off to get their drinks. Nadia looked around the room. "Oh, they've added pool since the last time I was in here." Two women played together, the one so intently focused on her next play that the other stole five bucks right from her friend's wallet.

"You play pool?"

"I had to do something to amuse myself at all the straight bars I went to in college."

Eva leaned against the bar. "Tell me more about college. Tell me all about that hot experimentation you did to decide your lesbian fate."

She was joking, but Nadia looked away. "It wasn't that interesting. I fooled around with some girls, but I mostly dated boys in college."

"Bummer."

"Not you, I bet. Probably a lot of women in your little black book from college."

"Hmm." Eva thanked the bartender again when they received their drinks. *Too much Coke, not enough rum.* "I had a lot of casual relationships, yeah. None of them were serious for a reason, though."

"Oh? Too much of a playgirl?"

"I suppose. But I only took on the playgirl image because I didn't have much choice."

"Oh…"

Eva shrugged, but it was the kind of shrug Nadia now recognized as a shrug of indifference, of the "shake it off" variety. "Nobody took a relationship with me seriously. I was their experimentation. I went to the women's college here, and everything you've heard about women's colleges is both true and a gross exaggeration. There is a lot of fooling around, but very few women who would actually call themselves lesbians. Or even bi, really. That made me both popular and one of the last people they wanted to hang out with."

Nadia sipped her drink. "I mostly had guys hitting on me for four years."

I didn't realize she took on the mantle of playgirl because she thought she had to. Did Eva think she had no other chance at a real relationship yet? Was that why she seemed so fascinated with what they had so far? Nadia couldn't believe it. Hadn't Eva been in serious relationships before? How could she not? She was rich. She was confident. She was damn good in bed and fairly easy to get along with, class differences aside. While Eva admitted to having "girlfriends" of the more monogamous sort in the past, she never mentioned love.

Oh, dear.

She was the type to put up barriers to protect herself, wasn't she? To think that she was already letting Nadia so far in… was it because of how long they flirted and crushed on one another? Or was it something deeper?

Was Eva *that* in love with her?

What surprised Nadia even more was how awkward Eva looked in a damn gay bar. The poor dear probably hadn't been to one many times in her life, even though she was one of the most famous lesbians in the region. *Is that why? Or is it because she feels unwelcomed?* She certainly had balked a little when Nadia suggested they come here for dinner and drinks. If anything, Nadia expected her girlfriend to be the life of the party, no matter how big or small it was.

Then again, she didn't seem to have a lot of friends, and few of them were gay like her.

Then again, she didn't seem to get excited about going to "gay" places.

Then again, Nadia sort of understood, even though she was coming from a different angle.

Dinner was robust if also a little on the stale side. The usual burger and fries fare. They could have gone to a fancy restaurant, or even a Mom and Pop ethnic joint on the corner of some street that had great Yelp! reviews, but Nadia was content to do something she suggested for once. Now that she saw how Eva drummed her fingers and rocked back and forth on that stool as if she would rather be anywhere else? It was particularly nice of her to come here.

Nadia, however, needed to do something about this discomfort.

"Play some pool?"

"Sure. I love wielding big sticks and balls."

Nadia laughed the whole way over to the nearest empty pool table. They grabbed some cues and set up the table while drinking beer right from the bottle. If Nadia weren't wearing her nice work dress, she would be feeling rather comfortable right now. As it was, any girl, no matter how athletic she was, would find it difficult to bend over a pool table to take a shot and *not* have her skirt ride up.

"No, no, I insist. Take another shot," Eva said, grinding the end of her cue against the floor. "In fact, it would work better if you leaned farther across the table. That's right. Get those toes off the floor."

"Perv!" Nadia cried, realizing that her ass was about to fall out of her dress. She spun around and smacked Eva on the hip. "If you wanna see my ass, just ask."

Eva pushed her aside and set up her next shot. "Maybe later. I gotta whip that ass at this game first."

Cute. One cocktail and a beer later, Eva was already losing her verbal faculties. "I'm not sure those words went in the order you intended, but I get the point."

Even though the place was relatively empty most of the evening, Nadia could safely say she had a decent time with her girlfriend. Until some of the regulars showed up.

Eva was in the bathroom, having had one too many beers and having them all catch up with her at once. *Or something. I think that's what she said.* Unfortunately, the worse her verbiage became, the better her pool skills got. Nadia briefly considered moving some of the balls on the table and seeing if Eva would notice.

"Now what's a pretty thing like you doing in a place like this?"

Nadia stood up straight before turning around. *Says a lot about me. I was expecting to see someone different.* The woman standing in front of her would not be considered conventionally butch. *Then again, neither is Eva.* Yet when Nadia looked at this woman, that was the first word to pop into her head. It was the way she moved, with a lackadaisical confidence that took over the room. Her shredded tank top outlined a pair of biceps that most lifters would kill for. Tattoos covered her skin, crawling up her long neck, and rounding her angular face. Long, stringy black hair was pulled back into a low ponytail. The way this woman looked Nadia's outfit up and down was both unsettling and kinda hot.

This was normally the moment where Nadia shut down. Did this woman want to flirt? Or… was she insinuating something that would not make Nadia feel good *at all?* Because she had been there. Been *here*… many times.

"Oh, you know…" Nadia employed the smile she kept in reserve for the receptionist's desk. "Having some beers. Playing some pool. Not sure I recommend the fries, though. Bit flat."

The woman was soon joined by two others sporting a similar style to her. Nadia instantly recognized the situation. *This is their Tuesday night hangout spot. Just got off work. I'm trespassing.* Straight, gay, people got weird in their haunts.

"You sure are fancy for someone around here."

Nadia leaned against the pool table with her cue between her legs. "Stopped by after work. I work downtown." That was often code for *I work in a high-rise office.*

"Hon, do you even know where you *are?*"

A hand clasped on Nadia's shoulder. "She sure knows where she is," Eva said, slamming her cue next to Nadia's. "It was my girlfriend's idea that we come here." Damn. Now there was a smile that could slay a woman where she stood. Must have come from living that rich bitch life. *Did she learn that from her family? Or from her experiences?* "Eva Warren. Pleasure. Who are you fine women?"

The woman in front snorted while one of the ones in the back let out a full laugh. "Eva Warren, huh? Heard of you. You're that rich chick!"

"Yes, my new friend, very rich. Very gay, too. Problem?"

"Hey, we ain't got no problem, as long as you know what you're about," the woman in front said. "Name's Sam. Welcome to our little hovel."

They grinned at Eva but sent Nadia cautious looks. *Of course.* Eva may be tipsy enough to make friends with the lesbian peasants, but Nadia needed five more beers to get over those looks of *You don't look gay enough to be here.*

It was the same wherever Nadia went. Back in college, she couldn't get a female date to save her life. A pity, since she was burning to kiss more girls and experience what their bodies felt like against hers. (Naked, of course.) Boys, on the other hand, were a dime a dozen when it came to their flirtations and come-ons. Even when Nadia went to her school's Gay-Straight Alliance, everyone assumed she was a part of the S. It was strange. She knew stereotypes abounded, but was it so strange that she could be gay *and* feminine to a fault? Most people were benevolent in their oppression. They didn't mean it *that* way. They didn't want Nadia to feel bad. They were confused, that's all! How often did one meet a lesbian who looked like a millionaire's trophy wife? *There are thousands of us out there.* The only time Nadia felt solace was when she found online communities dedicated to her dilemma… then she tried online dating and ended up in a circle again. And dating men. Again.

The looks these other lesbians gave her were much of the same looks she experienced before. Nothing else could possibly get Nadia sidling up to her girlfriend as much as she did now.

"Fun, huh?" Eva said after the end of the hour. The women had gone off to get more drinks, but Eva looked game to leave. "Shall we blow this place? One of them is looking at me like I've got a bottomless wallet she can take advantage of."

"That's what I've been using you for all day."

"Yes, but I like it when *you* do it." Eva pulled out her phone. "You wanna go dancing? I feel like dancing. I'll find us the nearest club that looks good. Stay here, babe."

They blew each other kisses while Eva wandered off to get better reception on her phone. Nadia took up the task of cleaning their pool table so it would be ready for the next group (whenever that would be.)

"…She sure has a nice ass, that's for sure."

Nadia pretended to not be listening. Surely, Sam and her friend didn't think they were audible.

"Which one?"

"Man, pick one! They've got asses with balls."

"They seem nice."

"Yeah, whatever. It must be a cold day in hell when a femme like that is in here. Thought they had all ran off because they were too good for us."

"You're mad because your last girlfriend was a femme and she left you for a dude."

"You think that Eva Warren isn't going to have that problem soon?"

"Whatever, man, she's loaded. She'll have another girlfriend lined up in no time. That kind of woman ain't single for long."

"You thinking of getting her number?"

"Now don't go putting ideas in my head!"

Eva reappeared at Nadia's side. "Ready to go?"

"Yes, please. *Please.*"

"All right! Got your point."

The club Eva picked was only a few blocks from her apartment. After the car was parked in her private garage they walked over, Eva going on about how she wanted to get drunk enough to not have anything to do with her car for the rest of the night. Nadia concurred. After the gay bar, she was ready to get properly loaded.

Good news? The club was upscale and kept careful tabs on who they let in. Bad news? Straight couples. Everywhere. *Surprised she would go for a place like this.* Eva must not have a lot of perv on the brain when she was drunk enough to dance like an idiot.

Oh. Nadia was incorrect.

"Why aren't you dancing with me?" Eva shouted over the dance beat. The music was so damn loud that Nadia could feel it giving her heart palpitations. *My heart is beating as if it's constantly looking at her.* That fluttering motion that had yet to let up whenever Nadia was around her beloved Eva. "Come on! I'm drunk on Smirnoff and want to dance with my lady!"

Nadia assumed they were safe in that dark club. After all, it was *dark* and people were preoccupied with their groups of friends or (heterosexual, of course) dates. Nobody cared about the pair of women getting down and dirty on the far side of the dance floor. While Nadia wasn't exactly her most mobile in that dress, Eva wasn't the most physically coherent after however many shots of vodka she had consumed. Throw in their height difference, and this created a perfect storm of stumbling, teetering, and one's incredibly bad breath hitting the other in the face. In short, it was the perfect evening.

"You are the sweetest girl in the world," Eva mumbled against Nadia's forehead as they swayed together during a slow RnB song. "You know how many women I can take drunk dancing with me? Not many!"

Nadia giggled against her girlfriend's chest. *I'm gonna fall asleep right here in her cleavage.* Eva didn't have a lot of cleavage, but what her bra created was more than nice to snuggle in. "You flatter me!"

"No, babe, you flatter *me* by even going out with me." Eva tilted Nadia's head back and gave her the lingering kiss of a lifetime. *Butterflies!*

Drunken heart palpitations! Same difference! "You wanna go back to my place now or later?"

"Depends. What are we going to do there?"

"Didn't I buy you a bunch of lingerie today?"

"Yeah, but we've drunk…"

"Hey, ladies."

Oh, no. Oh no. Who the fuck invited the frat boys?

That's what they had to be. A group of snickering frat fuckers who had as much to drink as Nadia and Eva… and had no idea how to handle it. *I know these types. I once dated these types.* Men who prowled parties and clubs, looking for women to screw for the night and to screw over for the rest of their lives. The way they leered, licked their lips, and watched their fingers itch in a great and mighty need to touch the lesbians in front of them reminded Nadia why she was surprised Eva brought her here.

Men. Men loved to fuck up everything lesbian, which was the kind of moment happening between Nadia and her girlfriend now. *Excuse you, we're having a very gay moment here. Could you please back off for a few seconds? Thanks.*

Eva's game plan was to ignore them. She swung Nadia around toward the corner and continued to canoodle her, although someone could easily feel how tense Eva became.

"Aw, come on. You ladies gonna stand there teasing us all night and not let us in on something?"

Eva, suddenly sober, craned her head around. "Let me let you in on a little secret, *boys.*" Oh, they really didn't like the way she said that. "Our relationship isn't for you to enjoy. We're here having a fun night together. It's our date night. That get your cocks hard, huh? I've got a hard cock too. You into it? Ask my girlfriend here how well I fuck in the ass."

Nadia's eyes widened. *I don't recall that happening!* But the guys each took a step back, their anuses probably clenching as Eva the big bad diamond dyke shot them an image they wouldn't be able to get rid of no matter how many drinks they downed.

"If you want someone to fuck you in the ass, honey," one of the guys said to Nadia. "Come home with me and find out how a real man does it."

"See, that's the thing," Eva snapped at him. "The whole point is that there are no men. Y'all ain't got what it takes to impress women like us. Oh, wait. You aren't looking for women anyway. You're looking for girls. Be on your way now. Shoo."

Nadia wanted to giggle at her girlfriend's overconfidence, but half the guys nearby did not look impressed with what she said. "Maybe we ain't interested in any other *women.*"

Eva's arms tensed around Nadia. "Come on," she muttered. "Let's get out of here."

The guys let them go without fuss, although Nadia could feel their leering clear across the main club room. They managed to make it to the front entrance without incident.

It was while crossing the second intersection en route to Eva's apartment that the first incident occurred.

"Fuck," Eva said, sending a scorching look over her shoulder. "They're following us."

"What!"

Eva grabbed Nadia's hand and hauled her across the street before any cars arrived. *They won't do anything, will they?* No way. Not in public like this. Would they? *Never put it past them.* Nadia had been stalked plenty of times in her life. It would not be the first time some brutes followed her home from a party or function and tried to get in her pants – with her consent or not.

"Shit, shit." Damn! Why did Eva have to be so tall, so athletic, *and* wearing practical shoes? Nadia struggled to keep up in her heels and constricting skirt. Didn't help her breasts kept trying to pop out of her bust every time she took a large stride forward. "You see them?"

Nadia didn't have much opportunity to look back. "I don't think so?"

They were at Eva's building, the doorman hurrying to open the door for them. Eva, panting, urged her girlfriend in and muttered something to the doorman. He hurried as quickly to close the door. "Good." Eva let go of Nadia's hand and went up to the security officer on duty at the front desk. Whatever she said to him, it was effective. The officer stood up and planted himself in front of the door, eyes on the lookout for men of a certain description. By then, Eva had taken Nadia into the elevator and forced the doors closed.

"What a night," Eva said, almost breathless. When she finally spared Nadia a look, her girlfriend nearly gasped.

That wasn't mirth in her eyes. Nor was it that look of *Guess that's over with finally. What now?* The only way Nadia could describe what she saw in Eva's blue eyes was…

Fear.

Not immediate fear. Not the kind of fear that would make her bar her door once they were inside. Nor was it the kind of fear that would leave her unable to speak for the rest of the night. But it *was* the kind of fear that took her back to a darker moment in her life. Nadia didn't have to ask what it was. Eva was a strong, capable woman who had put a lot of bad experiences behind her, but there was a reason Nadia was one of the only people who knew about her incident back at Winchester Academy.

"Hey," Nadia cooed, taking her girlfriend's hand in the middle of the dark apartment. "It's okay. They're gone. It's just you and me now."

Eva exhaled a pent up breath, but it wasn't enough to relieve her anxiety. "I know. Those guys, they…"

"They made you think of your soccer team." That was the easiest way to say it. For Nadia, anyway.

"Yeah. Guess so. Stupid of me, I suppose. But when I realized those guys were following us, I…"

Nadia squeezed her hand. "I think that's normal. Well, what they did was not normal. But your reaction to it is. I don't blame you at all."

Uneasily, Eva laughed. "No? That's comforting, I guess."

"Do you wanna take a shower?" Nadia removed the sweater draped across her shoulders. "Or are you too drunk?"

"Babe, I'm never too drunk to have a naked time with you." Eva was already ripping her shirt off her body. Could she slow down a bit? Nadia wouldn't mind helping her undress.

The double-jets of Eva's shower felt every bit as good as the woman's own hands felt on Nadia's naked body. As water ran down her skin, Nadia both volunteered to and was gently pressed against the tiled wall. Eva took her hands and flatted them above her head. Were those hard nipples pushing into her back? Oh, definitely.

"You're the best, and I love you," Eva said.

Nadia smiled. Water got in her mouth, but she didn't care. Smiling was better than spitting out the annoying water creeping between her teeth. "You make me feel comfortable to be myself around you. You have never questioned whether I'm actually gay or not."

"Why would I? I'm not that insecure. Not about that."

Nadia slowly turned, letting her arms loop around Eva's hips. "But you are insecure about some things?"

"Everyone is insecure about certain things, babe."

"That's true. But you don't seem the kind who is very insecure about anything."

"Aren't you insecure about things? Money doesn't buy you as much confidence as you seem to think it does."

"Of course I'm insecure. Are we talking in circles now?"

"Yeah. Less talking. More kissing."

"And nobody gets to watch."

"That's where you're naïve, babe. I've got cameras all over this place. Like you said, I'm a giant perv."

"Oh, care to see my ass now?"

Nadia knew that was going to get her a hard spank. Good. She wanted to feel her skin jiggle and the delightful, erotic pain shoot through her tender flesh. "I'm going to do all sorts of stuff to your ass tonight. You heard me back there. No one fucks a girl in the ass as good as I do."

"Have you actually done that before?" Nadia wasn't sure whether to laugh or run.

"Babe, I've done everything. But I haven't done everything with you."

"That could take a while."

"Oh," Eva kissed her, hungrily, their lips dancing together until she finally decided to finish her thought. "I've got my whole life."

Chapter 34

"There's a big fundraiser happening this weekend," said the text from Eva. *"I want to take you as my date. My very public date."*

Nadia sat at her desk during a lull in guests. As soon as someone walked through that door, however, she would have to put her phone away. Mr. Cole was back from his honeymoon, and while he was in a good mood, he wasn't about to put up with Nadia's unprofessionalism when so many people were demanding to see him.

"There will be press there. They'll want to take professional pictures of us for Page 6. I'm sure some tabloids will get the pics too. What do you think? It would mean a lot to me."

That text was sent two hours ago. Whatever Eva was doing, she could wait a little bit longer for an answer.

What do I want to do? They had long decided that they were in a semi-serious monogamous relationship. Nadia got her wish and spent every night with Eva the week before. They didn't always make love, but they did always have a little fun, whether Eva was on the phone for work or if Nadia was helping Amber with one of Mr. Cole's "Return to Work" presentations.

"Think I should do it?" Nadia asked Amber during lunch. They sat in the break room, Amber glued to her phone while Nadia also considered her own. "Kind of a big deal openly dating a rich lesbian, isn't it?"

"Girl, you are one of the only ones I know who isn't jumping on the opportunity." She laughed. "Who isn't in the closet, anyway. What's the problem? If you're planning to get serious with Eva, you should come out on your terms. Before the paps do it for you."

Nadia shivered. *She has no idea.* Eva and Nadia did appear in the tabloids. The only reason nobody identified Nadia was because of the carefully placed sweater over Nadia's head as they dashed for the Jaguar. "What about you? You still seeing Ms. Thomas?"

"Yeah, but that's different. We're not like you and Eva. You guys are like… really natural to look at. Does that make sense?"

Nadia cocked her head. "Not at all."

"What I *mean* is that you guys look so good together. You can tell there's something deeper between you two. Me and Adrienne? We're dramatic fuck buddies. I don't see us lasting beyond this year."

"That's…"

"Pathetic?" Amber shrugged. "I guess."

"Does that bother you?"

Amber put down her phone and lethargically stabbed her Caesar salad she brought from home. "No. Why would it bother me?"

Nadia noted the way her friend automatically got huffy and on the defensive whenever Adrienne was brought up. "No idea. It's not like she's using you for her own experimentation or anything."

"Who says she's using me? I'm using her for money. Goes both ways."

"Does it? And is that really healthy?"

"Hey." Amber put her elbow on the table and pointed an accusatory finger at Nadia. "It ain't about being healthy. I'm young enough to not give a shit."

"That's… insightful."

"Maybe the sex is good enough for me to not care."

"Maybe it is." Nadia opened her chat window on her phone. "*I'll say yes for now. You gonna buy me a new dress?*"

The response was almost instantaneous. "*I will buy you a whole new wardrobe yet* again *if it means I get to tell the whole world that you're my hot girlfriend.*"

"There," Nadia announced, showing Amber her phone. "I'm going to do it. I'm going to let her parade me around to a bunch of rich people as her girlfriend."

"Enjoy. And see you there. I've gotta work at that party."

"Who you working for?"

"Mr. Cole, of course."

"Uh huh."

"I've got a good thing going, okay? I don't technically work for Adrienne, so it works out."

"Does he know you're seeing his business partner on the side."

"Oh, I'm sure he does. Adrienne has insinuated that he knows."

"And he's okay with that?"

Amber rolled her eyes. "This is Mr. Cole we're talking about. He would be extra okay with it if we started fucking at a drop of a hat in front of him every ten minutes. Please."

Nadia had no idea what to say to that. Luckily, Amber changed the subject.

"It's Tuesday, right?"

"Yeah." One week since Nadia called in sick so she could go out on a hot, long date with her girlfriend.

"Sweet. The tabloids have updated."

"Can't believe you read that trash."

"How can I not? All the people I know are in it!"

Amber got lost in the words displaying on her phone. As she did every Tuesday at lunch, she laughed at bad photos, *ooh'd* at the gossip she hadn't heard yet, and pretended to be so damn involved in the personal lives of those in high society. While Amber also read the celebrity scandal rags, she was much more into the blogs like *The Daily Social,* which focused on regional high-society news. Country club and fundraiser gossip was the talk of the town on that blog. *They're the ones who keep taking pics of Eva and me.* The editors over there kept pulling out their hair trying to get a good enough picture of Nadia so they could be exposed before they were ready to announce their relationship.

"Um…" Amber dropped her phone on the table and braced her hands on either side of it. "Nadia!"

She likewise dropped her phone. "What?"

"Nadia!"

Would she calm down, or at least tell Nadia what was going on? "*Look!*"

Amber slid her phone across the table. Nadia snatched it before it could fly off and land on the floor.

She rather wished she had let it crack on the floor. Then she wouldn't have to see the horrors flashing on Amber's cell phone screen.

"*Warren Heiress Caught In Flagrante With Fiery New Flame!*" shouted the headline. The lead-in blurb continued, "*Heiress Eva Warren, known for her Sapphic philandering across the world, has been seen with a new honey these past few weeks.* The Daily Social *has recently acquired some photos you won't see anywhere else! Behold, the lesbian in her natural habitat… on top of a new woman! (Now set to Cantonese music.)*"

"Oh my God!" Nadia scrolled. Why did she scroll?

"Right? Oh my God!"

There they were. The pics Nadia had been told about, but had been led to assume were destroyed. Hong Kong. A few weeks ago. Eva naked on top of Nadia in the midst of one of many orgasms.

"She's got a nice O face at least?"

Was this really the time? Nadia shot Amber a horrified look before continuing to scroll. However the perverted cameraman managed to get these shots, it definitely had been creepy to the max. There were several photos, but they clearly covered only a minute or so. How long had the reel gone on? Were there more? Or did the cameraman only manage to get thirty seconds of sex and another thirty of pillow talk between lovers?

Wait. Why was Nadia most concerned about *that?*

"Ms. Warren's new redheaded flame has been identified as Ms. Nadia Gaines, whom some may recognize as being under the employ of megabillionaire Ethan Cole."

"No!" Nadia jerked up out of her seat, her purse knocked over and spilling her makeup. She didn't bother to bend down and pick it up, however. "Fuck!"

This wasn't happening. This wasn't supposed to happen to *Nadia.* This was bullshit that occurred to the heiresses like Eva and the billionaire heartthrobs like Ethan Cole, who also appeared in the high-society gossip rags like clockwork. *But has he ever had sex pics posted?* Nadia nearly dry-heaved her way out of the break room, pale as a fucking ghost as she launched herself at her desk to grab her sweater and call HR. If this didn't warrant taking the afternoon off so she could track down Eva and get some answers, then she didn't know what did!

So happened that was the moment Mr. Cole walked out of his office, cell phone flat in his hand.

"Oh… Ms. Gaines." Was he blushing? The fucker was blushing! "You'll never guess what crossed my desk."

"I can guess!" Nadia tripped over the legs of her office chair trying to get her sweater on. "Holy shit, please don't fire me!"

"Fire you?" Clearing his throat, Mr. Cole shut off his phone and pocketed it in his suit jacket. "It's clear there has been a gross invasion of privacy. You can be assured that I…"

"Gotta go! I'm taking the afternoon off!" Nadia couldn't look him in the eye. To be fair, he couldn't look her in the eye either. Nadia's body parts may have been blurred out in those photos, but it was enough to give Mr. Cole a whole new look at his receptionist.

Everyone was looking at her as she flew past them. The worst part? The elevator opening to reveal Adrienne Thomas, back from her lunch break and gawking between her phone and Nadia's person as it hurled toward the elevator.

"Since when are you dating Eva Warren?" Why the fuck wasn't she getting out of the elevator? No matter! Nadia slammed on the buttons… and promptly realized that she had forgotten her purse. Luckily, there was Amber, scurrying toward the elevator with Nadia's purse in her hand. "And who is your plastic surgeon? Good God."

Amber pushed the doors open and handed Nadia her purse. "It's all real, thanks." Nadia gestured for Adrienne to get the fuck out of the elevator. "Yes, even those bulbous tits. Now excuse me!"

She left Adrienne and Amber standing together outside the elevator. Joking about the situation was the only thing keeping her going at the moment. If she actually stopped and thought about what had happened? That everyone in the whole fucking building had seen her professionally shot nude body mid-coitus with another woman? Nadia was going to die. Full stop.

She couldn't die yet. She had things to do. Like track down Eva and find out what the *fuck* happened.

***

"That is definitely one way to come out," Kathryn said over the phone. "Damn. And I thought I had it bad with the press!"

Eva had Kathryn on one line and her PR manager on the other. Her heart raced so quickly that she felt like she was going to throw up every ten seconds. "Those photos were supposedly destroyed, okay?"

"So you knew about them?"

"Kinda. God, what the fuck am I gonna do! Nadia's gonna freak!"

"Have you talked to her yet?"

"No, but this has got to be her biggest nightmare come true. Right up there with breaking a fucking nail."

"Breathe, girl. Your manager will have those photos taken down by the end of the day. Just grease that editor with a few million more dollars."

By then the whole country would have seen Eva's tits. Again. At least this time the photos "only" showed her rutting against Nadia's delectable thighs and not receiving head from a Brazilian supermodel. That wasn't going to make Nadia feel better, though. In fact, the last thing Nadia probably wanted to hear right now was that her girlfriend was once papped getting head from a Brazilian supermodel! *And her life was ruined. God, what's going to happen to Nadia?*

Someone knocked on her door. Eva froze, phone glued to her head. Not just anyone was given access to her door like that. Usually the front desk buzzed her even when Kathryn had come to call. *It can't be a pap. Can't be.* Please, anything but that right now!

"Eva?" a masculine voice boomed through the front door. "You in there? I tried calling."

Eva simultaneously heaved a sigh of relief and steeled herself. *Henry.*

"I gotta go," she said to Kathryn. "I have some music to face."

"Good luck." That was the last thing Eva heard before hanging up.

She opened the front door after taking a deep breath. There Henry stood, removing his hat from his head and giving his sister a knowing look.

"Now's really not a good time," Eva said.

Henry helped himself into her apartment. *Fuck.* Eva closed the door. For Henry to show up at her apartment like this… *fuck.*

"Like what you've done with this place." He tapped the brim of his hat against his lips. "You're redecorated since I was last here, right?"

Eva sighed. "It's been months since you last dropped by. Who knows." She couldn't take this anymore. "You're here about the pictures."

At least he cringed when she asked. That was the only appropriate response her older brother could give. "Unfortunately. It's caused more than a few ripples already."

"I'm so sorry." What was she doing? Groveling? Already? She hadn't consumed dinner yet. *It's too early to start groveling!* Could she get some wine? "I have no idea how that happened, Henry. I've been careful since Rio!"

"I know." He held up his hands, as if that could stem the flow of Eva's words. "I'm not here to yell at you, Eva. I'm here to help."

"What the hell could you possibly do? Sue *The Daily Social* until they crawl into a hole and die?"

He shrugged. "That's a start, for sure. My lawyers are already on it."

"Your law…" Eva turned away. *This is my mess to clean up, Henry!* How often was her older brother going to sweep in and act like the savior come to claim the day as his own? Henry rarely had to deal with the paps. He wasn't as openly social as Eva. He preferred to stay behind the scenes, and so did his wife. The only times they were papped together were when they went to public functions that commanded a red carpet presence. As far as Eva knew, Henry had a sweet deal with the press that meant he made a monthly appearance, his terms, where they got to take all the pictures they wanted. How could Eva get a deal like that?

"I'm sorry that this is happening, Eva." Oh, no, he was addressing it directly again. "I can only imagine how embarrassing it is."

"It's even more embarrassing when your big brother keeps talking about it!"

He clamped his mouth shut. "I'm sorry. But it was better for me to come here instead of talking only on the phone. Eva, this has to be addressed."

"It is being addressed!" Was she, or was she not, still on hold with her PR manager? "Contrary to popular belief, Henry, but I *am* an adult and can handle some of my own shit!"

He gave her that look. *That* look. The disapproving parent look. With a whole decade separating them, it wasn't hard for Henry to look more father than brother. *God knows he's already a better father than mine.* Eva shuddered to think of her father's reaction to this. Knowing him, though, he had his head firmly in the sand and would only talk about the latest horse races. *Bastard.* Not that Eva wanted to talk about this junk with her father… but it was a miracle when he even acknowledged her existence. This was an instance where his will didn't count.

"I know you can," Henry said, his soft voice more infuriating than reassuring. "But *I* had to take action as soon as I found out. It's my job as head of this family now."

"Fuck you." Ah, shit, she was blubbering. *Why am I acting like this? It's Henry, not my father!* The man who wasn't shy to have sex in front of his friends and kinky colleagues had no business getting into her head over some intrusive photos. "You gotta make me feel worse than I already do?"

"That is not my intention, Eva. Believe me."

"It's what you're doing!" Her PR manager was calling her back. Eva shut off her phone. *Anything she has to say to me isn't enough.* Not when Henry was in her house and ready to rip her a new asshole with great courtesy. "You think I'm not embarrassed enough as it is? I haven't even heard back from my girlfriend yet! She's probably dead and buried right now!"

This wasn't happening. This was totally not happening. At all.

"I'm sorry, Eva. I didn't have a choice. When something like this happens, I have to take immediate action."

"Do you even understand how powerless that makes me feel?"

Ouch. She hit her brother in an appropriate spot, apparently. Henry shifted between his large feet and pretended to be fascinated with his gold pocket watch. "I truly am sorry, Eva."

"Do our parents know about it?"

His lips turned downward. *Shit.* "That's partly why I am here. I left Mother down in the car."

Eva didn't think she could be any more humiliated right now. *My mother. Is downstairs. In a car. She's seen. The pictures.* Eva sank into one of her chairs and covered her face with her hands. What would happen if she shoved her face into her lap? Could she possibly disappear? That would be great.

"Fuuuuck!" she moaned.

"If I hadn't acted, *she* would have. I also told her I would come up here and talk to you about it. So. Here I am. Is there anything I can do, besides go away and never acknowledge this again for both of our sakes?"

"Fuck off, Henry. My naked ass is in some skeezy pap photo fucking my girlfriend. This can never be erased from our lives."

"Well, yes. As they say, what has been seen can never be unseen."

"Fuck. Off."

"This is being taken care of, Eva. I guarantee you that. By tonight those photos will be down, and by this time next week that embarrassment of a so-called publication will be paying *us* compensation under pain of being sued into oblivion."

"But that's it! I took care of it already! Long ago!"

Henry stepped back. "What do you mean?"

Eva did her best to explain the call she got from her PR manager talking about the Cantonese publication that took the original photos. Something something… closed down… something… *after* she paid them off.

"Ah, Eva," Henry kept saying in that fatherly tone of his, "they were probably bought out by the company that owns *The Daily Social.* The payoff didn't extend to them."

"Apparently."

"This is most unfortunate. I…"

Someone else pounded on Eva's door. Both she and her brother turned toward it with trepidation.

"You better open it," Henry muttered. "Before she does it for you."

Eva, whose face was pale beyond recognition, cautiously approached her door and slowly opened it.

As she feared, her mother stormed through, practically knocking Eva over.

"How could you!" Isabella slammed the door shut, her tall, intimidating form overshadowing her daughter as she grabbed a coffee table for balance. "Do you understand what you've done to this family? Do you ever think about anyone but yourself? For God's sake, Eva, *nude sex photos?*"

"First of all," Eva began, pushing herself away from the doorway and seeking the refuge of her couch. "None of that was *because* of me, Mother. I'll have you know that I don't go out of my way to have toxic photos like that taken of me."

"I should hope not! I didn't raise a whore!"

Eva gasped. Henry stepped between them, hand on his mother's shoulder. "Eva and I have discussed this, Mother. She is not at fault. Those pictures were a gross invasion of her privacy, and she and I will deal with the publication that unjustly put them out there."

"How can you say that?" Isabella looked between her children as if they conspired against her. "How can you say this isn't her fault at all? Of course it's her fault! Her perversions are the whole reason we're even in this mess!"

"There's no reason for this, Mother. Society will forget about it in due time. It's only a matter of time before another scandal like this crops up in some other family. I hear the man you tried to set my sister up with has himself a new girlfriend to distract the press."

"Don't remind me! You think I don't spend every day as it is trying to find this hurricane a good match who doesn't laugh in my face when I bring it up? She's ruined our family's reputation!"

"I'm right here, you know."

Both Henry and Isabella ignored her. Eva slammed her body against a large pillow and let out a groan of humiliation. Did they have to do this in her apartment?

Apparently.

"Eva has done no such thing," Henry said, his tone becoming increasingly irate. "Just because you don't agree with who she is doesn't mean she's out to destroy this family, Mother."

"I can't believe you're on her side. You *always* take her side, Henry! Do you know what this does to me? It's not enough that you've gone and married one of the worst possible women on this planet, you're now condoning this debauchery of your sister's? I'd say I can't believe it, but I've apparently raised two of the stupidest assholes to ever grace this family. Guess I only have myself to blame!"

"If your biggest gripe about your children is that we're happy with who we are and the families we're building, then you haven't done *that* badly."

"Maybe if I were a peasant. But I am *hardly* some middle-class sow who can't rein her damn children in! I had one job to accomplish when I entered this family. *All* that was asked of me was raising children this family could be proud of. Look at you!" Who was she referring to? Eva? Henry? Both? "I tire of this humiliation. If it wasn't bad enough that my husband has shamed us into hiding for the rest of our lives, I have apparently raised a pair of real deviants! But at least you have the courtesy of not being a homosexual, Henry!"

"Never know, Mother," he said, dryly, "there's still time for me to divorce my wife and marry a man."

"Don't you even jest!"

"It's fine, Henry." Eva stood from the couch and faced her mother. Isabella met her incredulous look with sneering disdain. "I'm used to the icy freeze that is our mother's love. She's never wanted me." She looked her mother right in the eyes. Those beady, cold eyes that held as much love as a forgotten corpse. "I've known that since I was a little girl. Isn't that right, Mother? You never wanted me. I was the spare you had on a lark when you realized your precious little boy could die. Except I turned out wrong, didn't I? I was born *wrong,* and not only was I not needed after all, but I was more than useless! I was a broken piece of shit, wasn't I?"

Even Eva was shocked at how quickly she escalated to shouting at her mother, who remained resolute with her upturned chin and glower. Henry, on the other hand, stood with nothing but shock on his pale visage.

"You won't even deny it." Defeated, Eva sat back down. "My own mother. I bet you wish I wasn't even born."

A good mother would have said "*That's not true! I love you! You're my daughter!"* Yeah, a good mother. Then there was Isabella Warren, who only showed up when she wanted her children to know how much she disapproved of them. Oh, and their father disapproved as well, he was too chickenshit to say it. So much for that Warren pride.

"Evangeline," Isabella said with that haughtiness she always carried with her, "you are certainly no lady."

"Even if I were your prefect image of a feminine, darling, heterosexual lady, you would still treat me like shit, Mother. I haven't been anything but chattel since the day you found out I was female. My job, from the moment I was born, was to marry into some great, proud family that could bring us even more esteem. I've known that my whole life. Unfortunately for you, it doesn't matter how many men you throw me at. They don't want me, and I don't want them."

Isabella opened her mouth to speak.

"No, Mother. Stop it. I'm never marrying a man. Not even to boost this family's supposed honor. I would rather die."

"So dramatic."

"Me? I'm dramatic? It's not my fault you shoved yourself into a corner that you hate and can't escape. *You* did that to yourself. You could've left Father the moment he sank this family. A sinking that Henry and I saved you from, if I may remind you."

"Don't be so…"

"So what? So realistic? The reality is that you have your way of living, and so do I. So does Henry. You know what? It says a lot about you as a woman and as a mother when you can't believe we're happy and in love. I've felt more love from my girlfriend this year than I have from you my whole life. I'm sure Henry can say the same thing about his wife." The look she sent her brother said he didn't have to commit to an answer. "If you want to be miserable, Mother, no one is stopping you. But I'm not going down with you. I'm never going to be your perfect pawn to marry off to the best family. I'm going to do what makes me happy. The only person pretending to be hurt by that is *you*."

Isabella squared her shoulders, but her demeanor continued to falter. "You've made your point quite clear. No need to crow about it from the top of the tree." She straightened out her dress and picked some lint off the skirt. "It's also been made quite clear to me that I am better off staying in Montana and pretending this…" she motioned to her children, "is from another planet that I have nothing to do with."

"That's not necessary, Mother," Henry said. "You should stay and enjoy the birth of your first grandchild."

"And I will, as I have intended." Isabella sniffed. "But this," she gestured to Eva, "is dead to me."

Eva knew it was coming, and yet it was like a pick to her heart all the same. *I can't… she actually said it.* She picked up her pillow and held it front of her face. *Don't let her see you cry, Eva. That's what she wants.*

"That's so unfortunate," Henry continued. "Because as soon as she gets her degree later this year, Eva will become a prominent face in the family business. Haven't you heard, Mother? Eva's agreed to lead the jewelry project *you* pitched years ago."

"I… have?" Eva looked at her brother, who in turn gave her a solemn gaze that bolstered their mutual confidence. "That's right. I have. Jewelry. As of the new year I'll be helping Henry open Warren… Warren, uh…"

"Warren Jewels."

Really? That plain? All right. "Yup. Warren Jewels. I'm going to be president."

Henry swallowed a small protest. "Certainly. But we can discuss that more *later*."

Isabella bit her lip. "You two will be the death of me. Between the rumors I hear about you…" she pointed to Henry, "and the outright truths I see about *you,*" that was for Eva, "I'm going to have a stroke before your father can wonder where all his billions went." She turned, heading toward the door. "Get this mess cleaned up! Both of you!" It slammed with purpose.

"What a day," Eva squeaked. "Sex pics of me on the internet… my mother says I'm dead to her… I'm gonna be president of a jewelry enterprise…"

Henry put a reassuring hand on his sister's shoulder. "It's going to be okay, Eva. She didn't mean any of that."

"Yes she did. Don't lie to me. She blames herself for making me the way I am. All of the shit she throws at me is really thrown at herself." Isabella unfortunately came from another time when the way children turned out fell completely on the mother. Daughter born gay? Mother's fault. (And what a fault it was.) To top it off, Eva had to be one of those gross butches who made a mockery of the family every time she left the house. To have lesbian sex pics out there in the world? *Again?* It almost made Eva wish she was back in high school, when the veneer of concern for her well-being at least existed. "I'm used to it." So why were the occasional tears making their way down her cheeks?

Henry knelt beside her. "You going to be all right?"

Eva snorted. "Hardly. I've been humiliated beyond measure. Everyone and their mothers have seen my lesbian O-face." She glanced at him. "Including you and our mother."

"I will be pouring bleach into my eyes later tonight, rest assured." He patted Eva's back. "I'm sure she wants nothing to do with us right now, but you should invite your girlfriend to one of our retreats. Get away from the public eye until someone else's scandal takes over."

"Fuck, I don't even want to think about what she has to say to me right now."

"Then go find her and take care of her. It will be worth it. I promise."

Eva looked up at him with bloodshot eyes. "More like she would be taking care of me."

"Even more worth it, then."

They weren't a hugging kind of family. Even so, Henry gave her a tight squeeze before putting his hat back on and quipping that he was off to collect their mother and drive her back to the Estate. Or the airport, if that was what she preferred.

Eva was left with some frantic messages from her PR manager… and not a peep from Nadia. What time was it? Didn't matter. Eva couldn't stay in her apartment. She would find Nadia before the day was over.

Chapter 35

Nadia almost ran Eva over in the lobby of her apartment building.

"Oh!" Even with her black shawl over her head and dark sunglasses adorning her face, Nadia could still clearly see her girlfriend right in front of her. For the briefest moment Nadia lived in a wonderful world where something terrible hadn't happened. How could it, when one of the most visually striking women in the world was right in front of her and focusing all of her attention on little Nadia?

Right. Nude pictures.

"I was coming to see you," Eva hissed. She took Nadia's hand and pulled her to the farthest wall from the doors. "I was gonna call you before getting in my car. I… wait, what are you wearing?"

Unlike Eva, who was adorned in dark jeans and a black faux-leather jacket, Nadia had gone for the full *nobody can recognize me, right?* effect. First thing she did after leaving the office was hop in her brand new Fiat and race home to change her clothes and cover her hair. *Hair like mine? Everyone can recognize me!* Nadia wasn't used to being tabloid fodder. Then again, she also wasn't used to having everyone see her naked in the papers. Getting to the parking garage, past security guards and men in suits, was such a humiliating hassle! *Everyone* had looked up at her! Some had even snickered as she raced by!

Eva was going to make this better. Nadia didn't hide her need to hold her girlfriend and bury her covered face in Eva's chest. She was both grateful and beyond disbelief when Eva hugged her in turn.

"I'm sorry," Eva whispered, her hug tightening. "I don't know how this happened. I swear to you I had taken care of those photos."

Nadia swore she felt some eyes on her. Sure enough, when she turned around, she saw the concierge glancing at them – and it wasn't part of the job. "Can we get out of here? Please? People are staring!"

Eva swung her arm around Nadia's shoulders and directed her toward the parking garage. "Yeah. Let's go."

They kept their heads down as they escaped into the parking garage, bypassed security with barely a nod, and hopped into the Jaguar. Nadia's car remained protected in the visitor parking area. *Hope it will be okay there for however long we're gone.*

She waited for Eva to start the car and get them out of there.

Instead, Eva wrapped her arms around the steering wheel, put her head down… and cried.

"Eva!" Nadia threw herself on her girlfriend, shaking her shoulders and attempting to force Eva to look up at her. "Are you okay? Baby?"

Calling her that seemed to calm her down for a bit. Eva rubbed her face and sat up, sniffing a good amount of tears and whatever else. "Been a rough day!" she said.

Nadia took off her seatbelt and sidled up next to her girlfriend. Her black shawl fell down her head and revealed the top of her red head. "Me too. What happened?"

"You mean besides the dirty sex pics of us in Hong Kong being spread all over the internet and the humiliation we are currently suffering?"

Nadia cringed. "Yeah, that."

"My mother basically said that I am dead to her, so there's that."

That bitch! Nadia could see it playing out in her head right now. What a vile woman! "I'm so sorry. Oh my God."

"Yeah, well, what are you gonna do? My brother has sent his lawyer goons after *The Daily Social,* so hopefully those pics will be down soon."

Shudders passed between them. "It's too late," Nadia muttered. "It was too late the moment they went up and people started saving them to their… oh, God."

"It's all right." Eva patted her girlfriend's knee. "This will pass. I promise. Not my first sex pic scandal. Thanks, paps."

"Yeah, and what happened to that girl? She disappeared off the face of the earth!" Nadia sat back with a sigh. "What's going to happen to *me?* They knew who I was, Eva! The whole office saw those pics! Fuck!"

"They did?"

"Yeah! Know what Ms. Thomas said? '*Didn't know you were dating Eva Warren, har har.*'"

"Ms. Thomas can go suck herself off."

"Mr. Cole saw them too."

Eva looked as if she wanted to be shot dead right there and then. "Because it wasn't bad enough that my *brother* saw them!"

"Fuck!"

"Yup! That's what they saw!"

The two of them reoriented before Eva slammed her hands back on her steering wheel. Nadia, in turn, pulled off her shawl and used it as a handkerchief. "What are we going to do?"

"Ride this shitstorm out until the next scandal takes over the world. I give it a few days, though."

"A few… Eva."

"I know. I'm sorry."

"And what am I supposed to do? Fact is, everyone's seen me having sex with you, and it's been caught on film for everyone to *enjoy* for the rest of their lives. We're going to be on porn sites!" Nadia couldn't handle it. More than one person had insinuated she had a body for porn, but she would have never been able to do something like that and come out of it unscathed. *Trust me. I thought about it when I was twenty and struggling to pay bills.* Now she would join Eva and have her own "actress" page on all the main streaming sites.

Eva clutched the steering wheel as if it held the answers. "I honestly don't know what to tell you. I've been dealing with invasive shit like this since I was a little girl. First time I realized shit was fucked up was when someone papped my private horse riding lessons. This was before the state made it illegal to pap kids by themselves."

I vaguely remember that. Nadia hadn't grown up in this state, but that law going into effect years ago was talk even in her own household. *I think it was spearheaded because some celebrity's kid was papped on his walk to school.* Nadia had seen Eva's childhood riding pictures, too. There were a few in the Warren Estate. *Perfect little blond girl, like a doll.* Even back then Eva had long and gangly limbs that made her a natural rider. Apparently, though, she was no longer interested in horses.

Ah, it was nice to think about something else for a while.

"Let's swing by my place before going somewhere else," Nadia said. "I need a few overnight things."

Eva started the car. Nadia fixed her meager disguise and took a deep breath. *It's going to be fine. Come on. Not the end of the world. This shit unfortunately happens to people all the time. Not like I'm a celeb who stands to lose shit here. Maybe my job. My good job that pays well enough. Has benefits. Fuck.*

The drive to Savant's Town was almost too quiet. Eva fiddled with the radio before ultimately turning it off. Nadia turned off her phone and shoved it in her purse so she wouldn't be tempted to check up on what people were saying – or if those pictures were even still up. Occasionally she would look over at Eva and sigh. It was because of her girlfriend's infamy that they were even in this situation to begin with.

"Oh, no."

Eva's groan made Nadia snap her head up and check out the road before them. "Seriously?" she said in disbelief. Why was her street crawling in reporters? This was Savant's Town, not Beverly Hills! "The fuck!"

The Jaguar came to a complete stop. Eva put the car in reverse, turned around, and backed down a long, private driveway. Eva made sure they were hidden behind a large tree before shutting off the car.

"What now?"

"You can borrow my shit. I can get someone to buy you stuff to keep at the hotel. Maybe Kathryn will let me borrow her assistant. Nobody knows who she is or cares about her." Eva leaned back against the headrest. "But you can't go down there. Paps are camping out on your sidewalk in the hopes of seeing you. They'll yell some gross shit at you and get some pics. They'll take that and write articles about how you're ashamed and refuse to come out. Regardless of what the truth is."

Nadia put one hand on her face. "I *am* ashamed."

Hands went on the steering wheel, but Eva didn't start the car. "You ashamed of me?"

"No. I'm ashamed that people saw something so intimate. Add on the fact we're lesbians and… can you count the levels of fetishization?"

"Trust me. I've thought about almost nothing but."

"Have you? Because I'm not used to people seeing me like that."

"Oh, and I am?"

Nadia shook her head. "That's not what I meant. But you've got a thicker skin than me when it comes to these things. Your damn brother is apparently scaring these people into taking the pictures down… you're the whole reason this is happening."

"Yes, babe, I'm a hot, rich lesbian who is the heiress to an old and vast fortune. I have a lot of sex partners and like to be public with them. That puts a huge target on my fucking back. Trust me. I *know.* The editor of *The Daily Social* is an old fuck who probably goes home and beats off to fake lesbian porn on his laptop. When he heard that those pics were on the market, he probably popped off right at his desk."

"Shut up, Eva." Nadia was going to gag. "I don't need to see that in my head."

"Sorry. It's how it is."

"And you accept it?"

Eva lifted her head and gave her girlfriend a sour look. "Who the fuck wants this!"

Nadia looked out the window, at the large tree shielding them from the paps down the street. "I'm sorry too," she muttered. Eva sighed, completely turned away from her girlfriend. "I know you don't ask for this. I… don't know how to handle it."

"It never gets easier." Eva started the car. "We can't go to your house. I'll get us a hotel so we'll have a little more privacy. They might be camped out near my building too."

Like your security would allow that. Nadia couldn't say she had guards and concierge blocking her house from the paps. "I don't want to go to a hotel." She waited for Eva to look at her again, that sad visage hitting Nadia right in the gut. "We'll be fine at your place?"

That was a fake smile, but Nadia took the reassurance nonetheless. "Yeah, babe. We'll be fine. Let me text Kathryn real quick. Maybe she'll distract the paps at my place. I dunno, have a mental meltdown on the sidewalk or something. I'm sure she's due one."

Nadia shouldn't have laughed, but she needed the humor.

***

"Thanks for the help," Eva said, taking the last bag from Kathryn's assistant. "How's it look out there?"

The young woman couldn't look more different from Kathryn if she tried. Mousey brown hair, round face, and a department store chic that would've been nice if it wasn't obvious she bought everything off clearance racks. "It's pretty congested with photographers," the assistant said. "They didn't care about me, though."

All according to plan. Nobody suspected the plain woman shuffling through the lobby with bags full of clothes and hygiene products. All Eva had to do was call concierge and tell them to admit Kathryn's assistant. Voila! Nadia had some stuff to get her through the next few days until it was safe for her to go home again.

"Hopefully they don't give you any trouble on your way out, either. Give Kathryn my best when you get back to her. Tell her I'll pay her back." There wasn't enough time for Eva to send her credit card info over. Easier for Kathryn to pay as if she were shopping for herself. Wasn't like she couldn't afford to buy Eva's girlfriend a few outfits. *Still, I gotta pay her back.* Eva preferred it when she didn't have to look at receipts and could let her accountant deal with it. "If they do, remember, we're not here."

The assistant nodded. "If that's everything…"

Eva showed her out and sent Kathryn another thank you text. Behind her, Nadia began rooting through the bags for anything she would actually wear or use. The assistant had all the usual products, measurements, and brands Nadia lived by, but who knew what had been lost in translation?

"Is it okay?" Eva asked from her couch.

Nadia held up a conservative black dress and plopped it against her chest for inspection. Wow. Was someone heading to a funeral? "Kinda has to be, doesn't it?" Nadia folded the dress back up and placed it in its box. "Don't know if I can wear that one to work."

Shuddering, Eva turned back to her phone. *You'll be lucky if you can leave my apartment at all.* Nadia would need a private escort to get out of there. Coming back? Even worse. At least Eva didn't have classes to get to. Still, didn't mean she was looking forward to being cooped up in her apartment for who knew how many days. Nadia could say this apartment was huge all she wanted… for Eva, who liked to get out and walk around at least once a day, the walls were quickly closing in.

Her phone chose that moment to pop up with an email reminder.

"To Ms. Evangeline Warren: Please RSVP To The Animal Conservation Gala By Midnight Tonight."

Fuck. The gala.

There was always a gala. Always a fundraiser. Eva was invited to most of them, whether the people running the thing actually wanted her there or not. *Of course they want me there. Having a Warren attend something like that floats their little boats.* Henry and Monica were already confirmed to attend. Eva had no obligation to go. But…

That was the event she wanted to use to debut Nadia as her serious girlfriend.

It was perfect. Animal conservation was one of the safest topics around. People on both sides of the political spectrum could usually agree that endangered animals should be protected. It looked good to show up to that particular event and throw money. *Not to mention it's one of the most lighthearted events of the year.* Every summer the social elite could look forward to cute animal photos with a healthy helping of amazing food, live music and dancing, and catching up with those who decided to use one of the most popular events of the year to make a compulsory appearance. The media likewise would flock there. Certain members of the press would be allowed in to take flattering pictures and report on what this person wore and who danced with whom.

With such a good mood in the air, what better time was there to show Nadia off to the world as Eva's girlfriend? That was before those *other* pictures came out. Now Eva wasn't even sure it was a good idea to go. Damn. One of her favorite live jazz groups was going to be performing there.

"Do you still want to go to that?" Nadia asked, glancing at her girlfriend's phone. Eva shut it off and set it aside. "I was thinking about saying yes before… you know."

"Yeah. I know." Eva crossed her arms. "I was hoping you would say yes. Would've been the best way to do things on our terms."

"Not very much is on our terms now, is it?"

"Well," Eva began, passing through her living room en route to her bathroom. When she was anxious, Eva had a habit of washing her hands for a lack of anything else to do with her fidgeting extremities. Nadia followed her. "It would still sort of be on our terms. Once those disgusting photos are taken down, people will be hankering to get more of us. We should give them normal ones. Maybe it will disperse them for a while."

Nadia's fingers grazed Eva's behind as she soaped up her hands. As she ran her hands beneath the faucet, Eva's girlfriend hopped up on the counter and languidly swung her legs back and forth. *Why does she have to be so cute right now?* The faucet turned off. Eva grabbed a towel from its rack.

"I don't know if I want to go," Nadia admitted. "Even without this mess… it would be awkward for me."

"Who knew things would be less awkward if nobody knew you." Eva crossed her arms as she leaned against the counter. Nadia continued to swing her legs. "Not that I think a ton of people do."

"They may not know me personally," Nadia flipped her hair, "but one look at these locks and they're bound to recognize me from somewhere. They'll at least remember wanting to fuck me, even if they don't remember from where."

"*I* definitely wanted to fuck you, that's for sure."

"Hopefully more than fuck me."

"What do you call this?"

The shy smile that drew out of Nadia almost sent Eva to her knees.

"Tell you what," she said, making her way between Nadia's legs and wrapping two strong arms around her. "We'll kick some mad ass at the gala and become everyone's *it* couple, whatever that means. It changes every month anyway." Eva had seen every couple she had ever known be the paps' "it" couple for a hot fifteen minutes. Poor Kathryn almost died from anxiety when her scandalous relationship with Ian was made public. *Those fuckers got to do it on their own terms, though.* What Eva would give to do this all over again. For one thing, she wouldn't have taken Nadia to Hong Kong. She heard Japan was really strict about what and who could be photographed. Plus, they really didn't give a shit about the Warrens there.

If Eva learned anything from her Winchester classes about dealing with the press and the price of fame, it was that *any* bit of bad press could be turned into an advantage. Eva didn't have a brand, per se, that she was trying to uphold. She wasn't Kathryn with her endless charity cases that may be put off by their billionaire fundraiser being caught up in filthy sex scandals. Nor was she Adrienne Thomas, a woman who – by all accounts – was building a brand as one of the forefront CEOs in America. *Imagine her being caught up in a lesbian sex scandal. No wonder her one relationship with another woman is so unhealthy.*

So how could Eva and Nadia turn this unfortunate bullshit into an unwitting favor? Exploit it. Exploit the fuck out of it. Own who they were and not give a shit about what other people thought.

Easy enough for Eva to think. But what about Nadia?

“After the gala, I’ll take you to my family’s private island. You and me. Definitely no paps there. And if one of the employees talks? They’re fired before they can think about their dead retirement fund.”

Nadia picked beneath her thumbnail while making a face that suggested she didn’t quite believe her girlfriend. “All right,” she finally muttered. “I’ll go to the gala. You’re buying me a new dress, though.”

“I can get you one custom made beforehand. I know a gal.”

“That’s not necessary,” Nadia said, sheepish behind her curling knuckles. “It’s too much trouble. Seriously.”

Eva tightened her hold. “Oh, babe,” she muttered in her girlfriend’s ear, that soft red hair tickling Eva’s nose, “nothing is ever too much trouble for you. Seriously.”

“Hm…”

Nadia yelped when Eva dragged her off the counter, carrying her with nary a struggle across the bathroom and toward the bedroom. *I’d have even less trouble if you stopped squirming.* Nadia could save the squirming for when they were in bed. Eva *loved* it when her girlfriend squirmed beneath her. *I’m stronger than I look, I swear!* All those soccer and badminton matches meant Eva didn’t spend much time sitting on her ass. Besides, didn’t sex count as a vigorous workout? *It should.* Men weren’t the only ones who got to show off their virility in the bedroom.

“Know what we should do?” Eva dropped Nadia onto the bed, delighting in the way everything shook and jiggled on her girlfriend’s body as she bounced in the middle of the mattress. "We should do way more incriminating shit than what was in those pictures. You and me, babe. We’ll rock every world that needs to be rocked.”

Nadia pushed herself up on her hands and bit her lip. *Ow. My heart. My loins. Everything hurts.* The view of her cleavage helped. “Do you want to end every day with sex?”

"*How* is that a bad thing?" Eva leaned down, hands joining Nadia's on the bed. Slowly, Ms. Gaines found herself in a supine position, Eva's lips only a single breath away from kissing the sides of a pair of breasts that demanded to fall out of Nadia's dress. "Especially when there is still so much for me to show you."

"Oh?" Mischief colored that fair complexion. "Like what?"

Uh oh. There was a nipple popping out. Nadia should spend most of her life lying down. Gravity did wonders for Eva's libido whenever that happened. "Quite a few things that would definitely give my mother a heart attack," she muttered, biting that nipple and refusing to think of her mother for the rest of the evening.

Chapter 36

Nadia should have guessed that Eva only cared about upping the ante whenever her sexuality was challenged – let alone by the media.

"You're a danger to the both of us, Ms. Warren." Most women in possession of large breasts took their share of pleasure from watching them rise and fall whenever moments heated up like this. Nadia was no different. Her whole body, currently clad in nothing but her black and red accented lingerie, was a reminder that she was a feminine beauty who had the ability to seduce one of the most powerful lesbians in the country. That was no small feat. It was one thing for Eva to have a passing interest in her. It was quite another for Ms. Evangeline Warren, all-around playgirl who quoted Sappho in billion-dollar executive offices, to confess love and a willingness to have a serious relationship… on top of the kinky sex.

Ah, kinky. Who knew Nadia could get into it?

"I'm only a 'danger' because you won't sit still." Eva was still dressed in her jeans and T-shirt as she sat back in a chair by the window. Sure, she had a great view from *there.* For the past five minutes Nadia's hands had been bound above her head and attached firmly to the headboard. This whole situation began because someone got horny while being undressed. Eva had stopped at her girlfriend's lingerie and *commanded* her to put her arms up and hold them until a piece of silk fabric could finish the look.

One thing Nadia could say was that her worldly girlfriend knew how to gradually introduce things to their sex life. And she didn't do it every single time they made love – only when the moment truly called for it. Eva told the truth when she said she wasn't into lifestyle bondage and submission play. She also told the truth when she said she was into the kinkier sides of sex and appreciated exploring them with the woman she fancied. For all her apprehensions earlier on, Nadia couldn't figure out why, for the life of her, she ever considered this something to be nervous about.

Not like Eva would ever *hurt* her. Emotionally or physically, for that matter. Only sweet, succulent promises of heart-fluttering and thigh-wetting pleasure Nadia didn't even know she was capable of experiencing.

So when Eva smacked a wooden paddle against her palm, redness spreading across her white skin, Nadia knew there was only one way to shudder.

With sheer anticipation.

"Tell me what you want," Eva said, slender legs crossed and exuding a bravado only men usually got away with. *Fuck me, fuck me, she's so hot, I can't stand it.* Now that Nadia knew what her girlfriend was truly capable of in bed… nope. Couldn't stand it. Why wasn't she paying physical attention to her now? "What do you want me to do to you, my lovely little dove?"

"I should be asking you what you want, Ms. Warren." Nadia was ready to give up anything. She was so fueled with desire that those paps would have a hard time justifying what they saw through Eva's tinted windows. *But that's why she has tinted windows, even this high up.* After all, there was another apartment building across the street. What was stopping a pap from popping in there and using a high-res camera to look through *these* windows? Oh, right. The tint. Technology hadn't caught up to that yet. She hoped.

Eva held a long finger up to her lips. She was a woman of little detail when it came to her fingertips. Other women of her stature, regardless of how feminine they usually presented, often went around with the fanciest nails. Or they went for understated French-tips. Not Eva. She kept her pink nails perfectly buffed, each one the same short length. That turned Nadia on more than a flash of her girlfriend's cleavage – although she got some of that as well. That was quite the plunging V-neck Eva wore.

The only way she could be hotter was if she were wearing one of her designer suits. But Eva didn't need a suit to get her point across.

"No, babe, I'm the one doing the talking. Unless you're answering my questions." The paddle spun in Eva's hand before tapping against her leg. "Last I checked, I had asked you a question. So spill. What do you want me to do to you?"

As she spoke, her finger slowly trailed across her lips, tugging at the corner of her mouth and showing off her pearly white teeth and long, pink tongue. *What do I want? You on top of me!* What was this? Rocket science? Sheesh.

"I want you to do whatever you want to me, Ms. Warren." God, she felt so naughty calling her girlfriend that. Being in nothing but lacy lingerie had that effect, too.

"No, precious, that's not a proper response. I want you to be specific. It's not all about me, you know. You have your own wants and desires too. I want to hear them."

"Does it matter when you've got that paddle in your hand?"

"This thing?" It tapped against Eva's dimpled cheek. "Consider it inspiration. Lots and lots of inspiration."

"You want to spank me, don't you?"

A look of disbelief clouded Eva's face. Right. Nadia was supposed to be answering questions, not asking them. *You need to train me better, ma'am.* God! Nadia was starting to sound like the women she often bumped into! This shit was infectious, wasn't it?

"Do you want me to spank you?"

Nadia rustled against the bed. "Maybe."

"No maybes. Yes. No." Eva held up the paddle. "Those are your options. When we play, babe, there are no gray areas. No room for miscommunication. I don't want to hurt you or scare you. I need to know exactly what it is that you want. I want to hear you beg and plead for me to do things to you, even if they're things I hadn't even considered doing. Do you understand?"

"Yes, ma'am."

"So do you want me to spank you?"

Nadia couldn't stop biting her lip. "Right now I want to look at you."

"And I want to look at you. What a happy coincidence."

They gazed at each other for a few minutes, Eva perfectly still – paddle twirling excluded – and Nadia continuing to shift around as if she were going to run away at any moment. *I'm not going anywhere.* She was nervous. Excited. Eager to be touched with more than a sultry, smoldering gaze. There was something extra delicious about a pair of icy blue eyes leaving scratches all over her exposed skin. And Nadia had a lot of exposed skin. It helped when her movements caused her bra to slip down her breasts and expose the same nipple Eva bit earlier.

"That's a hard nipple you've got there, babe," Eva mused. "Makes me wonder what other parts of you are ready for me."

All of them. No wonder Nadia needed strapping down. Eva would strap her down every time they played like this until Nadia could learn to sit still. That would *not* be today.

"You're free to come over and find out anytime."

She expected another reprimand. God knew she deserved one. Instead, Eva stood up, her limbs moving effortlessly as she took two long strides to the bed and kneeled on the edge. Her presence was palpable enough to caress.

"I'm not going to get straight answers out of you, am I?" The tip of the paddle touched Nadia's outer thigh. "I should ask yes or no questions. Like… do you like it when I spank you?"

She asked it so damn sweetly that Nadia could hardly believe what she said. "I like it a lot more than I thought I would." So true. A year ago, someone asking Nadia if she liked spanking would have made her turn her nose and pretend she didn't think of her boss and best friend's interoffice hanky-panky. That was something straight people did, because men were possessive assholes. Or so Nadia presumed. Who knew she could feel this good with another woman doing that to her in the privacy of their bedroom? "So, yes."

"Do you want me to smack you with this paddle?" Eva tapped her harder. "Do you want me to smack you, finger you, and make you come? Or I could make you come from this paddle… maybe I'll kiss you, too."

What a cheeky grin. *Know what else is cheeky? My ass.* Too bad Eva didn't flip Nadia over and start smacking it.

However, she did pull Nadia's legs open and expose the crotch of her lingerie. Whatever she saw down there made her smile even wider. "That's exactly what I wanted to see, babe. See? Looking at me does make you wet."

Nadia forwent rolling her eyes in favor of smiling back at her girlfriend. "Like that's difficult to achieve. I look at you and all I can think about is snuggling and sex."

"Fancy that! Those things can happen at the same time. Snuggle me hard enough and I'll start fucking you. Almost like I can't help myself."

Nadia didn't need her girlfriend to open her legs for her. She could do *that* herself as well! Nice and wide. So wide that her underwear strained against her skin. How was that for a show? "Is there a problem with that?"

The paddle gently landed on Nadia's thick thigh. So close to a forbidden place. Not that it was really forbidden… more like… too much too soon. Eva knew that as well.

"No problem. But I'm a woman who likes to practice *some* semblance of control. Why do you think I'm the one with the paddle and not you? If I gave it to you, you'd start smacking everything within your reach. I can't risk that. I need to know I can trust you, like you trust me."

"Please," Nadia batted her eyelashes. "You want to smack some of my skin and watch what happens. It gives you a thrill. You get off on it."

"And you don't?"

Nadia glanced at the paddle resting on her thigh. "Try me."

The paddle hovered over her skin. "Try what? Come on, you can be nice about it. I'm not sleeping with someone with no manners. Show me that sweet, needy side of yourself. Make me feel like there's no option but spanking your hot skin until it's as red as your hair."

Nadia sucked in her breath. Her breasts raised up, spilling from her bra and enticing both her and her girlfriend. "Please," she whispered, drawing her legs up until her knees pierced the air. "Do it."

"Do what?"

Eyes closed, Nadia shoved her head back into the pillow beneath her. "Spank me."

"Why?"

"Because it feels good."

"As good a reason as any." Eva curled her hand over Nadia's knee and gave a hearty tap to her thigh.

It wasn't painful, yet, but it did send a thrilling chill through Nadia's lower body. Through her legs. Through her abdomen. Through her gut and to her loins. Apparently it reached her torso as well, for her nipple was even harder than it was before. The gasp emitting from her body coincided with her curling toes.

"Again?"

"Yeah," Nadia whispered. "Again."

The paddle smacked her, harder, sending more than a chill through her now. That was shock. Those were tingles. That was her body getting so turned on by wood hitting her skin that she barely knew how to control herself. No wonder she was tied up!

"Again!"

Every consecutive hit was harder than the last, building Nadia up to taking a full, carefully placed smack from an experienced Domme. If Nadia were going to participate in something like this, what better way to cherish it than with a woman who knew what she was doing? Eva knew how to place a smack, how to control the strength and use the right amount of force to neither hurt nor hinder her beloved. The amount of trust Nadia placed in her was unprecedented. What other person could she do this with? Her ex-girlfriends? No way. They were as closed-minded to this sort of play as Nadia used to be. Her ex-boyfriends? God, no! Further proof that Nadia was better off without any of them.

"Oh!" That garbled sound ended that round. Nadia snapped her legs shut, basking in the feelings overwhelming her. Eva stood up and took in the sight she helped create. *Oh,* indeed.

"You're a dirty one, aren't you?" Finally, Eva rolled her girlfriend over, the silk strip twisting with the motion. Nadia lay on her stomach, legs still spread and a gorgeous blonde straddling the left one. Eva was deceptively heavy. A woman that tall and athletic was bound to be. *Ah, bound. My new favorite word. Right up there with paddles and spanking.* "You like it when I assert my nature, don't you?"

She said it so sweetly! What a trap. What a *bitch.* God, what was wrong with Nadia? Eva was doing this on purpose, and it was turning her girlfriend on! "Yes," Nadia said, meek but not weak. "I love it!"

"That's what I like to hear." Eva shifted herself until she was straddling Nadia's back instead of her leg. But she wasn't facing forward. As her thighs settled on either side of her girlfriend's back, Eva leaned forward – the perfect position to caress Nadia's ass with both hand and paddle. Wasn't it nice that Nadia wore a thong that day? Her cheeks were right there, ready to be spanked! "Naturally, I like it when my lady is enthusiastic. It's music to my nasty ears."

She bent down lower, breath hitting Nadia's skin, traveling from the top of her ass and toward her slit. Fingers kneaded her flesh. A frisky tongue circled the area Eva intended to smack first. Nadia knew this, because as soon as Eva sat up, she smacked that ass with enough intent to make a seasoned sub blush.

"Oh my God," Nadia muttered into her pillow. "You're killing me!" Killing her with lust. Would it be too much to ask to have Eva stick her finger somewhere? Preferably down low, where all the wet was?

"I've got you right where I want you, babe." Eva moved the paddle across Nadia's ass, lingering on both cheeks before stroking the back of her thighs. "I'm thinking about all the ways I want to touch you and make your skin a pretty shade of pink. You know, my favorite shade." She chuckled. "I could do it here…" Her ass. "Or here." The back of her thigh. "Even here." The side of her thigh. "I know how to do all three. But let's start with the basics. We'll work up to the harder stuff some other time. I'm sure I'll get my fill from your awesome ass."

Words. She said a lot of words, didn't she? But did they actually mean anything? Because Nadia wasn't sure they meant a damn fucking thing other than *you're hot and I want to fuck your brains out.*

"Spread your legs. Get wetter every time I strike your ass."

The way she said *strike* had Nadia quivering before the paddle came down on her skin.

"Oh!" Now that was pain. The good kind of pain that made her nipples peak and her face rub against the pillow. Hands clutched the sheets. Toes continued to curl. And, yes, her thighs were wetter than ever before. "That's good."

"Good? Just good? Are you kidding me?" Laughing, Eva spanked her again, this time *her* crotch rubbing against the curve of Nadia's back. She had her own heat that emanated from her body. Her jeans couldn't hide that! *She wants me. She's so turned on. She's restraining herself to toy with me a little longer.* "I want to be the best you'll ever have." Eva yanked on the tiny strip of fabric that called itself a thong. It had to be soaking wet. Sure enough, Eva's nose appeared close to Nadia's wet slit, tempting her with penetration. *Think you could stick something in me* and *spank me?* Was that too much to ask? Was Nadia allowed to request something right now? Or was this the Eva Warren Show?

Haha. Like she had to ask *that!*

"You are," Nadia moaned. "You're the fucking best."

"What was that?" Eva sat up, spanking Nadia with her bare hand. It wasn't as intense as the paddle, but it was certainly more intimate. "I couldn't hear you, babe."

Nadia pushed herself up enough to make her intentions known, but not enough to knock Eva off. "I said you're the best!"

"Of course I am. So happens that you're the best too." Eva grinded her hips against Nadia's bare skin, every little swirl of movement sending Nadia farther back down into her pillow. "Suppose I should reward you for that display of affection. What do you want me to do, babe?" Her finger was right on the edge of Nadia's opening, ready to plunge in. She knew what Nadia wanted! She was teasing her, as always!

"Fuck me," Nadia whimpered. "Please. I want you inside of me!"

"Want?"

"Need!" That was the magical word, wasn't it? "I need you inside of me, please!"

Eva didn't say anything, but she obliged. Before Nadia could beg again, a finger slid into her. Deep. *Deep.*

It felt good, but it wasn't enough. Nadia was so wound up that she needed more than one finger. What was this, a warm up? Ha! She was a seasoned pro at fucking Eva Warren now. Her appetites had grown. She wasn't satisfied with some feeling up and a pussy rub. If Nadia wasn't biting her pillow and digging her nails into the mattress, then it was all wrong!

"Holy shit, girl, you're *wet.*" Still laughing, Eva smacked her girlfriend's ass. "You definitely want to get fucked, don't you?"

"Yes!"

"Fine, my lovely little dove." Oh, God. A second finger. Now they were talking. "I'll give it to you."

Nadia was lost to everything. The world, her girlfriend, even the bed beneath them. As soon as Eva began fucking Nadia with her fingers – in between spanking her with the paddle, of course – Nadia was gone with the wind and riding high in the sky. *What? I can only think in clichés right now!* Every spank brought a numbing desire to her body and a cry of pleasure to her throat. Every thrust of Eva's fingers made her squirm against the silk holding her wrists together. Nadia didn't hold back her demands. *Fuck me. Spank me. Own me. Use me. Make me feel like that slut everyone saw in those pictures today.* There was empowerment lurking within that thought. Something intimate had been stolen from them, to be made entertainment fodder for the whole world. Nadia wanted to take some of that back. She wanted to feel like it was okay. That it didn't matter if her boss accidentally glanced at some pictures that would make him blush around Nadia for the next ten years. That it didn't matter if dysfunctional assholes like Amber and Adrienne expressed utter disbelief or thought it was funny. Who gave a fuck? It was sex! *Awesome, mind-blowing, life changing sex!* Nadia wanted it. She wanted to feel like this every time she made love to her girlfriend. Maybe not always with the kink, but definitely with this amount of passion and intimacy between them. Nobody could snatch the way they felt for one another. Funny. Who knew that getting spanked and finger-fucked could make Nadia so aware of *love?*

"You gonna come?" Eva pulled her girlfriend wide open and licked the wetness coming from her body. "You're gonna come. Excellent. See if you can hold off until I tell you to come."

Madness!

Eva was relentless after that. The paddle landed on the bed, hands the only things touching Nadia's flesh. One fingered her, hard, fast, while the other intermittently spanked her. It was the best fucking combination in the whole world, and nobody could tell Nadia otherwise!

Of course, she wanted to come. She wanted to fling herself into orgasm the moment Eva spanked her with two fingers still inside that tightening cunt. She even commented on it! "*Babe, if you get this tight, you're going to come. I haven't told you to come Wait for me, lovely. I know you can do it.*" Fuck her! Who was she to say when Nadia could or couldn't *come?* Wasn't part of the fun spontaneously orgasming? Wait, that sounded weird…

But not as weird as the sound ripping itself from Nadia's throat. A long, tumultuous whine that ran a full octave before echoing in that corner of Eva's apartment. She couldn't say words anymore. Nadia was nothing but a giant sound box that writhed in anticipation of orgasm.

Eva clamped her thighs on her girlfriend's back. "All right! Come!"

Nadia was way ahead of her. She was undulating back and forth, Eva's fingers constantly inside of her, binding her to Nadia and turning her into a prisoner of lust.

Eva was never going to get those fingers back.

"Holy *shit.*" That laughter was no longer the carefully crafted tone of dominance. It was pure amusement – and arousal, if that heat emanating through those jeans meant anything. "Look at you go, girl! You're fucking hot."

Nadia was fucking, all right. Hot? Yeah, she was sweaty. How could a girl not get sweaty even in an air-conditioned apartment?

Eva swung her leg off Nadia, eventually landing both feet on the floor. "Ready for another?" That was a zipper. Nadia didn't have to lift her head to know her girlfriend was disrobing. "Because I am. You're not the only one around here who gets to climax."

She plopped on the bed next to Nadia. After untying her girlfriend's wrists, Eva propped herself up against the head board, her bare legs spreading as wide as Nadia's was a while ago. "Hey, babe." The paddle was back. But instead of smacking Nadia's ass, it tipped her chin up. "Come here and give me a kiss."

That kiss was the perfect display of their roles that afternoon. Eva, upright, dominant, in control. Nadia, on her hands and knees, head thrown back and deferring to her girlfriend's demeanor. Eva stroked Nadia's hair, fluffing it as they kissed, one's tongue more vibrant than the other's. Nadia was drunk on her orgasm. How could she be expected to kiss like Eva right now?

Not that she wanted to, anyway. What she wanted to do? Was the very thing Eva asked of her two seconds later.

"What are you waiting for?" Eva purred. "Get between my legs and make me feel like a fucking queen."

"Absolutely." Nadia braced herself against Eva's spread legs. "Whatever you want, Ms. Warren."

Eva hid her sweet smile behind the paddle. But Nadia could still see it: the gleam in her eyes. Not just sexual dominance. A need to be in love.

Oh, Nadia would love on her, all right. She would keep her eyes locked on those icy – but warming – blues as she lowered her face and took in the scent of a woman ready to be pleasured.

Nadia had always enjoyed going down on other women. (It was definitely preferable to doing the same for men. That much she could say with authority.) Every woman tasted and smelled different, their folds intricate mazes of awaiting pleasure. But there was also something that was always the same between them. Femininity incarnate. Every woman Nadia had pleasured like this before quivered when she got near. They all let out the same soft moan when she gently licked their first fold. They all instinctively grabbed her hair when her hand wrapped around their thighs and she teased their clits with lips and tongue.

The scents and tastes were different. The womanhood she encountered? Always familiar. Nadia loved it. She especially loved it when it was Eva on the other end of her tongue. Eva pulled up her T-shirt and groped her own breasts with one rogue hand. Her other hand? Deep in Nadia's hair as Nadia dove deeper into her girlfriend's intoxication.

Yet somehow it's so different with her. It wasn't mere love. It was a constant exchange of power. A back and forth of wills and whims. One moment Eva was totally in-control, gazing down at her sexual servant and reaping the benefits of being a powerful heiress. The next? She crumbled. She was as much Nadia's toy as Nadia had been her toy five minutes ago. Those glimpses of vulnerability were what spurred Nadia on to a new level of devotion as she pressed her lips against flesh and sent her tongue after the essence teeming from the woman beneath her.

Eva was hers to control now. Nadia may have been flat on her stomach, feet kicking up in the air in time with her flicking tongue, but it was Eva who was at her mercy – not the other way around.

You wanna come, huh? The intense scent, the tightening of muscles, the flushing heat covering her skin… Eva didn't need to say she wanted to come to make it known. But Nadia did appreciate the sweet sounds gracing her ears every time she did something Eva liked.

Yet like how Eva made Nadia temporarily wait out having an orgasm, Nadia could do the same. As soon as Eva was on the brink of coming, Nadia pulled her tongue away, letting her nose be the only thing to touch her girlfriend there. The tip of her nose wandered up and down Eva's quivering skin, inhaling heady scents and getting high off promises of more sex. The hand in her hair tightened. Eva's hips buckled, sliding farther down the bed as she gasped in defeat.

"Do you feel like a queen yet?" Nadia asked the thigh beneath her face. "Or does your ego need more convincing?"

Her head was shoved forward, Eva's lips instinctively kissing the folds before them. Oh, Eva need more convincing. Or maybe not convincing. She demanded worship. A goddess always knew her worth.

"Don't stop until I come." Her voice was raspy, demanding. "Not until I come all over that face and make you indisputably mine."

Nadia had to oblige. She *had* to. Slam her face right against that wet skin and work it until the world ended around them. Fine thing, too. Nadia had no problem heaping positive attention on her girlfriend.

So much attention.

So. Much.

She wasn't simply right there when her girlfriend started to climax. She was a willing participant, washed away on the winds of heat. Eva's essence exploded from her, like she exploded in shakes of the limbs and womanly moans that crashed right into Nadia's brain. They were going down together. Nadia may be the one *going down,* but Eva was going to join her.

Now.

"Fuck!" When Eva whined, Nadia knew she had done a good job. Even without looking up, she knew that Eva had her eyes squeezed shut and her mouth hanging open in an eternal cry. "*Fuck!*"

Nadia only came up for air a few seconds later, when Eva practically pulled her girlfriend's hair away from sensitive places.

For a second, she thought they were finished.

Only a second.

Eva was on top of her, thrusting against her, pulling Nadia into pure hedonism. Their kisses were brazen. Their tangled limbs made their own separate kind of love. Their bodies and minds were one, but their spirits had no idea what to do with themselves. Come together? Remain separate, cautious? How deep did these feelings go? Was it about abandoning oneself to sex, or…

Or was this the purest form of physical love?

Even after they both orgasmed again, Nadia's body so worn out that she finally noticed how sore her ass was, did they concede it was time to bring this to an end. Eva collapsed on top of her girlfriend. Nadia splayed her arms out, too tired to hold anyone, even the woman pressed against her. They shared a few gentle kisses before sighing.

Nadia fingered the soft T-shirt within her grasp. Eva kept her face nuzzled between two pushed-up breasts. They never fully undressed. Somehow, that was sexier than being naked.

"I fucking love you," Eva said, rolling over and folding her arms on her abdomen. "You know that?"

Nadia cuddled up next to her. "I know. I love you too. I've gotta love you if I didn't run off screaming after what happened today." She drew her fingers up and down her girlfriends arm, then her stomach. "I think you're worth it, though."

She had said it sarcastically, and Eva took it that way, snorting with the last of her strength. "Good. 'Cause I'd probably be a mess without you now."

They remained lying there until the evening, Nadia dozing against her girlfriend's shoulder and being filled with the kind of reassurance she craved every single day. Not just when something happened to shake her trust in the world. Every. Day.

Their hands intertwined as Nadia slipped into a fitful nap. Eventually, she was going to give Eva a taste of her own medicine. *I can already see it now. Make her feel the way she makes me feel. Truly.* Maybe no paddles involved… but Eva was a fool if she thought her girlfriend was a mere feminine plaything who always fell in line. Nadia may have enjoyed her primary role in the bedroom, but sometimes? Things needed to flip.

Next time. Because there *would* be a next time.

***

Nadia didn't show her face outside of Eva's apartment until she went to work Friday morning. Mr. Cole had been nice enough to give her a couple of days off until the scandal cooled down a bit. The way Amber told it over the phone? Nadia was lucky. Because more than one pervert showed up for unannounced appointments, obviously sniffing around Nadia's desk in the hopes of seeing her. Mr. Cole never deigned these people with his presence. They would go home, completely disappointed.

The way *Jasmine* told it at lunch that Friday?

"I haven't heard anyone talking about it," she said with a hilarious amount of authority. She was Mrs. Cole now, after all. Her name carried no weight earlier that year. Now? Everyone played nice around one of the richest wives in the city. Nadia could barely give a shit about the details of her friend's marriage, but she was grateful to hear that Mr. Cole agreed with his wife to do some damage control on Nadia's behalf. That didn't stop the conversations they privately had in the corner of a rooftop restaurant, though.

"People are talking about it." Nadia's voice couldn't be flatter if it were steam-pressed. "They're simply not talking about it in front of *you*." To be fair, people rarely talked about things in front of Jasmine… although she had the uncanny ability to overhear shit never meant for her.

Blushing, Jasmine made a flippant comment about her orange juice.

Nadia glanced around the room. Jasmine's status commanded her access to one of the most private corners in the restaurant, but Nadia's hair made her a beacon for prying eyes. *Is anyone staring at me?* The few other diners in the restaurant couldn't be bothered with her, but that didn't mean anything. Maybe they were waiting for her to look away again. *You know, that big fat lesbian who is fucking Eva Warren and getting caught on camera in Hong Kong. Christ.*

"Welcome to the world of dating a billionaire, I suppose." Jasmine and Nadia didn't only have similar styling interests, but both heads of hair were wild and wavy. Jasmine's ebony black hair was overshadowed by Nadia's red locks, so when they both threaded fingers through their hair at the same time, only one of them drew the attention of the waiter floating through the restaurant in search of someone to help. Nadia went ahead and ordered another Diet Coke. This was on Jasmine's dime anyway. "Everyone is suddenly in your business. I don't know how many times those awful paps have invaded my privacy, let alone Ethan's."

Nadia kept her thoughts to herself. *You're not a giant gay-wad, though. You've got a man to "protect" you. You're the image of a beautiful, rich couple.* There was no sense getting into those politics right now. Jasmine meant well. She was oblivious to a lot of Nadia's bullshit, but she meant well. Sometimes intent really was enough.

"Can't wait for more invasions of my privacy." Nadia held off more comments until her Diet Coke was in front of her. She smiled at and thanked the waiter before he left. "It's going to be a lot of fun being in a relationship with her. So fun."

Jasmine added more dried tomato flakes to her salad. Nadia didn't even know restaurants offered shit like that until she started working for Mr. Cole. She had a feeling that Jasmine hadn't known either. "So it's serious between you and her finally?"

"What do you mean finally? It's been serious for a while."

"At the wedding…"

"It was serious before that, but things got twisted." Nadia looked away. "You've been gone, so you don't know. But Eva and I are sort of… um…"

"Yeah?"

"You know…"

"*Yeah?*"

Lord, she looked like a twelve-year-old waiting to hear about getting a puppy. Nadia shifted back and forth in her seat. "We're kinda in love."

There it was. The squeal Jasmine was really, *really* trying to keep in her throat. It eked out of there anyway. For a woman who had been playing matchmaker between Eva and Nadia for a hot minute… no wonder she was excited. Not that it made Nadia feel any better.

"That's awesome! Good for you."

"Yeah, I guess. Her parents hate it, though."

"I can't imagine Henry and Monica having a problem."

"They don't. But they're not technically the heads of the family." Nadia wasn't sure how the family worked at that level. Henry may have been in charge of the holdings and money-making now, but Gerald and Isabella were still granted many privileges by right of progenitor. Their opinions mattered, even if Henry was the only one signing papers at the moment. "There's a lot of tension over her sexuality. But… I probably shouldn't say more. We've got enough drama at the moment."

"I suppose so. Those paps are ruthless. I'm surprised they didn't stalk me on my honeymoon. Some of the stuff we did…" Great. Heterosexual giggling. Something churned in Nadia's stomach – cause she totally wanted to imagine whatever images were beaming from Jasmine's brain. "I told you that I accidentally bought that resort, didn't I? That would've been embarrassing for them to find out. Everyone already paints me as a total ditz."

Nadia sighed. "You can't really compare the two things. You've never been papped in such an intimate way." Or at least Nadia couldn't recall any horrors related to Jasmine and Ethan Cole being photographed mid-coitus. *God! Gag!*

"No, that's true. I think I would flat out die if that ever happened. I can't even bring myself to do much with him in that club everyone goes to. You know." Jasmine lowered her voice. "The sex club."

Nadia rolled her eyes. Everyone in a certain world knew of The Dark Hour, a club of depravity that was full of public sex and was a popular hangout for those into BDSM. Eva had been open with her membership there. Nadia didn't care. She wasn't about to go there herself, though. Eva could have all the drunken fun she wanted as long as she didn't touch anyone. Not like that, anyway. In fact, hadn't she said something about going there tonight to see some of her gal pals? Whatever. Not the point.

"Again, it's not the same. You don't get it. You're straight. It's different."

Jasmine's movements slowed.

"I don't want to hear about how you experimented with that girl in college. Unless you actually ID as bi or something… fuck it, it's still not the same and you know it. You're married to one of the most celebrated men in America. You're beautiful and so is he. People say shit about you? It's because they can't think of anything better to pick on. So I don't really want to hear it, Jasmine. I wasn't papped because it's fun and scandalous to get papped having sex with someone you haven't gone public with yet. We were targeted because we are lesbians, and society loves nothing more than fetishizing us. It wasn't just a misogynistic attack. It was homophobic. *Lesbo*phobic. You ever hear that word before? No? So yeah, I don't wanna hear it. If I were with a man, the outcome would've been different. Those pictures probably wouldn't have even been published! You know Eva had already paid off the Hong Kong tabloid to destroy them? If she had been a man, that would've been enough. But *The Daily Social* caught wind of them and couldn't help themselves. They specifically picked us because they knew we were extra vulnerable. So… shut up, Jasmine. You can't relate at all to how I feel right now."

Boy, that did *something* to Mrs. Cole. Jasmine's cheeks were so red that she was probably about to pass out from embarrassment. *She may have nice intent, but she's so dumb sometimes.* Not dumb enough to warrant high society painting her as a stupid trophy wife, but when it came to these matters? She really didn't know what the fuck she was talking about.

"I'm sorry," Jasmine meekly apologized. "I hadn't thought of it that way."

"Yeah, well, you've never had to. Not only did I not want to deal with the crap of dating a billionaire, but… fuck, Jas! It's so embarrassing having everyone giggle over our relationship! If you knew some of the other shit Eva's had to deal with in her life… I feel so bad for her. I don't want it. I'm only sticking this out because I'm stupidly in love with her." Nadia picked up her napkin and dabbed her eyes. Jasmine offered her another napkin. "I don't know how she's put up with it. This is my first real time and I feel so lost and attacked by the public. I can't deal with the misogyny and homophobia at the same fucking time."

Nadia stopped most of the tears before they erupted, but some of the damage was already done. She sniffed, wiped her eyes, and struggled to regain her composure. Fuck. This is what dealing with shitty assholes did to her. And she didn't even know what those assholes looked like! Just as well.

"I may not know your exact predicament, no," Jasmine began, "but I know what it's like to feel overwhelmed by people's opinions once you start dating someone of that stature."

"Yeah, sorry." Nadia left her crumpled napkin on the table. "I know you do. Sorry."

"If there is one piece of advice I can give…" Jasmine's trepidation after Nadia's rant was tangible. "It's that dealing with the bullshit is totally worth it. If you love the person as much as you say you do, and they love and take care of you in return. A lot of it is still new and scary to me. I can't even imagine what other layers of bullshit you have to deal with. I can't imagine you at the country club for one."

"Yeah, I bet they'd love us there." *Country Club* screamed images of raging homophobes. Only thing worse would be the racetrack.

"But if Eva really has been through this before, then she knows what to expect. If she tells you something is going to be fine, you have to believe her, you know? The money isn't enough for most of us, I suppose. I know that if Ethan didn't support me so much, I'd be gone long before we got married. It's not just about the sex, money, and the rest of the lifestyle that comes from dating people like that. They offer a very unique love and perspective on our lives. If it's worth it to you, then it will keep being worth it. Does she love and respect you?"

Was Nadia supposed to answer that? "Yeah."

"Then keep at it. I've almost let go of my relationship many times, you know. But every time I imagined life without him, I felt even worse. In the end, it wasn't worth losing him in order to lose the crap. They come together. Eventually you figure out what works best for you in dealing with it. I guess it's especially hard for us since we didn't grow up in it. Not like Eva."

"And she's had to deal with very different shit from even her best friend."

"I guess so, huh?"

Jasmine would never know about Eva's more harrowing experiences. Or at least she wouldn't learn about them from Nadia. *Not my place to share those personal things.* From the sounds of it, the only people who knew about what Eva had been through were limited to her closest friends and family. The fact that Nadia belonged to that prestigious circle… shit, Eva really did love and trust her, didn't she?

The thought of living without Eva – not that Nadia had been considering it anymore – hurt her more than the dirty looks she got when she went out. It hurt more than thinking of what people had seen in that paper.

"I guess tomorrow will be the real test," Nadia said. "I'm going to that gala with her."

"Really? I'm going too!"

Of course you are. Jasmine was stepping into charity work ala Kathryn Alison. Of course she would be dragging her husband to one of the biggest fundraising galas of the year. It wouldn't be their first official appearance since their marriage, but it was the most high profile one. The cameras would be all over them too.

"I'm supposed to go pick up my dress at her place tomorrow."

"Is that what you were getting fitted for yesterday?"

"Yup."

"What brand?"

"Gucci. She's wearing Gucci too."

"Aw, you two are already coordinating!"

Nadia loved her friend, but sometimes she was really, really tempted to smack that slumber party grin off Jasmine Cole's face. There weren't enough eye rolls in the world.

Chapter 37

It had been way too long since Eva spent some quality time with the ol' gang of Dommes.

Used to be they hung out every other weekend, tearing up the clubs and bars while throwing around money as if it were nothing but cheap paper. Eva didn't even mind that everyone but her were straight and searching for submissive men of varying flavors. That wasn't the point. The point? Oh, the *point* was hanging out with women who shared her love for taking charge in the bedroom. Watching men get on their knees and attempt to please cackling women in heels the size of their egos was dinner entertainment.

They also didn't give a shit about her sexuality. Half of them greatly enjoyed it when Eva sniped a girl from some bigshot Dom. Men *hated* that. They hated "losing" to a butch lesbian and having their precious manhood challenged. If she were drunk enough, Eva would shout at them that she knew how to please women the best. Most of those women never complained, even if they were too drunk to figure out what they were doing once they went home.

These days, though, the gang didn't get to hang out nearly as much. Most of the members had moved to other cities around the world. That's what happened when powerful, rich women were aggressive enough to be Dommes in their personal lives. Their ambition carried them all across the globe. It was a miracle when they happened to be in town at the same time. The day before the biggest gala of the year? Hell yeah!

The six of them hit up a couple of bars before meandering over to The Dark Hour, the best place in the city for them to strut their stuff and put some fear into the men around them. The fear was for the Doms who thought they were going to spend their Friday nights relaxing with beautiful women who wanted nothing more than to wait on them. Joke was on them. Six of the baddest bitches in power suits and bondage gear showed up to be as loud and rowdy as possible. The bouncer at The Dark Hour called them trouble before letting them in with a grin. Eva clung to Kathryn's arm as they blew kisses to the coat check girls and specifically asked for a server who wouldn't mind six screaming banshees who were all about grabbing cock and spanking male ass.

Eva may not have been much into touching men, but she didn't mind watching Dommes go to town on them. When one old friend, Mariel, hooked up with a frat guy and made a show of him on the public stage, Eva was the first to applaud and buy her friend a drink. When Lily Kat – not her real name, of course – tied up a guy until he couldn't reach his dick even if he wanted, Eva planted the first kiss on the man's cheek. She wasn't sexually attracted to these men, but she enjoyed lording over them once in a while. As a lesbian, it was a simple pleasure in life.

Cocktails, half naked men in bondage gear, and six women all with something to prove? Just another night in The Dark Hour as far as Eva was concerned.

Aside from her and Kathryn, the other women turned into pumpkins around nine and either went home to their families or grabbed a private room with their subs of the night. That was where Eva's interest in events ended. Before Nadia, she may have looked for a sweet woman to make hers as well, but the thought was blasphemous now. And Kathryn? Taken as well. Not that being left alone was anything to them. The two were as likely to come to the club on their own for drinks and chat.

However, Kathryn was already fairly tipsy while Eva was already sobered up again. Poor Kathryn was everyone's favorite punching bag at these get togethers now. She had gone from being a full-time Domme to a switch in her relationship, which got her endless amounts of teasing from the others. But when they heard that things had swung the other way while Kathryn and Ian were in Paris a while ago, they made Kathryn take a shot for everything she described. Eva had to check out when she was forced to imagine Ian on his hands and knees being ridden like a damned horse. *I have to have meals with the guy. No thanks.*

"This is the best," Kathryn said, leaning back in a large white chair while she shared a cigar with Eva and sobered up with a Coke. "Just some gals being pals."

"You're full of yourself 'cause you finally got to brag about how you're halfway to pegging your boyfriend's ass."

"Oh my God!" Kathryn sat up, her makeup smearing against her left eye. "You think he'd let me? It's only fair, right? He's stuck it up my butt a couple of times!"

Too much info. "I don't understand the point of having a male sub unless you get to fuck his ass." She was glad she was into women. No asses required. Except for spanking. *Pussy is the premium shit.* If only she could get these other women to understand. Those who were curious enough to try it always said they liked dick too much to give it up.

"Holy shit, can you believe it?" Kathryn gestured over Eva's shoulder and to the main part of the club. "Monroe got himself a girlfriend."

Eva was in no hurry to turn around at the sound of that name. *Thanks, Mom.* She took a drag of the cigar and craned her head around. Sure enough, there was Damon Monroe, the man Isabella tried for a hot minute to get her daughter to marry. No surprise to see him here. He liked BDSM and he *owned* half this club. What was surprising, however, was to see him already bringing a date in. Usually he stayed stag or took home a random woman he met. Not tonight. That was a scantily clad woman on the other end of his leash. That alone was enough to make Eva roll her eyes. Then she noticed that this woman had light blond hair.

"Someone has a type." Eva passed the cigar back to Kathryn. "Clearly he's not over me yet. Hmph."

"I still can't believe your mother and his father tried to set you up."

"You should've seen his face. He was as fucked up over it as I was."

"He's so him and you're so *you.*"

"Even if I were straight, I'd run. No way, man. Not a guy like that."

"Oh, I dunno." Kathryn took a healthy drag of the cigar before finishing her Coke. "There's a lot of be said about a man of that caliber of masculinity."

Ew. Could Eva wrinkle her nose any more than she did? "Yeah, I have no idea. I'm not the one who fucked him."

"Let me tell you, that was a good night."

"You didn't actually date him, though. Couldn't have been that good."

"Oh, please. Like I could date a man like that. He's way too intense."

"Apparently!"

"Besides, the both of us are spoken for now. Wouldn't do us any good to date around, no matter how good they are in bed."

"Is that why you still won't sleep with me?"

Kathryn blew a circle from her mouth. "Play your cards right and I'll let you sleep with me tonight, stud." Her half-drunk wink was hilarious with that smeared makeup.

"Not sure Nadia's into swinging. Though she's the one with experience with men, and your boyfriend seems the type to enjoy a curvy redhead."

"Yeah, he's jealous of you. Everyone is."

"Huh?"

Kathryn leaned forward. Her hair had been in an elegant French twist when the night started, but now it was so frayed that a diamond clasp was about to snap out of her thin hair. "You have one of the hottest girlfriends. You know how many men want to tap that hot ass?"

"I'd rather not think about it." The last thing Eva wanted to ponder was how many *men* wanted to fuck her girlfriend. Nadia obviously didn't want to think about it either. So why would Kathryn bring it up? Ugh. Straight women. Even when they meant well, they still thought the ultimate flattery came from men. "As long as she wants me tapping her ass, that's all that matters."

"I'll drink to that."

After they ordered another round of drinks, Eva mentioned the gala the next day. Kathryn moaned that she would probably have a headache through the whole thing due to how much she had drunk recently. She wasn't twenty-one anymore. What the fuck was she doing drinking like she was a teenager? *And she used to drink like crazy. And fuck dudes like crazy.* If anyone thought Kathryn was a party animal *now,* they had never met her when she was in Winchester or doing her undergrad studies. Not even Eva could keep up with how much liquor Kathryn put in her liver and how many boys she put in her pussy back then. Seeing her as such a mature adult with a steady boyfriend was *hilarious.*

"You think going to the gala is a good idea?"

Kathryn waited to answer. After all, their shots had arrived. One, two, *swallow!* Yikes. That shit burned. "That place is going to be crawling with photographers. I actually had to consult a stylist about what I should wear," Kathryn finally said. "Paps are tracking my ass this year too. I'm glad they never found out about Vegas."

Oh, that thing where she and Ian got drunkenly married and had it annulled in one week? That shit was public record, so it was only a matter of time before someone tipped the paps off. Kathryn better be for-real married by then so she could save some face.

That drink was enough to tip Kathryn toward drunk again. Didn't help she ordered a vodka and topped it off with a whisky sour afterward. Great. Eva was going to be the babysitter again. While Kathryn laughed at a comedic bondage show on the stage, Eva began counting down the minutes until they could hop back in a cab and go home.

"Hi."

Eva leaned her head back and found a tall, Slavic beauty hovering over her. Clad in nothing but a thin black negligee, the woman may have been large, but her body language and the sweet smile on her face screamed submissive on the prowl for a partner.

"Danica," Eva said. The woman touched her new friend's nose. "Long time no see." The last time… three times… they saw each other? Eva was scraping herself out of a hotel room bed and doing a hearty walk of shame while Danica slept in the beautiful nude. Nothing ever serious between them. Just a mutual love for Sapphic hanky-panky.

"Have you missed me?" Danica sat on the arm of Eva's chair, her breasts ceremoniously pushed up in her lingerie. They had nothing on Nadia's though. *Oh, my lovely lady.* They were spending the night apart since Eva had this girl's night out planned far in advance. Nadia had stopped by Eva's place after work to pick up her Gucci dress for the gala, but aside from some sweet kisses and groping each other, nothing got beyond second base. Now Eva wished she was going home to her girlfriend. *I should go to sleep with my face plastered in her tits.* That was the definition of a good life.

She wasn't stupid, though. She knew what Danica wanted. There was only one reason a woman like her came over to interrupt Eva's conversation with her friend. *To get in my pants.*

"I always miss a woman who can pull the stem out of a cherry with her tongue." The things a woman like that could do to another's clit? Yowza. "Unfortunately, I'm a bit taken now."

Danica glanced at Kathryn. "She finally giving you what you need?"

"No, not her." Eva snorted. "You must not have seen the pictures."

"Oh, those? I didn't think anything of them. Other than they turned me on and I was awash in memories of what you can do to a woman's nether regions."

"As my girlfriend continues to discover."

"Pity." Silky fingers caressed Eva's chin. "I came here specifically to find you."

"Don't you know how to inflate an ego?"

Danica twiddled her fingers goodbye. "If you ever decide to get back to your single playgirl ways, give me a call."

Kathryn watched this all unfold with a mischievous grin. "Girl, you're in bad love. You're freaking me out a bit. I'm not used to this side of you."

"You know better than anyone else that sometimes you have to wait for the right one to come along to turn you into a monogamous monster."

"You happy with that?"

Eva held up the last shot of the night as it came to her on a platter. She barely noticed the hot server carrying it. "Yeah. I'm happy."

"Hope you knock them dead and on their asses tomorrow. Cheers."

Yup. Eva could drink to that.

***

They stumbled into Eva's apartment an hour later, Kathryn so sloshed that she was already half asleep and needed Eva to drag her across the living area and to the bed. Not the first time this arrangement had occurred. Unless otherwise requested, it was better to take Kathryn back to Eva's place where the latter could keep a better eye on her blacked-out drunk best friend.

"There you go." Kathryn flopped onto Eva's bed with jacket and pants off. Eva pulled a quilt over her friend's legs and removed the hair suffocating her face. Already Kathryn was snoring. "Don't throw up on my bed. The cleaning lady won't be here until Monday."

Eva popped into the shower with a soft groan of fatigue. When she came out, toothbrush stuck in her mouth and towel wrapped around her body, she realized the whole place reeked of alcohol breath. *She and I are gonna have a talk about this tomorrow.* Depending on the size of Kathryn's hangover, anyway.

She climbed into bed after turning off the apartment lights. Kathryn had pulled the quilt up over her head and snored so loudly that Eva considered finding her earplugs. But the alcohol had caught up with her as well. As soon as her eyes closed, her body turning toward Kathryn's, Eva was out like the lights around her. Here was hoping Nadia didn't show up unannounced the next morning and found them in this suspicious situation. That would be a wild way to start their first day as the newest power couple around.

Chapter 38

When the biggest high society event of the summer was going on, downtown closed.

The traffic was completely stalled starting from four in the afternoon, the exact moment Nadia stepped out of her shower, grabbed her altered Gucci dress from its hanger, and started detangling the mess that occurred on top of her head while in the shower.

She peered out her bedroom window. For the first time in days, not a single paparazzi loitered on her street – probably because they were all down at the city's red carpet. Nadia wasn't taking any chances, though. The sun may have been beautiful in her bedroom, but she closed the curtains and got dressed on the far side of the room. Her dress was on her body when Eva texted her to say she had arrived for the pickup. By then, it was five, and they had an hour to get through the tough traffic.

"Whoa." Eva leaned against Nadia's bedroom doorway, grinning at the image of her girlfriend twirling in front of her mirror. "When the stylist sent me a picture of the dress and shoes I bought, I was kinda afraid. Gucci is super hit or miss depending on the woman."

She was telling Nadia! When the stylist took a look at her measurements before dragging her to the nearest Gucci boutique, she almost had a heart attack. She was expected to wear *that?* Nadia had never been able to pull off those types of designs. The first dress she tried on was a floor length pink thing with a giant bow right beneath Nadia's breasts. *I never wear pink for a reason.* It clashed horribly with her skin and hair. The boutique manager told Nadia she looked absolutely radiant, but even the stylist was quick to rip it off Nadia's body and head for the opposite end of the color spectrum.

Now she stood in a blue chiffon gown. The gala was a big event, but most women would show up in cocktail dresses and other flirty pieces that were meant to show off their personalities. To make up for the floor-length skirt – covered in threaded gold swirls, even – the stylist hired a last minute seamstress to hem it up until it rested atop Nadia's knees. The gold swirls dipped beneath the hem and created the illusion that they were caressing her thighs. Flirty, for sure.

"Like my cleavage?" Nadia asked. The plunging V-neck showed off the curves of her breasts. The gold bow and the sequined appliques brought more attention to her breasts than Nadia usually liked. Fashion tape was the only thing keeping them secured in her strapless bra. "I feel like I could smuggle some dinner in it."

"Cleavage is God's gift to women like me." Eva kicked off the doorway and went to Nadia. Arms covered in black silk encircled Nadia. Sure enough, a tight squeeze meant Nadia's breasts pushed up higher. Eva was the only one grinning. "You should wear a plunging necklace."

"I still need to put on my shoes." Nadia walked away, already dreading the blue sandals she bought to go with the dress. Blue romain satin criss-crossed over pale feet, while the galvanized heels glittered with silver and purple snakes. Separately, the dress and shoes seemed like night and day. Together? The heels were higher than Nadia liked to wear, but they *somehow* went with the crazy designs on her dress. Somehow. Nadia's hair already looked crazy enough with the whole look that she decided to go with it.

Besides, it wasn't like Eva wasn't wearing some interesting design choices too.

On the surface, it was a simple two-piece suit coupled with a white blouse and a skinny black necktie. However, gold accents adorned the cuffs, ankles, and glittered on the collar. A gold chain dangled from one side of the jacket to the other in lieu of buttons. Large gold hoops hung from her ears. Strappy black heels gave Eva an extra feminine flair.

"We are so going to be the best looking couple there." Eva picked up her girlfriend's blue Gucci clutch and handed it to her. Nadia's wallet, makeup, and tissues were already packed in there. "Ready to go? We need to get moving if we only want to be fashionably late."

She extended her arm to Nadia. *Do I need to be led out of my own house?* One step, and Nadia was hobbling in her shoes. Oops. Apparently she did need assistance.

***

An hour later, Nadia could see the venue outside of the Jaguar window, but they weren't any closer to actually pulling up and getting out of the car.

Fine with her! The place was a mess! Valets worked tirelessly to drive off with cars if someone didn't use their personal driver. The moment a man – let alone a *woman* – stepped out onto the sidewalk, security advanced to keep the photographers back. Reporters held the front line along the ropes. Some guests walked right past them, but most lingered for good photo ops and to answer a few questions before going inside.

The whole process terrified Nadia.

Eva was half asleep at the wheel, fingers tapping against it while an RnB song quietly played on the radio. They hadn't moved in five minutes. One of the guests was apparently a starlet, and not only did everyone want her picture, but she was inclined to give a full interview while limos honked and bodyguards got out of the fronts of cars to find out what was going on. When they saw the brunette Hollywood star, they turned around and got back in their cars.

Nadia scratched her arm through the sleeve of her dress. *So scratchy!* How was she going to last the night? Her stomach growled. Were they going to have dinner be able to eat? How much did it cost per plate, again? Not that she had any reason to believe Eva wasn't paying for her girlfriend's plate. *Maybe I want to get this over with.* On the other hand, Nadia was dreading getting out of the car and facing the vultures that had seen her in one of the most compromising positions possible.

"Any minute now," Eva grumbled. "Her movies ain't even that good!"

The starlet finally moved on. A black limo pulled up curbside. Eva snorted when a driver both she and Nadia recognized got out and opened one of the back doors.

Monica stepped onto the carpet before her husband appeared beside her. A million lights went off again. "Should've grabbed a ride with them," Eva said. She lightly stepped on the gas so they could proceed two feet. "That would've burned my mother."

"Is she going to be okay?" Nadia hadn't seen Monica since that ill-fated dinner date. Now she looked ready to give birth at any moment. Her black evening gown highlighted her bulge while showing off most of her back. The reporters were especially intrigued with getting solo shots of her and with Henry. *Everyone loves babies.*

"She said this is her last public appearance until she gets off maternity leave." Eva snorted again. "You know, in a month?"

They were now three cars away. Nadia continued to shift in her seat. Were her nails clean? Was her hair brushed? Her tits weren't totally hanging out of her dress, were they? Was she going to trip in these shoes?

"Showtime, babe."

Holy shit, that was fast!

The Jaguar idled. Out of the corner of Nadia's eye came a valet. He bypassed her door. Instead, a big, sunglassed security man approached Nadia's door.

Oh my God. Her heart fluttered. No. No throwing up right now!

Eva was out of the car and the valet getting ready to enter the driver's seat. Nadia's door opened. *Wow. Apparently this car is super soundproofed.* Rabble hit Nadia's ears. She was blinded by the cameras. Her hand searched for anyone's in a great need to be helped. Eventually she found the security guard's hand and stood up without ever falling over.

"Thanks. I've got it from here." A familiar arm looped around Nadia's. She released the guard's hand and heard the car door shut behind her. When she finally opened her eyes again, she looked down a tunnel of reporters, all of them scrambling for a good shot of her and Eva. "Follow my lead," Eva said into her girlfriend's ear. "We'll be fine. I promise."

Her arm fell to her side, hand taking Nadia's. Together they walked, Eva's posture straight but her aura effortlessly casual. She was retreating into herself, calling upon all the training she went through as a young girl growing up in a world that demanded nothing but ladylike perfection from her. She may not be the lady everyone expected her to be, but she was still quite lady*like*. Not a thread was out of place. Her hair was combed down to give her a softer edge as she strolled in that stark Gucci pantsuit highlighted with gold. Nobody was shocked that she was seen with Nadia.

In fact, they were calling her name.

"Nadia! Ms. Nadia! Ms. Gaines! Over here, please!" Even the newspaper reporters, who she assumed would be more professional than the everyday tabloids, shouted this at her. Nadia fell for it the first time, not at all expecting to hear her name. While it was not her first time appearing at a function, she was never a focal point, outside of someone commenting on her hair or dress. They didn't care about her identity. Who she was. Her name. She was *that girl who worked for Ethan Cole. You know, the hot one at the front desk?* Nadia was not arm candy. Nor was she at the forefront of any industries or trying to make a name for herself. So while many people may have recognized her from somewhere they couldn't quite remember, she was never in danger of being the center of such commanding attention.

Until now.

"What do I do?" Nadia whispered. Could Eva even hear her?

Her girlfriend's hand gave hers a squeeze. "Charm them. Flash them a smile or a wave. You're my girlfriend, babe. Let them see what I'm so in love with."

A smile and wave? How about an awkward twitch of her lips and a half-assed attempt at twiddling her fingers at one photographer? *Shit.* This wasn't going to work. Nadia couldn't fake the nerves away. These people knew her name! "*Nadia Gaines! Over here, Nadia Gaines!*"

"This way." Eva deftly spun Nadia around, forcing her to face one older gentleman in a tuxedo and holding analog reporting equipment – a pad and pencil. "Meet Mr. Reynolds. Lead society writer at *New England Times.*"

The man gave her a grandfatherly smile. "I should hire you to do my introductions everywhere I go, Ms. Warren." That smile turned toward Nadia. *Do we trust this guy? At least as much as we can around here?* "This must be the lovely young woman causing more waves for you than usual. You're stunning in that… Gucci, is it?"

Nadia laughed, nervously. "Yeah, it's Gucci." *Wow, way to sound elegant.* "Her idea."

"Sure, blame me if everyone slams you in the fashion columns tomorrow."

Nadia froze. "I'm gonna be in fashion columns?"

Eva wrapped an arm around her midsection. "Babe, have you seen us? We're gorgeous! We're taking *over* the fashion columns tomorrow!"

Laughter erupted around them. More cameras were held up. Men and women behind the ropes hurried to write down Eva's quote before they forgot it.

"Hasn't that dress been altered?" Piped up a woman from behind Mr. Reynolds. "Isn't it usually longer?"

"Y… yes." Nadia didn't continue to speak until Eva nudged her. "This way you can see my shoes better." She put her hand on her waist and puffed out her chest. Was this how women carried themselves at these things? It would have to do!

Cameras pointed downward. Better than at her chest!

"Very elegant," Mr. Reynolds commented. "Now, you two have been quite the news lately. Ahem."

Eva narrowed her eyes. The man did not relent.

"Is there anything you would like to say? An informal statement, of sorts?"

"The only thing we have to say is that we're greatly disappointed that certain publications have taken it upon themselves to show their true colors." While Eva spoke, Nadia wondered which one of these reporters worked for *The Daily Social.* "I'm especially disappointed in how they have handled my dear girlfriend. She's given up a lot of privacy to be with me. I am grateful, though." Her softened voice floated into Nadia's ear as Eva leaned down and lightly kissed her cheek. "She's got a will of steel. We're a perfect match, aren't we?"

"Thank you, Ms. Warren. Do enjoy the gala. You too, Ms. Gaines."

"We will, thank you." Eva urged Nadia to continue walking. "Let's head inside, babe. I think the Andrews have arrived behind us, and they don't like to be kept waiting."

They hurried past the last line of reporters and entered the venue. A comparatively quiet place, filled with live piano music that provided the backdrop to hundreds of attendees socializing in the lobby or making their way into the ballroom, a place where dinner, entertainment, and speeches of gratitude were to commence.

"Ah, Ms. Warren," said an usher the moment the couple arrived at the ballroom entrance. "Right this way, please. You've had seats reserved on behalf of Ms. Alison."

"They're already here?" Nadia asked.

"Of course. Kathryn's peripherally attached to this charity. She's been here since she slept off her hangover at my place this morning."

She said that so dryly that Nadia almost didn't double-take. "At your place, huh?"

They were following the usher between tables stuffed with designer dresses, hair coated in hairspray, and enough cologne to set off everyone's allergies. Nadia hid a sneeze while she waited for her girlfriend to explain.

"We got trashed last night and she slept over at my place. It happens."

"I *see.*" Nadia wasn't jealous, especially since Kathryn had to be one of the most heterosexual women on the planet, but it was good to know that drunken sleepovers happened more often than not. It was *especially* funny to imagine that happening the moment they approached a circular table hosting none other than Kathryn and her boyfriend Ian.

"Hey!" Kathryn leaped up, probably blasted on caffeine for her to be that excited. She wore a knee-length, strapless, cream-colored sheath dress accented with gold jewelry and plain, nude heels. Her boyfriend, on the other hand, was casually handsome in a three-piece suit. *Couples.* Ian Mathers' vest was a deep, royal purple with swirls that matched his girlfriend's dress. Was that done on purpose? Probably. "You're earlier than I expected. So… wow, is that Gucci? This season?"

Nadia looked right down into her cleavage. "Yup. It doesn't look garish, does it? I'm not used to wearing stuff like this."

"Garish? You pull it off better than Eva could!"

"Excuse you."

"Please. Everyone is used to you wearing off-the-wall fashion." Kathryn sat back down in her seat. "Anyway, hope we get to eat soon. I hear Chez Blu is catering." She shot a smile in her boyfriend's direction. "I love French food."

"Oh, gag." Eva pulled out a chair for Nadia. As soon as they were seated, she continued, "It's a good thing we showed up. Looks like things were about to get *gross* over here."

"Was not."

"Was too."

Always good to see that the rich could be as petty with high-school prattle. Nadia shared a look of *see what we have to deal with?* with Ian the moment another usher arrived with one last couple.

"Whoa! Fancy seeing you here!" Jasmine slammed against Nadia, nearly knocking her out of her seat – and definitely mussing up her dress. *Thanks, friend.* Nadia checked her hair as soon as Jasmine was off her. "We're even wearing the same color!"

Not really. Jasmine was in a bright, baby blue halter dress cinched with a diamond belt. Her long black hair was pulled to one side, a carefully placed curl dangling before her face. It bounced every time she moved. Which was a lot, because Jasmine could not sit still when she was excited. Behind her, Mr. Cole – right, that was Jasmine's *husband* now – pulled out his own chair and sat down. "I asked for us to be sat here," he mumbled. Jasmine didn't hear him.

"You knew I was going to be here," Nadia said.

"Yeah, but I didn't know we would be sitting next to each other! Do you know what's for dinner? I'm starving. I hope whatever it is won't make me bloat. This waistline is *tight!*"

She could say that again. Nadia was also dreading trying to eat anything aside from some veggies and *maybe* a piece of lean protein. If she developed a food baby, or, gasp, got bloated? That dress was going to be absolute hell against her stomach. "I have no idea. Something French? Anyway, I've now learned that I should always wear an empire waist to dinners." She looked to Eva. "You have to buy me empire-waisted dresses now."

"Oh, great, so everyone can think you're constantly pregnant with lesbian babies. I mean, it's your funeral in the press, babe."

Their waiter appeared, offering a choice of chicken, steak, or fish. No one ordered the steak. It was five plates of chicken and one of fish for Ms. Alison, who said she couldn't look at a chicken without feeling drunk. Something about fried chicken the night before?

"When did we have fried chicken?"

Kathryn blushed. "You weren't there."

"What?"

Before she could get an answer, the waiter returned with a complimentary bottle of champagne for the table to share.

At least the format of the evening was something Nadia anticipated. Once the appetizers began to roll out, speeches commenced on a stage. Boring topics, to be sure. Lots of thanks. A promise of a fun night full of music, dancing, and videos of cute animals on the big screen. Volunteers would be making the rounds during dessert, offering chances to win amazing trips (because people there apparently couldn't afford their own) and other prizes – all they had to do was pledge a donation of a minimum $10,000. Nadia had a headache thinking of that number. That was how much debt she was still in before Eva paid it off for her.

Dessert was something Nadia could not pretend to pronounce. Most of the table opted for cinnamon rolls topped with ice cream. Nadia couldn't stand to look at it without feeling bloated in her dress, so she shared hers with Eva, who insisted she wasn't that much into cinnamon. Yet she ate most of the dessert anyway!

"Good evening, ladies and gentlemen." A woman in a simple black dress appeared by their table. In her hands was a silver tray topped with a glass vase full of crystal straws. Each straw held a folded paper flower on top. "A pledge for a donation allows you to pick one straw. There are all sorts of prizes included. Trips around the world, new cars and yachts, even shopping sprees." She chose Nadia to be the target of her wink. "Who would like to start?"

Ian raised his hand. "I'll do it. Put me down for twenty. Does that get me two straws?"

"Sorry, sir. It's one straw per person."

"Fine. Kathryn, pledge half so we get two straws."

She rolled her eyes. "I'll get my own, thanks."

Someone wrote down Ian's pledge for twenty (grand, was it? *Sheesh,)* while the platter of straws was presented to him. He attempted to get his girlfriend to choose for him, but Kathryn reiterated that she was going to get her own. Besides, it might have been a gift certificate for manscaping, and that would be awkward.

"All right, let's see what I've got." Ian unfolded his chosen paper flower and read aloud, "A weekend for two in…" He tossed the flower onto the table. "Vegas."

Kathryn's face faltered; Eva laughed so loudly that Nadia wondered what was funny.

"Classic," Eva muttered. Kathryn made her own pledge and grabbed a straw. "Love it."

Kathryn won a complimentary consultation with one of the most elusive stylists in California. Nadia didn't recognize his name, but the way people talked about him, it sounded like he styled a lot of big Hollywood stars and more than a few Silicon Valley princesses. Jasmine was already giddy by the time her husband made a pledge and asked her to pick a straw for him. Who knew tax write-offs could be so exciting?

By the time Eva's turn came around, Nadia was already on her second glass of champagne. She needed more alcohol if she was going to get through this rampant display of wealth. All around her millionaires and billionaires were paying the equivalent of her college debt to get prizes that were worth half that at best. The prizes weren't the point, however. These people could afford weekends here and there without batting their long eyelashes. A weekend in Vegas was nothing, regardless of what transpired there. Okay, so maybe getting a consultation with a reclusive stylist was intriguing, but someone like Kathryn had enough money and social pull to get that on her own if she really wanted it. She didn't even have to do it herself. Didn't she have an assistant to arrange those things on her behalf?

"Pick a straw, babe," Eva said, her immaculate nails gesturing toward the tray of vases. "Whatever it is, it's yours. Unless it's a ticket to see Kate Bush in concert. Sorry, I'm taking that."

Nadia ignored her and plucked the first straw she came into contact with. Half the table waited with bated breath while she slowly unfolded the pink paper flower and read the words *Dinner For Two at* Le Magnifique *In Monaco.* Fucking Monaco!

"Wow, that's the place where you can order whatever you want from anywhere in the world and get it in fifteen minutes. I've always wondered how they pulled that off," Kathryn said. "Lucky." She nodded to Nadia. "Now you need to make her take you to Monaco. Better than *Vegas.*"

"Talk about a pretentious place," Eva mumbled. The woman carrying the tray thanked everyone for their generosity and congratulated them on their prizes. After she left, a waiter came by and cleared the empty dishes. The live jazz band began to play, and guests were encouraged to dance on the big open floor in the midst of the round tables.

Nobody got up. Not only at Nadia's table, but at any of the tables.

Everyone was too preoccupied with who had shown up fashionably late.

***

"There you are!" Adrienne Thomas cried, slapping her hand on Ethan's shoulder. "Sorry we're late." Shoulder-length hair tucked behind her ear, she squeezed the hand she held. "You know how it is. Those limos, right? So private."

Amber Mayview, the woman in a gold dress who looked half-mortified, hid her face behind her clutch.

"Well," Kathryn said. "This is interesting." She glanced at Eva. "Know anything?"

About this catty lesbian bullshit? All Eva really knew was filtered through Nadia. Now looking at the pair – the very public pair, since everyone with working eyes was staring at them – she saw the makings of a couple with plenty of chemistry but no chill between them. (This was totally different from how things were between her and Nadia, of course.) Their body language looked more like sorority sisters up to no good than two women on a formal date. "I know Amber's hot," she muttered back at Kathryn.

Nadia glared at her. *What? Like I've hidden that opinion?*

"Your dress is gorgeous," Amber said to Nadia. "What is that? Dolce & Gabbana?"

"Gucci," Nadia corrected. "Yours?"

"Dior."

Haha. Oh my God. Of course. Adrienne loved her Dior like Eva usually loved her Givenchy. That dress was bought on a shopping date to a boutique, and nobody would be able to tell Eva otherwise.

"Surprised to see you two so out in the open here," Eva braved saying. Both Amber and Adrienne looked at her as if she should *shut up*. "And here I thought my girlfriend and I would be the star lesbian couple of the evening."

"Can't have everything, now can we?" Adrienne waved her hand in dismissal. "Suppose you could say we were *inspired* by recent events. Girl power, and all that."

Groan. It was either that or crack up laughing again, and Eva had a feeling that wasn't a great idea at the moment. "You two are a lovely couple." Five other heads hurried to nod in agreement with her statement. "Be sure to give the paps our love." Eva could squeeze her girlfriend's hand too, and stew in the fact that they were a more natural looking couple. Amber was dragged from table to table as if Adrienne had something to prove to the world. Ethan Cole's poor assistant spent more than a few words blushing in embarrassment.

"Someone explain to me why I feel so weirded out by that," Ian said. "Because normally I am *all about* that girl power stuff."

"Because Adrienne's up to something," Ethan replied. "She's been one bit of bad press away from having a total breakdown. Not sure this is the best way to avoid it."

"Oh, there is going to be press about *that,*" Eva said. She didn't have to elaborate. Even Nadia had a look in her eye that said she understood. *She understands too well.* Eva leaned over and kissed her girlfriend's cheek. "They're doing us a favor, huh?"

Kathryn chuckled. "With any luck, they'll be next week's big scandal. Soon enough the public will have their fill of drooling over lesbians."

"If you ask me," Eva stood and extended her hand to Nadia, "one can never get enough lesbians. Care to dance, babe? This party needs to get started and we can't be upstaged by *them.*"

Initially, Eva fretted that Nadia would turn her down. Then that silky soft hand touched hers, and Nadia was up, hemmed skirt flirtatiously floating around her knees.

"Why don't we look that good together?" Kathryn said with a smack to her boyfriend's shoulder. "You gotta be more suave. Come on."

"Why? Do *you* wanna dance?"

"Hell no! I'm still digesting dinner! I start dancing and they'll be picking up Kathryn chunks off the dancefloor…"

Eva tuned that out with a face of repulsion. She instead smiled at her girlfriend and led her to the middle of the empty dancefloor while the jazz band played.

"Ready to blow their minds with how great we are?" One hand clutched Nadia's while the other fixed her hair. Red locks settled on her shoulder and blended beautifully with the blue fabric of her Gucci dress. *Hell yeah I picked the right designer!* "I'll lead."

"Of course you will." Nadia balanced her elbows and bestowed a glowing smile upon her girlfriend as they swayed together to the soulful vocals of a woman on the stage. "You've always got to be in control, don't you?" She said it with such sweetness that Eva couldn't take offense.

"I also had formal lessons for *years.* Part of my finishing. You'd never guess, I know, but I was often picked to lead in the all-girls classes." *And this was before I cut off my hair and started dating girls.* Some women had that aura about them. Eva was more than happy to take up that role. And, yes, she did like having control, even on the dance floor. All the better to gaze down at her girlfriend and become absolutely enraptured with that smile.

Some people stared at them. Others ignored them. Those who would have stared but currently did not were too distracted by the spectacle that was Adrienne and Amber stumbling around and catching every photographer's attention. *That is not going to end well.* Eva didn't know what their problem was, but she was grateful to look "normal" for once.

Slowly but surely, other couples got up from their tables and danced around Nadia and Eva. No other female couples, but it was a healthy mixture of older, younger, and even a smattering of people who could not easily be called Caucasian. *The Johnsons are laughing these days.* Twenty years ago, when Eva was a small girl going to Tuesday brunch at the country club with her mother, the big scandal was investor Kevin Johnson meeting a hotel hostess in the Caribbean and bringing her back to New England to marry. For the longest time, she was the only black woman at the club. A place she always returned to even though everyone spoke behind her back and even made racist comments to her face. But Bernadette Johnson was not going to back down. Eva had always admired that, and now she felt no ill-will toward seeing the middle-aged Johnsons laughing and enjoying themselves on the dancefloor. Nobody gave a single shit about them. Nor did they spare a second glance for their biracial son and daughter who also shared a dance – on the other side of the dancefloor of their parents, of course, because otherwise it was just weird. *Teenagers.* Eva would never want to be one again.

"Did you know," she said to her girlfriend, "that we're the best looking couple at this event? I mean, look at you. You're so gorgeous it's driving me insane!" Did any other woman look as striking as Nadia did in this beautiful blue Gucci dress? No? Did anybody have that same button nose? No? Okay, so some women had the same kind of breasts, but Nadia's were special. Why? Because Eva knew every inch of them by now – and how they responded to her touch. *We better be having sex tonight. I'm gonna be so ready.* Eva dropped Nadia's hand and pulled her into an embrace instead. *Ah, yes, head on chest and boobs against my abdomen. This is the life.* She was pretty simple, in the end.

"I feel beautiful when I'm with you," Nadia said.

Aw, was that a tear in Eva's eye?

A professional photographer for the city newspaper finished setting up his tripod at the edge of the dancefloor and took his first shot. It was directed at Eva and Nadia.

"We're going to be all over the papers tomorrow. You okay with that?"

Nadia nodded her head against Eva's chest. "I'm okay with this."

"This?"

Nadia's forehead lifted, those swirling eyes of endless mischief meeting Eva's so intimately. "You know I've thought about nothing but how I would handle all the attention since the day I decided to go on a date with you. I've always had a crush on you, Eva. But aside from knowing what a silly teddy bear you are beneath all the glam and sophistication, I worried that I wouldn't be able to handle being the girlfriend of a billionaire. I see that shit all the time, you know? Just watching Jasmine go through the bullshit gives me a headache. But you know what she told me yesterday?"

"No, what?" *This oughta be good.*

"She said that it's worth every bit of stress and invasion of privacy if you really love the person. That such a life is better than not being with them at all. When I think about not having you anymore, I don't know what to do. I want to be with you, Eva. I love you, even with all the bullshit and your mother causing trouble. Really."

"Really really?"

"Really really."

Their tepid kiss was more cute than hot, but the cameraman went for it anyway. *I'm gonna call up the editor of the paper and tell him to send over the master copy so I can have it framed.* There would be plenty of chances for Nadia to be the most beautiful woman in the room. But this would probably be the only night she was this *kind* of beautiful. Newly in love and emerging from her shell to take her place as the irreplaceable girlfriend of some bigshot everyone rolled their eyes at but said nice things about anyway.

"You can handle it, huh?" Eva teased. "You gonna be the wife of a billionaire one day?"

Nadia's lips puckered. "Why? You asking me to marry you? That would be a way to round out the night. You getting on one knee and proposing to me. Adrienne and Amber might have to call over a priest to marry them right that second to keep the attention."

"No marriage yet, babe. Let's take our time and enjoy ourselves. Besides, I've got to finish my degree. I ain't got time to plan a wedding!"

Nadia's face fell halfway through that response. "You're serious? Marriage?"

"I said let's wait…"

That smile returned. "You're getting me all giddy."

"Good. You should be giddy every day you're around me. It's the only way I want you."

"You know I'm not always going to be giddy? If I have to get used to living your kind of lifestyle and having all this attention on me, then you have to get used to my mood swings and all the other bullshit *I* have."

"Your mood swings? What the fuck do you think I've been experiencing for the past several months!" Did Nadia miss those weeks, no… months… of endless drama and going back and forth on whether they should date or not? Or did she think that was the status quo? *She better not. Otherwise I won't survive!*

"Look at you. All bluster around a pretty girl."

"You have no idea. Fuck you and the spell you cast on me. I was living a pretty good life playing around and doing my own thing."

"But were you happy?"

Eva delighted in stroking that soft hair. "I was content, which was fine for the time. But I'm happy *now.*"

Nadia squeezed her as the song came to an end. "We can do this. If only out of spite."

"See, now you're speaking my language. I love running on spite."

"I thought your language was sex and tits."

"Like those are separate?"

Nadia winked at her as they held hands on their way off the dancefloor. "Not around you."

They returned to a table missing an extra two people. Eva glanced over her shoulder and saw the Coles enjoying the next round of dancing. They were positively disgusting with their canoodling and private laughter. Suited Eva fine, though. She was ready to sit down and make fun of Kathryn for not moving from her seat in an hour.

"I'm going to go find the ladies' room," Nadia said with a touch to Eva's arm. "See you in a few. Or maybe a half hour. Depends on how long the line is. Also will depend on whether or not the you-know-whos are fucking in a bathroom stall."

"Ooh." Kathryn grinned. "I have an idea."

"I wanna fuck there," Ian whined to his girlfriend. "We never have fun anymore."

"Grow up, loser."

"Yeah, grow up, loser."

Nadia was gone by the time Ian gave both remaining women a derisive gaze. "I'm writing about this on Twitter."

"You don't have a Twitter."

"Fine. Facebook."

"You don't have that other."

"Fine! Instagram." Ian whipped out his phone and set it to selfie mode. He leaned in toward camera and held the phone above their heads. "Angles, babe!"

"There you go. You definitely have an Instagram."

The camera phone clicked. Ian sat back up and sent the photo to Instagram, probably littered with a million dumb hashtags. *I've seen his Instagram. It's all cats.* Maybe Ian really was a bigger lesbian than Eva. "Hell yeah, the porn stars love me on there."

"Those are bots."

"Don't care. They love me. I enjoy the validation."

The couple shared a knowing smile about something Eva was not privy to. Whatever. She would happily sit and check her phone messages while she waited for Nadia to come back from the bathroom. Whenever that would be. Like she said, those lines could be ridiculous. And now that horny lesbians were taking over stalls across the country? Whelp.

Someone approached their table. At first, Eva paid the woman no mind, but then she was called out specifically.

"Eva Warren! So good to see you! It's been years!"

That voice was vaguely familiar. Eva was not inspired to look up when nothing but chills went down her spine. The kind that screamed at her to ignore the harbinger of bad memories.

"Oh." Her throat went dry when she finally looked up. Teeth gritting, Eva tapped into her auto-pilot formalities drilled into her since her days at Winchester. The same place this woman went to. "Hi. Long time no see, indeed. Since what? Graduation?"

"Since Winchester!"

Ian and Kathryn gave their attention now. "Do we know you?" Kathryn asked.

"Kathryn Alison, right? You probably don't remember me. I was in Eva's class." Silky brown hair gained air when the woman turned her head with too much gusto.

Two sets of pleading eyes looked at Eva.

"Kathryn, Ian," she began. "This is Jenny Myers, captain of the Winchester Girls' Varsity Soccer Team, Class of 2009." And she could take a quick trip to hell, as far as Eva was concerned.

Chapter 39

Jenny had barely aged since eighteen. She still had that oblivious smile and the brown hair that made so many boys fall over – for whatever reason. It wasn't as straight as it used to be, but Eva assigned that to changing times. Back in 2009, most of the girls at Winchester had straightened hair they wore down or in high ponytails. *Didn't Kathryn start that trend?* Probably. Kathryn was one of the queen bees of Winchester by her junior year. Eva barely knew her back then. *We didn't become acquaintances until her senior year, and we didn't become friends like we are now until we were in college.* Unfortunately, Winchester had fostered the same kind of cliquing that most public high schools dealt with – just with so much cocaine that a student was more likely to pass out with a nosebleed than alcohol poisoning. *Never forget the Winter Formal.* Eva, in her pantsuit, sitting next to a sophomore she barely knew who was in dire need of 911. The girls' restroom had been nothing but powdery lines and girls screeching that it was getting in their cleavage – and then deciding that was for their boyfriends to enjoy.

Anyway, Jenny Myers… Why wasn't Eva surprised that Jenny chose now of all times to come walking back into someone's life? This wasn't a coincidence. They had been to many of the same functions over the years, and they *never* even exchanged nostalgic smiles. Not that Eva had anything to be nostalgic about. Was Jenny still with that douchebag who broke into the girl's locker room one day and threatened to rape Eva if she didn't effectively quit playing soccer? Because that's how a girl knew she *really* had a keeper in a boyfriend.

"So you're the infamous Jenny," Kathryn said with her fake nicey-nice voice. *She gets it.*

Jenny's nervous chuckle was almost worth this awkward moment. "Infamous?"

"Oh, sorry, I meant famous! I was thinking of some other Jenny."

The silence befalling the table was exactly what Eva wanted. *You come over here to say hi after seeing what happened to me this week, huh?* Jenny was like that, wasn't she? Always wanted to start shit but unable to effectively do it on her own. She was the type to need others to do her dirty work for her. Unfortunately for her, she didn't have any backup today. Was she still with that loser, or did that go by the wayside once she got into Yale using the extra-curricular Eva genuinely wanted?

"It's good to see you," Eva said through a dire smile.

"Jenny Myers, huh?" For all his buffoon-bluffing, Ian was a sharp-witted man. "Soccer captain? It's always good to meet another captain, even if we're not the same gender."

Jenny smiled in relief. "You must be Ian Mathers. Charmed."

"Indeed. A couple years before you went through Winchester, but we captains stick together." He nudged Eva. "I love giving her crap for not making captain. Didn't know you were the one she lost out too."

"Eva is a very formidable player."

"Oh, I know. She kicks my ass regularly, *and* she'll be wearing heels. Funny that. I was the MVP two years in a row, and this gal can make me feel like junior varsity in those silly heels you ladies wear." There was nothing friendly about his demeanor. "It must be her lack of leadership skills that kept her from being captain."

"As I recall, Eva didn't go out for captain…"

"Nope, I sure didn't," Eva corroborated. "I was inspired not to. Rather convincing argument those people made, too."

"So, anyway…" Jenny waved. "Be seeing you around… bye…"

Three sighs erupted around the table. "Good Lord," Kathryn muttered.

"I don't know who that woman was, but I don't like her."

"You can guess who she is."

"Hm. Yes."

They both looked at Eva, whose head was in her hand and phone shaking in her lap. No, not her phone. Her other hand, holding her phone. *That's* what was shaking. *Because nothing feels as good as being reminded of that time a bunch of guys threatened to hurt and traumatize you.* Eva knew she would probably never really be over that moment. But she had hoped there was no actual trauma related to it. Seeing Jenny Myers sauntering up to her like that? It was a miracle Eva hadn't pissed herself.

"You okay?" Kathryn asked.

"Oh, fine. Super peachy. Yup." Eva shoved her phone into her pocket so she would stop fiddling with it. "Thinking about super unpleasant things. Whatever."

She didn't know why she was so messed up over it. It happened years ago. She was able to talk about it with her girlfriend and best friend without having a freak out. Yet something about seeing Jenny strolling up to her… knowing *damn well* what she had done to Eva back in high school… as if nothing had happened. Had she come to intimidate her? Make her feel bad? Say that she was sorry? *Yeah, right.* Why had she done that? Why had she bothered her? Tonight of all nights? *I'm trying to have a good time with my girlfriend. We had a pretty rough week, as the whole world knows by now.*

"You need someone's ass kicked?" Ian asked.

"You're about seven years too late for that offer."

Kathryn reached over her boyfriend's lap and steadied Eva's shaking hands. "Anything we can do?"

"Yeah." Eva stood up, collecting her things. "Get me a lobotomy. I'm gonna go find Nadia and see if she wants to go home. I'll text you if we decide to leave." Eva had put in her time and money for the cause. She could leave whenever she wanted. Beat traffic that way.

Eva didn't find Nadia in record time. She found a meltdown unfolding in front of a group of people gathered around the *real* entertainment that night.

"Stop. Using. *Me!*" Amber the young blond assistant had never looked so menacing. Adrienne stood before her, arms crossed and nose turned up in the air. *Ooh, what's this? Some real drama worth watching?* Eva was down for some entertainment.

"What's going on?" she whispered into Nadia's ear. The redhead jumped, hand clasping her chest as she craned her head around and noted Eva's presence. "For once we're not the ones creating a scene?"

"It ain't a wedding, so no." Nadia kept her voice lowered, not that she needed to. Adrienne and Amber were so damn loud that the jazz band could probably hear them. "Someone is tired of someone else's shit."

"I should've brought the popcorn."

Before them, Adrienne threw her hands up in defeat and turned away from Amber. The blonde went after her, insisting that they were *not* done talking. "I'm tired of being the one who's convenient for *you!* Don't tell me you think the sun rises and sets on my ass and then ignore me for two weeks straight! You're either in this or not, Adrienne!"

Chatter rumbled through the small crowd. Eva picked up the usual mess. "*Women are so dramatic, aren't they? I could never be a lesbian for that reason. Men are so much easier to deal with!*" As if that made a difference in drama levels.

"Yes, you'd love that, wouldn't you?" Adrienne hissed back at her on-again, off-again girlfriend. "You'd love it if I gave you everything you wanted. You think I don't know that you're using me too? Don't play coy! You've been playing me since the day I asked you out! Before that! You think I didn't realize what you were doing when you were shoving your tits in my face and batting those eyelashes of yours? I've heard all about you, Amber Mayview. You're a gold digger, and you should admit it!"

"All right! So I flirted with you so I could have some fun! Could you blame me? You're a gorgeous, successful woman who knows how to spoil a girl. Why wouldn't I flirt with someone like that who shows interest in me? Fuck! That's all you wanted me for, anyway. To assuage your fragile-ass ego because you're jealous that your ex-boyfriend got married."

"Go to hell!"

"I'm already there!"

"Piss *off!*"

Adrienne stamped off. Amber, humiliated and the more vulnerable one since hardly anyone knew who she was, stumbled back and took one look at the crowd before hurrying into the women's restroom. Where else was she going to go? Adrienne's car?

"Shit." Nadia turned to her girlfriend. "I better go check on her." The crowd was starting to disperse. "Did you need something?"

"I was going to ask if you were ready to head back to my place."

"All right. After this." Nadia nodded toward the exit Adrienne took.

"Shit. Fine." Eva rolled her eyes. "I'll go check on Crazy McInsecurity. Catch up with you in a bit."

Eva dragged herself through the exit, instantly hitting a private courtyard populated with only a few people out for a stroll. One small group laughed in between swigs of champagne. Another couple canoodled beneath a tealight covered tree. Eva followed the stench of tobacco to find Adrienne having a smoke by the guardrail overlooking a pond.

"Can I help you?" she snapped at Eva.

Not if you're going to be a bitch like that. Eva leaned back against the guardrail. Damn these warm summer nights. Her jacket was going to suffocate her. Adrienne had the right idea. Short and sleeveless. She was one of the few women around who could wear such a skimpy dress and still look business-chic. *It's the hair and makeup.* Dark, slick, and nothing out of place.

"Dunno." Eva stretched her arms above her head. "I was told to come check up on you. My girlfriend is friends with yours, in case you've never noticed." From what Eva gathered, Adrienne never noticed much at all. Unless it had to do with her own little world, anyway. "Unless she's not *really* your girlfriend, in which case you should probably inform her."

"Ha! What are you, the lesbian love doctor?"

"No, but I'd bargain that I've been around the ol' box block a few more times than you. This is all old hat to me. You're like a fish slappin' on land trying to make sense of a world without water. Or air. Not sure which."

"So you came to give me advice? Not necessary. It's officially over now."

"After all that work you put into making sure everyone knew about it? Nobody does that without feeling it's real on some level."

"Is that so? You're the expert, huh?" Adrienne blew out a drag of her cigarette and stared at nothing but the tranquil water in front of her. "Why are you over here? You don't know me."

"Maybe not, but women like us have to look out for one another." *I guess.* The world was a lot different from even a few years ago, but the amount of out lesbians or bisexual women could still be counted on one of Eva's hands. That was including herself, too.

"Women like us." Adrienne put out her cigarette beneath a Louboutin. "Women like *us.*"

"That's what I said. Hon, you ain't playing around with a girl like Amber for so long if you don't feel inclined to call yourself a certain way."

"I don't believe it. First it's Ethan, and now it's you. What business is it of anyone's what I do in my personal life?"

"I'm guessing it's Amber's."

"Like I said, she's a gold digger. That's been pretty clear since the beginning. She basically trades sex for spoiling. You know how much money I've spent on that girl? More than she makes in her salary."

"And you're duly rewarded, I'm sure." Eva was on a different wavelength. *I never think of casual dates that way.* She certainly had her fair share of supposed gold diggers who only wanted anything to do with her if shopping, dinner, and hotels were involved. Sex? Oh, that was okay, one supposed. Took Eva a few years to start spotting those women *before* they ended up in bed – and sorely disappointed. "She obviously thinks more than that of you, though. Otherwise she wouldn't be so upset about being your public arm candy and possibly nothing more."

"You want to know the truth?" Adrienne glared at Eva from the corner of her eye. "We've broken up about five times now. Then I get sucked back in and it starts all over again. Every time I'm sucked in a little deeper. It's like she wants to wipe my head of any sense."

I know those types of women well. Sounded quite familiar. One moment Eva was looking for a lay with Nadia, and the next? Thinking about forever! From 0 to 60 in about seven months. Better than most people those days, Eva supposed…

"You in love with her?"

Adrienne turned her head away. "I barely love myself first, honestly. Not exactly in a place to be loving anyone else. Maybe that's the problem."

"At least you admit it. You know, it was pretty brave of you being so out in the open tonight. I bet most of the people in there had no idea you were involved with a woman."

She got the reaction she expected. Adrienne shuddered, fingers linking as she stared into the pond. "I was brash when I decided to do it. I decided at the last minute to invite her. Thought that maybe this was a good time to test the waters. You know, with you being so public with Nadia…"

"Not on my terms."

"No." Adrienne gave her a sympathetic look. "I suppose not."

"So you thought you would beat the paps to their own punch? Ballsy. You're definitely upstaging my girlfriend and I tonight as the 'it' lesbian couple. I should probably thank you."

"You're welcome. Now they can report that we're officially broken up again. I should ask Ethan to fire her and save everyone's sanity."

Because that's super fair. Adrienne was like everyone else sometimes. Someone was causing her issues at work? Fire her! What was the problem?

Wasn't that what she was supposed to do? But one could not easily break it off with a woman who worked in the same exact office. No wonder they kept hooking back up again. Eva and Nadia had enough push and pull to last them a lifetime without that shit!

"From one queer to another," Eva said, "the sooner you accept who you are and what that means for your public *and* personal life, the sooner you start handling it better. 'Cause it's gonna suck. A lot. Might even be worse if you're bi. I dunno. People are super closeminded, especially around here. They will treat you like a freak show."

"Gee, thanks."

"Just saying. Part of the reason that girl is so frustrated is because she wants you to own up to who you two are. If she were using you for your money, she wouldn't even have come with you tonight. I bet you got her hopes up that this was going to be a huge turning point for your relationship. Now she's in the bathroom crying. Good job."

"You don't know the details of my relationship."

"No, but it's probably not good."

"Shut up, Warren."

"You first, Thomas."

Adrienne stood up, scuffing one shoe against the ground. "I didn't start indulging in this bullshit until this past year. She was right. I was jealous that Ethan was getting married the moment I walked back into his life. We used to date, you know."

"Uh huh." Everyone knew that. Big whoop.

"For some reason I thought the best way to rebound was by finally fooling around with women. Took a lot of nerve. I hadn't really done that before, but I had always wanted to."

"Uh huh."

"You really should feel kinda bad for Amber. She was a convenient target, but I never intended to have any feelings for her."

"So you better own up to them. Either let her go and let her have peace, or do the right thing by her. That means no more hiding and being afraid. Okay, you should be a little afraid. Keep you on your toes for when the assholes come out. You know what I mean."

"I've been working on it. Not being afraid, that is."

"Trust me, nobody knows better than me how scary it is coming out. Tonight I saw the girl who made my life hell in high school. That stuff happens." Eva hid her shudder beneath her jacket. "You never really get over it, but you learn how to deal with it."

"I hope so."

"Come on, you dumb dyke, let's go get your woman."

Adrienne stood back with a start. "What the hell did you call me?"

"Get used to it. It's what everyone's thinking, so you better start owning it."

Scoffing, Adrienne walked ahead of Eva back into the venue. It didn't take them long to find Nadia and Amber in the bathroom. By then, Amber had finished drying her eyes and gave Adrienne a look of hope mixed with trepidation. Another look Eva knew well.

"Hey," Adrienne said softly. She and Amber kept their distance. "I'm sorry. Let's go home and talk this out. I've been…" She closed her eyes and exhaled. "A big dumb dyke."

Apparently that was some sort of breakthrough for them. Maybe not the *dyke* part, but Eva would hazard that Adrienne referring to herself as something like that was a pretty big deal. Had she ever called herself anything but straight before?

"Yeah, you have been." Amber's hands were on her hips. "Okay. You get one *last* chance, Adrienne. I'll go home with you. And you get to grovel. I'd like to hear *you* do that for once."

Sounds like my kind of night. Eva had half a mind to slap Nadia's ass. *Let's grovel. Fuck yeah.* "All right. Shall we go?"

Adrienne extended her hand. Amber stared at it before linking her fingers with Adrienne's. "Sure. You're ordering us some of that gelato, though. I want orange flavor."

"One 'I'm sorry' cup of gelato coming up." They sauntered out of the restroom.

As soon as they were gone, Nadia asked, "What did you say to her?"

"To buck up and stop being an asshole."

"Succinct."

"I try to be. Now, how about *we* go home? I'll even get you some gelato too."

Nadia kissed her girlfriend's cheek. "No need. I'll take you."

"Now that's what I'm talking about." Eva looped her arm around Nadia's waist and led her out into the hall.

"Did you see those women?"

They stopped. Down at the other end of the hall were Jenny and another woman who suspiciously looked like someone who was Team Jenny all the way.

"Seriously, what is with all the gay shit lately? Don't they have any shame? Their parents can't be pleased about that."

"Women like Adrienne Thomas can do whatever they want without pissing off the parents. They're self-made billionaires. Bitches."

"At least there are ways to deal with them."

Eva had no idea what they meant. A reference to what happened in high school? A business venture? Getting money from Adrienne? It didn't matter. Those terrible words reminded Eva of what happened several years ago.

It wasn't fair, was it? No matter what, Jenny Myers had gotten into her head and… for more than a moment… made her feel unsafe as both a woman and as a lesbian. No. Not tonight. Not after all the drama of not only tonight, but the whole week… the whole *year* so far!

"Come here, babe." Eva pulled Nadia into her arms, dipped her, and planted a hearty kiss right on her lips. A muffled cry erupted in her mouth. Frisky hands clasped behind her neck. Giggles tickled her skin. When she popped Nadia back up, both Jenny and her friend gaped at them in a mixture of shock and disgust. *Their loss. Women are fun to kiss.* That was a truth Eva would hang on to for as long as she lived.

Time to go home and make good on it.

Chapter 40

"Something troubling you?" Nadia asked, hands snaking up her girlfriend's chest. They had arrived at Eva's place, one light on and no clothes off. After putting their clutches and wallets down on the coffee table, they remained in the living area, gazing into one another's eyes with that silent form of flirtation between them. However, Nadia had picked up on Eva's stiffness the moment she touched that golden chain hanging between lapels. "You're so tense."

"It's nothing." Eva grazed her knuckles against Nadia's chin. "Not with you here. Nothing bothers me when we're alone like this."

Nadia couldn't help but close her eyes and smile at words like that. *Could she be any more romantic?* Seemed impossible. Almost felt like Eva had taken classes at Winchester to cover all her seductive bases. *Instead of shop classes, she snuck into "How to get into a woman's pants" classes.* No wonder Nadia was constantly smitten. "I'm glad to hear that."

"The only thing that could be possibly be bothering me is the fact you're still wearing this obnoxious dress. And I only call it obnoxious because it's on you. I want you naked, babe. Now."

Their lips met in a soft yet needy kiss. "That can be arranged," Nadia mumbled. "Then let's work on getting this tension out of your body."

"Shower?"

Nadia grinned. "A shower would be awesome. I'm sore and sweaty from the gala. I want to be soft and clean when we make love tonight."

"Or we could make love now…"

"Shower first." Nadia kicked off her Gucci sandals and left them in the middle of Eva's living area before wandering toward the bathroom. "Come help me take off my clothes. We should be naked. *Now.*"

To say that slowly undressing one another near the bed was one of the hottest acts of foreplay did a disservice to every sensation flooding Nadia's mind and body. Nothing could knock her out of that moment. The touch of Eva's hand… the gentle way she pulled up that dress and sensually unsnapped the bra… her breath on bare shoulder and throat alike. Magnificent. Not earth-shattering, no, but that could come later. For now, Nadia wanted the work up to having a fantastic orgasm with the love of her life.

Shower first.

Nadia was halfway into the shower, the water already spraying and fogging up the glass, when Eva finally started losing her clothes. Black silk hit the bathroom floor. Gold earrings and chains *clanged* on top of the sink. Nadia pressed her lips against Eva's cleavage as she slowly wove every button through their respective loops. Who needed a blouse anyway? Not Eva. She was meant to be as free as Nadia was right now. And wet. *Say goodbye to this underwear. Now come do me in the shower.*

"Your hair is going to get all wet like this." Eva withdrew a claw clip the size of Nadia's hand. *Oh, good, she knows how heavy this shit on my head is.* Eva may have been divorced from her long hair for several years, but the woman had not forgotten what a pain in the ass holding up thick, wavy hair was. "Turn around. I wanna look at your awesome ass anyway."

Giggling, Nadia turned, leaning against the shower doorway and letting the showerhead spray her breasts with hot water. Might as well get some of the grime of the day off… *and* get more aroused. Because why not? When the best girlfriend in the world was piling hair on top of one's head to keep it from getting soaked in the shower…

"Do you know how hard it is for me to keep my hands off you?" Those hands descended Nadia's sides, feeling up her hips, her outer thighs, and the seemingly infinite curve of her ass. "I didn't have a type before I met you."

"Is that a compliment?" To be fair, Nadia's idea of a "type" had changed drastically since going out with Eva as well. *I never realized how much I would enjoy a woman who likes to take control and has that air about her.* Eva wasn't the first butch Nadia had ever dated – but she was the first to completely own who she was in such a devilishly seductive way. There was no forcing it. No faking it. Eva had plenty of opportunities to tone down her style and mannerisms to make her life easier. Yet she had never taken those opportunities, because it would have gone against who she was. Nadia admired that before she admired the beauty and elegance Eva conducted herself with – even when she was hellbent on making a woman orgasm.

"You bet it's a compliment. I've done nothing but compliment you since I first saw you." Nudity surrounded Nadia as Eva helped herself into the shower and slid the door shut. "I'm still in awe that you're all mine."

Eva reached for the body wash on the ledge. By now the shower was so full of steam that Nadia couldn't tell what was humidity and what was sweat. A good amount of it was sweat, she would guess. It had to be. She was so full of anticipation that sweat gleamed on her brow before the steam hit it. Eva had that effect on her. "Goes both ways, you know?"

Nadia wasn't surprised when body wash drizzled on her shoulder and slid down her back. Yet she shivered nonetheless, hands instinctively splaying against the marble of the shower.

"Of course I'm yours too. But right now I'd rather celebrate how much you're mine. This time tomorrow everyone's going to be wishing that they had you. Men, women… the men will curse themselves for never having a chance with you, and the women will wonder why they never thought about playing for the home team. We caused our own kind of mayhem tonight."

Hands massaged the body wash into Nadia's skin. She tilted her head back, the pile of red hair on her head bumping against Eva's forehead. "You seriously overestimate how much people want me. You're the one with all the money and know-how. I was just born with this body that is apparently so…"

"Fuckable?"

Nadia laughed. "I was going to say *distracting,* but if you insist."

Eva's fingers curled around Nadia's thighs. No soap in that area, but that wasn't the point. The point was to rile her up and make her think about all the sex they could be having.

"I think you're a lot of stellar vocabulary words. But it depends on my mood. Right now I'm hung up on how much I want to indulge in you. So, fuckable will have to do."

"Synonyms are nice too."

A sweet moan escaped Nadia's lips when she was pressed to the wall, her nipples hardening against tile and her toes pushing her body up. Eva nipped her girlfriend's ear alongside a well-timed thrust of her hips. "How's that for a synonym?"

"My, your vocabulary is indeed strong, Ms. Warren."

"Every time you call me that, I get chills. I don't know why." The showerhead dislodged from its holder. Gone was the water spraying upon Nadia. She already missed its heat. "Lots of women have called me that. Some even earnestly. I thought it turned me on then, but now? I think it's because you were never into it before you met me. That goes to a girl's head."

"Does it?" Nadia was a million miles away already. She knew where that spray of water was going. Her feet scooted apart, careful to not slip, but eager to be far away from each other. "What happened back at the gala? I didn't think you were in this kind of mood today."

The silence lasted a little longer than Nadia anticipated, but as she was about to be concerned for Eva's well-being, her girlfriend said, "If I'm around you long enough, I'll enter this mood. Can't be helped. I'm overwhelmed with the desire to make you hot for me and come."

"Does your vocabulary start dying around that time too?"

"Don't make fun of me for being riddled with hormones. I'm young and dumb. My brain has only finished developing like… earlier this year."

"You're too much," Nadia mumbled. "What are you going to do with that showerhead?"

"What do you think I'm going to do?"

Nadia's fingers curled against the tile. "Something naughty."

"Go ahead and say it. Ask *real* nicely. I love it when you show me that side of yourself."

Didn't realize I had something to show. Nadia quivered as she thought of the water touching her in places Eva should be touching. Instead it was like indirect sex. More distant than sex toys, yet somehow more intimate than watching each other be naughty.

What Nadia ended up asking for probably wasn't what Eva had in mind. "Do whatever you want with it. I'm sure I'll love it."

She did, too.

Nadia had never been a woman for vibrators. Something about them irritated her after two seconds of shocking pleasure. Then it was like being *tortured*… and not in the fun way! So while most of her toys went without batteries, she had to admit that feeling the spray of shower water directed at her folds – and not to mention her clit – was one of the best sensations in the world. Or was that only when coupled with leaning back against Eva's chest, head thrown back and endless moans spilling from her lips? Was it the way Eva groped Nadia's breasts, pinching her nipples and making them rub against the tiles? Or was it the way she spread those folds apart and slowly sank a single finger into the one place begging for penetration? Hard to tell when Nadia's brain was about to explode and her body was prepared to follow suit.

"Are you going to come for me?" Every touch of the water was like a prick both in Nadia's loins and in her head. Hearing Eva's voice like that? On top of everything else? A damn hammer! "Or do I have to take you into my bedroom and fuck that orgasm out of you?"

Nadia's imagination went right to it, conjuring up scene after scene of what "fuck that orgasm out of you" meant. Eva was a goddess whether she used her own fingers or recruited aid from the nightstand. One was certainly more intense than the other. Right now? Nadia imagined lying down, legs spread wide and girlfriend slamming her hips down with such a fervent grace that Nadia could barely keep up. *Take me and break me in half. Sounds good.*

And what else sounded good?

That climax finally claiming her, of course.

"Eva!" Nadia's hands slipped against the tile in front of her. Her feet arched until she was completely dependent on Eva keeping her balanced. The water was relentless against her slit. Shivers turned to shudders, and shudders turned to shaking. Eva dropped the showerhead with a *clunk!* and shoved Nadia against the wall, attacking her clean skin with kisses and rubbing her whole body with fingers that begged to be inside her.

But something had clicked inside of Nadia's brain as soon as she came down from her high. She shrugged Eva off her. The two of them stumbled for a moment, Nadia turning everything around and slamming Eva against another wall. She hurried to pick up the showerhead and shove it back into its proper place.

Oh, good. The water rained upon Eva's body, dripping between her breasts, rounding her navel, and disappearing between her legs. Her chest begged to be fondled. Her hips ached for attention. How could Nadia stay away? She wanted to devour Eva.

Except Eva liked to think she got to be in control. The dominant one. The woman who always had someone to do her bidding, whether she realized it or not. Such a sweet, spoiled heiress. The dear was daft, wasn't she? This was the fool who thought Nadia's bathroom was a hell-spot because it didn't look like *this* one. Nadia could only roll her eyes at it now.

But sometimes? Eva needed to be put in her own place. The only way she understood.

"Shit," she muttered, and she must have been given quite the sight. Nadia on her knees, not giving a single damn about how the tiles felt against her bones as she grabbed Eva's thighs and pried them apart. Somebody wasn't getting away unless she begged to.

Eva wasn't going to beg for anything but more of her girlfriend's tongue on her pussy.

Water got all over Nadia's messy bun, but she didn't care. All she cared about was burying her face in Eva's folds, getting drunk on her chemistry, and feeling her tremble in orgasm. Eva wasn't a one-shot climaxer, though. Nadia had been with those women. The ones who came so suddenly that it was like being smacked in the face with heat and wetness when going down on the girl. As fun as that was, Nadia discovered she much preferred Eva's style of orgasming. Her folds swelled on Nadia's tongue, Eva's clit also becoming more prominent and easier to suck between pursed lips.

That was only phase one. Phase two was the sweetness beginning to cover Nadia's tongue, long before Eva got the signal in her brain and began trembling like a virgin having her first orgasm. Hands clasped around Nadia's head, hard and strong, bringing her face forward and burying it in slick heat. Nadia clung to her girlfriend's hips and darted her tongue into the source of all that sweetness. A little bitter, too. One could not adequately compare the taste of a woman to the taste of a man – as someone who had done her fair share of orally pleasuring ex-boyfriends, Nadia was well versed in what it meant to experience that intoxicating moment preceding a partner's full climax. But even though the two could not be adequately compared, Nadia could say that without a doubt she much preferred being on the other end of a female orgasm.

Come for me, my love. Use me as I was meant to be used in this moment. Men had the habit of being the *aggressors* during sex. Even when lying down, they thrust into Nadia's mouth, forcing her to acclimate to *them.* With women? Nadia got to retain all of the control. She had to seek out the parts of Eva's body that begged to be stroked. Lips on clit. Tongue in body. Ducking here, darting there, searching and unyielding. Even when Eva thrust her hips against Nadia's face, she was still at her lover's mercy. It was up to Nadia to make sure her girlfriend rode the wave of pleasure cresting over her body. Sex had never felt so egalitarian as when Nadia was with another woman… and that was accounting for dominant women like Eva.

Because, after all, she was a kitten like the rest of them when it came to coming.

"Fuck!" The clasp tugged against Nadia's hair as hands yanked on it. Pain screeched against Nadia's poor scalp, but she pressed on, happy to feel the force of her girlfriend's sensations. This was almost as good as fingernails raking her skin! "Don't stop! I'm coming!"

Funny, that. Nadia knew Eva was coming long before *she* did!

The roar of the water drowned out Eva's dirty words. Nadia did not doubt that her girlfriend said filthy things deserving of soap. But by then she was so intoxicated that the words made no sense. "*Fuck me, baby. Drink my cum. Take it all.*" What did it mean? They were words that were hotter to hear the cadence of than the meanings themselves.

Kind of a shame. Nadia loved hearing dirty talk when she was having sex. *Especially* from women. They always meant it the most.

Her knees reprimanded her when Nadia kissed her girlfriend's mumbling lips. She ignored the pain, the stiffness of her joints after spending a few minutes kneeling on a tiled floor. It was worth it to feel and see how Eva continued to shudder even after her orgasm concluded. Nadia was ready to relax. They could go to the bedroom and take things more slowly…

Eva shut off the water and wrapped Nadia in a sudden embrace. "You've gone and done it, babe. Now I want you even more. No mercy. I'm not going to be finished with you until your throat is worn out from all the screaming I'm going to make you do."

Nadia's eyes widened. That better be a promise.

***

It was! It was definitely a promise!

She was pinned beneath Eva's body, head permanently slammed against pillow and legs so wide that her *thighs* were the first things to scream for relief. Not that either Nadia or Eva gave them any relief. Once they were opened, inviting another woman between them, well, that was the end of that.

Instead of being calmed in the shower, Eva was in overdrive. Like her orgasm had clicked something in *her* brain too. She barely gave Nadia time to dry off before hauling her into the bedroom and consuming her on the bed. Nadia was a willing participant in all of it, of course. In fact, it was so damn scorching hot that Nadia found herself begging, pleading, *demanding* that her girlfriend be anything but forgiving when it came to making love.

Rough love, but love nonetheless.

Eva had something to prove. Nadia could only grasp at what there was for someone already claiming her girlfriend's heart to prove to the world, but she would offer herself up as the willing sacrifice. *Fuck me until I can't stand the feeling of my own sweat anymore.* They both bathed in it, so soon after a shower, too! *Yes, baby, you're the best lover I've ever had. Make sure I feel it, too.* Nadia could barely speak. Her words were an incomprehensible medley of moans, cries, and phrases that would have bolstered Eva's ego should she be able to understand her girlfriend. Eva was not on this planet anymore, though. The moment she was between Nadia's legs, thrusting, groping, and leaving hickies everywhere, she was fulfilling whatever fantasies she harbored and Nadia was still not quite able to understand.

That didn't mean she reaped no rewards, though. Rewards like being taken to a place so full of emotional and sexual pleasure that she too retreated to another world where she loved everything for what it was. This was particularly possible when Eva rolled over for a whole five seconds to pull something out of her nightstand.

See, she was *amazing* with a strap-on.

Not good. Not great. *Amazing.* She was everything Nadia wanted from intercourse from men but was never able to get. Even when she convinced herself she loved those men, she wasn't able to enjoy them like she thought she deserved. Something was always missing. Probably because they had no damn finesse. All they cared about was getting in, fucking, and getting off. Sometimes they felt bad about it and made sure Nadia was adequately pleased in bed, but it wasn't what she wanted. She *wanted* that intense, physical connection until she too came. Either those men were incapable… or they didn't care. This was rarely an issue with women, and Eva never made it an issue at all.

She may not have been able to feel the cock plunging into her core, but that made her more mindful of it. How it curved. How it filled it. How it touched her G-spot and transformed her into a pathetic mess. Eva knew how to move her hips and use the friction of sex to both of their advantages. Especially Nadia's. Bless her.

Every thrust brought them closer together, even if they were in their respective galaxies. Eva couldn't stop moving or kissing her girlfriend. Nadia couldn't stop hungering for more of what Eva offered once they began. Feeling her girlfriend fill her body like that was better than what happened in the shower. Apparently her loins agreed. The one time Eva pulled out to flip Nadia over and take her from behind, the bed became so wet that Nadia almost refused to believe that was all her coating the sheets.

How many times did she come? What counted as coming? Did all the little climaxes count as separate orgasms? Or was it one long, drawn out orgasm from Heaven that undulated in tune to their thrusts? Nadia hated being dislodged from her girlfriend, but she loved feeling the head of Eva's fake cock graze her G-spot even more. In a brief moment of clarity, Nadia wished that they would have the strength and fortitude to do this all damn night.

Instead, Eva was determined to finish Nadia's pussy off.

"Do you feel that?" Such a raspy voice was not unheard of during their times together. But this was one of the only times it held such conviction, so much desire to be told "*Yes, baby, I feel it.*" "Do you feel me all the way inside of you?"

Their hands fumbled next to Nadia's head. Pillows were so handy, weren't they? They muffled sounds of joy when it was pertinent to do so.

They also added a lot of comfort for someone getting pounded from behind. But now that pillow's sole purpose seemed to be suffocating poor Nadia as she struggled to respond. "Yes," she whispered, stroking the web of skin between Eva's fingers. "I feel all of it." Wasn't it wonderful that all people had the opportunity to fill their lovers in such wonderful ways? Eva didn't need to be born with certain body parts to accomplish what they both wanted to feel. The best part? It wasn't even about being male or female. It was about sharing something that was so intrinsic to how they wanted to express their love for one another.

"Good. Because I feel all of you with me." Eva's fingers crawled up Nadia's throat, encircling her tender flesh and pulling against her bottom lip. "Every little bit of your body. Every inch of your skin and the flesh inside of you. If I push hard enough…" Nadia went down, gasping into the pillow as Eva's hips surged against her from behind. *Oh my God. Oh my God!* It hurt, but in that delightfully pleasing way. The kind of pain that didn't leave any lasting marks, other than the passion fueling her desires. Eva knew how to get that reaction too. "I can feel your heart too. It's beating so quickly. Beating for me, yeah?"

"Yeah…" Nadia pressed her cheek against the pillow. A kiss touched her skin.

"You want me to possess this body of yours? Make it mine? Mark it the only way a woman like me can do?"

"Absolutely." How did such a complicated word escape Nadia's lips? "Do your worst. I mean your best. I mean…"

Lips touched hers. "I'll do both? How about that?"

"Good."

Eva released her. Nadia's face fell back into the pillow, her hands free to grab the sheets beneath them while the lower half of her body was both used and venerated. It was as much about Eva's pleasure as it was about Nadia's. Of course, Nadia assumed she was getting the better end of the deal, but she wasn't Eva – the woman who needed infinite control handed to her on the silver platters of her youth. Perhaps she didn't get as much physical pleasure out of this as she did mental. What a sight Nadia must have been! What a delight it must be to grab her hair and pull it. Nadia pushed herself up on her hands, head tilted upward, eyes closed and mouth falling open as her splitting legs accepted whatever Eva gave her between them. One could never underestimate how much strength an athlete possessed.

"Come for me," Eva growled, stilling inside Nadia. *Holy shit! Completely spear me, why don't you?* Nadia quivered on the silicon cock filling her as if it had every right to do so. Who had given it that right? Besides the two of them, of course. "I come for you? You come for me. I want to see you completely lose your mind."

Easy enough to do. The moment Eva moved again, Nadia ran toward the edge of the proverbial cliff and jumped.

She screamed into the air, since her fingers were busy mangling the pillow. Warmth did not spread from her core as she was used to experiencing. *Heat* blasted through her instead, decimating every part of her until her nerves cried in blissful agony. A spank hit her ass, interrupting her scream and sending her into a spiral of groans that pushed her back down to the bed. Eva was on top of her, fucking her with a heavy yet sensual motion that coaxed Nadia to spend the last of her orgasm knowing what it felt like to have her girlfriend as such a fixture in her body. All while never once touching her clit.

Damn, she's too good.

Nadia's last sound was a moan reverberating against the bed. Eva slowed her motions before withdrawing her cock and letting it rest atop Nadia's ass. Still hard. Still so wet.

Eva didn't need masculinity to be as virile as she was. So what if that wasn't her real body part? She knew how to use it. How to make it convey what she felt inside her heart. A woman through and through… but a woman who was fluent in the language of sexual implements and all that they implied.

"I'm still hard for you, babe," Eva muttered. "You feel that? That means I still want more of you. But I think I got you good already. You look like you've been fucked since Sunday."

"I feel like it." Nadia rolled onto her side, finally taking in the beautiful look of her girlfriend. Sweat streamed down Eva's angular face. Her hair was plastered on her head so long after getting out of the shower. And, yeah, that countenance screamed that she was pretty pleased with herself for fucking her girlfriend like that.

It made Nadia want to give her thanks in ways Eva hadn't even asked for yet.

"Hi," Nadia said, drunk on how good she felt. "You look like someone who needs someone to make you feel good again too."

"Oh?" Eva flopped down onto the bed, propped up on her arm. Lying like that, languid and perfectly happy with her lot in life, made her look like the sex goddess she probably thought she was. "Tell me more."

"Why tell you?" Nadia grabbed the hard thing between Eva's legs. "When I can show you?"

Eva's eyebrows shot up her forehead. "Then get to showing, babe."

Nadia found it easiest to give herself over when she was already hungover on the best parts of sex. Two orgasms later – one *much* harder than the last – she was prepared to do anything that came to mind. Right now? Her mind told her to bend over her girlfriend's torso and put her mouth to work… and not with kissing pretty pink lips.

It was a lovely lull in between bouts of intense lovemaking. Nadia's body was so relaxed that there was no question that she could take all of Eva into her mouth and throat. Sure, it was sometimes weird that the fake cock had almost no give, but at least she knew what to expect in size and rigidity. That would never change. She also didn't have to anticipate any surprises, unless Eva got some crazy ideas about what to do with her hips. Nadia didn't think that was going to happen. Her girlfriend was content to close her eyes and let Nadia do whatever.

"God, you are so beautiful." Eva's fingers lightly combed Nadia's hair. "How did I get such a gorgeous girlfriend? What have I done to deserve such special treatment in life?"

She was always a laugh, wasn't she?

"You got me because I fell in love with you. That's all there is to it."

"Uh huh. Is there a reason you stopped doing that down there?"

Nadia sat up. *Look at her.* So cocky. So arrogant. So dashing in her femininity and the way she smiled like a kid having the best day of her life. Yet there was still something hanging between them. Something that prevented Eva from thoroughly enjoying this moment they shared. It was the same something Nadia sensed when they first came home and undressed in the living area. *She's uptight about something. Remembering that something. Did it happen tonight?* When Eva came to find her outside of the women's restroom, she had that look on her face that said "Let's get out of here. Now." Nadia wished she knew what was wrong. But unless Eva was willing to open up – and good luck with that – then her girlfriend would have to find other ways to make her feel better.

"What do you think?" Nadia straddled Eva's waist, the thick rigidity of their mutual friend pressing against her eager cleft. *I hadn't thought about fucking like that again… but now that you mention it…* Neither Nadia nor Eva protested when it slipped back inside. "Like what you see here?"

"If I had a sight like this every day, I would be the happiest woman."

"You mean you're not already?"

"I'm not walking into that trap." Eva reached up, squeezing Nadia's tender breasts. Her nipples had been perpetually hard since the moment they got in bed. Was that ache because of them? Or because she still desperately wanted to be touched? It certainly felt nice, with her legs spread once more and her body filled with the one thing connecting them outside of love and fancy. "You know what I mean."

"And what do you mean?" Nadia rotated her hips in slow, sensual circles. It was enough to keep her aroused, but not enough to send her into another orgasmic fit. Eva bended her knees and brought them up into the air. Nadia would take the opportunity to lie back and brace herself against her girlfriend's sturdy limbs. "Come up here and kiss me."

Eva did. She shot up, clutching Nadia in her embrace and covering her with the heaviest kisses to grace those lips. Their tangled limbs brought them closer together now than they had been minutes ago. Still, Nadia giggled, happy to feel that hot breath against her throat once more.

"I love you," Eva murmured. "I'd do anything for you. I want to do everything with you."

"Really? Then tell me all your secrets." When Nadia received an incredulous look, she continued, "All right, you can keep some to yourself, but I want to know what's going on in your heart. It passes on to me, you know. So what's bothering you?"

"Who said that anything was bothering me?"

"I'm to the point in this relationship where I can tell that something is bothering you." And something was bothering Nadia right now. Namely that fucking cock still inside of her. Were they going to keep doing it, or was this about something else now? "You should tell me so I can help you feel better. That's part of my job as your girlfriend that loves you so much. What's up, buttercup?"

"God, why do you have to be so adorable right now?"

"Because we're having sex, and I want you on your toes so you'll give me pleasure."

"Deal."

Nadia pecked her girlfriend's lips. "But first you have to tell me what's on your mind. Don't hold back, baby. Tell me so I can make your night even better."

"Ah…" Eva pushed her forehead against Nadia's chest. Did she enjoy pushing her face in big tits, or was that a happy byproduct of biology? "When you were gone at the gala earlier, that girl I told you about… the one who became soccer captain… she came by our table to get a rise out of me."

A stone sank in Nadia's stomach. "What? That's awful. If I had been there, I would have socked her."

"I would have loved to have seen that." Eva's smile was tenuous at best. "But I don't think it would have helped, unfortunately."

"Aw." Nadia cupped her hands around her girlfriend's face. "Yet I could have still tried."

"You're doing more than enough right now." Their noses rubbed together. "I enjoy being with you more than you can know."

"You sure about that? Because I'm pretty fond of being with you as well."

"It's different."

"How so?"

"It just is."

Fine, if she was going to be that way… "You were really into what we were doing earlier. You associate taking control in the bedroom with taking control of your past, don't you?"

The candid look on Eva's face faltered. "I thought we've already talked about this before. Besides, don't I have a dick up inside of you? Shouldn't we be talking about that instead?"

"Hon, unlike you, I've been with men. Trust me when I say what I'm feeling right now isn't that much different from some of my ex-boyfriends." She made it sound like she had so many. Some of the men in that count weren't even really boyfriends. Just… men she had been with, for better or for worse. *None of them felt as good as any woman, though.* She reaffirmed that to herself with a kiss to Eva's brow. "You associate what we're doing right now with taking control. Maybe you're not taking it from me, per se, but you're yanking it from the universe. You're reclaiming the control you lost a long time ago."

Eva looked away. "Sheesh. What are you? My shrink?"

"No. I'm your girlfriend. Sometimes that's the same thing, though." Nadia traced her girlfriend's cheek bone. "You ever think about letting me have some control for a while?"

"What do you mean?"

The way Eva looked at her implied that she damn well knew. With a flirty kiss, Nadia climbed off her girlfriend's lap… and unsnapped the straps around her waist. "It feels good to give up control. Let me remind you. Please."

Chapter 41

Somehow, Eva had known that this day would come.

Nadia was a lot more fluid in the bedroom than most of Eva's previous partners. Nadia didn't question what they did or how often they did it. She was as likely to suck a dildo she had been fucking as she was to yank those straps off her lover's body and put them on for herself. Eva had introduced her to a more structured world, where roles were defined for a set amount of time, but she hadn't flipped the script aside from showing her more vulnerable sides of her girlfriend. What was more vulnerable than giving up control?

"You even know how to use that thing?" Eva's unease wasn't supposed to be so apparent. A laugh. Play it off with a laugh! So much for that. She sounded like she was braying instead. *This should be hot. I should be turned on by the sight of my hot girlfriend wearing a strap-on.* It was good enough the other way around, wasn't it?

Nadia shot her a devilish look as she secured the straps around her voluptuous waist. Indeed, she had to loosen the straps to make them fit comfortably. What had looked fairly large on Eva's thinner body was much more proportional on Nadia's. Yet it supposedly felt the same? "You think I've never fucked a girl with a strap-on before? Please. I can give as well as I can get. Ask my ex-girlfriend Shari."

"I've never heard of this Shari." Eva drew up her legs, protecting her crotch with her feet. "She as good looking as you? Paint me a picture, babe."

Nadia crawled forward, face nuzzling against Eva's arm. "Don't be nervous," she said softly. "I can't believe you've never done it like this before."

"Of course I've done it." Apparently that was as preposterous to assume as it was to think that Nadia never wielded a cock before. "Just… never on the fly like this."

"Oh?"

Eva looked away again. "I've done it more than a few times, with varying success." She couldn't do it with anybody. And she was a lot more opened to doing it when she was younger… before that incident happened. Her first real girlfriend was all about experimenting with lesbian sex toys. Eva had more fake cocks in her than most of her classmates had real ones. Hell, it wasn't the first time she enjoyed such company with Nadia. Just… not like this. *I fucked myself for our mutual enjoyment, but she didn't do it to me. Not without me directing her.* Eva loved that. She loved having a pretty woman lick one of those things and then shove it deep inside – either of them. Didn't matter. Hot either way.

A strap-on was a different story. Eva hated to admit it, but it reminded her of *men.* Men who used their cocks as instruments rather than body parts. *Tools of violence. Tools of oppression.* That was her only relationship to them, aside from being those things that made babies and helped men pee. Not that she ever thought about that either. Gross. But as a woman who had no interest in sex with men, having her girlfriend put on a strap-on and give her *that* look was something else entirely.

"You usually plan it out, huh?" Nadia really was perceptive, wasn't she?

"Yeah. Usually I know we're going to be doing it."

"Ah, I see. You're not used to your girlfriend springing it on you. Not that I think I'm springing it on you." Nadia stroked Eva's face in an effort to placate her. It worked. A little. "I don't want to do it to lord it over you. I want to do it because I want to share something like that with you. But if it really bothers you…" Nadia unsnapped one of the buckles. "We could do something else. I don't really mind."

"No, no…" Eva put her hand on Nadia's. "Let's do it. Give me a moment to reorient my poor brain. I'm still stuck on fucking yours out."

"Trust me, love, I don't think I can take much more right now. Let me do you for a moment. Ahem."

It wasn't that Eva was turned off by the prospect. *How can I say no to this image coming for me?* That gleam in Nadia's eyes screamed to be obeyed. Every day. *Obeyed.* Ah, perhaps that was the issue. Eva didn't like obeying. Not only did it go against her nature, but in situations like this, it gave her bad memories. *I get caught up thinking about what could have happened in that locker room. Just because they didn't touch me doesn't mean they didn't affect me.* And that fuckin' Jenny Myers… she knew what she was doing! All these years later… she should have stayed away and lived her own life. Eva was willing to forgive (but maybe not forget) but Jenny had thrown that prospect away by approaching the table and talking about soccer.

"Eva," Nadia softly said. "Relax. Look at me, baby."

She did look at her. Nothing was more pleasing to look at than Nadia Gaines, the woman who had played an arousing game of hard to get for so long. *Now I've got her. No, now she's got* me. What a thrilling feeling! Eva didn't hand her body and soul – or her heart for that matter – to just anyone. Trust was earned through many encounters. Eva trusted her girlfriend enough to let her in like this, but it would take that dreaded communication to make it go off without a terrifying hitch.

"Could we turn off the light?" Eva asked. "Or at least this one. Sorry."

"Don't be sorry." Nadia climbed over her girlfriend and shut off the lamp next to the bed. The light was still on by the door yards away. A soft golden glow illuminated Nadia's hair from behind. Before her? Shadows. Eva was in enough darkness to create the illusion of protection. How funny. She needed to feel protected.

Somehow, this level of vulnerability seemed unheard of. *Get over yourself, Eva. This isn't the first time you've taken some girl's dick. Let alone your own! Hey, come on, you know it's not like that with Nadia of all people! If any woman is going to fuck you like you fuck them, it better be her.*

Was that it? Was it because of who Nadia was? She wasn't a friend with benefits that Eva trusted enough to give her a good time. Nor was she a one night stand who specialized in such things – and Eva knew that going in. This was the woman she wanted to spend the rest of her life with. The woman she was making suffer with the rest of the Warrens and the paparazzi so they could be together. That wasn't fear in Eva's heart, sinking her into the bed.

That was excitement.

"You're mine." Nadia eased Eva's legs opened and kneeled between them. "I'm the last woman you're going to be with. I'm going to prove to you why I deserve that position."

"And this position, I'm sure."

Nadia smiled. Loving, nurturing… Eva had never felt so cherished. "You wet for me?"

"When am I not?"

"You can make all the jokes you want." Nadia leaned down, trapping Eva against her bed. Her hips instinctively raised to meet the head of Nadia's – because it was hers now, wasn't it? – cock. "But I'll have you know that this is serious. I'm gonna prove everything that needs proving."

"Like what?"

They shared a long and sumptuous kiss as Eva eased open. *Oh, fuck.* Yeah. Yeah, that felt pretty damn good. Inch by inch Nadia entered her, slowly, seducing her over to the idea of making love like this.

"You know what, Eva." Nadia undulated her hips once more. But instead of riding her girlfriend's lap, she entered her, filled her, and tenderly made love to her. "Quiet, now. No more talking. Concentrate on *us.*"

"Okay."

"Okay?"

Eva nodded. "I'm okay."

"Good." That was the last thing Nadia said before increasing her thrusts.

She had been right about a lot of things. Like how there were things that still needed to be proven. Or that Eva would be more than able to enjoy herself while being on the receiving end of Nadia's control. For she did control this, from beginning to end, taking Eva on a journey she never anticipated that night. *I wanted to take control tonight because I had something to prove to myself. But what was I proving to her? That I can make her feel good? She could prove the same thing to me.* Of course, that was only possible with so much love and trust blossoming between them. The love had already been there, whether it appeared in the form of will-they-won't-they or sharing a bathtub together. Ah, and the trust! Eva hadn't realized she needed a girlfriend she could trust so wholeheartedly. It certainly made life sweeter, didn't it? This whole business of looking into each other's eyes and finding nothing but consecrated bliss.

"You like it?" Nadia had found a steady rhythm that kept Eva's eyes rolled back until that moment. Now she was forced to focus on her gilded beauty, those curves so damned luscious as they rolled in the shadows. Hair fell to the side. Eyes glistened in arousal. Hands fondled Eva as she had fondled Nadia not so long ago. Breasts bounced slightly enough to keep Eva's focus on those two hard nipples dotting mounds she wanted nothing more than anything to bury herself in again. Hips? Damned hips. Always rolling, always pushing forward and making Eva feel good. She was right. She was experienced at this. Maybe not as much as Eva was, but damn well good enough to make her forget what they were doing and damn well experience it!

"Hell yes," Eva whispered. Her eyes slammed shut as the first shudder wracked her body from within. It was easy to match Nadia's rhythm. She pushed forward, Eva pushed up. She pulled back, Eva lowered her hips. Simple enough. Yet it was the most glorious feeling in the universe at that moment. How in tune were they with each other? "You feel good inside of me."

"I'm glad." Nadia hovered over her, hair tickling Eva's shoulder and eyelashes kissing skin. Her hands folded beneath Eva's head and brought it up for a kiss. "I love you, Eva. You can always feel safe with me."

That was the moment Eva was supposed to use to say "*And you too, you know.*" But this wasn't about Nadia's safety. This was about Eva's. This was about Eva learning to trust her girlfriend so unconditionally that nothing would ever come between them. Things certainly did not come between them right now. Not even that pesky thing called friction.

"I love you too." Eva wrapped her arms around Nadia and brought her down. "Fuck me."

She was glad she asked to turn off the bed enclave light. The sweetness of the shadows added to the passion erupting between them. Seconds passed. Seconds became minutes. Those minutes were full of the easy kind of lovemaking Eva desperately needed right now. The more they made love? The more she gave herself over, declaring her heart to be Nadia's now, then, forever. She didn't once question whether or not she had Nadia's heart. How could she, when Nadia gave herself so readily over? She was willing to try anything. To put up with anything. To imply that she couldn't handle what Eva dealt with every day… well, some days would be harder than others. But they would get through them. They would find a way to not only love each other even more fervently, but to overcome whatever obstacles were thrown at them.

They were worth it.

"I must be so deep inside of you," Nadia whispered in Eva's ear. "Am I? Can you feel me near your heart?"

Eva gasped. Where were her hands? Her legs? The rest of her, floating on a cloud? All she could feel was the beating of her happy heart and the good sensations flooding her abdomen. "Yeah." That was accompanied with a groan. "I can feel you everywhere."

"Are you going to come?"

"Only if you do too."

"Of course. But that means I have to fuck your brains out. I've been holding back this whole time."

"Don't hold back. Don't ever hold back with me."

"You sure?"

"*Absolutely.*"

Nadia was relentless. It must have been the last of her energy reserves. It *had* to be. Nadia had taken everything Eva had thrown. They had been having sex for almost two hours straight! Was this it? The finale? Were they going to be so spent that Eva wouldn't be able to move for a week? *God, I hope so.* That was the best way to declare love for another woman.

Nadia sure was virile, wasn't she? Eva knew better than anyone that virility had nothing to do with gender or its entrapments.

"Oh, *God!*" No surprise when Nadia came first, her sweet voice raining honey in Eva's ear. The woman was inspired by her own good feelings to plunge hard and deep into Eva, consuming her every crevice and drawing out every last drop she had to give. Everything – *everything* – was on fire around them. Where did one's voice end and the other's begin? Was there an ending? A beginning? Or were they experiencing something that went beyond what most humans were able to comprehend?

Eva didn't give a fuck. Orgasm made sure of that.

And the utter peace they both experienced moments later made sure that they knew what it meant to be one.

***

"I have to say, Eva, I'm excited to see how your project goes this term." Prof. Davis sat back in her office chair and bestowed a grin upon Eva's anticipating form. "And I don't say that to most of my students. You've always been ambitious, and that's exciting."

Eva released a pent up breath. She could never tell what Prof. Davis was going to think of the projects she wanted to accomplish every term. "Adding up all those figures every week is going to be a pain in my ass, but I'm willing to do it. To impress you, of course."

"Impressing me is half your score, obviously." That droll humor was infectious on the graduate campus, particularly in the business department, a towering ten-story building downtown. Urban campuses tended to suffer from a lack of greenery, but this graduate off-shoot of the local private university that constantly hit the national top 10 lists made up for it in cute, green parks and cozy cafés full of students cramming for their next midterm or final. The law students had it the roughest. Then there were masochistic dumbasses like Eva who made her programs tougher than they were on paper. Her last term was to commence in a month. Like hell she was going to take the easy way out! "That said, I do hope you're willing to put in all the work. Not that you've given me reason to doubt you before."

"I can assure you that I'm ready to start, but I'm going to take a huge vacation first. And after. By graduation this Christmas I'm probably going to be half-drunk already, but I hear that's normal in my world. I wouldn't know. It's all normal to me."

They shook hands before Eva picked up her bag and sauntered out of her professor's office. The campus was particularly dead that time of summer, but Prof. Davis made a habit of being in her office every morning and sometimes afternoon. When she had half a dozen scoundrels like Eva to keep track of… well, she was a bit busy.

Eva stopped off at her favorite student café and bought a drink for herself and for Nadia, whom she was en route to see at Cole's executive office. *Bastard has her working on a Saturday.* Darling Nadia was making up for an emergency office closure on Tuesday thanks to a prank bomb scare. Appointments had been shuffled and Adrienne Thomas was taking over for the weekend. Eva decided to make it up to her girlfriend by arranging for reservations at one of the nicest restaurants in town.

The top floor office was buzzing with more life than Eva anticipated. Adrienne stood in her office doorway happily chatting with a man in a three-piece Bespoke suit. More men headed toward the elevator as Eva got off, holding the button until they were all in and thanking her for her trouble. When they weren't gawking at her semi-garish white Givenchy pantsuit, anyway.

Then there was Nadia, the only one sitting at a desk. She was wearing a black Queen Anne dress with a ruby-studded belt that Eva had bought for her a week ago. *Saw it in the window, knew she had to have it.* That was the best perk about being so rich! Nadia had two dozen designer dresses in one of Eva's closets now. Pretty soon they would migrate to the Warren Estate, assuming Nadia would set foot there again.

"Hey, stud," Nadia said, leaning back in her seat in a *much* more pleasing way than Prof. Davis had. For one, Nadia had amazing cleavage, especially in a Queen Anne dress. *Yow. Za.* "Come to flirt with me again? Because I'm not buying anything."

"The hell you're not." Eva sat on the edge of the receptionist's desk. Yup. Mighty fine view of cleavage from up there. It almost made her jealous that she didn't have any to match. "I didn't come up all this way for you to turn me down. I'll have you know that after you get off work here you're coming with me to dinner. I made reservations. So there."

Nadia tried to hold her disinterested façade, but it crumbled the moment Eva told her that. "Aw, really? That's sweet. Since, you know, I only get one day off this week. Tuesday didn't count. Bit stressful." She glared at the work still left on her computer.

"I know, babe. That's why I'm going to pamper you all night and all day tomorrow. We're not leaving my apartment the moment we get there. Not until you have to go to work Monday morning."

Nadia propped her head on her hand. "Pamper me, huh?"

"Anything you want. We'll order in all the food you want…"

"Maybe I want you to cook for me."

Eva flinched. "You need that extra carbon in your diet, huh?" Eva was a master at volcanic-inspired cuisine. Everything turned to ash at her touch!

"Maybe I want to cook something together."

"The whole point is to *pamper* you so you don't have to lift a finger."

The glass door to the office opened. Eva paid the visitor no mind at first. Then Nadia glanced away, frowning.

"What is it?" Eva looked over her shoulder. There was Amber, bedecked in a casually stylish maxi dress topped off with a thin leather jacket. Wasn't she hot in this summer weather? "Thought she had the day off since you said Cole wasn't coming in." The bastard. Made everyone but himself work on Saturday.

"Don't think she's here for that..."

Amber looked around until she met Adrienne's gaze from her office. The CEO stopped chatting with her guest and acted as if she had never seen Amber. *Just in time for the drama.*

"What's going on with them?" Eva asked, lips close to Nadia's ear.

"They've been cordial since the gala. Don't know if they're still going out, though."

The man excused himself and nodded to Amber on his way out the door. She glanced at Adrienne again before pulling something out of her Louis Vuitton purse and extending it to the CEO ten yards away.

It was a key.

"What have I done to deserve this?" Adrienne plucked the key from Amber's fingers. They smiled at one another. "Changed your mind about giving me your house key?"

"It was my roommate's idea. He said he wants you around often. He likes your perfume."

"And I like his omelets, so we're even." Adrienne planted a gentle kiss on Amber's cheek. "Tell me he's doing dinner for us."

"I'm sure it can be arranged."

They looked in the receptionist's direction. "What are you two lovebirds doing for dinner?"

"She got us reservations."

Eva coughed. "Pussy."

"Eva!"

Adrienne rolled her eyes. "Dinner of champions around this place."

"'Cause we run the world."

Adrienne Thomas didn't smile very often, but when she did – genuinely, anyway – she looked closer to Eva's age than her brother's. "Give me a few years to buy out my business partner. I'll keep the spot open for you, Ms. Warren."

"As long as I still have a job," Nadia said.

"Ms. Gaines, if you can have your tits and O-face plastered all over the internet and still have a job here, I'm sure a little corporate upheaval won't have much effect either."

Nadia turned toward her work computer, blushing. *There's not enough work in the world on your computer to take your mind off what you're thinking about.* Or what Eva was thinking about. Sure, her imagination was flooded with those pap pics that showed as much of her as they did her girlfriend. But Eva was to the point where she was able to think of nothing but her hot and naked girlfriend writhing on a bed in a Hong Kong hotel. *Most excellent fantasy, yes.* It had already gotten her through a few nights away from Nadia.

"You two have a pleasant evening. I think we're heading out." Adrienne popped out of her office wearing a light sweater and carrying her purse. She locked her office door behind her. "Close up for us, would you Nadia?"

"Of course, ma'am."

Amber and Adrienne walked out of the executive office hand-in-hand. It almost wasn't fair. Eva had spent most of the year trying to make her and Nadia the star lesbian couple of upper society, but in one night those two bisexual supermodels had managed to upstage every dyke trying to leave her mark on the world. That was great for Nadia, who was quickly forgotten by the press and most of the perverts sniffing around the office. Not so great for Eva, who had long learned to use the media to her advantage. Besides, not like she was shy with showing off her tits… enough drunken nights at The Dark Hour sex club revealed that about her.

Her phone rang in her pocket as Nadia opened her mouth to say something.

"Hang on, babe, it's Henry." Why in the world was he calling his sister at this time of day? They hadn't spoken since dinner last Monday night. *What is there to say? He's got his life and I've got mine.* By the time Eva held her phone up to her ear, she was already convinced that Henry was warning her about their mother's new machinations.

Not quite.

"Hello, dear brother. What can I do for you?"

"Eva!"

Whoa! Who had woken up the frenzied side of Henry Warren? "That's me! You being kidnapped or something? Sorry, don't have any ransom money on hand."

"Monica's in labor!"

In that case... Was she supposed to be surprised? Monica was a week overdue already. "How about that! Someone's gonna be a daddy today!" And Eva was going to be an auntie, but she didn't think about that. "Should I meet you and our parents at home?" Monica had been planning her wondrous home birth for months. Midwives and doulas everywhere.

"No, because you know how Monica is. She's at the Château."

"She's *where?*"

"I told her to come home sooner, but she didn't listen to me..."

Eva didn't have the heart to tell him that she wouldn't be listening to him about a many good things in their marriage. Monica may have been a lifestyle submissive that Eva could never in a million years relate to, but she was stubbornly independent in a lot of ways. Insisting on working until the day she literally went into overdue labor was one of them. Didn't help that her place of business was an isolated manor up in the fucking mountains, hours away from the city!

"Give us a few minutes and I can come get you. You shouldn't be driving."

"Don't worry about it. The Coles are giving me a ride."

"The Coles, hm?" Eva glanced at her girlfriend, who waited patiently to be told what was going on. "Then you're in good hands. Tell you what. Nadia and I have dinner reservations in an hour. We'll head up to the Château afterward." Least she could do. "Oh, and do text me if it's born before I get there. And remember that you owe me twenty grand if it's a boy."

"Thanks. Our parents will be staying here, so it will be good to have family up there."

"Aw," Eva smiled at Nadia, "Henry called you family."

"Eva?"

"Yeah, yeah, what are you doing talking to me? You've got an overnight bag to pack and a car to jump into. I'll see you later!" Eva hung up before Henry could keep himself further distracted from the matter at hand. *You know, the fact that his wife's having their first child as we speak.* "Slight change of plans, babe." Eva leaned across the desk. "After dinner we need to go see my brother and his wife. They're apparently about to be parents."

Nadia dropped her pen. "Shouldn't we go now? I can go ahead and close up the office."

"Nah. You know how babies are. Could be a few hours… could be a day… they'll be plenty distracted. Not like we'll run out of daylight going up there at this time of year."

Nadia shut down her computer and stood up, jacket quickly covering her arms. "You're going to be an aunt!"

Eva waited until her girlfriend had rounded the desk before responding. "In a way, so are you. By proxy."

Nadia's purse strap slipped down her arm. "I've never been an aunt before. I don't even have siblings."

"Then aren't you lucky to have me! I'll share all my little nieces and nephews with you. It'll be great. We'll be the Gay Aunts every child deserves to have!"

Eva swung her arm around Nadia's shoulders as they wandered out of the office. Nadia shut off the lights and pulled out the keys to the doors. "This is pretty exciting, though. Your parents will finally leave."

"Ha! They ain't even going to be there!"

"Why?"

"Because Monica is a workaholic and still up at the Château. Can you believe it? Giving birth to an heir in a courtesan house. Seems fitting."

Nadia stopped halfway to the elevator. "I've never been there before."

"Never? It's doubly your lucky day. That place is a trip. Plus your boss and friend will be there. Let's get going! I'm hungry."

Eva had to practically drag Nadia into the elevator. After assuring her girlfriend that she highly doubted any straight hanky-panky would be happening up in the mountains while one of the most important women in the city was in the middle of giving birth, Nadia still looked at her as if going up there to join the fun was the dumbest thing in the world.

Then, she said, "We're taking my car."

"Why would we do that? We'll take mine. I know the way."

"Didn't say you wouldn't be driving, hon."

"Then why *your* car?"

"Because when you meet your niece or nephew, they're going to see you rolling up in a black Fiat. They'll have years to deal with your ego. Might as well start things off humbly."

"The fuck about a Fiat is *humble?*"

Nadia raised one of her red eyebrows. "Compared to a Jaguar convertible?"

"The kid is going to be one of the richest, most spoiled heirs in the *world*..."

"Like I said. Start off humble."

They got into the elevator as the doors closed again. Nadia punched the lobby button. "You're going to be *that* aunt, aren't you?" Eva asked, arms crossed.

Nadia sidled up next to her. They were quite the distorted sight in the elevator doors' reflection. "If there's anything I've learned from your sister-in-law, it's that you Warrens need some wrangling now and then. Privileged idiots, the lot of you."

"Says a lot about you dating one, then."

Eva hadn't quite expected Nadia to pull her into a kiss that lasted the whole ride down to the lobby, but hey, she wasn't going to protest, either! Kissing was a great way to feel humble, after all.

Or was that fueling the ego? *Hm.* Eva would have to keep the kissing party going to do further research.

Epilogue

The gentle lap of ocean waves touched the sandy beaches so tenderly that Nadia could close her eyes and feel like she was in a rejuvenating cocoon. Her skin, judiciously covered in sunscreen, warmed beneath the Caribbean summer sun. If she didn't return from this weekend getaway with a new tan that was sure to disappear by October, then she hadn't lived her life right. *I could stay here forever.* She thought that every time a hand stroked the top of her head.

Eva was behind her, propped up on their beach towel and reading a novel. They wore the same linen shirt, buttons open to reveal their respective bikini tops, but Eva went with cotton shorts while Nadia rocked flirty bikini bottoms. Every so often Eva reached down and tugged on one of the strings keeping the fabric covering Nadia's most sensitive areas.

"What did I tell you?" Eva said with a sigh. Nadia shifted her body so she could better hear her girlfriend. *She speaks quietly, yet it sounds like screaming over the peace of this island.* "Having your own private island rocks."

If by private she meant *nobody else on this beach,* then yes, she was right. But the island was far from *private.* Year-round staff kept the guest houses ready, and that didn't include the daily delivery people who rode over from the main (public) island with provisions, their boats laden with tropical fruit, fresh fish, and a daily copy of *The Wall Street Journal.* None of these people bothered the Warrens and their guests unless asked, but still, totally not private.

"I am definitely getting used to this." Nadia stretched her arms behind her, indirectly inviting Eva to touch stomach and cop a feel. *Don't give me ideas about beach sex.* They had only been on the island twelve hours, having flown in late last night after Nadia got off work, but Eva was already antsy about being as naughty as damn possible. She claimed that the hot tub with the great view of the sunset had their names on it. There was a reason the fool was reading an erotic romance novel.

Or at least she *was.* Now Eva was texting on her phone. So much for attention.

"I have a surprise for you, pretty dove," Eva said. She nicked Nadia's chin. "To make up for how busy I'm going to be this term."

Eva started her final term of classes next week. Nadia was not looking forward to the late nights apart and how stressed out dear Eva was probably going to be, but it was going to be worth it… that's what they both told themselves. Besides, they were comfortable enough in their relationship that half a week apart here and there wasn't going to break them. Sighing, Nadia sat up and took off her sunglasses so she could get a better look at her girlfriend's glowing countenance. "What is it? You only call me dove when you're buttering me up."

A man descended the wooden stairs leading to the beach. Balanced on his hand was a silver tray carrying something Nadia could not yet make out.

"A surprise."

"That's what you said."

The man stood behind them. His smile was a careful mixture of practiced and genuine. He was either *that* good at faking mirth, or he really did feel giddy over what Eva had planned. This must've been the first time the Warren heiress surprised a girlfriend on the island like this.

He lowered the tray so it was at Nadia's eye level. A red box wrapped in white ribbon waited for her to pluck it off the silver tray.

"Go on, babe. Happy birthday."

Grinning, Nadia took the box and marveled at its feathery weight in her palm. "My birthday isn't for another month!"

Eva shrugged. "Sounded good in my head. Open it."

The man nodded before taking his leave. Nadia tore the ribbon and popped the lid off the box. "Oh my God," she gasped. "You're kidding me!"

Eva snorted before removing her sunglasses so she could get a better look at her girlfriend's gift. "You like it?"

Nadia pulled out the ring and held it up to her eye. "Is it a ruby?"

"Red beryl, actually."

"Red… *beryl?*"

"Told you I was into gemstones. When I saw it in my collection, I knew I had to have it set and sized for you. Consider it a promise ring, babe."

Nadia's hand was shaking too much to put such a precious gemstone on her finger. *This must be worth a fucking fortune!* Nadia knew the bare minimum about gemstones before dating Eva. Now she knew enough by osmosis. Like how red beryl was so rare that it was only mined in Utah. *Utah!* "A promise for what?"

Eva kissed the top of her girlfriend's fiery red head. Was that what made her think of Nadia when she saw this gem? *In her collection, no less! What other prizes does she have in there?* "A promise to think about you every day for the rest of my life. Here." Eva leaned down, taking both the ring and Nadia's hand. "See? Perfect fit."

The ring slipped effortlessly onto Nadia's left ring finger. "You can't put a ring like this on a girl's wedding finger and say something cheesy like that."

"I think I did.'

Nadia pulled the ring off and threatened to put it on her right ring finger instead. "You gotta do better than that if you want me to wear this on my left hand. Everyone's gonna talk, and I ain't gonna tell them that this is anything less than a *real* promise ring."

"A promise ring for what?"

Nadia narrowed her eyes. "Don't be daft. You know what."

"Hmm." Eva's long and nimble fingers tugged on a tuft of red hair. "Wouldn't it be cheesi*er* if I chose now to propose to you?"

Nadia swore that was the sun making her so red… not blush. Nope. "I didn't say that. I said you should make a real promise."

A kiss dotted her lips. "I promise to be your faithful sugar mama girlfriend who spoils you with new cars, new clothes, and an endless supply of hot, invigorating orgasms. There. How's that?"

"That's what I'm talking about." Nadia leaned into her girlfriend's sideways embrace. "That sounds way more like you."

"Can you put it back on now? I wanna see it on you."

Nadia held out her hand so they could both admire the red beryl twinkling on her pale hand. "I love it," she said. "Thank you, Eva."

They were about to kiss when the rumble of a boat from the main island interrupted their slice of paradise.

"What the hell?" Eva turned toward the docks on the other end of the beach. "We're not supposed to have any other deliveries today."

The boat pulled up to the dock, where a small crew of staff people awaited the first person to get off. Eva stood up with a start. Beneath her, Nadia scrambled on her beach towel to stand up as well. "What is it? I mean, *who* is it? Your brother?"

"No way. He's too busy playing papa back home."

Both Nadia and Eva took off down the beach, kicking up sand and weaving in and out of palm treed shadows. Someone walked up the dock carrying two expensive suitcases marked with the initials IW.

"Oh, *fuck!*" Eva came to a halt as her mother emerged on the dock.

"I should have guessed!" Isabella called. "I leave one home because of all the noise and come here to find even more noise!"

"What are you *doing* here?" Eva's posture matched her mother's. When they were both prompted, mother and daughter would follow a mental game of Simon Says until someone finally gave in. "I thought you were going back to Montana!"

"Your father went on ahead. I decided to swing by here and take in some salt and sun before punishing myself with Montana weather. It's *so* hard on my skin." Isabella's sandals slapped against the wooden dock as she approached the couple already inhabiting the Warrens' Caribbean oasis. "And I really do deserve a quiet week after all that screaming I put up with."

"You mean your grandchild?"

"Yes, her."

You ever pay make good on that bet with your brother? Nadia nudged her girlfriend. Someone owed Henry twenty grand after the newest Warren heir turned out to be an heiress.

"Don't know how you deal with *two* of your own, then. And aren't you staying in my wing? Unless you're babysitting – and I can't believe that you are – I don't know what the hell you're complaining about."

"I'm complaining about whatever I damn well please." Isabella stopped before them, taking in their relaxing beachwear. Nadia closed her linen shirt over her bikini. Didn't stop her thick thighs from spilling from the hem, however. "Like you. I'm complaining about you next."

"Can't wait."

"For one, I bet you've set yourself up in the main guest house." What a dramatic sigh! Nadia *almost* felt sorry for the woman. "Guess I'll stay in the second house. It has a better view of the main island anyway."

"I also ate all the grapes. There won't be any more until provisions arrive tomorrow."

"How dare you."

If Nadia didn't know these two had such a strenuous relationship, she would think that this was the sarcastic banter that kept their family afloat. "We won't trouble you for long, Mrs. Warren," Nadia braved saying. "We're leaving tomorrow evening."

Isabella gave her a cursory glance. Or at least it would have been cursory until she saw the rock on Nadia's left ring finger. "What is *that?*" She snatched Nadia's hand and then gaped at her daughter. "What have you done!"

"What do you mean? I gave my girlfriend a ring! Who gives a shit?"

"Evangeline Madeline Warren, I swear to all gods pagan and Abrahamic that if you're putting me through another circus of a wedding so soon after your brother's that I will… I will…"

"Calm down, Mother." Eva put a sturdy hand on her mother's shoulder. "There's time for us to have a shitshow wedding over the next few years. For one, I can't knock her up, no matter how hard I try."

"*Evangeline!*"

"I'm too ladylike, Mother. I keep fucking this poor girl, but still no more little Warren heirs yet. My fingers aren't as potent as my brother's, I guess."

Nadia was going to die right there on a Caribbean island! But Eva got the reaction out of her mother that she wanted, and within two minutes Isabella was marching toward the secondary guest house mumbling about terrible daughters and what a curse they were. All the better for the Heavens to curse her own son with…

"Ms. Warren."

Eva pivoted on her bare feet to meet a courier from the boat. "Yes?" One would have never guessed that she implied such sexual things to her own conservative mother. Nadia couldn't decide if that made her more attractive or not.

The courier handed her an envelope with Henry's personal seal emblazoned on it. "For you. Mr. Warren made it clear that you were to receive it before we shipped out."

"Thank you." Eva tipped the courier with the few bills she had in her pocket and took the envelope a few feet away. Nadia followed. Eva did nothing to hide the contents of Henry's letter as she held it out for both pairs of eyes to see.

"Eva,

First, my sincerest apologies about our mother. When she made the decision to fly to the island this morning, I tried to dissuade her, but she was adamant. I hope that she will not be too much trouble, but it seems that being a grandmother is not a role that naturally suits her. I for one am shocked since she was such an upright beacon of maternity when we were growing up.

I hope you are enjoying your reprieve with Nadia, and I further hope that she likes the ring you gifted her. It's a marvelous piece. After considering the photos the jeweler took and forwarded to me, I've decided that it's time you and I had a serious talk about your future in our family's company. As you know, we have often off-handedly discussed you spearheading a jewelry division. Your eye for stones and design comes to no surprise to me, but I am surprised that we haven't done something with it yet, no matter what we've told Mother. If you're up to it, stop by my office tomorrow night when you get back. Or we could arrange to chat on Monday.

Best wishes on your sojourn. Your niece misses you already. Aside from Monica, you are still the only one who knows how to hold her without sending her into an utter fit. I think our mother is personally offended, so go easy on her.

Henry"

Eva lowered the piece of paper and pulled Nadia into a hug. "We're stuck with her until we leave tomorrow. I propose we have loud and obnoxious lesbian sex so she can't sleep tonight."

"I'm fine with your mother never knowing details of our sex life." Nadia squeezed the torso within her grasp. "Congrats on the job offer?"

"That's not a job offer. That's my brother finally pulling his head out of his ass and realizing that I exist outside of being his quirky lesbian sister everyone gives him a hard time about. Being a father has softened the darling dolt."

Nadia was pretty sure it was more complicated than that, since Henry had never hidden his admiration for his sister's ambition. *Whatever helps her cope, I guess…*

"On that note, I'm thinking that since my mother is hogging the compound, we have dinner down here by the docks and then retire to our room for some you-know-what." A comical wink almost sent Nadia back howling in laughter.

"And what is this you-know-what? Stop being so cryptic. If you wanna bang me, say you wanna bang me!"

"Oh my God, I've been *saying* that I wanna bang you for over a year now! Maybe I got tired of saying it!"

"Only took a few tries for me to get used to the idea."

"Thank goodness, too. I was about to lose my mind for the rest of my life if I couldn't have a taste of you."

"Instead, I played hard to get."

"Did you really?"

Nadia pushed herself up on her toes and kissed Eva's lips. "Maybe. A little. I wanted to make sure you actually wanted me that badly."

"Actually wanted you that… oh for fuck's sake."

"Now your mother is the one playing hard to get with me. Don't worry. I'll have won her over by the time we get married."

"That's *not* an engagement ring." Eva was still smiling. "When I get you one of those, it'll be a diamond. One I've picked out on my travels. Only the best for my pretty dove."

"When will this engagement happen? I heard what you said to your mother. You can't knock me up without a turkey baster, and I'll know if there's a turkey baster in our bed."

"I will find a way." Eva grabbed her girlfriend's ass and squeezed it. "It may take a lot of trying, but I'm sure you'll be up for it. I gotta handcuff you to my bed until we come up with an heir to rival my niece."

"Handcuff me to your bed and fuck me until you're too worn out to continue? Baby, that's a normal Friday night."

"We'll have to double our efforts!"

"Seriously, though." Nadia fingered the lines of her girlfriend's linen shirt. Wooden buttons tapped against her fingernails. "What if we do want to have children one day?"

Damn, did she know how to make Eva let her go and take two big steps away or what? "Why you gotta bring *that* up right now? I'm too young for that! *You're* too young for that!"

"Think about it, though. If we're not adopting, then we have to find a donor! And you know how your mother is. She would have a heart attack if it wasn't genetically related to her. Are *you* going to be knocked up? Hm?"

"Don't even!"

"I figured. You're going to make me be the pregnant one. So you know what that means?"

"Don't. Don't go there, babe."

"We'll have to get your brother to donate the genetics! I'll be knocked up with your brother's sperm! Your children are your nieces and nephews!"

Eva was either going to laugh or scream, but she wasn't going to commit to anything yet. She would instead already be halfway down the beach, getting as far away from this talk of marriage and babies as possible. *She called her brother the dolt?* Nadia kicked up a large wave of sand as she chased after Eva, shouting things like, "My lease is up at the end of the year! When are you going to buy us a townhouse to live in together! Eva! Baby!" But Eva ran faster, using her ridiculously long legs to carry her farther than Nadia could cover with thighs that chafed at the mere thought of *walking.*

"I'm too young and free-spirited for townhouses and babies!" a shrill voice echoed between palm trees and across somber ocean waves.

"It's a small island, Eva! I'll catch you eventually! Then we're talking about whether you're wearing a white or black tuxedo to our wedding!"

Did someone drop a soccer ball in front of Eva? Because she was running as if the Gold Medal depended on it!

So who was playing hard to get now?

Cynthia Dane spends most of her time writing in the great Pacific Northwest. And when she's not writing, she's dreaming up her next big plot and meeting all sorts of new characters in her head.

She loves stories that are sexy, fun, and cut right to the chase. You can always count on explosive romances - both in and out of the bedroom - when you read a Cynthia Dane story.

Falling in love. Making love. Love in all shades and shapes and sizes. Cynthia loves it all!

Connect with Cynthia on any of the following:

Website: http://www.cynthiadane.com
Twitter: http://twitter.com/cynthia_dane
Facebook: http://facebook.com/authorcynthiadane

61281617R00280

Made in the USA
Lexington, KY
05 March 2017